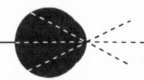

**This Large Print Book carries the
Seal of Approval of N.A.V.H.**

JUSTICE FOR SARA

Erica Spindler

CENTER POINT LARGE PRINT
THORNDIKE, MAINE

Chapter One

Katherine McCall stood at the broken front gate and stared at the words that had been spray-painted in black across the yellow clapboard siding. Simple. Ugly. A warning.

We know u did it

No surprise there. Kat shifted her gaze. The once sunny yellow had turned forlorn. The white trim was peeling, the gardens overgrown and overrun by weeds. She pictured it as it had been the last time she'd seen it, ten years ago. The cute gingerbread cottage with the white picket fence, gardenias in bloom, their fragrance potent in the June sun.

Not her childhood home. No, that had been a grand estate on the Tchefuncte River. Plantation grand—with white columns and a double gallery, a sweeping expanse of lawn with ancient live oaks and century-old magnolias. A swimming pool and cabana. A guesthouse and tennis courts. A home befitting the owner of McCall Oil.

No, this had been her sister Sara's cottage. Her first home, her pride and joy.

As it had turned out, the only home Sara would ever own.

Regret and grief washed over Kat, as piercing as a fresh wound. If she hadn't been such a selfish little shit back then, maybe Sara would be alive today. Maybe her murderer wouldn't have had the opportunity.

Kat reined in her thoughts, the regret. She couldn't change the past, no matter how hard she fought accepting it, no matter how far or fast she ran from it.

Being back in Liberty was an acknowledgment of that.

Kat unlatched the gate and stepped through. She'd thought she would never return. She had promised herself she wouldn't.

Yet here she was. The scene of the crime. The place her life had come to a bloody, screeching halt.

She started up the walkway, heartbeat quickening. Breath coming fast and thin. Kat forced herself to keep moving, to put one foot in front of the other. She reached the porch steps. Three of them, though it could have been a hundred by the way she dreaded climbing them.

She did anyway. Crossed to the front door. With unsteady hands, she fit the key into the lock, turned it and stepped into the foyer.

Cousin Jeremy had opened the cottage and had it cleaned for her. The smell of the polish and cleaners still hung in the air. She closed the door behind her but didn't move.

Her gaze went to the spot where she'd found Sara. In a crumpled heap, blood pooled around her in the shape of an amoeba.

An amoeba. Kat remembered thinking that. She had just studied the single-cell organisms in science class.

She stared at the floor, unable to tear her gaze away. The blood had subtly stained the honey-colored wood, creating a faint but permanent shadow.

Or was that her imagination?

The doorbell sounded.

Startled, she jumped, then, hand to her chest, peeked out the sidelight. A man. Dark hair. Good-looking. Holding up a badge.

The sight of it knocked the breath out of her.

"Miss Katherine, I'm afraid you're going to have to come with me."

"Ms. McCall? Sergeant Luke Tanner. Liberty P.D."

Kat gazed at him, suddenly seeing the resemblance. Now, there was a name she had never wanted to hear again.

She nodded and opened the door. "Hello, Sergeant. Did you say Tanner?"

"Yes, ma'am."

"Any relationship to Chief Stephen Tanner?"

"His son."

"Perfect." The sarcasm slipped past her lips before she could stop it. "Sorry, your dad and I have some uncomfortable history together."

"Funny, he and I do as well."

She surprised herself and smiled. "How can I help you, Sergeant Tanner?"

He motioned to the graffiti across the front of the house. "I heard from Mrs. Bell across the street that you'd had a little trouble already, thought I'd stop by and check it out."

"Iris Bell's still alive? I thought she was a hundred ten years ago."

Kat could see he wanted to smile but thought better of it. His brown eyes crinkled at the corners. He cleared his throat. "Probably just kids, but we'll be keeping a close eye on the house, stepping up drive-bys and the like."

"I appreciate that, Sergeant Tanner. And I'm sure Iris Bell will be stepping up her surveillance as well."

Again, he struggled not to smile. "This is a small town, Ms. McCall, everybody knows everybody and their everything. To that end, you might as well call me Luke."

"I remember you now. Local football hero. You were off to college before I got to Tammany West High." She cocked her head. "You were a bit of a hell-raiser, am I right?"

He laughed. "So now you understand my comment about bad history with my dad. We all carry our pasts around on our backs."

"Or written on our foreheads," she said. "A bloodred 'M' on mine."

He glanced toward the graffiti, expression serious. "Yes, well, don't hesitate to call if something comes up."

She followed him onto the front porch. He stopped when he reached the stairs and turned back to her. "I don't know why you came back to Liberty, Ms. McCall, but little towns have long memories. People don't forget. You'd be wise to keep that in mind."

She watched him drive off. How could she not? She had the longest memory of them all.

Sara McCall
2003

Four days before the murder

Sara stood on the front porch, waiting for Kat. She glanced at her watch. Just past four thirty. Any moment, her sister would come trotting around the corner. Bubbling over about how well softball practice had gone. Playing Miss Innocent to the very hilt.

But she hadn't been to practice. Not today. Not once. Lying little sneak.

On cue, Kat arrived, baseball bat propped on her right shoulder. She was smiling.

Not for long. Sara struggled to control her anger. She shook with it. Deep down. All the way to her core.

She needed her wits about her when she confronted her sister. Kat was going to pitch a holy fit. It could get really ugly. If she let it.

Calm, Sara. In control. You're the adult.

The truth was, she didn't have the heart for this right now. She didn't have the energy. Not with everything else going on. But she didn't have a choice. She was Katherine's guardian.

"Hi, Sissy," Kat called, jogging up the steps.

"How was softball?"

If Kat heard the sarcasm in her tone, she didn't show it. "Great. I'm getting really good."

"Yes, you are." Sara held out her hand. "I'll take the bat."

She looked confused but handed it over. "What's up?"

"Jig's up, kiddo. You're grounded."

"What! Why?"

"Why? Let's try that you've been lying to me. I found out everything, Kat. What you've been doing and who you've been doing it with." She paused, watching as the reality of what she was saying sank in. "He's twenty years old. You're seventeen. No."

Kat's expression darkened. "You can't tell me what to do or who I can see."

"The hell I can't. I'm your guardian and that's exactly what I'm doing."

"That's not fair!"

Sara almost laughed. "Tough. Life's not fair." And boy, did she know it. If it was, their parents wouldn't have died and she wouldn't have been saddled with raising an obnoxious teenager.

"I hate you!" Kat shouted. "You're ruining my life!"

Sara didn't even flinch. It wasn't the first time her younger sister had shouted those words at her. She was certain it wouldn't be the last. "Stop with the drama, Katherine. If anyone's life's being ruined, it's mine."

"Then emancipate me."

They had been here before, as well. "Emancipate yourself. You're seventeen."

"Then I won't get my money."

"That's right, little sister. So, either go without 'your' money or live by my rules."

"I wish I'd died with Mom and Dad! Then I wouldn't have to live with you!"

It took every scrap of Sara's self-control not to shout back that she wished that too. That she wanted her life back. That caring for Kat had become like a prison sentence.

But she didn't. She loved her sister—at least the kid she used to be. In the past year, that girl had disappeared and this *creature* had taken her place.

"Wow, Kat, I love the way you're playing the victim here. You're not the one who's been lied to for weeks. Girls' softball? You didn't think I'd find out eventually? I've got to hand it to you, though, our trip to the sporting goods store to get everything you needed was pretty convincing."

"Thanks."

Sara wanted to slap the smirk off her face. "What were you doing all those afternoons you were supposedly at practice? Were you with this Ryan boy? Or that group of kids I told you to stay away from? They're bad kids, Kat."

"You don't know anything about them!"

A breeze stirred the azalea bushes beside the porch. In full bloom, they provided a brilliant shock of color; from the magnolia blossoms on the tree to her right floated a sweet, almost lemony fragrance.

Sara breathed in the colors, the smell, using nature's beauty to calm her. She was the grown-up here, she reminded herself. Kat had been through so much.

"Kit-Kat," she pleaded, using their mother's pet name for her, "I'm worried about you. The girl I know doesn't do things like this. Talk to me. No problem's too big we can't work it out together."

Kat's face softened, tears filled her eyes. "You don't know what it's like. All the other kids have their moms and dads. And mine—" She choked on the last, a tear rolling down her cheek.

Sara's heart hurt for her. She held out a hand. "I know what you're going through. I'm going through it, too."

"You don't know. I was twelve when they died, you were grown up."

Just out of university, at her first teaching job. Barely on her own two feet. "But I still needed them, too. I miss them every day."

"Why'd they have to die?"

She started to cry and Sara took her in her arms. "I don't know. And I wish I could change things, but I can't."

"I'm sorry I lied to you. It's just that—" She sniffled, her face against Sara's shoulder. "The only time I'm happy is when I'm with my friends. They understand me. They make it . . . stop hurting. That's why I lied about where I was."

Something in her sister's tone didn't ring true. A cloying quality. Sara frowned as a suspicion wormed its way into her head: *Was she being played?*

Kat went on. "You don't know them the way I do. They're really good kids. Please don't take them away from me, too."

Sara's resolve wavered. She'd heard things from the other teachers about the group. They had warned her to keep Kat away from them. But that was all secondhand information. There was a reason the courts didn't allow hearsay as testimony, right?

Sara glanced across the street. Old Mrs. Bell stood on her front porch. Listening to every word. Or trying to.

"I tell you what, Kit-Kat, have them over here. Let me get to know them. If they're the kids you say they are, I'll feel comfortable letting you hang out with them."

"Really?"

"Sure." She smiled. "I just have to know you're safe."

"You're the best!" Kat hugged her. "Can they come over tonight?"

"You're still grounded, Kat."

"But you just said—"

"That I'll give your friends a chance. And I will. After you do your punishment."

"No!"

"Two weeks. And I'm taking your phone, car and computer."

"You can't do that! How am I supposed to get to school?"

"I'll drive you." Kat looked horrified. "And the answer's still no about you and this Ryan dude. He's too old for you."

Before her sister could squeal her protest, she dropped the final bomb. "Cousin Jeremy suggested I start drug-testing you. And I think he's right."

"What?" The one word conveyed outrage and innocence. "I can't believe you don't trust me!"

"Are you kidding? Really?" Sara folded her arms across her chest. "If you've got nothing to worry about, what's the problem?"

Kat stared at her, her face an open book as she stuttered and searched for the right response.

She had been playing her. Little brat.

"Give me your car keys." She held out her hand. "Now."

"I lied before. I wish you were dead. Then I wouldn't have to put up with your shit!"

"Want to say it a little louder? I don't think *all* of Liberty heard you."

"I wish you were dead!" she screamed, turning toward the street. "You hear that, everyone? I wish my stupid sister were dead!"

Kat threw the car keys. Sara reacted just in time not to take them square in the face. They grazed her cheek before hitting the wall and dropping to the floor. It stung; her eyes teared up and she brought her hand to her cheek.

But instead of apologizing, Kat stormed past her into the house. A moment later, she heard a door slam.

Sara sank onto the porch step and dropped her head into her shaking hands. What was she going to do? She was frustrated. Overwhelmed and exhausted. And it wasn't just the situation with Kat. It seemed every part of her life had spun out of control as well, situations that made dealing with a rebellious teenager a piece of cake.

Mom, Dad, why'd you have to go out that *night? Why'd your path have to cross that drunk's?*

She couldn't do this alone. But who could she trust? It seemed like everyone had either turned against her or had their own agenda. If ever she could have used a miracle, it was now.

Chapter Two

Monday, June 3
10:40 a.m.

Luke glanced in the rearview mirror. Katherine McCall stood on her porch, watching him drive away.

He'd finally come face-to-face with Liberty's version of Lizzie Borden. He'd expected her to be harder, not so young and certainly not so wholesome-looking.

He pictured her: shoulder-length medium brown hair, pulled back into a ponytail, pretty brown eyes, a smattering of freckles across her nose. The quintessential girl next door.

He supposed that was the point—she was the girl next door. And she very well may have beaten her sister to death and gotten away with it. The way ninety-nine percent of Liberty thought.

A jury of her peers had found her not guilty. Case closed, as far as he was concerned. His job was to make certain somebody didn't turn all that misguided fervor into vigilante justice.

Luke eased around the bend, heading back toward the Liberty town square. He wouldn't let those big brown eyes fool him. She was angry; she had a chip on her shoulder. Both had been obvious. He didn't blame her; he'd be pretty pissed off, too.

She'd come back to town for a reason. An important one. Otherwise, why put herself through this? 'Cause it wasn't going to be nice— or easy. The graffiti, he feared, was only the beginning.

Although she'd seemed more resigned than rattled by the vandalism, it could be she didn't realize how hated she was here. Rumor had it she planned to open a bakery. Did she think cookies would change people's minds?

He eased to a stop at the light at Main and Church streets. When he'd heard she was coming back, he'd done a little homework. Katherine McCall had walked out of the St. Tammany Parish jail at eighteen, with almost no family and a ton of money. She'd headed to the Northwest and settled in Portland.

The case that had been such a big deal down here had hardly made a blip on the radar up there. She'd gotten a job with a baker and had eventually opened up her own place: the Good Earth Baking Company. She had six outlets in the Portland and Seattle areas.

It didn't make sense. Why leave the comfort of there to come here?

His radio crackled. "Liberty Twelve?"

He answered. "Twelve here."

"One-two-eight Big Bear."

Luke smiled. Trixie had worked for his dad for twenty years. After all those years reporting to him, she couldn't bring herself to openly report on him. So they had come up with a code. His dad was Big Bear, 128 his office. They had others as well, plus they improvised as they went.

"Ten-four, Trix. See you in five."

Like many small southern towns, Liberty had been built around a town square. Back in the day before malls or the Internet, the square had been the center of town life. The courthouse, post office and police station were located on the square. A bed-and-breakfast, several shops and a couple restaurants as well. In the center of the square was a lovely gazebo, which had hosted weddings, spring and fall festivals and countless other civic and private events. Liberty's first church, St. Margaret's, was just one block over.

The Liberty P.D. was located on the square's northeast corner. Luke parked in his dedicated spot and climbed out. Two elderly women strolled past: one had attempted to teach him piano when he was in the second grade, the other had had the unlucky job of being his seventh-grade English teacher.

Luckily, neither woman held a grudge.

"Morning, Luke," they called in unison.

"Ladies," he responded. "Beautiful day."

"Bit warm for this time of year," said one.

"Unseasonably," agreed the other.

"Global warming," the first said. "Where do you stand on the issue, Luke?"

No way he was getting pulled into that hornets' nest. He knew those two—sweet, retiring little old ladies they were not. More like tag team wrestlers. Get sucked in and he was dead. An hour gone, minimum.

He smiled winningly. "I'd love to discuss the subject with you, but it's going to have to be another time. Duty calls."

His old teacher touched his sleeve. "You heard she was back, didn't you?"

"Kat McCall," the other said, voice hushed. "I suggest you don't sleep. She strikes at night—"

"—when no one's watching."

He wanted to laugh at their drama. Instead, he assured them he would, wished them a good day and slipped into the P.D. Trix was waiting, expression anxious. "How's the weather?" he asked.

"Stormy," she said, handing him his messages. "Thunder and lightning."

23

Luke thanked her and headed to his office. His father sat, back to the door, as he rummaged through a file cabinet.

"Hey, Pops, what're you doing here?"

He swiveled to face Luke. "I'm still chief of police, aren't I?"

Seeing him there, shrunken and gray, affected Luke like a punch to the gut. His larger-than-life dad had always dominated the big chair and desk.

Now they dominated him.

Luke cleared his throat. The most recent round of chemo had really taken it out of him. "You're not supposed to be driving."

He looked irritated by the comment. Luke wasn't surprised. "Never expose your weak spot," his dad had always preached. "It gives your enemy the best place to strike."

But he shouldn't be the enemy, Luke thought. He was his son. "You badgered Mom into bringing you down, didn't you?"

"Sweet-talked," he countered.

Luke leaned against the doorjamb, arms folded across his chest. "What can I do for you?"

"I hear she's back in town."

Luke played dumb. "Who's that, Pops?"

"Her. That murdering McCall girl."

"She was found not guilty by a jury of her peers."

"Jury of her peers?" He snorted in disgust.

"Hardly. A bunch of New Orleans liberals. Democrats, I'd bet. Every last one of them. Besides, not guilty isn't the same as innocent."

Luke could've pointed out that the Constitution covered all Americans, not just the ones with the same social and political leanings as Chief Stephen Tanner, but that would've been a waste of breath.

"She seemed decent enough."

"You talked to her?"

"Some kids vandalized the cottage, so I stopped by to check on her. Assured her we'd be keeping a close eye on the place and told her to give us a call if she needed anything."

"Why'd she come back?"

"I didn't ask."

"You should have. I don't trust her."

"And I got the feeling she doesn't trust you."

That stopped him a moment. He narrowed his eyes. "Good. She knows I've got her number. I'll be watching."

"It's been ten years, Pops. She was acquitted. Isn't it time to let it go?"

He flushed. The angry color made him appear healthier. "She beat her sweet-hearted sister to death with a baseball bat. On my watch. And I let her get away."

"You didn't let her get away. It went to trial—"

"People don't see it that way. They figure if I'd done a better job investigating, there would have been more for the prosecution to work with."

"How do you see it, Dad?"

"What kind of a bullshit question is that?"

His dad's face went from red to purple and he started to cough uncontrollably. Luke didn't rush to his side; he would only push him away, the same as always.

Luke crossed to the watercooler and got him a cup of water.

After a few sips, the coughing jag eased a bit. Luke stood back, giving him space, watching as he fought weakness. That was his dad. Stubborn. Pigheaded. He refused to step down. Refused to admit his leave of absence was anything but temporary.

Six months ago, after his dad's diagnosis, Luke had left the St. Tammany Sheriff's Department to join the Liberty force. As his father's condition had worsened, his "help" had turned into the role of acting chief.

It hadn't been easy. His old man resented Luke's help and grumped at and badgered everyone. No going peacefully into the night for Chief Stephen Tanner. No, he would be kicking and complaining up until his last breath.

Finally, the coughing ceased altogether. His dad sank back in the chair, looking old and beaten. He passed a trembling hand across his face. "Both McCall and Wally," he said suddenly, "the same night. Wally was a good man. A real good man."

"I know, Pops. I remember."

"There was nothing I could do. It wasn't even my case." He sighed, the sound weary. "Sheriff's Department botched it. Not me. But I was the one who looked bad. He was one of my guys. On patrol."

"Nobody blames you. You're too hard on yourself."

He went on as if Luke hadn't spoken. "Two unrelated and unsolved murders in one night. In Liberty, son. Population seven hundred and fifty. How the hell does that happen?"

Officer Wally Clark
2003

The night of the murder

Liberty, Louisiana, police officer Wally Clark liked working the graveyard shift. By the time he came on at 11:00, little ol' Liberty had rolled up the sidewalks. A town of families with young kids and retirees, for any kind of entertainment you had to go ten minutes up the road to the metropolis of Covington or Mandeville.

Wally eased his cruiser along Front Street. He scanned both sides—on his right, the Tchefuncte River, on the other, shops, cafes and other small businesses asleep for the night.

Not a creature stirred, not even a mouse.

Wally grinned. Most folks would be bored brainless by this gig; he found it peaceful. He'd patrol the streets, munching on carrot sticks and sipping his Yoo-Hoo chocolate drink. Every so often, he'd get a call about kids parking on Bayou Road or a domestic disturbance, he'd even had a couple break-ins to investigate over the years, but most of the time he just cruised, waiting for 4:00 a.m. to roll around. That's when he'd swing by the Tasty Cream to say hello to Miss Louanna and get fixed up with the first dough-nuts of the day.

Wally took the bend where Front Street stopped following the river, slowing in the curve to shine his spotlight into the cemetery. All quiet. Just the way it was supposed to be.

Wally's thoughts moseyed back to Miss Louanna and her prizewinning doughnuts. He figured she was a little bit sweet on him, and he'd considered asking her out, but he sorta liked being a bachelor and he figured that Louanna just might be the one to change his mind 'bout that.

No sense rushing. He had all the time in the world for marriage and a family.

Chief had told him to cruise by the McCall place. A couple neighbors had reported hearing another argument over there. He shook his head. Poor Miss Sara. She had her hands full with that wild sister of hers.

Truthfully, both of 'em deserved his sympathy. He'd never forget the night their parents had been killed in that crash. The whole town had been in mourning. He'd seen the photos. Peter McCall had gone through the windshield and his wife, Vicky, had been crushed. Awful. Still cropped up in his dreams now and then.

He came upon the McCall place and slowed to a crawl. A couple lights burned inside. Miss Sara was still up. He wondered if she was grading student papers or waiting up 'cause her sister had sneaked out again.

Or maybe she had company, he thought, noticing an unfamiliar car parked nearby.

He peered at it as he passed. Empty. Most probably belonged to one of Barbara Russell's "friends." She had a lot of visitors at night.

But maybe he'd just loop around the block anyway? Swing by a couple more times, just to make certain all was good?

Wally did, but as he made the block, he saw the unfamiliar vehicle had pulled away. It was at the end of the block already, turning left.

Wally frowned. Now, that wasn't right. Not at all. His cop senses tingling, he fell in behind the vehicle, the McCall place disappearing in his rearview mirror.

Chapter Three

Kat had wanted to beg off dinner with Jeremy and his wife, Lilith. Between the strain of being back where her life had gone so terribly wrong and of being constantly on edge, afraid to go out for fear of a confrontation, she was exhausted.

Word was definitely out. She'd been hyper-aware of the parade of cars passing the cottage, of the way each vehicle slowed to a crawl in front of her place to gawk.

But canceling hadn't really been an option. Jeremy had been so good to her. And to Sara after their parents' deaths. He was the only family she had left.

Jeremy and Lilith lived in a gated golf community in Mandeville. Kat stopped at the gate; the guard checked her name against his list, then waved her through. Jeremy had given her detailed directions, as he lived at the very back of the large development on one of the waterfront lots.

After only a few wrong turns, she found Riverwood Lane. It, too, was gated, though this time with a call box instead of a guard.

"Hi, Lilith!" she said when the woman answered the call. "I'm here."

"Great. I'll buzz you in."

A moment later, Kat rolled through, keenly aware of the gate swinging closed behind her. As it clanged shut, she was reminded of the old Eagles tune "Hotel California" and its creepy lyrics about checking into a beautiful reality but never being able to leave.

These homes were grander, the lots more estatelike than the ones at the front of the development. She found Jeremy's drive, protected by another iron gate, though this one stood open.

As she pulled through, she was struck by a bittersweet sense of déjà vu. The setting—expansive grounds dotted with oaks and magnolias, the columned house at the end of the winding drive—reminded her of her parents' home and those carefree days.

She parked in front of the house and breathed in the evening air. The scent of the flowers and the river, of southern summer, lush, fecund and brimming with life.

Jeremy burst out the front door, all smiles. Lilith followed more slowly. "Cousin!" He hugged her. "I never thought I'd see the day."

She smiled. "Truthfully, I never thought I would either."

Lilith reached them and kissed her cheeks. "Welcome to our home."

"It's beautiful." She turned back to Jeremy. "You've done so well, Jeremy. I'm happy for you."

He beamed. "Lilith is half this equation. She made senior partner two years ago."

Kat looked apologetically at the other woman. "Of course. I'm sorry, Lilith. I really did mean both of you."

"Don't think a thing of it; I didn't."

Everything about Lilith was elegant. Her voice and mannerisms, the way she carried herself. Clothes, jewelry, even the way she styled her chin-length dark hair.

"Come, let's have a cocktail on the back veranda. Have you ever had a lemon drop martini?"

"I haven't, but it sounds delicious."

The two made a great pair, Kat thought, surreptitiously studying them as they fixed drinks. A real power couple. Where Lilith was elegant, refined and introverted, Jeremy was larger than life, boisterous and outgoing. He, the quintessential public servant. And she, the power behind the throne.

Jeremy handed her the drink. Like everything else about the pair, it was beautiful—from the glass's sugared rim to the cocktail's pale, translucent yellow and the perfectly executed lemon curl garnish.

She took a sip and made a sound of pleasure. It

was as delicious as it looked—tart, sweet and chilled, perfect for a June evening in Louisiana.

"Sorry about all those gates you had to drive through," he said. "Lilith lives in fear some voter will show up with a gun and a bad attitude."

Although his tone was light, something in it suggested this had been a bone of contention between them. But as someone who had been a victim of a violent crime and lived with threats, she got that.

She changed the subject as they made their way out onto the veranda. "Your home is beautiful, Lilith." And it was, every bit as lovely and elegant as its mistress. Not one knickknack out of place, not one false note.

Lilith smiled, pleased. "I just knew enough to hire the best. In fact, your old friend Bitsy Cavenaugh was my decorator."

"Bitsy's an interior designer?"

"A really good one. Her work's been featured in *Southern Living*. Among others."

Jeremy frowned. "When's the last time you talked to her?"

"From jail."

He looked distressed. "You were such good friends."

"When we were young." Kat sank into a chair that faced the river. As relaxing as the view was, she suddenly felt agitated. "Bitsy chose not to ride the crazy train with me. Wisely, I might add."

"The crazy train?" He took the chair to her right.

"Mmm." She sipped the lemon drop. "Rebelling. Against everything. Cutting class. Drinking. Smoking weed. She wanted no part of that."

Kat thought of that time, that crowd, and an almost smothering wave of guilt enveloped her. She looked away. "I was such a creep."

"But not a murderer."

She jerked her gaze back to her cousin. "Is that a question?"

"Of course not." He reached across and squeezed her hand. "A reassurance, Kit-Kat."

Sudden, surprising tears stung her eyes. "I keep wondering if I could have prevented it."

"Really?" Lilith leaned forward. "How's that?"

Jeremy looked sharply at his wife. "Of course she couldn't have."

Kat wished she felt so confident of that. She thought of the people she had been hanging with back then, the way she had shot her mouth off about the things she and Sara had, about the money she would inherit when she turned twenty-one. Or if Sara died.

And then she had.

"Why'd you come back, Katherine?" Lilith asked. At her husband's shocked expression, she went on. "I think it's a fair question, sweetheart. It's been ten years. And I'm sure Kat knew the people of Liberty weren't going to greet her with open arms."

"It doesn't matter why," he said, "we're glad you're here."

Ever the politician. She smiled at her cousin. "It's okay, Jeremy. It *is* a fair question. And that it's been ten years is the point, don't you think? Sometimes you have to look back before you can take a step forward."

Lilith looked unconvinced. "And that's it?"

It wasn't, not by a long shot. But it was all she was going to reveal for now. She changed the subject. "I'm meeting with the commercial Realtor tomorrow, the one you recommended."

"You'll like her," Jeremy said. "She's a real go-getter."

Lilith sipped her cocktail, expression thoughtful. "You really think an organic bread store and bakery will go over here in south Louisiana? We're not health-conscious Portland."

Kat didn't take offense. This was Lilith. She followed her head, not her heart, and measured her decisions against logic, not desire.

"Yes, it's healthy. But it's delicious, too. A few will come in because it's whole grain and organic, but the rest will come in because it tastes good."

"I don't know." She frowned. "This is beignet-and-king-cake country. I just hate for you to waste your time and money."

Jeremy stepped in, looking irritated. "Your instincts haven't failed you yet. Six Good Earth

Baking Company stores in six years. It's phenomenal. I'm really proud of you."

"But why Liberty?" Lilith persisted. "We're so small. And off the beaten track. I think you'd do better in Mandeville or Covington."

This argument was nothing new. Her business manager had said all the same things to her. "I probably would," she agreed. "At least for the walk-in business. But the walk-in business is only a small part of what I do. Supplying restaurants and cafes is a bigger part. And I see opportunity here."

"Maybe so."

Kat smiled, considering even that a win from Lilith. "How about we revisit this after I've been open six months?"

She laughed. "You've got it. I'm making a notation in my BlackBerry."

They joined her, their laughter breaking the tension. Kat used the opportunity to change the subject. "Those kids I was hanging with back then, any of them around anymore?"

"I'm sure there are," Jeremy answered, then paused as if running names through his head. "That one, Debbie Holt, who testified at your trial, she and her mom run the Sunny Side Up cafe."

Dab. Testified. Against her.

"The Sunny Side Up was on Riverview, wasn't it?"

"Still is."

"One of the properties I'm looking at is on Riverview. Maybe I'll stop in for a cup of coffee."

He and Lilith exchanged glances. "You sure you're ready for that?" he asked.

"Why wouldn't I be?"

"The kind of people who graffiti houses are regulars at the Sunny Side."

"Luke Tanner believes kids did that."

"You know what I mean. The kind of folks who send threats."

She reached across to grasp his hand. "Liberty folks," she said softly. "I'm here, Jeremy. I can't hide forever."

At that moment, dinner was announced. As they dined on grilled redfish and roasted vegetables, they left Kat's past behind to discuss Jeremy's future. He had decided to run for state senate in the next election. Kat was grateful for the distraction. But even as she joined the conversation, a part of her attention was on visiting her old friend Dab.

And finding Ryan.

Ryan Benton
2003

Two weeks before the murder

Ryan had no intention of screwing this up. She was rich. And one hot piece of ass. She'd thrown herself at him. She was that kind of a chick. Wild. Wanting to do anything and everything. Including fuck him.

Unfortunately, she was only seventeen.

"I love you, I love you . . ." She rubbed herself against him, her lacy bra tickling his chest. She kissed his mouth, then his neck, then his shoulder, using the opportunity to bite. She loved to suck and bite. He was covered with hickeys.

No hickeys for her. No way was he going to chance that. San Quentin Quail, that's what she was. Sheriff Tanner would like nothing better than to toss another Benton into jail. Knowing this town and the McCall name, he'd fry, no doubt.

Ryan fired up a joint. It wasn't their first, so when she tried to take another hit, he took it away. "Oh, no, you don't. You need to be able to shimmy back in that window without killing yourself."

"I wanna stay with you. All night. Forever. And I don't care who knows it!"

She yanked the door handle, popped open the

door and leaned out. "I'm in love with Ryan Benton!" she shouted.

He grabbed her and pulled her back in. "You're out of your fucking mind."

"From fucking you." Laughing, she slid out of his grasp and out of the car. She landed in the soft grass, then got to her feet and twirled around. "I'm in love . . . I'm in love . . ."

He'd parked at the very end of Bayou Road. A dead end, isolated but not unknown as a make-out spot. The Liberty cops made occasional runs up here to stir things up.

He leaned over and held out his hand. "C'mon, sugar, you don't want my ass hauled to jail, do you?"

"I don't want us to be a secret anymore. We're together and I want everyone to know it." She twirled again, a spectacle in her bra and panties. "I'm in love with Ryan Benton," she shouted.

"Dammit, Kat. Get in the car!"

"You want me, come and get me."

A part of him thought he should leave her. Just drive off, teach her a lesson. But that could turn out even worse.

Ryan climbed out of the Mustang and took off after her. He could picture how this would look if one of Tanner's hick deputies pulled up now, Ryan Benton chasing a nearly naked girl around his car. He suspected the deputy would shoot first, ask questions later.

He finally got his arms around her, brought her to the ground. She squirmed beneath him, teasing.

Furious, he pinned her arms above her head. "Let's get something straight, little girl. I'm not going to jail for you or anyone else. Got that?"

The laughter died on her lips, her eyes welled with tears. "We're not doing anything wrong!" she cried. "We're in love!"

Stupid teenage girls. Spoiled brat. If this one wasn't about to inherit a whole shitload of money, he'd be done with her.

"The law says we are."

"But our hearts—"

"Don't mean shit to a judge. Get a clue."

"We could run away," she whispered. "Then we could be—"

"Not without your money. I'm not stupid."

She started to cry. He wanted to slap her until she shut up. Instead, he coaxed, "It's okay, sugar. Shh . . ." He kissed her tears. "C'mon, baby. It's just for a little longer. I have a plan for us. You trust me, right?"

She nodded.

"Good girl. Now," he said patiently, "we've talked about this. You're seventeen. In the eyes of the law what we're doing is wrong."

She opened her mouth to argue, he laid a finger against her lips, stopping her. "Statutory rape. Or carnal knowledge with a juvenile. I'd have to register as a sex offender. Do you want that?"

She shook her head, eyes welling with tears again. "I'm sorry."

"You're going to do what I say?"

"Yes," she whispered.

"Good girl." He stood, then hauled her to her feet. "Let's get you home."

Chapter Four

Monday, June 3
10:10 p.m.

It was nearly ten o'clock before Kat left Jeremy and Lilith's home. She made it home without getting lost in their sprawling neighborhood, despite the glass of wine with dinner. A significant feat. She'd been teased for her ability to get lost in an elevator.

Kat stepped inside her house and stopped cold. As if some sixth sense had kicked in and sounded an alarm, the hair at the back of her neck prickled.

Something was wrong.

Her gaze dropped to the shadow on the foyer floor, the spot where Sara's blood had pooled. *Just a shadow.* Swallowing hard, she closed the door behind her, listening intently. It was pin-drop quiet.

She rubbed her arms as she crossed the foyer

into the front parlor. She flipped on the overhead light, then switched on the table lamp, flooding the room with light. Nothing out of place. Not there or in any other room. Everything was as she'd left it.

Until she reached her bedroom. She frowned when she saw the door was closed. She had left it open. She was certain of it.

Heart thundering, Kat stared at the paneled wooden door. The old-time glass knob.

Do not open that door, Kat. Call the police. Now.

And tell them what? That some *sixth sense* warned her something was wrong? Right.

She closed her eyes, took a deep breath. She had been here before, many times. Afraid of the shadows, her imagination running away with her.

But the boogeyman hadn't jumped out at her, not once. She had shut the door without thinking. It was an old house. The heavy panel had swung shut on its own.

What an idiot. Open the damn door, Kat.

She grabbed the knob and twisted, the glass cool against her palm. As the door creaked open, her doorbell chimed.

Startled, she snatched her hand back and swung around. The bell chimed again, followed by firm knocking.

"I'm coming!" she called, hurrying that way. She peeked through the sidelight and saw Luke

Tanner standing on her doorstep. "Sergeant Tanner?" she said, cracking open the door.

"May I come in?"

She stared at him, surprised silent. "I'm sorry," she said, when she could speak, "it's just so weird to have you show up at my door right now."

He looked beyond her, into the house. When his gaze returned to hers, she saw concern in his eyes. "Is everything all right?"

"Yes, I'm fine. I'm just—" She stepped aside so he could enter. "Come on in."

He did, though she noted how his gaze scanned behind her and his right hand hovered over his gun holster. "I got an anonymous call. Caller said you were in trouble. Have you been here all evening?"

An anonymous call? Rubbing her arms again, she shook her head. "No, I had dinner with Jeremy and Lilith. At their place. I got home a few minutes ago."

She glanced over her shoulder, in the direction of the bedroom, picturing the closed door.

"What?" he asked.

"It was silly. At least I thought it was." He waited. "Don't laugh, but I had this weird, creepy feeling something was wrong."

His lips twitched. "Normally weird, creepy feelings aren't my area, but I think in this situation I'd better make an exception. How about I take a look around."

"I already have. Everything was fine except—" She hesitated a moment. "The bedroom door was closed and I remember leaving it open."

"Let me check it out. You stay here."

He drew his gun and made his way almost silently down the hall. Ignoring his order, she followed, cursing every creaking floorboard. How had he managed to avoid them?

When he reached the door, he motioned her to stay back and to the far side. In case an intruder burst out. The same reason he flattened himself against the wall. And moments ago, there she'd been, ready to simply open the door and step inside, totally vulnerable.

"Police," he called out.

She held her breath. Only silence answered.

He called out once more and when he again got no reply, he inched the door open with his foot. She watched as he stepped inside, gun out, then as he swung from right to left. He moved beyond her vision, then reentered it a moment later.

Kat swallowed hard. She felt a little like a character from a romance novel—admiring a man's backside when she should be afraid for her life. But he did have an amazing backside. And watching him do his cop thing had been kind of sexy.

"All clear," he said, lowering the weapon.

She cleared her throat, flustered. Until now, she hadn't had any use for cops—she'd hated them mostly. And here she was, feeling flushed and aware of one—who happened to be the son of the very cop who had made her life a living hell ten years ago.

"I knew I was being ridiculous," she said. "I hope you don't hold it against me."

"Actually, you weren't. At least I don't think so. You better take a look at this."

She crossed to him, legs unsteady. He indicated her bed.

Lying across her pillow was a baseball bat, a bloodred bow affixed to the grip.

Chapter Five

Monday, June 3
10:35 p.m.

Luke kept his gaze trained on her face. Her expression registered horror. She went white. He grabbed her arm as she swayed slightly.

Without speaking, Luke led her back out to the front porch. "Sit," he ordered. "I'll be right back."

He went to his car for a flashlight and scene kit, then returned to the bedroom and did a second search. Window was locked. No footprints or other debris on the floor near the window or the bed. Earlier, he'd checked under the bed and in the closet; he did so again in an abundance of caution.

Nothing.

He trained the flashlight on the bat. Peeking out from under it was something he hadn't noticed before. A plain white envelope.

He slipped on latex gloves and eased it out. A standard legal-size envelope. Loosely sealed. Nothing written on the front or the back.

He returned with it to the front porch. Kat hadn't moved.

"Are you okay?" he asked. "Do you need some water or something?"

"I'm fine," she answered. "Thanks."

"I found this on the bed. Under the bat."

She looked up at him. "What is it?"

"You tell me."

Recognition crossed her features, but she shook her head. "You open it."

He carefully unsealed the envelope. Inside was a single folded piece of paper. He slid it out. Three words: *JUSTICE FOR SARA.*

Luke gazed at it. Not kids this time. Too thought-out. Slick. And not just mean. A threat. Meant to terrorize.

"May I see it?"

He held it out for her to read. She made a choked sound and looked away. "He found me. I suspected he would."

He shifted his gaze to hers. "Who?"

"My fan." Without further explanation, she stood and went back into the house. He followed and watched as she crossed to the hall closet and removed a plastic bin. She carried it to the living room, set it on the coffee table and removed the lid.

It was filled with other envelopes. Other correspondence. Neatly lined up. "They're all from him? Your fan?"

"Yes, except for a few pieces of random hate mail."

Random hate mail. She said it so matter-of-factly. As if hate mail was expected, a part of everyday life.

For her, it was. He wondered what that felt like. How it had affected her. "May I?"

"Sure. They're organized oldest to most recent. I don't know why I kept them. Ghoulish masochism, maybe."

"Or maybe you thought you'd need them someday?"

She hugged herself. "Yeah, maybe."

Luke sat on the sofa. He began at the beginning. Hatred. Vitriol. Threats of violence. Old Testament Scripture about the Lord's vengeance. Reading them turned his stomach. He'd done a stint with the NOPD, he'd experienced evil. He'd seen firsthand the cruelty one person could inflict upon another. The hatred rooted in it.

This was like being hammered with it.

She sat quietly beside him. Every so often she glanced at him, or peered over, reading with him, commenting. She did that now.

"That was one of my favorites," she said. "The irony of it, you know. Quoting the New Testament, then damning me to hell."

"Which is so Old Testament."

She looked at him as if surprised he got it. "Exactly."

He refolded the page and slipped it into its envelope. "You seem pretty calm now. But before, you were scared. What gives?"

"I'm okay now because I know he left it."

He frowned. "I don't get that."

"This has been going on for ten years. There's over a hundred letters in there. And I'm still here."

Alive. Unharmed. He nodded, understanding.

"When did you begin receiving them?"

"Within a month of my acquittal. They came frequently at first, then slowed to a trickle. I always get at least one on the anniversaries."

"The anniversaries?"

"Of Sara's death and my acquittal."

"You showed these to the police?"

"Of course. Right away. I was terrified. They weren't too worried. They assured me that this sort thing was expected to happen to people in my position."

"In your position?" He thought of his dad. "You mean, acquitted of a crime the general public is convinced you committed?"

"That's the one." She smiled slightly. "They

48

also said that the type of person who writes threatening letters rarely takes it any further. The letters satisfy their aggression. If they'd wanted to physically attack me, they knew where I lived.

"At first, I didn't trust them and I moved. Somehow they found me. The letters started again. After the third move, I figured the cops were right and went on with my life."

"How did this fan keep finding you? Didn't you change your name?"

She shook her head.

"Why not?"

"My name was all I had left of my past. The good part of my past." She met his gaze, the expression in hers defiant. "And I didn't do anything wrong."

"Why'd you come back?"

"It was time."

Time for what, he wondered. To set the record straight? Face her accusers. He thought of the message: *Justice for Sara.*

Could that be why she was here? For justice?

But for whom? Her or her sister?

"Did the police warn you that this type of perpetrator often escalates their campaign of terror?"

"Yes. But they haven't."

"Until now."

She frowned and he turned to fully face her.

She had her hands folded in her lap; he covered them with his. She looked startled, which was good. He'd wanted her full attention.

"Kat, whoever this person is, they were in your home. They left you that bat. Why?"

"Sara was beaten to death with a bat. One just like that."

He waited for the information to sink in. For her to realize that this message was unlike any that had come before it.

Her fan had escalated his campaign of terror.

He knew the moment the realization hit, when her hands trembled beneath his. She jerked them away and jumped to her feet. "Why'd you have to tell me that? This whole thing, coming back here to . . . it's hard enough. I didn't think I'd have to worry about this . . . freak."

He stood to face her. "I'm not trying to scare you, or make your life more difficult. But in this case, ignorance is not bliss. You need to be careful."

"Dammit. I'd rather be pissed."

"Go ahead. Just be careful while you're at it." He shifted his gaze to the front door, then from one window to the next. An old place like this had a lot of them. In the days before air-conditioning, folks relied on fans and a crossbreeze.

"How'd this person get in? Your doors were locked?"

"Absolutely."

"Windows?"

She hesitated. "I can't say positively because I haven't had any open."

They checked. And found two unlatched. The first was a small window in the kitchen, above the sink. The second was in the back bath, above the old-fashioned claw-footed tub.

"This is the window I used to sneak out of at night."

The tub had been rigged with a spray nozzle and circular curtain rod to create a shower. Luke pushed aside the curtain, lifted the window and peered down.

It was a bit of a drop. Even though a single-story home, like many of the homes in Liberty, it had been built on brick pilings because of the threat of flooding.

"Okay," he said, nodding, "you stood on the edge of the tub and pulled yourself through. You were young." He looked over his shoulder at her. "But how'd you get back in?"

"I'll show you."

He followed her outside and around to the back of the house. The top of a brick piling jutted out from under the house, creating a step.

"I'd grab here"—she showed him a notched piece of siding—"use this as a step, then pull myself up and through."

"Who knew about this?"

"All my friends. My boyfriend." She lifted a

shoulder. "I was pretty much a complete ass-hole."

The words were flip, but the emotion behind them heartfelt. He heard her regret in them and felt bad for her. He'd been a jerk at seventeen, too. But his parents had lived long enough to see him through it.

"We all are at that age. I was the reigning king of assholes. Just ask my dad."

"I'd rather not, but I'll take your word for it."

Apparently, she and his pops felt exactly the same way about each other.

They went back into the house. He locked the bathroom window. "No climbing out windows at night, okay?"

"I don't know if I can make that promise."

She said it with such seriousness, he had to grin. "Well, don't call me if you break a leg."

"First person I'm going to call."

He laughed. "I have a little work I need to do here, including collecting the bat and letter, see if we can get anything from them. I'll try to be out of here as quick as possible."

"No worries. Being alone tonight isn't at the top of my list."

He'd done all he'd needed to in thirty minutes. As he was saying good-bye, he sensed she wanted to ask him to stay awhile. Have a cup of coffee or cold drink. But she didn't.

Luke wondered why.

"I'll follow up on the anonymous call, maybe we'll get lucky and it'll lead us to him."

"You'll keep me posted?"

"Absolutely."

"Good night then," she said, standing at the door. "Thanks."

The expected "Anytime" jumped to his lips. He swallowed it. "You realize there's a good chance your fan's from Liberty?"

"I figured he was."

"But you still came back."

She paused a moment, then met his eyes. In them he saw steely determination. "Because he challenged me to."

Chapter Six

Tuesday, June 4
4:07 a.m.

Kat's eyes flew open as something was pressed over her mouth. Tape, she realized, horror rising up in her. Figures around her bed. Hands holding her down. She tried to struggle, to scream, but couldn't.

The room was dark; she strained to make out her attackers' faces. Were they wearing hoods? Masks? Why couldn't she see their features?

As if a cloud had been obscuring the moon, the

room suddenly brightened. Light streamed through the window, starkly silhouetting the person at the end of the bed. He held something in his hands, but she couldn't make out what.

"Justice for Sara," he said.

The others nodded and repeated the words in unison, "Justice for Sara."

"Now," the leader said. "Finally. After ten long years."

"Justice for Sara," the group said again. "Justice for Sara."

Their words rang in her head. The leader raised his arms. A bat, Kat realized. Not any bat, *the* bat he'd gifted her that very night. Its red bow caught the light, winking at her. No, Luke had taken the bat with him, as evidence. It couldn't be.

He turned slightly. The moonlight caught his face. *Luke*.

Suddenly all their faces were clear. All were familiar. Jeremy and Lilith. Ryan. Mrs. Bell and Bitsy. Dab. Sheriff Tanner.

All the people of Liberty. Her accusers. They began to chant. "Justice for Kat . . . Justice for Kat . . . Justice for Kat . . ."

No, she silently pleaded, eyes moving from one to another. No . . . please don't. I'm innocent . . . I promise . . . I'm—

Her gaze stopped on Luke. Smiling grimly, he reared back with the bat and swung.

Kat screamed.

And sat bolt upright in bed, her screams bouncing off her bedroom walls.

It took her a moment to realize it had been a dream. That she was safe, the house empty. Trembling, she pulled the bedding to her chin, eyes darting around the room, assessing the dark corners. Looking for her accusers, hidden there. In the shadows.

It'd been so real.

Luke. The bat. All the people of Liberty. Everyone.

Her accusers.

Kat pressed her face into the bunched-up bedding, struggling to get a grip. She concentrated on controlling her breath, slowing her heart. A dream, she kept telling herself. Only a dream.

After several moments, the physical manifestation of her terror eased. But the dream remained vivid, her accusers' chants still resounded in her head.

Justice for Sara.

Justice for Kat.

Wasn't that why she'd come back? For justice? And because he'd challenged her to. Her fan. The freak.

She grabbed her cell phone off the nightstand and checked the time. Just after four. No way she could go back to sleep.

Kat climbed out of bed. Her legs were wobbly, the wooden floor cool against the bottoms of her feet. She slipped into light sweats, visited the bathroom, then headed for the kitchen to start a pot of coffee.

What had brought on the dream wasn't a mystery. The letter. The bat. Luke's warning to be careful. She stood a moment at the black-and-white-checked tile counter and watched the coffee drip into the glass carafe, then filled a small saucepan with milk. She heated the milk, then when the coffeepot chirped, she simultaneously poured the coffee and the milk into a mug.

Cafe au lait. A south Louisiana tradition. One she'd been brought up on. When she was a little girl, her mother would heat a cup of milk for her, then add a splash of coffee. Coffee milk, she had called it.

Kat carried the mug to the table and sat. She trailed her fingers over the table's reclaimed cypress top. She'd always loved this table. Even when she'd been an out-of-control teen who hated everything.

It'd been in her parents' breakfast nook, and after they'd died, Sara had moved it here. Every morning it had seemed to greet her like a hug from her mom.

No blood on this table. Thank God. She didn't know if she could have borne it.

There'd been so much blood.

She glanced toward the living room. She could

see the plastic bin, sitting on the coffee table where she'd left it. Lid off.

She stood and slowly crossed to it. For long moments, she stared at it. The neatly organized letters. When she'd boxed them up, she'd boxed up her fear of their writer, as well. She'd labeled it *upsetting but harmless.*

Not harmless. Not after last night.

He'd been in her house. In her bedroom.

She retrieved two letters from the box. The two most recent before last evening's. Luke hadn't looked at these. And she hadn't offered them.

But they were important.

Kat brought them back to the kitchen and laid them carefully on the table. One she had received on the tenth anniversary of the murder. The other, exactly one month later, on the ninth anniversary of her acquittal.

She took a sip of the now-tepid cafe au lait, then set the cup aside and opened the first, pulling out the single sheet of paper.

What About Justice for Sara?

Those words, on the tenth anniversary of losing her sister, had affected her like a kick in the teeth.

What about justice for Sara?

What about justice for her?

She'd sat and stared at the words, tears rolling down her cheeks. Those tears had become sobs. Uncontrollable. As if she had pent up everything—anger, grief, confusion, disbelief—for ten long years. And now, finally, was releasing it.

She'd cried for two days straight, then on and off for a month. And then the second letter had come.

She picked it up, eased it out of the envelope.

Coward. I Dare You.

Tears had turned to realization. One of life's *aha* moments.

Ten years had passed and she hadn't moved forward with her life. She'd matured, started a successful business, made friends. None of that mattered. Essentially, she was in exactly the same place as the day she walked out of the St. Tammany Parish courthouse a free woman.

A coward, she was. She'd run away from Liberty and her accusers; she'd run away from the truth.

And from her guilt. The almost paralyzing fear that her sister was dead because of her.

Going back, she'd realized in that moment, was the only way to move forward.

So here she was. Kat narrowed her eyes. The police, in their rush to judgment, had missed something. Something that would exonerate her and lead to the guilty party. The killer was still here in Liberty. She believed that to the very core of her being.

In a strange way, the letters proved it.

Her fan. Why had he urged her to come back? To kill her? The baseball bat seemed to confirm that notion. So why hadn't he done it? He could have. A hundred times.

Maybe he'd wanted to witness her terror first-hand. Like a cat playing with a cornered mouse.

The thought sent a chill up her spine. She stood and crossed to the front window, pulled the drape aside and peered out. He could be any-where. Anyone. He could be old Mrs. Bell from across the street.

She dropped the drape. Or maybe he wanted something else from her. But what?

Chapter Seven

Tuesday, June 4
8:10 a.m.

Luke sat at his father's desk—he still thought of it that way—surrounded by files, case notes and crime-scene photos. On the computer monitor were the results of his search: *The People of Louisiana vs. Katherine Ann McCall.*

Though he hadn't slept, he felt wide awake and energized. He'd left Kat McCall's place and come directly here. He'd been off at LSU when the murder occurred. The trial had come a little over a year later; he'd still been at school, partying his way toward flunking out.

The trial hadn't even been a blip on his radar. And after spending time with Kat, after seeing the anger that had been—and still was—being directed at her, he'd wanted the particulars.

Truth was, he didn't get it. She didn't seem like a cold-blooded killer to him—his father's words—or a lying, sneaky snake, another description he'd overheard.

He liked Kat. She seemed remarkably calm, considering. And she still had a sense of humor. In fact, he hadn't picked up on any of those unfortunate characteristics acquired by people who'd been through great trauma. No, Kat McCall seemed to have both feet planted firmly on the ground.

Though, as he was sure his father would point out, he didn't know her very well. They'd spent, all combined, maybe an hour in each other's company.

He'd like to spend more time with her. He rubbed his stubbly jaw. He could just imagine, that would probably send his old man straight into orbit. Or directly into the ground.

One corner of his mouth lifted in wry amusement and he shook his head. Just a few years ago that would have been reason enough to get involved with her. It'd been reason enough for most of the ridiculous things he'd done.

Luke shifted his gaze to one of the framed photos that graced the big, old desk. His brother, Stevie. Holding up the prizewinning bass he'd caught on his tenth birthday.

The same summer he drowned.

The summer that everything changed between him and his dad.

With a familiar pinch in his chest, Luke dragged his attention back to the information spread before him. Forced himself to focus. He'd wanted the particulars to understand the level of fury directed toward Kat McCall. His father's. Those people who had written with such hate. The folks of Liberty who refused to forget or accept. This "fan" who had followed her for ten years.

Had the jury botched the verdict that badly? Or had the prosecution blown it?

Luke looked down at the crime-scene photos, fanned out on the desk in front of him. Awful. Gruesome. Whoever had killed Sara McCall had beaten her to a pulp, even bashing in her face. The pathologist had confirmed that the perpetrator had continued to beat her after she was dead.

That was pure rage. Personal. Directed against Sara McCall.

She had known her attacker. A stranger didn't do that.

Strike one against the angry little sister.

Kat had found the body. That'd been another strike. She'd called 911 but hadn't sounded upset. In fact, she'd sounded calm, some had thought happy. Her story about sleeping through the murder had seemed farfetched; later she changed it, then changed it again. More strikes.

61

The prosecution had laid out a parade of witnesses who testified Kat and her sister had fought constantly, that Katherine McCall had publicly wished her sister dead and had told friends she wanted her inheritance, that it wasn't fair that her sister wouldn't give it her.

The bat had belonged to Kat. Four days before the murder, Sara had discovered her sister had been lying to her about going to softball practice. She had confronted Kat and grounded her, which had led to a shouting match on Sara's front porch.

Four days later, Sara was dead. Beaten to death with the softball bat.

But that was all they'd had. No bloody finger-prints. No bloody tracks leading from the home. No blood-spattered clothes. No DNA evidence on the bat. And Luminol tests on all but the kitchen sink had been negative. If Kat had been covered in blood, she hadn't showered it off at the scene.

Luke sat back. Circumstantial. All of it. Weak. In his opinion, if the jury had found her guilty, it would have been a huge miscarriage of justice.

Yet everyone in this town, including his dad, thought she'd gotten away with murder. They'd been so convinced, they never pursued other suspects. Why?

He frowned, remembering something she'd said. She'd used the bathroom window to sneak out to meet her boyfriend. But no boyfriend was mentioned anywhere in the case notes.

"You look like hell."

He glanced up. His father stood in the doorway, using a cane for support. "Like father, like son."

He snorted and made his way into the office. He lowered himself into a chair, bushy eyebrows drawn into a scowl. He gestured the cluttered desktop. "What're you up to?"

"Familiarizing myself with the McCall case."

"I heard you were over there last night."

"Did you?" Luke folded his hands on the desk in front of him. "How, Pops?"

He bristled. "You think I'm so old and sick I don't have eyes and ears anymore? That I don't have friends anymore?"

Why wouldn't he give him a straight answer?

The anonymous call. *There's trouble over at the McCall place.*

"I'm worried about you, boy."

"Me," Luke said, surprised. "Why?"

"You're my son. The only one I have left."

Several emotions hit Luke at once, anger the strongest of them. He struggled to keep it leashed. "Really, Pops? You're going to pull out the 'only son I have left' card? Already?"

"You could at least listen to what I have to say."

"Fine. I'm listening."

"Don't get sucked into her stories. She's a liar." His motioned the paperwork strewn across the desk. "Read the transcripts."

"I have."

"Then you saw how many times she changed her story."

"Katherine McCall was seventeen years old," Luke said, indicating the information spread out on the desk between them. "And, I imagine, pretty damn traumatized."

His dad made a sound of disgust. "I should have known you'd take the opposite stance from mine. You always do."

Luke narrowed his eyes. "Nobody can have a different opinion, right, Dad?"

"I don't have to take this crap." He got up, his gruff words belied by the way he struggled to gain his footing. "If I wanted someone chewing on my ear, I'd have stayed home with your mother."

"This isn't about you."

"To hell with this." He started for the door.

"Why didn't you interview her boyfriend?" Luke called.

His old man stopped. Turned. "She didn't have one."

"That's not what she told me. She used to sneak out of the house to meet him."

"Or so she told you. She changed her version of what happened the night of the murder four times!"

"The notes here say three times." He paused. "I'm reopening the case."

The words flew out of his mouth, surprising him. Until that very moment, he hadn't realized that's what he intended to do. "In fact, I'm reopening both of them."

With his free hand, his dad grabbed the door-jamb for support. "How could you do this to me?"

"Do to *you,* Dad? You should be pleased. McCall was Liberty's only unsolved murder. And Wally Clark was one of your men."

"I know who Wally was and what a black mark McCall was against me. I don't need the criticism. Especially from you."

Luke shook his head. "Not criticism. A fresh perspective. It's been known to work on many a cold case."

"I solved the McCall case but the jury bungled the verdict. As for Wally, that wasn't ours. Look to the sheriff's department."

"Have you ever considered the two crimes might be related?"

"You don't think I looked into that?"

"Did you?"

"Son of a bitch, boy! What kind of lawman do you take me for?"

"A good one. But even the good ones miss things."

"What could I have missed? The two murders had nothing in common. Wally was shot on the road, McCall was beaten to death with a bat."

"Nothing but the fact they happened on the same night, less than five miles apart. Besides, like I said a moment ago, this isn't about you, Pops."

"The hell it isn't. The only reason you're so interested is because it's my failure."

"Not true, Pops. Maybe once upon a time it would have been, but no more."

"You're my own flesh and blood. Why can't you leave this alone?"

"Because two people died. They deserve justice."

His father seemed to crumble, all bravado sucked out of him. Luke moved to help him, but he angrily waved him off.

Luke watched as his father limped slowly out. Why did his old man feel so strongly about the case being reopened. Was it his pride? Or was he hiding something?

Chief Stephen Tanner
2003

The morning after the murder

A swimming pool, bright blue water like glass. The sun reflecting off it, almost blinding. No adults. Just two boys.

His boys.

Laughing. Daring each other to swim to the bottom. Touch the drain. Whoever stayed under longer won.

Typical Stevie, oldest and boldest, jumped in first.

Stephen Tanner sat straight up in bed. "Stevie!" he screamed. "No!"

The warning reverberated off the bedroom walls. Heart thundering, disoriented, Tanner looked frantically around. Dark. His bed. Alone. Margaret, where—

At her mother's, he remembered. For the week.

He brought his hands to his throbbing head. His mouth was dry, his stomach rolled. Its contents lurched to his throat, and he climbed off the bed. His right foot caught a bottle, sending it spinning.

An empty bottle.

Captain Morgan spiced rum.

His stomach protested again and he stumbled to the bathroom. He reached the commode just in time, bent over it and retched. Stomach empty, he dragged himself up, crossed to the sink. He rinsed out his mouth, then splashed his face.

His haggard reflection gazed back at him. Unshaven, pale. Bloodshot eyes.

The reflection of a man who couldn't stay sober. A man who hadn't been able to protect his family.

He curled his shaking hands into fists. Chief Stephen Tanner. The great pretender.

Tanner turned away from his reflection. No. It wasn't true. He had everything under control. Liberty and her citizens were safe under his watchful eye.

Tanner returned to the bedroom; the empty bottle mocked him. He scooped it up. One fall from grace. It'd been months. That wasn't so bad.

A man in his position had to let off some steam every once in a while.

But Margaret couldn't know. She had warned him what would happen if he started up again. That she would leave him. Then everyone would know. They would see what he really was.

Margaret didn't understand the pressure he was under. So many people depended on him to be strong. Her. The citizens of Liberty. His son.

His only son.

He would bury the evidence deep in the trash.

The phone rang. He frowned, glanced at the bedside clock. Barely five. Not the time of day for a social call.

He cleared his throat, snatched it up. "Tanner," he said.

"Chief, it's Trixie."

The night clerk. She manned the phone and the station from 11:00 p.m. to 7:00 a.m. She never called.

Her voice was thin, shaking.

"What's wrong?"

"It's Wally, he . . ." She started to cry. "A sheriff's deputy called . . . he said . . . he said—"

He tamped down the panic that wanted to

rise up in him. "Pull yourself together, Trix! Tell me what's happened."

"He's dead."

Tanner frowned. She couldn't have said, she didn't mean—"Who's dead?"

"Wally!" she wailed. "Somebody shot him!"

For a split second he was certain he had misheard her. Or that it was a sick joke. She couldn't have said—

But she had.

"Quickly, Trix, tell me what happened."

"He called in. At two forty-six. About a car with no plates at the side of Highway 22. He was going to investigate."

"That's it?"

"That's what he said. Didn't he call you?"

"Why would he?"

She whimpered. "He said he did."

Tanner worked to pull together his scrambled thoughts. "The phone didn't ring," he snapped.

"I could be mistaken, I'm not . . . That's what I thought he said."

"Judas Priest, Trixie! Pull yourself together!"

She started to cry again. He cut her off. "Where did they find him?"

"On 22. A hundred feet from the Liberty line."

"Their jurisdiction? Or ours?"

"Their's. They made that clear."

"Nothing else?"

"Miz Bell called. Said she thought something was going on over at the McCall place."

"She always thinks something's going on over there."

"She said she saw Miss Katherine sneaking out of the house last night."

"And last week she reported a peeping Tom that turned out to be a raccoon."

"She was insistent. Said she would have called it in sooner, but that she wasn't feeling so well—"

"Dammit, Trix, focus! Wally's dead, nothing else matters."

She went stone silent. He'd never raised his voice to her and he knew he'd hurt her feelings. But he couldn't worry about a rebellious teen-ager or her nosy neighbor right now. "What else did the sheriff's deputies say?"

"That he'd been . . . he'd been shot. That's all."

"I'm heading to the scene. Keep this under wraps until we know for sure what happened."

Chapter Eight

Tuesday, June 4
9:15 a.m.

Kat had arranged to meet Jeremy's Realtor at the first property. She'd left early enough to stop at the Sunny Side Up first. Although their three-egg scramblers and Applewood smoked bacon were two of the most delicious things on the planet, she wasn't looking to have a late breakfast.

She wanted to have a word with her old friend Dab.

Kat parked her Fusion hybrid, angling it in between a Suburban and an F-150 pickup. It was amazing how many people still drove gas-guzzling trucks and SUVs down here. In Portland, compact, efficient and hybrid were the norm. Of course, if you Googled "southern transportation," it'd pull up a picture of a big ol' truck.

Riverview Street was the most picturesque in Liberty. Only three blocks long, it fronted the Tchefuncte River. The riverside was dotted with magnificent live oaks, the other side with cafes, shops and other businesses.

Good Earth Bread Company would be a perfect addition to the other businesses. Her other choice of location was the town square.

Kat reached the cafe. Sunny Side, as the locals called it, had been a Liberty tradition for as long as Kat could remember. When her mother had been a teenager, the Sunny Side's soda fountain had been their after-school hangout. By the time Kat made high school, coffee drinks had replaced ice cream creations and she and her friends had stopped in for lattes and granitas.

As Kat entered the cafe, the bell over the door jingled. A friendly welcoming sound. Folks glanced her way, their smiles fading as they recognized her. One by one, they fell silent and stared.

Not so friendly now, she thought. Not welcoming.

Could one of these people be her "fan"? Was he staring at her now, thinking of the bat and imaging her reaction? Getting off on the idea of her terror.

She wouldn't give him, any of them, the satisfaction. Kat let the door swing shut behind her. "Hi, y'all," she said brightly. "Yup, it's true. I'm back."

She saw that there was room at the counter and headed that way. It was a weird feeling, all those gazes on her back. She was tempted to look over her shoulder and catch them staring, but figured it'd only serve to give them more to talk about.

She took a stool. The waitress approached. Kat recognized her. She'd manned this counter ten years ago as well. She'd been a classmate of Sara's, had married young and lost her husband in an oil rig accident. "Hi, Mary Lee," she said. "Coffee would be great."

Mary Lee silently filled her cup.

"Is Dab around?"

The waitress looked surprised. "She is, but—"

"Could you let her know her old friend Kat's here to see her?"

Mary Lee hesitated, then shrugged. "Sure. I guess so."

A moment later Dab stepped out from the kitchen. She was flushed from the heat. And very pregnant.

Kat tried not to stare. She tried not reveal how upended she was, how startled. Had she expected time to stand still for Dab, the way it had for her?

"Hello, Katherine," she said. "I'd heard you were back."

"Bad news travels fast in Liberty."

"I don't want any trouble," she said softly. "I'm due any day now, I shouldn't even be working but Mom had a heart attack. If you start something, I might just drop this baby right here behind this counter."

Dab had always been the honest one. Kat had liked her for it. "I don't want any trouble. Why would I?"

Dab lowered her voice even more. "The trial? My testimony against you?"

"You told the truth, didn't you?"

Dab held her gaze a moment, then looked over her shoulder. "Lyle, honey? You think you can manage a few minutes without me?"

He said he could and she motioned to the door at the back of the restaurant. "Everybody's way too interested in what we might say to each other. Besides, I've got to get off my feet. C'mon around."

Moments later, they reached Dab's cramped office. With a sigh of relief, Dab lowered herself to her chair. An engineering feat, Kat thought.

"Is this your first?" she asked.

"It is." She beamed. "We're so excited. It's a boy. Lyle couldn't wait to find out the sex."

It took Kat a moment to find her voice. "Lyle's your husband, then?"

"Been married four years." She held out her left hand, wiggled her fingers. "How about you, Kat? You married? Have any kids?"

Questions any old school chums would ask after ten years, not much more significant than *How's the weather been?*

Not for Kat. For her, they dug deep. Her life, the direction it had taken, so much of it hadn't been her choice.

"Nope," she said lightly, "still single."

They fell elephant-in-the-room silent. Dab broke it first. "I only told the truth, Kat."

"I know." She paused. "I looked pretty guilty."

"I never said you did it, only that you talked about it. About wishing she was dead, I mean."

"I know," Kat said again. "But I didn't do it."

Dab shifted her gaze slightly.

She didn't believe her.

It took Kat's breath away. "I didn't," she said again. "And I'm going to prove it."

"I've got to get back in the kitchen, Kat. It's been real nice seeing you."

When all else fails, fall back on good, old-fashioned southern manners. As disingenuous as they can be.

"Wait." Kat pulled a Good Earth flyer from her purse. "I'm thinking of opening up one of my bread stores down the street." She handed her the flyer. "A big part of my business is supplying restaurants with healthy, whole-grain alternatives. I hope you'll be open to me calling on you."

Dab skimmed the information. "Sure. Of course. I get requests for this sort of thing."

"Any of the old gang around?" Kat asked as they stood.

"Some. I don't see 'em much anymore. I'm pretty busy."

"What about Ryan?"

"Ryan?"

"Benton."

"Oh yeah, him." She laughed self-consciously. "It's been ten years, hard to remember every-one from back then."

Unless back then was when your life came screeching to a halt.

"He owns an automotive repair place up on 59 in Mandeville," Dab said. "R and B Imports."

Chapter Nine

Tuesday, June 4
10:00 a.m.

Kat and the Realtor simultaneously arrived at the storefront. Tish Alexander was not what Kat had expected. Since Jeremy had recommended her, she'd pictured classic professional, like Lilith. Instead, Tish was tall with a big voice, big chest and long blond hair.

"Katherine McCall," she greeted Kat with a distinctive Texas twang, "Tish Alexander." She stuck out her hand. "Pleased as punch you called me."

Kat smiled and took her hand, immediately liking the other woman. "Thank Jeremy, he couldn't say enough good things about you."

"That man is as sweet as my mama's peach pie. I was able to fix him up with office space, then the perfect location for his campaign headquarters."

"I can't believe he's running for state senate."

"I can." She nodded as if for emphasis. "And

he's gonna win, too. You just wait and see. C'mon, let's take a look at this place."

Tish kept up a running commentary while she got out the key and opened the door. "Most recently, it was a restaurant. So it has a kitchen already, though I'm sure you'd have to build it out to your own specifications. Why don't we start there."

Kat stood in the center of the kitchen and did a slow three-sixty. She *would* need to build it out, Kat thought. But the layout was good and the size was right. The ovens were her most expensive pieces of equipment. The better the oven, the better the bread.

As Kat inspected the kitchen, she started forming a list: sinks could stay, so could the counters. New fans, ovens and coolers. The commercial dishwasher, surprisingly, was adequate.

She looked at Tish. "Why didn't they liquidate the fixtures and appliances?"

"They own the property. Figured it might help rent it out."

"But they're willing to sell?"

Tish hesitated, then nodded. "Yes, absolutely."

Kat frowned at her tone. "Is there a problem?"

"No, not at all. It's just when Jeremy contacted me, he thought you were looking to rent. He thought—"

"That it would be wiser, considering my history? That sounds just like Jeremy."

"I'm sorry, you're my client, not Jeremy."

"It's all right. I suppose it does seem a little crazy. What with people wanting to tar and feather me."

"Tar and feather might be an overstatement."

"More likely an understatement." Tish didn't ask what that meant and Kat didn't offer.

As they walked through the other rooms, Kat imagined her bread company here. What had been the dining room was big enough to serve as a storefront that included a small cafe area. She planned to serve sandwiches at lunch. And although most folks grabbed a pastry to go, in a setting like this, some would want to stay and enjoy the day, sitting outside and watching the river.

She stood on the covered front porch, the breeze stirring her hair. She smiled. "I like it. A lot."

"Good."

"I'd want to add a deck area, for additional outdoor seating. Over there." She indicated a spot on the left side of the porch. "I wonder about the setbacks."

"I'll find out. The owner is motivated."

"When you inquire, don't use my name. Just the corporation's. If I decide this is the one, I don't want who I am to become a factor in the negotiation."

"I think that's wise. You still want to look at the other two properties?"

She nodded, and less than an hour later, they stepped out of the second one. Both would do, Kat thought. Being located on the square would offer walk-in traffic, by her estimation, and these two properties would require less of a build-out investment. But she didn't like either as much as the waterfront option.

Although this one sat directly next to the Liberty P.D., which could come in handy, considering how many people in this town hated her guts.

Plus, she'd probably run into Luke daily. She'd found him popping into her thoughts here and there, enough that she had begun to notice. And to worry about it.

Getting involved with the son of Chief Stephen Tanner, the man who, more than any other, had wanted to see her fry, was an impossible idea.

"Hey, Kat."

Think of the handsome devil, and up he jumps. She turned. Luke strolled toward her.

"What're you doing down here?"

"Looking for commercial space. I'm opening up a bread store and bakery."

"I'd heard that." He slipped his hands into his pockets. "I'm awfully fond of cookies."

Charming. Dammit. She laughed. "I warn you, my cookies would be good for you."

"But tasty?"

"Very."

Tish cleared her throat, then stuck out her hand. "Tish Alexander. Front Door Realty."

She had forgotten the other woman was standing beside her. Heat stung Kat's cheeks. "I'm sorry, I assumed you two knew each other."

"Nope." He shook her hand. "Sergeant Luke Tanner. Great to meet you."

"Likewise." His cell phone sounded and Tish turned back to her. "I'll get that information you wanted. Call me if you think of anything else."

"I will, Tish. Thanks."

Luke was still on his call; he signaled her to wait. Kat studied him while he talked. Dark hair and eyes, wicked smile, he reminded her of Hugh Jackman without the stubble. She remembered being in junior high and seeing him, around six feet tall, with a lean, muscular build, and his jock friends throwing the football on the square, and being awestruck. They'd been like rock stars to her.

Today he wore jeans, a chambray shirt and a rather battered sports coat. A much more casual approach to dress than his father'd had. She'd never seen Stephen Tanner in anything but his uniform.

Luke ended the call and smiled at her. "Sorry about that."

"No problem. What's up?"

"If you have a minute, there're a couple questions I wanted to ask you."

She said she did and he led her into the station. For a split second, she couldn't breathe. It all came crashing back, the shock and disbelief, the fear and nightmarish reality of it.

She wanted to turn and run. Leave this place—and Liberty—far behind.

He touched her arm, snapping her back to the moment. "You all right?"

"Am I that obvious?"

"Sorry."

She forced a laugh and felt better for it. "First time back, that's all."

"First is the worst."

"You're a poet and don't know it."

He laughed and she realized he had chased the ghosts away. A moment later they faced each other across his desk. "I'm surprised your dad lets you get away with dressing like that."

He looked down at himself. "Pops? Yeah, he's a bit of a uniform nazi. But there's not much he can do about it. I'm acting chief, and the city bylaws don't require the chief to dress out." He grinned. "It drives him crazy."

"Why do I suspect that's part of the reason you do it?"

"Not at all. I'm over the whole rebellion thing. Long time ago."

The twinkle in his eyes told her otherwise. She laughed. "Right. I see that."

A framed photo of a young boy holding up a

big fish caught her eye. She picked it up. "Is this you? Cute."

"Nope. My brother. Stevie."

"Stevie?" She frowned. "I don't remember you having a sib."

"He was a year older than me. He drowned. The summer of '92."

She set the photo down. "I'm sorry."

"Stuff happens." He changed the subject. "So, you think Liberty's ready for a healthy bakery?"

"You sound like Lilith. And yes, I do."

He cocked his head. "If I asked you out, would you say yes?"

Her pulse fluttered. "Are you? Asking me out?"

"Thinking about it."

"Don't burn any brain cells over it. I'd say no."

"Have you ever been to Pontchartrain Vineyards?"

"A vineyard? Here? As in wine?"

"Crazy, but there is. Off Old Military Road." He held her gaze. "They have this Jazz in the Vines thing once a month. I wondered if you wanted to go."

"With you?"

"Yeah."

"Didn't we just cover this?"

"Not to my satisfaction."

"I don't date cops. Too much history."

"Sounds like an unreasonable bias."

"It is. No argument from me there."

"Good news, I'm not a cop. I'm acting chief. Big difference."

"You're a Tanner. Even worse."

"Another unreasonable bias. I'm not going to give up."

Kat decided she liked that. "Whatever. Your brain cells."

He laughed. "I've got a question for you."

"Another one?" She sat back. "Shoot."

"Last night, you mentioned sneaking out to meet your boyfriend. Who were you dating?"

He continued to surprise her. She narrowed her eyes. "Why do you want to know?"

"Because I'm reopening your sister's murder investigation."

Chapter Ten

Tuesday, June 4
1:00 p.m.

Kat wanted to talk to Ryan before Luke did, so she headed directly there from the police department. R&B Imports wasn't the small-scale operation she had expected, but a big, impressively slick one, from the contemporary leather seating in the waiting room to the complimentary beverage center, complete with an espresso machine.

She greeted the blond receptionist. Young, very.

Looked bored. Kat smiled. "I was hoping Ryan was in?"

"He is."

That was it. No smile or offer of help, borderline rude. Kat wondered if Ryan encouraged the attitude as a way of discouraging unwanted visitors or if she was just that clueless.

"Is he available?"

"Do you have an appointment?"

"Tell him Kat McCall's here to see him."

Her expression changed subtly, sharpening with interest. "If this is about your car, one of the mechanics—"

"It's personal. I think he'll want to talk to me."

For a split second, the girl looked as if she might refuse, then she picked up the phone.

Moments later, Ryan met her at the door to his office. He didn't look happy to see her. Kat acknowledged a perverse pleasure at the thought she might be totally screwing up his day.

He closed the door behind them and faced her. For a long moment, they simply gazed at each other.

She had wondered what he'd look like after all this time. If he'd be as handsome or if he'd have gone soft and begun to lose his hair. She had wondered if she would still respond so forcefully to being near him.

The answer to the first was yes, he was still

handsome. Lean and muscular with a full head of dark hair, though he had changed dramatically in other ways. Before, he'd been a young rebel, the quintessential town bad boy. Now his demeanor shouted success, confidence and . . . caution. The new Ryan Benton cared what people thought.

And the answer to the latter was no—the sexual tug she had felt for him back then was gone. All that remained was a smoldering anger.

"Ballsy move coming here," he said.

"I grew a pair in the last ten years."

He released a bark of laughter. "Wild-Kat McCall, all grown up."

Wild-Kat. He used to call her that sometimes. She'd liked it. The name had made her feel adult. Like her own person. What a joke.

She swept her gaze contemptuously over him. "Rebellious Ryan Benton, tamed."

He didn't like that. "Why're you here, Kat?"

"Wow. Really? After ten years, that's it?"

"I don't know what else you could expect after all this time."

"I was madly in love with you. I gave you my virginity. Maybe an 'It's great to see you' or a 'You look great'?"

"You do look great," he said softly. "But I'm not going to pretend to be happy to see you. You shouldn't have come here and you shouldn't have come back to Liberty."

"And why's that?"

85

"Let's not play games. People haven't forgotten. And they won't forgive. Not here."

"And what about you? Why don't you want me here?"

He narrowed his eyes. "I'm a businessman, Kat. This"—he motioned around them—"is how I make a living. People in small towns talk. They judge. I can't let you damage my reputation."

Her? Damage his reputation? That burned. She was the one who had thrown everything away for him. "You sound like a man who has something to hide. Or one who's a coward. Are you a coward, Ryan? Funny, back then, I thought you were a hero."

"You were very young."

She moved farther into the room, crossing to a series of framed certificates on the wall. Several 'Best of the Northshore' awards, association memberships, diplomas from the Mercedes training program, a photo of him with a race car driver she didn't recognize.

She turned back to him. "You're still in Liberty, still working on cars. I'm surprised. I remember you telling me that was the last thing you wanted to do." She couldn't resist the dig, though it brought nothing to the table.

"Overseeing work on cars," he corrected tightly. "What do you want, Kat?"

"I didn't kill Sara. But I intend to find out who did."

"Good luck with that." He motioned the door. "If you don't mind, I need to get back to work."

She didn't move. "I kept our secret, Ryan. But maybe I shouldn't have."

"Big secret. We had a fling. Kids do that."

He'd taken advantage of her youth. Her vulnerability and need for love. She'd been a piece of ass to him.

She'd finally realized that after she'd been cleared of all charges—and he still hadn't come for her.

"I sat in jail, day after day, wondering where you were. Why, if you loved me the way you said you did, you didn't come to see me."

He averted his gaze. Yes, she decided, a coward. And weak. What had she ever seen in him?

"I thought you'd save me, Ryan."

She cleared her throat, surprised by the lump of emotion that settled there. She didn't care anymore. Not about him or how he had hurt her. So why did the memory of that desperate and heartbroken girl still have power over her?

"I worried something had happened to you," she went on. "Or that you'd found someone else. Did you even think of me and what I was going through?"

His silence was her answer and sudden fury rose up in her. "I'd lost my sister, my only family. Then I was charged, arrested and thrown in jail. Where were you? I had no one. I told myself I had to keep us a secret, to protect you. What were you doing to protect me?"

"I was young, Kat. I—"

"I don't want to hear about how *you* felt!" She curled her hands into fists, wanting to hit him. "I found her body. That morning I got up and—"

The horror of the memory momentarily choked her. She fought it off. "After a while, I started thinking of the last time we were together. Remember? Two nights before she died. What you said."

He remembered. She saw it in his eyes. But she wasn't surprised when he played dumb. "I'm sorry I hurt you, Kat. I am. I was a selfish prick."

His words rang as true as a tin bell. But an apology, heartfelt or not, wasn't what she was after. "Not good enough. Tell me you remember that last night we were together."

"Sorry, none of those days or nights stand out to me. They were all the same."

"Lucky you, Ryan. Some are burned on my memory."

"What do you want from me, Kat!" The words exploded from him. "I said I'm sorry. If you hadn't been so young, you would have recognized me for what I was."

But was he a murderer? Would she have seen that?

"You're right. I was an idiot teenage girl. Such

an idiot, I was completely loyal to you. You told me if anyone knew about us, we couldn't be together. So I told no one. Not even my lawyer. My story kept changing because I had to take such a big piece out of it—you."

His expression tightened. "This trip down Memory Lane's been real, Kat, but it's time for you to go."

She wasn't going anywhere, not yet. "You know what was really idiotic, Ryan? I was so madly in love, it never even occurred to me that you might have done it. What we talked about. That last time we were together." She paused. "You suggested we kill her."

Something dangerous crept into his eyes. He leaned toward her. "You're mistaken."

He spoke through clenched teeth, his tone low, menacing. That move might have worked back then, but no more. She held her ground, meeting his gaze evenly. "I thought you were joking, remember? I suggested we push her in front of a bus."

"You were stoned. So was I."

"You said you had a plan for us to be together. That I should trust you. What was that plan, Ryan?"

"I had no plan. I just said that so I could keep banging you and keep you from shooting your mouth off. Jail wasn't an option." He walked to the door. "Time for you to go."

She didn't move. "You talked about killing her. And then she was dead."

For a split second, as his smoldering gaze landed on hers, she was reminded of the boy he had been all those years ago. And of the dangerous hold he'd had over her.

"Did you kill her, Ryan?"

He didn't look shocked, or even surprised. But she sensed his panic, the way one animal did another's. Only this time he was the one in a corner.

And a cornered animal would fight for its survival.

He took a step toward her. "Do not fuck with me, Katherine. You understand? I have a lot to lose and you won't like what happens."

"You didn't answer my question."

"Hell no, Kat. I didn't kill her."

"Luke Tanner's reopening the case. Expect a visit from him."

She started for the door, he blocked her exit. "Why would I kill her? Yes, we talked about it that night. We were stupid kids. It was just stupid talk."

"And then she ended up dead. That's a crazy coincidence, don't you think?"

"If this gets out, it'll incriminate you, too."

"Double jeopardy, babe. Law says I can't be tried for the same crime twice."

This time he didn't try to stop her exit. Kat

stepped out of his office. The receptionist glanced her way.

The petite dark-haired woman she was talking with followed her gaze. "Katherine McCall?" she said. "Oh, my gosh, it is true! You *are* back!"

Kat stopped. "Bitsy?"

Her old friend closed the distance between them to give her a big hug. "I'm so glad to see you! It's been too, too long."

Kat smiled and hugged her back. "Other than Jeremy, you're the first person to say that to me."

"Well, maybe I just better say it again, then. It's good to see you."

The elfin girl had turned into an exotic-looking woman. Short black hair styled into a mass of soft, fat curls; large gray eyes, dramatically outlined in kohl; a mouth that was too big for her face. Funny how those same features on a child could be awkward to the point of homely.

"I hear you're an interior designer. Famous, even. You got to use your artistic talent, after all."

"And you're a successful entrepreneur."

Kat laughed and shook her head. "A baker," she corrected. "That's the way I think of myself."

Bitsy's smile faded. "I'm sorry I haven't kept in touch."

"I didn't expect you to." Kat became aware of the way they had drawn attention, including from Ryan, who had appeared at his office door. "I should go."

"I'll walk you out."

Bitsy linked their arms. "It's like the old days."

Kat laughed again. "Well, not just like—Oh my gosh, is that Merlin?"

Her father's 1960 Mercedes 220SE Cabriolet. They'd named it Merlin the Magic Car because seeing it always put Bitsy's dad in a good mood.

"It is. They passed, you know."

"I didn't. When?"

"Dad five years ago. Just as I was starting my business. Mom last year."

"I'm sorry."

"Thanks. It was difficult, but that's life." She shook off her melancholy. "We have to get together. Catch up."

"I'd like that."

"Lunch?"

"Anytime."

"How about tomorrow? Noon at Cafe Toile?"

Kat hesitated. Cafe Toile. They'd toasted Sara's closing on the cottage there. It'd been the last time they'd celebrated as a family. Not long after, her parents had been dead.

Another memory to be faced.

Kat agreed, and as she drove away she saw that Ryan had joined Bitsy beside Merlin. They stood beside each other, watching her drive off. The image of them struck her as wrong. Both intimate and wary.

It occurred to Kat that she hadn't asked Bitsy

why she had been there. She'd simply assumed she had brought Merlin in for servicing.

Could Bitsy and Ryan be friends now? No, never. The Bitsy she'd known had hated Ryan Benton's guts.

Chapter Eleven

Tuesday, June 4
2:45 p.m.

"Luke, Ryan Benton's here to see you."

"Thanks, Trix. Send him back." Luke hung up the phone and leaned back in his chair. *Ryan Benton.* It was the second time today he had heard that name. The first had been from Kat McCall's lips when he asked who she'd been dating all those years ago.

And now he was here to see him. Interesting.

The man tapped on the door; Luke stood to greet him. "Ryan, man. Good to see you."

He crossed the room. "Hey, Luke, good to see you, too."

They shook hands. Luke gestured to one of the chairs in front of the desk, then sat. "How've you been? I don't think our paths have crossed since Mardi Gras."

"Doin' good. The shop's been busy. You?"

"Hangin' in there. What can I do for you?"

He didn't answer, instead moved his gaze over the office. "Weird déjà vu thing going on for me. I spent a good bit of time in this office."

Luke laughed. He and Ryan had been in the same graduating class at Tammany West High School. He had been a star athlete, Ryan an ace hell-raiser. Although they hadn't traveled in the same circles, they'd had an odd, mutual respect for each other.

Ryan steepled his fingers. "The sheriff's kid and the kid the sheriff was always cuffing. And here we are."

"But that's not what brought you here today."

"No." He paused. "Katherine McCall was in to see me at the shop. She was saying some pretty crazy things, so I figured I better come in. I don't want any trouble. I'm not that dude anymore."

A surprise move by McCall. And Benton. Luke took a notebook, laid it on the desk. "For the record, you and she were seeing each other at the time of her sister's murder."

"Yes."

"And what kind of crazy things was she saying today?"

"That I had something to do with her sister's death."

"Something to do with?"

Ryan let out a long breath. "That I killed her."

"Did you?"

"Hell, no. I didn't even know the woman."

"Did she tell you I'm reopening the case?"

He looked annoyed. "She did. That's why I'm here. I figured I'd better come in and set the record straight."

A strategy. He figured it'd look better if he came in. It did in some ways. In others, not so much. "I appreciate that, Ryan." Luke glanced down at the notebook, then back up at the other man. "So what do you want to tell me?"

"Man, I hate being in this position. Shit." He shook his head. "I was messing around with a seventeen-year-old girl. I shouldn't have been." He lifted a shoulder. "I was a punk."

"You were never interviewed by the cops or the defense lawyers? How come?"

"Nobody knew about us."

"Nobody? That seems hard to believe."

"She was underage."

"Surely you told your friends or she told hers. Underage doesn't mean jack to them."

"It did to me."

"Was your relationship sexual?"

"Yes."

"Did you supply her with alcohol?"

"Yes."

"Drugs?"

"Weed." He spread his fingers. "Like I said, I was a stupid, punk kid. I don't do that shit any-more."

"Go on."

"If we'd been found out I would have been charged with contributing, at the very least. So I convinced her to keep her mouth shut."

Luke drummed his fingers silently against the desktop. Teenage girls didn't keep secrets. They gossiped, confided, wrote in their journals. She had to have told somebody.

"Even after she was arrested," Luke said.

"I never saw her after that. Never spoke to her."

"Why's that?"

He looked surprised. "Are you kidding? I didn't want anything to do with that. Plus, I figured she did it."

It was Luke's turn to be surprised. "You thought she was guilty?"

"She hated her sister. Wished she was dead. I thought maybe they got in a huge fight and she . . . did it."

"Because that's just one small step. Between talking and doing?"

"Yeah. I suppose."

It wasn't. It was a huge step, one most people would never make. "But she wasn't guilty."

"According to the jury."

"But you think they got it wrong?"

He lifted a shoulder. "Maybe. Yeah, I do."

Luke tapped the pen against his thumb, thoughts racing. "If that's true, why did she come back? And why accuse you of doing it?"

"I don't know."

Luke kept his gaze trained intently on the other man's even as he maintained an almost casual tone. "Let's say she is innocent. Why would she think you had something to do with murdering her sister?"

"Again, I don't know. Maybe she's playing a game with me. Punishing me for dumping her. Maybe she thought I did it for her."

"Why would you?"

"What?"

"Do it for her?"

"Why, exactly. It makes no sense."

He leaned forward. Luke decided schoolboy earnestness didn't play well on Ryan Benton. Came off smarmy.

"Here's the deal with me and Kat. I figured she was my ticket out. She was going to be rich. At eighteen she'd get a chunk of cash, then the rest of it at twenty-one. She was pretty, fun and a good lay. I was in for the long haul."

"Then what happened?"

"She was arrested for beating her sister to death with a baseball bat. I didn't want any part of that."

"Even after she was acquitted?"

"Like I told you, I thought she was guilty. Would you want to live with a chick who could do that?"

"Lots of teenagers hate their folks, wish they were dead. But they don't kill them. Seems you two had a pretty good thing going, sneaking around. Why would she kill her?"

He shook his head. "Her sister had found us out. They fought about it and she forbade Kat to see me again. Next thing I hear, Sara McCall's dead."

"Earlier you said no one knew about you two."

"That's right."

"But Sara knew."

"She'd just found out."

"Maybe someone told her?"

"I don't think so. Kat thought she may have seen us. Or maybe found something in her room. A note, her diary or something."

He was lying. And not well, at that. "Nothing like that ended up as evidence."

"I don't know what to tell you, man."

"But you did see her again?"

"Pardon?"

"After her sister forbade her to see you."

"Yes, once."

"And she told you about the fight?"

"Yes."

"How did you respond?"

"Why does that matter?"

Luke smiled easily. "Just filling in the blanks."

"I told her to be cool, everything would be okay."

"That's it?"

"That's it."

"And she believed you? Just calmed right down?"

"I thought so at the time. Until I heard her sister was dead."

"Let me just throw this out there, Ryan. Maybe you two talked about it, made a plan. She let you in the house and you beat Sara McCall to death. So the two of you could be together. You said it, she was your ticket out."

He flinched slightly. His tone changed. "No way, man. See, I didn't care that much. I wasn't about to put my neck on the line for a piece of ass."

"Or her bank account? You could have had the money right away. She inherited it all. The entire pot of gold."

"But I could have also been charged with murder and ended up rotting in jail. It makes no sense. All I had to do was wait a few months and get what I wanted without any heat."

"Ten months."

He shrugged. "To me, a year was no time to wait. For her, a week was too long."

"Her sister had found you out. She would have broken you up."

"She couldn't have. Kat was too far gone on me. She might have kept us apart awhile, but the minute that girl turned eighteen, she'd be back."

Arrogant jerk.

"Did you contact her when she was in jail?"

"I told you before, never."

"And never after?"

"That's right."

Luke shook his head. "I still don't get that. She'd been acquitted. And she had all the money. That's what you wanted."

"Again, would you want to sleep with a woman you thought capable of beating you to death? I didn't want anything to do with her."

"I'd like to provide another scenario, if I may?"

Ryan glanced at his watch, then nodded. "The floor's yours, dude."

"You're here today for damage control. Katherine's back, she knows something we don't—or didn't ten years ago—and you're covering your ass."

"That would make me smart. Not a killer."

"Let's say you did do it. You're under our radar, all these years. Now you're threatened."

"But I didn't kill her."

"How do I know that?"

He leaned toward him. "What would be the friggin' point? Kill her, then not collect?"

He had a point.

"Besides, I'm not that guy."

"That guy?"

"I'm a lover, not a fighter. A baseball bat?" He shook his head. "Who does that? Intense, man. It's not normal."

"As if murder ever is."

"Of course." He laced his fingers together. "We about done here?"

"You came to see me, right?"

He laughed. "You've got me there. Are we good?"

"For now." He stood. "Thanks for coming in."

Ryan followed him to his feet. They shook hands and Luke walked him out. When they reached the sidewalk, Luke stopped him.

"Did you know Officer Wally Clark?"

Ryan looked surprised by the question. "Who?"

"Officer Wally Clark. He was killed the same night Sara McCall was."

"Oh yeah, I remember that." Ryan narrowed his eyes as if in thought. "Somebody shot him, right?"

"Right."

"But the two murders didn't have anything to do with each other."

"We didn't think so at the time."

Ryan waited for an explanation, but Luke let it hang out there. "But you knew Officer Clark?"

"Sure." For the first time he looked truly uncomfortable. "I knew all the Liberty officers. That was just the way I rolled."

Luke laughed. "True that, man."

Ryan drew his eyebrows together. "Weird, but I hardly remember Wally getting killed. What happened with that? You guys ever figure out who did it?"

"The sheriff's department investigated that one. But no, they never got the guy." He held out his hand. "Again, glad you came in."

They shook hands again. "No problem."

Luke watched as he strolled to his car, a sleek Audi sedan. "Tell Bitsy I said hello," he called.

Ryan looked back, expression strange. "I will."

He smiled. "And I'll tell my dad you said hello."

Ryan laughed, slid into the sedan and a moment later drove off.

Funny, Luke thought, watching him. Benton had gotten his rich girl, it just hadn't been the one he'd started out with.

Chief Stephen Tanner
2003

The morning after the murder

Tanner pulled his cruiser to a stop in front of the McCall place. Officer Guidry parked directly behind him. His hands shook; his heart raced. Most cops dealt with violent death on a daily basis. Shootings, stabbings and suicides, overdoses and gang wars. But not Tanner. In his twenty-five years on the force, he'd investigated five.

Until now. Two murders in one night. That didn't happen. Not in Liberty.

Wally had been shot dead. Two bullets, one to the chest, the other to his face. He had dropped where he stood. The image of Wally at the side of the road, lying in a pool of thickening blood, filled Tanner's head.

An ambush, the deputies thought. Wally hadn't had a chance.

Tanner blinked, forcing the image to the back of his head, focusing on the one before him. Little Kat McCall sat on the top porch step. Not so little anymore. Not the wide-eyed waif he remembered from her parents' funeral. She was dressed for school. Her backpack rested on the step beside her.

She was just sitting. Staring blankly at him. He had expected hysteria. Tears. Her sister was dead. She had nobody now.

He climbed out of his cruiser. His boots landed on the pavement with a thud, one that seemed to resound in his head. Not a nightmare. Real. This was happening.

He met Guidry at his vehicle. "Stay a few steps behind me. I don't know what to expect. Miss Kat's most likely in shock and I don't want us to upset her."

Guidry nodded, his adam's apple bobbing along with his head. He looked more upset than McCall. Like he was torn between bolting and puking.

Tanner started cautiously up the brick pathway. McCall followed him with her eyes but didn't acknowledge him in any other way. He found it weird. Unsettling and just plain strange.

He stopped in front of her. "Miss Kat? It's Chief Tanner, you know me."

She blinked up at him. "I didn't do it."

Of all the things she could have said, he hadn't expected that. He squatted in front of her and took her hands. They were cold and had what looked like bloodstains on them. *Why would that be?*

"Do you know who did do it?" he asked.

She shook her head.

"Can you tell me what happened?"

"I found her."

"And called 911."

"Yes."

"Tell me about that."

"When I got up for school. There she was. I'm late now. I'll be in trouble."

Still, no emotion in her voice. Nothing. Gave him the creeps. "Don't you worry about school, Miss Kat. I'll take care of that."

"Thank you, Chief Tanner."

"Did you touch her?"

"Who?"

"Your sister."

She shook her head again. "No."

"You have bloodstains on your hands, Kat. How did that happen?"

She held up her hands. Looked at them. "I don't know."

The paramedics arrived. "They can't help her," she said.

"You're sure?"

"She's dead." She made this sound then, like a strangled laugh. Or twisted giggle. It made the hair on the back of his neck stand up.

Tanner stepped aside so the paramedics could get by them. They weren't in the house three minutes. Tanner looked up at them as they exited. Their expressions said it all.

No helping this one.

He refocused on McCall. "I've got to go inside now. Officer Guidry here will stay with you. If you need anything, you just let him know."

He stood and crossed to the door. She didn't move, didn't watch him go. But he had a sense she was smiling. He shook that off. Crazy. Why would she do that? "Miss Katherine?"

She looked over her shoulder at him. "Maybe you should call your cousin Jeremy."

"I don't have a phone."

"Guidry will call for you." He paused. "How did you call 911?"

"I used Sara's cell."

"You don't have one of your own?"

"She took it away from me. I don't know where she put it."

He and Guidry exchanged glances. Every one of his internal alarms sounded. Two murders. One night. A rebellious teenager, being punished by her guardian.

Could the two murders be related? Could Wally have seen something?

Tanner forgot about all that when he stepped into the house. A scene from a horror movie greeted him, one of those gory flicks to which teenagers flocked.

Sara McCall had been beaten to death. There was blood on the walls, floor, ceiling. Bits of flesh and bone and brain matter.

It looked as if her attacker had continued to pummel her after she was dead.

The breakfast sandwich he had wolfed down an hour ago began to come up. He struggled to hold it back. A guy twenty-five years on the job didn't puke at the sight of blood. He would never live it down.

It kept coming anyway. He darted back out to the porch and heaved over the side. As he did, he imagined the sheriff's detectives he'd met with over Wally laughing at him.

"Chief?" Guidry said, sounding shaken. "You okay?"

He couldn't speak. Tears stung his eyes and he cursed them. *I didn't sign up for this shit. That's not why I live here.*

Tanner considered just walking away. Saying good-bye to this crime scene, Liberty, police work. But it was too late. He'd never be able to wipe the sight of Sara McCall's pulverized face from his brain.

Behind him he heard Guidry crossing to the door, stepping through. He wished he could spare him what he was about to see, but he couldn't.

"Holy Mary, mother of God!"

A moment later, Guidry was beside him at the porch rail, bent over it, heaving.

And still, Kat McCall sat motionless on the steps.

Anger surged up in him. He wanted to shake her. Demand to know what had happened, who had done this?

If she had done it.

He wiped his mouth and crossed to her. "What happened?" he asked.

"I told you."

"Who did this?"

"I don't know."

"Dammit, Miss Katherine! You tell me what happened, right now!"

From the street, he heard the slam of a car door. He looked over his shoulder. Jeremy Webber, striding up the walkway, expression panicked.

Tanner stood and went to meet him. "Jeremy, thank you for coming."

"Of course I'd come. What the hell's going on? Officer Guidry called. He said Sara—" His gaze shifted to Kat on the porch step. He leaned closer. "That Sara had been murdered. Is it true?"

"I'm sorry."

Tears flooded his eyes. He blinked them back. "Does Katherine . . . does she know?"

"She found her and called 911."

He nodded, visibly pulling himself together. "Excuse me."

A moment later, he was drawing the girl into his arms. "Katherine, sweetheart, are you all right?"

She buried her face into his shoulder and began to cry. "I didn't know what to do."

"Of course not." He rubbed her back. "It's going to be okay, Kit-Kat. I promise."

Tanner watched the two and thought that it most definitely was *not* going to be okay. Problem was, he was unsure whether he was thinking of Katherine's life or his own.

Chapter Twelve

Tuesday, June 4
7:30 p.m.

What a day it had been, Kat thought. So many memories confronted. Being back. Seeing Ryan. And Dab.

She sat on her front porch, night falling around her, the darkness gathering. She'd long ago drained her glass of pinot grigio, but hadn't gotten another. Instead, her thoughts had kept her anchored to the spot. Every argument the prosecution had used against her was burned onto her brain. Day after day of the trial, she had been pummeled with the "facts" of the case.

At the time, she had wished she could close her ears and eyes, pretend it wasn't happening. Escape. Now she gave thanks that hadn't been possible.

Those inescapable facts, branded on her psyche, would lead her to her sister's murderer.

The pathologist had set the time of death between 10:00 p.m. and midnight. He'd made that determination from three postmortem factors: rigor mortis, lividity and the body's internal temperature at the morgue. He had explained to the jury that the longer a body sat, the harder to pinpoint the exact time of death.

The mosquitoes began to bite, motivating her to finally go inside. Kat flipped on the foyer light. Her gaze went to the shadowy stains on the wooden floor. She crossed to them, bent and trailed her hand over the darkest of them, picturing Sara—or what had been left of her—sprawled across the polished cypress flooring.

Sara had known her killer. That's what the prosecution's experts had said. With no signs of a break-in, she had opened the door of her own free will. Judging by the location of the body, she hadn't simply opened the door, she had invited her murderer into her home.

Kat closed her eyes, remembering. The foyer at the edge of the front room. Facedown. Head toward the door. Blood. Everywhere.

She shook her head. *Don't dwell on that, Katherine. No emotion. The facts as the prosecution had presented them.*

Sara had been struck from behind, which suggested her killer had been in the front parlor and that she had been walking him, or her, out. Kat shifted her gaze to the corner where the bat had been propped. Right there, by the entry between the foyer and parlor.

After their fight, Sara had set it there. Kat didn't know for certain why. Perhaps to remind herself of Kat's lie? Or to remind Kat of why she was grounded? Or maybe she had simply set it there, meaning to store it away later.

But later hadn't come.

Kat's throat tightened. Would her sister be alive today if the bat hadn't been there? Had the murder been a crime of opportunity? If the weapon had been something other than a bat, could Sara have fought her attacker off?

Kat dragged her hands through her hair, hating the questions. Ten years of them, battering her. Day and night, invading her sleep, stealing her quiet. Robbing her of any, every moment of peace.

The time had come to answer the questions.

Kat stood, turned toward the front door. Sara had invited the person in. Not a huge deal in a town like Liberty, even at night. Liberty wasn't Atlanta or New Orleans. Everyone knew everybody. Everybody trusted everyone else.

This crime had been highly personal. Isn't that what the experts had said? You didn't attack someone that way unless it was. That's why her face had been obliterated. It's why the killer had continued to beat her after she was dead.

That narrowed the field. Not just an acquaintance. It had to be someone with an axe to grind. Big time.

Hatred. Rage boiling over. Someone who wanted to erase Sara McCall from the face of the planet.

Kat remembered the prosecution's lead attorney saying just that during his opening arguments. Then he'd pointed at her. *"And no one had more anger directed at Sara McCall than her sister, Katherine McCall. No one had as much to gain at Sara's death as her sister. Take a good look at her, ladies and gentlemen. Don't be fooled by her youth or pretty face. She wished her sister dead."*

Kat squirmed, remembering that moment. Every eye in the courtroom turned to her in accusation.

Until that moment, she had naively believed the police would realize their mistake. She didn't kill Sara. She couldn't kill anyone, especially her sister.

Innocent people didn't go to jail.

Until that moment, Kat thought again. When the prosecutor had pointed at *her*.

And all her lies had come crashing in on her. Her defiance and rebellion. The circumstances. How it all looked.

She remembered numbly thinking: How could they *not* think I'd done it?

Kat opened the door and stepped out onto the porch just as Iris Bell's front-room light snapped on. The killer was someone from Liberty. And she would bet that the person still lived in the area. People from Liberty planted roots. You didn't settle here if you were a corporate executive who moved every couple of years.

She didn't know why she was so certain of that, but she was.

Maybe because her life had stopped with her sister's murder and she thought the killer's should have as well.

Kat sensed that her neighbor was watching her and lifted her hand in greeting. Mrs. Bell had testified against her, as well. But how could she hold that against her? Just like Dab, she hadn't lied.

Kat dug her cell phone out of her back pocket, checked the time and walked back into the house. There, she dialed the Liberty P.D.

"This is Katherine McCall," she said. "Is Sergeant Tanner still in?"

"I'm sorry, who did you say—"

"Kat McCall."

"Kat? This is Cindy Widmer. Well, LaGuarde, now. I married Rene."

An image of Cindy popped into her head. Short reddish blond hair, freckles. They'd been friends in junior high.

"Wow, Cindy," she said. "How are you?"

"Good. Pregnant with my first."

Another one. What was with the water in Liberty? "Congratulations."

"We're really excited. My mom's over the moon. You know how—"

She fell suddenly and abruptly silent. As if she had just remembered who she was talking to and that this wasn't a social call.

"Luke's already left for the day," she said, sounding like a stranger this time. "Is this an emergency?"

"Not at all. But I would like to speak to him tonight."

"You can catch him at home. Or on his cell. I can give you that number, if you like?"

In the end, Cindy gave her his address, too. As she stood on his front porch, she wondered if he had an Iris Bell living across the street. If he or she was peering out the window, taking notes. The quintessential small-town pastime.

Luke swung open the door. Dark hair slightly mussed, hint of a five o'clock shadow, wearing shorts and bright white T-shirt. Seeing him that way caused the strangest little hitch in her breathing. She noticed he didn't look surprised to see her.

What the hell was she doing?

"Hey," he said. "What's up?"

She corralled her runaway thoughts. "I have a proposal for you. Can I come in?"

A slow, sexy grin spread across his face; he swung open the door. "How could I say no to that?"

Chapter Thirteen

Tuesday, June 4
8:00 p.m.

Luke Tanner's house was cozy and cluttered and smelled really good. Like a Sunday afternoon with something in the oven. She sniffed. "What is that?"

"Jambalaya."

"You can cook?"

"I learned out of self-preservation. Pizza and burgers got old pretty quick."

She followed him to the living room. He cleared a bunch of files off the sofa. "Have you eaten?"

She hadn't. And she was hungry. But showing up at his house without warning felt sketchy enough without eating his food, too.

He laughed when she told him so. "Look, I have plenty and I'm starving and won't eat in front of you, so I'm fixing you a plate, sketchy or not."

When they reached the kitchen, she saw it was small but well organized. "I see you're a clean-as-you-go cook."

"I am." He opened the fridge and held out an Abita Amber. "Beer?"

"Thanks."

He popped the cap on the bottle and handed it to her. Then got one for himself. "I have to say it, Kat, that was an odd thing to notice."

She laughed. "I work in a commercial kitchen. There's no room for slobs or creative tornadoes. I had to go against my nature to learn that."

He took a swallow of the beer. She watched him, finding something sensual about the way he brought the bottle to his lips, the tip of his head, the arch of his neck.

She jerked her gaze away, not wanting him to catch her staring. "Can I help you with anything?"

"Just take a seat. Make yourself comfortable."

He gathered up the utensils they would need, then served up two bowls of the jambalaya. He placed them on the table, then took a seat. "Dig in."

She tasted, then fanned her mouth. "Spicy!"

He looked sheepish. "Sorry, I should have warned you. I like my food hot."

She took a gulp of the beer. "It's perfect. I love it."

He laughed. "Liar."

"I do. Actually, I really missed Louisiana food when I moved to Oregon. I just need to build my tolerance back up."

"Small bites and big sips, that's the way to go. In my opinion, anyway."

She tried it and it worked, though she emptied her beer in record time. She switched to water, standing and doing it herself.

"Tell me about your bread," he said when she sat back down. "What makes it special?"

"That it's delicious *and* healthy."

He cocked an eyebrow. "Yeah, right."

"It is. I promise. Here's the deal—" She leaned forward, warming to the subject. "I make it with all whole ingredients, as close to nature as possible. Nothing processed. Grains are nutritious. Chockablock full of B vitamins and folates. Fiber and protein.

"The reason bread gets a bad rap is because we've stripped everything nutritious out of it, stuffed it with preservatives and shoved it into a plastic bag." She paused. "And don't even get me started on the whole plastic thing."

"Okay, I won't."

She frowned. "You're laughing at me."

"Hell, no. We should all feel so passionate about what we do. And I'm a believer now. Get your store up and running, I'll be your first customer."

"I'm going to hold you to that."

His smile faded. "As much as I'm enjoying this, I know you didn't come here for jambalaya and small talk."

"No." She regretfully laid down her fork, reminding herself of why she'd come here in the first place. "Like I said, I have a proposal for you."

He leaned back in his chair and waited. She knew she should choose her words carefully, wrap it all up neatly with a bow. Instead she just blurted it out. "I think we should work on this case together."

"This case?"

"Finding my sister's murderer."

"That wasn't the proposal I was hoping for," he said lightly. "Give me another."

When she didn't reply, he frowned. "You're not serious."

"Dead serious."

He shook his head. "No."

"Why not? It makes perfect sense."

"It makes no sense." He leaned toward her. "I'm the cop. You're not. End of story."

"What if I have information that could help?"

"Then you're obligated to hand it over."

"I help you, but you don't help me? Not happening."

"You're not a cop, Kat."

"I have to know the truth."

"I understand that. I do. I'm reopening the case. That should make you happy."

"It does. But that doesn't mean I'm going to stop. I'm doing this with or without you."

"Do you really think you can do something the law couldn't ten years ago? Or do something that I can't now?"

"Yes."

His eyebrows shot up. "Really? Why's that?"

She dropped her hands to her lap and curled them into fists. "Because ten years ago your dad decided I did it and never looked any further. And everyone else associated with the 'law' went right along with him."

She could tell that got his back up. "My dad was a good lawman. He has the respect of this community. A community he served for thirty-five years."

"Bully for them and you, but he doesn't have mine. My sister was murdered; her killer is still free."

"And you assume he, or she, still lives around here."

"Yes."

"Because of the letters?"

"Yes. And other things."

"And what if you're wrong? What if we don't nail the bastard? What if her killer is long gone? What will you do then?"

She paused. "The truth?" He nodded. "I haven't even considered that an option."

"Maybe you should."

She stood. "Thanks for dinner."

He followed her to her feet. "Kat. Wait." He motioned her to sit back down. "Please."

She hesitated a moment, then sat.

"You're talking about going after a killer. Someone who has held their secret for ten years. They're not going to give it up easily."

"You're not going to change my mind."

"What makes you think they won't kill you if you get too close?"

She hadn't considered that. In her head, it was all very easy, clean. But she wasn't about to tell him that.

She tilted up her chin. "They won't."

"Now you're just being stupid."

Kat flushed and stood. "What was stupid was thinking you'd help me."

He caught up with her before she reached the front door. "I have all the files here. The crime-scene photos. Do you want to see them?"

She looked him square in the eyes. "Yes."

"Really? You're that positive?"

"They're not new to me, remember? I sat through every minute of the trial. I saw every piece of evidence. I see those images in my dreams. Do you?"

He led her to the living room. He told her to sit,

which was a good thing because she was stubborn enough to try to stand and her legs were already rubbery.

He sat on the couch beside her and handed her the envelope of photos.

She'd been wrong, Kat acknowledged moments later. It felt as if she were seeing them for the first time.

She broke down and cried. A few tears at first, but before long, a river of them. Sara, her sweet sister. Reduced to . . . that. She couldn't bear it.

Arms around her middle, she doubled over, sobbing.

He came and sat beside her, drew her into his arms. She clung to him and cried for what seemed like forever. To his credit, he didn't squirm or stiffen, didn't try to move away. He simply held her.

Comforting. Solid and strong.

Her sobs came to a slow, shuddering stop. Still she clung to him. She breathed in his clean, male scent and wondered if she would always associate it with him and this moment.

"Are you okay?"

She shook her head no.

How could she have acted so disassociated at seventeen? Kat curled her fingers into his T-shirt. *No wonder everyone thought she'd done it. No wonder they hadn't moved on.*

No wonder she hadn't.

"What are you thinking?" he asked softly.

Kat softened her fingers, smoothed them over the crumpled fabric, feeling the strong beat of his heart. She drew regretfully away. Met his eyes. "That this doesn't change anything."

He caught her elbow, stopping her. "You're putting pressure on someone who's very dangerous, Kat. This person won't hesitate to attack if they feel threatened."

The baseball bat. Waiting for her. A warning.

"Let me do my job." He searched her gaze. "I promise I'll do it well, to the best of my abilities."

"I can't do that."

"Yes, you can." He closed his hands over hers. "I won't be able to protect you."

She pulled herself together. "I'm not asking you to."

"You are. By putting yourself in harm's way." As if realizing her mind was made up, he sighed and released her hands. "Where are you going to start?"

"That's called cooperation, Tanner."

"You still want to look at the files?"

She did, and for the next two hours, they sat side by side, reading. He looked at her when she caught her breath. "What?"

"I forgot about the bloody footprints," she said. "How they abruptly stopped. It was so creepy."

"Not magic, just a smart killer."

A smart killer, Kat thought later as she let herself back into her house. Dangerous. Desperate to keep his secret.

She stopped in the foyer, gaze going to the spot where her sister had died. Where her blood had poured out. Anger rose up in her. Fury. White-hot.

"Not smart enough," she said, fisting her fingers. "I promise, Sara. The son of a bitch isn't getting away with it."

Chapter Fourteen

Wednesday, June 5
9:00 a.m.

The St. Tammany Parish Sheriff's Department was located in a new, state-of-the-art facility on Brownswitch Road in Slidell. Luke remembered when they'd moved from the cramped, antiquated facilities in 2009; they'd all felt like they'd hit the big time. The euphoria had worn off, but those first couple months had been pretty cool.

Luke tapped on Sheriff Walt N. Johnson's door. The man smiled and stood. "How are you, Luke?"

"Good, Sheriff. Thanks for seeing me."

They shook hands, then sat. "How's your dad?"

"Ornery as ever. Holding the cancer at bay."

"I'm not surprised by either. He's one tough old bird. What can I do for you?"

He'd always liked Sheriff Walt, straightforward

and no-nonsense. But with a heart as well. A tough feat in the world of law enforcement. "I'm reopening the McCall case."

"Interesting. I'd heard she was back in the parish."

"I want to review your file on Officer Clark's murder. They happened the same night, and I can't help but think there may be a connection."

"You're welcome to the information, Luke, but we worked that angle hard and came up empty."

Luke laced his fingers. "I respect that. As one of your former deputies, I know how thorough this department is. But to do this right, I've got to consider everything."

The sheriff stood. "I'll get you set up."

"Thank you, Sheriff."

"Take all the notes you'd like, make copies, but the originals don't leave the building."

Two hours later, Luke stretched, then leaned back in his chair. The STPSD had done a thorough job. Every "t" crossed and "i" dotted. They'd reopened it twice over the years, both after local drug busts.

Neither had gone anywhere.

It'd been an ambush killing, cut and dried. Officer Clark had approached the parked vehicle, the driver had lowered the window and shot him. Twice.

Clark hadn't gone for his weapon. It had been securely tucked in its holster. The murder had occurred in the early morning hours, yet Clark's flashlight had been affixed to his utility belt.

What did it mean? That Clark hadn't felt threatened? Maybe he had recognized the vehicle and its driver? Or simply a reflection of small-town, sloppy policework?

Luke frowned. He leaned toward the latter, though the sheriff's investigators had gone the other way. In truth, it was probably a combination of both. A big-city cop would approach his mother fully loaded.

Luke returned his attention to the case notes. Cruiser lights and searchlight had been on, the vehicle left running. He'd called in, before the stop. Given a description of the vehicle. All by the book.

The description. He flipped through the report. Ford Taurus. Silver blue. No plates. Nothing for deputies to go on.

Generic. A million of them on the road. But no plates? Small-town cop or not, that would've sounded alarm bells for Clark.

A vehicle at the side of the road, no plates. That's what he called in. Stopping to investigate.

He would have had his flashlight in hand, for a view of the car's dark interior. His other hand would have hovered on his weapon.

Luke thrummed his fingers on the desktop. How did you recognize a generic vehicle, in the dead of night, without plates? How could Clark have recognized the driver, coming up, as he had been, from the rear?

No wonder the STPSD investigators had gone for the sloppy-policework theory. Luke narrowed his eyes. But he knew his dad. That didn't add up for him. Small-town familiarity, a family atmosphere, sure. But they'd been trained to be cautious. To cover their asses.

Could Clark have forgotten all that? A cop twelve years on the force?

Something didn't add up. Not for him. He meant to find out what.

Chapter Fifteen

Wednesday, June 5
Noon

When Kat arrived at Cafe Toile, Bitsy was already there. She saw Kat and waved.

"Sorry I'm late," Kat said when she reached the table. "I thought I remembered how long it would take to get here, but boy was I wrong." She slid into the booth. "When did traffic in Mandeville become such a nightmare?"

"It's awful, isn't it?" Bitsy smoothed her napkin across her lap. "I blame all the strip malls."

Kat glanced around. The restaurant hadn't changed: booths covered in French toile, the same map-of-Paris wallpaper and black-and-white tile floor. The menu appeared the same as well, fresh salads and imaginative sandwiches, all with a French twist.

"Sara loved this place," she said softly. "I swear, she used to drag me here almost weekly."

"I'd forgotten," Bitsy said. "I should have picked somewhere else."

She shook her head. "No, this is fine."

"Do you mind if we order right away?" Bitsy asked, squeezing lemon into her iced tea. "I've got a two o'clock. Sorry."

"No apologies. That's perfect."

Bitsy motioned the waitress over. Kat ordered an iced tea and the shrimp remoulade salad. Bitsy ordered as well, then the waitress walked away.

An awkward silence fell between them. A moment before it became excruciating, Bitsy cleared her throat. "How are things? Being back, I mean."

"About as good as I expected them to be."

"Cryptic."

"Trying to be positive."

Bitsy smoothed her napkin in her lap again, then toyed with her flatware, straightening it. She used to do that, Kat remembered. Fiddle when she was nervous.

Kat told her so, and Bitsy looked surprised. "I can't believe you remember that."

"How could I not? It used to drive me crazy."

"The teachers, too."

"The more nervous you got, the more you'd fiddle. We never got away with anything."

Bitsy laughed. "Undiagnosed ADHD."

The waitress brought Kat's tea. Kat sweetened it, something she had never outgrown. "It was crazy running into you that way," she said. "Small towns."

"I was glad you did."

"Me, too."

Again they fell silent. Again, Bitsy broke it. "I asked you here for a reason, Kat."

"Not just to catch up?"

She shook her head. "It's about Ryan."

"Benton?"

She nodded. "We're together."

Kat thought she had heard her wrong. "Did you say you're—"

"Together, yes. He and I. We're engaged." She held out her hand. A huge rock sparkled on her fourth finger.

R&B Imports. Ryan and Bitsy. Of course. No doubt Bitsy had financed the business. Probably the ring, too.

"We're getting married over the Fourth of July. In Hawaii. Kauai."

"You and Ryan. Wow." She shook her head. "That's weird, Bits."

Bitsy stiffened. "Why's it weird?"

"Last time you mentioned his name was to tell

me what a bad guy he was. You warned me to stay away from him."

"But you didn't," she said, the edge in her voice unmistakable. She smoothed her napkin again. Her bangle bracelets clinked together. "I'm sorry if you're upset."

"I'm not upset."

"Tell me the truth, Kat. Did you come back hoping—"

"God, no."

"If you hoped to get him back," she continued, "it's too late. He's mine now."

This conversation felt surreal. Bitsy and Ryan. Together. Her territorial words, the warning in them.

"That ship sailed a long time ago, Bits. I promise you that."

The waitress arrived with their salads. She set the bowls in front of them. As she moved out of earshot, Bitsy leaned toward her. "You're saying you have no feelings for him?"

Kat laughed, the sound spontaneous. And incredulous. "None. That's not what he told you, is it?"

"We don't keep secrets from each other. Total honesty, always."

Kat doubted that was completely true, but kept her thoughts to herself. "Then you know why I was there?"

"He told me what you talked about." She leaned

forward, eyes narrowed. "But I want to hear it from you."

"Really? You want me to tell you that your fiancé suggested we kill my sister?"

"That's not true."

The words came out low. And angry. Kat sensed that Bitsy would do anything to protect her man. Anything. The realization left her uneasy. And wishing she was anyplace but sitting across a table from her.

She pressed on anyway. "Luke Tanner reopened Sara's murder investigation. Did you know that?"

"Yes." Bitsy's hands shook. She dropped them to her lap. "Why, Kat? Why are you doing this to us? Why now?"

"I'm not doing it to *you*, Bits. This is about me. And Sara. It's about justice for Sara," she finished softly.

Something like recognition—or shock—crossed Bitsy's features, then was gone. For the first time, Kat wondered if Bitsy could be her "fan."

"You always got everything you wanted, Kat. Everything."

It was her turn to feel shock. "Me? The one who lost everything. Really?"

Bitsy went on as if she hadn't spoken. "The pretty one. The popular one. You got the grades, the friends. You even got the guy. Then. But now *I* have him." She pressed her fist to her chest. "Me. Bitsy Cavenaugh, the ugly duckling."

Kat looked at her, momentarily startled silent. Then she shook her head. "The ugly duckling? I never thought of you that way."

"Sure, you didn't. Poor, awkward, uncool Bitsy. That's why you stopped hanging out with me when we got to high school."

She hadn't had any idea Bitsy felt that way. And she couldn't be more wrong. "You stopped hanging out with me! Because I went off the rails. Started hanging out with a wild crowd and—"

"He didn't do it," she said. "He didn't kill Sara."

"You're so certain?"

"I know him, Kat."

"You didn't back then." Kat held her gaze. "He was everything you warned me he was."

"Don't make trouble for him."

"I'm not here to make trouble. For him or anyone else. Unless they're a murderer. I just want the truth, Bits."

The truth. What Bitsy had said a moment ago, about Kat having gotten the guy back then, suddenly registered. "What did you mean, I got the guy back then? You knew I was seeing Ryan?"

"How could I? He told me about the two of you. After we got together."

He may have, but she had known long before that. This kind of anger and bitterness didn't spring up from a fresh cut.

This was an old wound.

"You had a crush on him, didn't you?"

"Stop it. He was cute. *The* cutest. That's all I meant."

"You're the one who told Sara about us."

"That's stupid."

"Were you following us? How'd you do it?"

"Again, you're being ridiculous. Sara told *me*. I ran into her. She was upset. At the end of her rope, actually. She told me she was thinking of sending you away to school."

Yes, Sara had been thinking about boarding school, but she wouldn't have shared that with a teenager. Which meant Bitsy was lying. But why? What difference would it make now?

The truth hit her hard. It would make a difference only if Bitsy had something to hide. Or someone to protect.

Bitsy believed Ryan had killed Sara. Or worried that he might have.

And yet she still defended him. Still planned to marry him. It was sickening to Kat, who pushed away her untouched salad. "I seem to have lost my appetite. I'll let you buy, Bits."

Kat collected her purse and stood. Bitsy caught her hand in a viselike grip, stopping her. "Leave him alone, Kat."

"Sorry, that's not up to me."

"We know a lot of people . . . we have a lot of friends. Ones who will look out for us. They can make your life very difficult."

Kat narrowed her eyes at the threat. She freed her hand. "Do you like letter-writing, Bitsy?"

"Excuse me?"

"You get your jollies from it?"

"I don't know what you're talking about."

"I'm not going anywhere, old friend. Tell your husband-to-be he has nothing to worry about." She paused. "Unless he killed my sister."

Ryan Benton
2003

Two nights before the murder

The interior of the Mustang was hot, the air humid. Kat's hair stuck to the back of her damp neck. She struggled to shimmy into her jeans while Ryan fired up a joint. The acrid scent stung her nose.

She looked at him. He lay back in his seat, shirtless, eyes hooded as he watched her. He was so handsome. She couldn't believe he was with her.

"Can I test positive from just breathing in the smoke?" she asked.

"No way, babe. You're good."

"Are you sure, because I feel sort of high?"

"Go with it."

She giggled. "'Kay."

She got her shirt buttoned and scooted across the backseat to snuggle up to him. "I hate her. She doesn't understand anything."

"You're here. Don't worry about it."

"Only because she had a fight with her stupid boyfriend. I wouldn't have been able to sneak out otherwise." She puckered her lips, recalling their raised voices, the roar of his truck driving off and the sound of her sister's sobs. "I wonder what they were fighting about. She was really upset."

"Who gives a shit? Not me, that's for sure." He sucked on the joint, held the smoke in a moment and then let it out in a long stream.

Kat tried not to breathe in too much of the smoke. "I wonder who told her about us."

"Maybe that nosy old bag from across the street."

"Dunno. Maybe." Her head was spinning. "That's what I'm trying to figure out." He didn't respond and she added, "I won't let her break us up." She tilted her face up to his. "We could just run away together?"

He met her eyes. "Big problem, babe. You said it yourself, you do that, you don't get your money."

"Would that be so bad? We'd have each other."

"That's all good, but we gotta eat, babe. You've always had everything you wanted, you don't know what it's like. It's tough out there."

"You're really good at working on cars."

He stiffened. "Really? You think so?"

She bit her bottom lip and nodded apprehensively. He scared her when he got this way. Angry at her for something she couldn't even name. Sarcastic and mean as a cottonmouth.

"News flash, little rich girl, I don't plan to be working on cars the rest of my life. And this shit-hole, hick town? I want it in my rearview as soon as possible."

She blinked against tears. She didn't understand him. All she'd done was tell him he was good at something.

"Gonna cry now? Poor little rich girl."

"I don't like it when you call me that. It hurts my feelings. Stop it."

"Why should I? It's true, right?"

She tried to move away; he held her, his arms like a vise. "You really wish she were dead?"

"Yes! You know how much I hate her."

"So, maybe she should have an accident?"

For a second she thought he was serious, then she realized he was messing with her. "Like walk in front of a bus?" Kat giggled. "Good-bye pain-in-the-ass big sister."

"There're no buses in Liberty, idiot."

She snuggled into him, brain humming. A hummingbird, she thought. So light, it seemed to hover above her. "Here's an idea. Fix her brakes. You could do that. When she tries to stop, she can't. She'll barrel down the mountain—"

"No mountains in Louisiana, babe. Not even bunny hills." He looked at her. "You're stoned."

"Mmm . . ." She leaned her head against the seat back; she could see a strip of the star-dusted sky through the back window. "How 'bout a skydiving accident? We make certain her parachute doesn't open."

"Does she skydive?"

"Nope." She giggled. "Do you?"

"Time to go home."

She pouted. "I don't want to. I wanna stay with you. All night."

"Imagine," he said, voice silky, "if you never had to go home. And if we didn't have to sneak around. Wouldn't that be great?"

"Mmm . . ."

"But your bitch of a sister won't let us do that."

"She's so mean."

"That could be us. Together every night. All night." He lowered his voice. "We could get married. Live happily ever after."

Happily ever after. With Ryan. She sighed. His arms felt so warm around her. So comforting.

He turned her face toward his. "We just have to get rid of her and we have it all."

Kat blinked, something in his tone threading through her drug-induced brain fog. "What are you saying? You're for real here? You want to kill her?"

His lips curved into a slow, sexy smile. "You're cute when you're loaded."

"I don't want to be cute. I want to be sexy. Hot."

He laughed and dragged her onto his lap so she straddled him. His arousal pressed against her. She felt like she couldn't breathe.

"Don't worry, babe." He started to unbutton her shirt. "You are."

Chapter Sixteen

Wednesday, June 5
12:35 p.m.

Kat walked away from Bitsy, head held high, pace brisk but measured. Inside she was a mess. Trembling. Disbelieving.

Of all the people she had imagined might be her enemy, her childhood friend's name had never even crossed her mind.

It was so weird. Bits and Ryan. Together. Engaged to be married.

All she felt was pity for the other woman. Ryan had said it—he hadn't wanted Kat without her money. Would he want Bitsy without hers?

Kat neared her Fusion and fumbled in her purse for her key. She reached the car and stopped. Someone had keyed the driver's door panel.

BITCH

She stared at the epithet a moment, then lifted her gaze. Slowly, she scanned the parking lot. He would be watching. He would want to see her reaction. Know he had upset her. Why else do it?

She wasn't about to give the bastard his jollies.

The shopping center was a busy place. Folks coming and going from the restaurant, the shops surrounding it. No one jumped out at her. The vehicles parked around hers were empty.

What had she expected? A neon *Here I Am* sign?

She unlocked the car, slid inside. Only then did she allow herself to let go. Her hands began to shake. She clasped the steering wheel. Who would have known she was here? Ryan, obviously. And the sentiment fit.

Who else? She hadn't mentioned the lunch to anyone. It could have been someone who had seen her alight the Fusion, recognized her and went to work. Or someone who had followed her.

With that thought an uncomfortable feeling settled in the pit of her gut. Kat shook it off. She wasn't afraid. And she wasn't about to let this go. She dialed Luke.

"Tanner."

"Luke, it's Kat. Just thought I should let you know, someone keyed my car while I was having lunch with Bitsy Cavenaugh."

"Where are you?"

"Cafe Toile parking lot."

"I'll be right there."

137

Ten minutes later, Luke arrived, a Mandeville cruiser with him. *A lot of manpower for simple vandalism.*

Not so simple, she thought. Not when it came to her. He climbed out. "Are you okay?"

"I'm fine, though my car has been better."

He looked at the damage and frowned. He motioned the Mandeville officer over. "Canvas the immediate area, see if any other cars have been vandalized."

The officer walked away, and Kat turned back to Luke. "No other cars were vandalized."

"You checked?"

"Come on, Luke. This is personal."

"Who knew you were coming here today?"

"Bitsy. And, I'd bet, Ryan."

"That's it?"

"As far as I know."

He snapped a couple pictures of the damage. "Whose toes have you stepped on since last night?"

His eyes crinkled in amusement. Disarming, she thought. And too damn sexy.

She looked away. "Nobody's. Although I'm still breathing, which seems to be enough to piss some people off."

"What about Bitsy?"

She met his eyes again. "She didn't do it. Although I'm sure she would have liked to."

"I hope that comes with an explanation."

"I was a spoiled little bitch who always got everything she wanted, including the guy."

"Ryan?"

She nodded. "Until today, I had no idea she felt that way." Kat rubbed her arms. "But here's the interesting part. I think she's afraid her honey did it."

"It?"

"Killed Sara."

He seemed to digest that.

"She warned me to leave Ryan alone. They have a lot of friends, she said. Ones who would come to their aid."

"Did it sound as much like a threat when she said as it did just now?"

"Oh, yeah. Can I go?"

"Free to, Ms. McCall."

She climbed in. He motioned her to lower the window. He leaned down. "Thought any more about Saturday night?"

"Saturday night?"

"You and me. Food. Wine. A good-night kiss."

"I don't date cops, remember?"

He ignored that. "Where are you off to now?"

"The high school."

"Summer school started Monday."

"So I learned."

"Principal Bishop is still in charge," he said.

"Sara's old boss. I learned that, too."

Luke narrowed his eyes. She could almost

see him thinking. "Danny Sullivan's head of the athletic program now."

Sara's boyfriend at the time of the murder.

"You don't say?"

"He was never considered a suspect."

"Only one person ever was."

He searched her gaze. "Be careful. Like you said, you seem to piss folks off."

She said she would and eased out of the parking spot. She looked back and saw him picking something up from the ground where she had been parked. He was frowning.

What, she wondered, had he found?

Chapter Seventeen

Wednesday, June 5
1:00 p.m.

Danny Sullivan. Sara's jock boyfriend. Big man in a little town. Had played ball for LSU and never let anyone forget it—even though he'd gotten minimal playing time and never started.

She hadn't liked him. And she hadn't kept it a secret from Sara. Of course, back then if it hadn't been about her, for her or worked to her advantage, she'd had no use for it.

Had her dislike of him been about anything more than that?

Kat thought back. If Sara had talked to her about her romance, she hadn't been listening. She had overheard a few arguments between them, a particularly explosive one just two days before Sara's murder. The last time she had seen Ryan.

She rubbed her temple, working to remember the details. She'd been grounded. No phone, computer or TV. Sulking in her room. Pissed at Sara. Growing desperate. What would Ryan think when she didn't show up for their "date." Would he be angry? Would he dump her for a girl closer to his own age, one who didn't have an overprotective sister?

Then Danny was there. He always tooted his horn when he arrived. She'd listened at her door. At first, all she'd caught was the murmur of their voices, then an occasional laugh.

Quickly, the mood had changed. Raised voices. Her sister crying. Saying something about not being able to trust him. Him begging, apologizing.

Sara kicking him out; the squeal of his tires as he drove away. Her sister's bedroom door slamming shut. Then . . . silence.

She'd felt bad for her sister. Figured Danny had cheated on her, and thought about checking on her. The thought had been chased away by a realization: this was her opportunity to sneak out. Find Ryan. Explain why she hadn't answered his calls or texts, why she'd stood him up.

Her opportunity to be with him.

Kat frowned. What had they been fighting about? Twenty-four hours later her sister had been dead.

It could be nothing. It could be *the* thing.

Who else would know?

He was probably a pretty decent guy. Had treated Sara well. Had seemed to love her.

He'd testified at her trial. Sara had been worried about her sister. She had cried to him over the things Kat had said and done. She had been looking into boarding schools.

That had been a shocker. Kat hadn't had any idea.

Danny had broken down crying. He'd gotten a ring for her. He had planned to propose.

Or so he had testified.

The prosecution had held the ring up for the jury's inspection, entered the sales receipt into evidence.

Had he asked and she turned him down? Is that what their fight had been about? Or had they fought, perhaps over an infidelity, then he'd gotten the ring?

She meant to find out.

Tammany West High School serviced the western edge of the parish, not only Liberty and surrounding communities, but taking in all the unincorporated areas as well.

Home of the Gators. Kat parked in a visitor's spot, stepped out of her vehicle and gazed up at the school. It brought back so many memories. A blur of them.

A blur. Because her life had been spinning out of control. She had been spinning out of control. Way before her sister had been murdered.

She made her way inside, to the principal's office. Mr. Bishop was talking to the receptionist. Mrs. Lange. Another thing that hadn't changed.

They both recognized her. Mr. Bishop greeted her warily. "How can I help you, Katherine?"

Not much of a welcome back, but then she hadn't expected much. "I'm looking for Danny Sullivan."

He frowned. Mrs. Lange looked like a deer frozen in the headlights of an oncoming truck.

"I'm sorry," he said, "I can't allow you to wander the school halls."

As if she'd want to. "I'd like to speak with Danny, if he's available."

"He's not," Mrs. Lange chirped. "He's in class."

Summer school for P.E. Amazing. Unless the requirements had changed since her days here, to pass one had only to show up and dress out.

"When do classes end?"

The two exchanged glances. Fred Bishop cleared his throat. "He doesn't deserve more heartache, Katherine."

Condemnation in both their gazes. If they only knew she considered Danny a suspect. "And I don't want to cause him any. Could I leave him a note?"

Bishop hesitated, then nodded. "Fine."

She scribbled a note, folded it and handed it over. "You'll make certain he gets it?"

This time he didn't hesitate. "I'll personally see to it."

"Thank you."

She started off; Bishop called after her. "He never married, you know. Nobody measured up to Sara."

Kat didn't stop or look back. Didn't comment. What could she have said? She agreed.

June in south Louisiana could be brutal, scorching hot and suffocatingly humid. Today lived up to its reputation. After grabbing her thermos of water, she found a shady spot at one of the picnic tables to sit and wait.

She had a clear view of the faculty parking lot and had gotten a bead on which vehicle she figured was his. A Ford truck. Blue and in need of a wash. With a gun rack and a trailer hitch. Danny had liked to hunt. Men in the South did that. Duck. Deer. Whatever moved.

And from this truck's hitch hung a pair of balls—Truck Nutz, they were called. Did they have those anywhere besides the South? she wondered. She had never seen them in the Northwest, that was for sure.

Kat soon discovered she'd been wrong about which vehicle was his. He drove a Fusion Hybrid, just like hers. Even the same color—dark gray.

He walked toward her, sun glinting off his Ray-Bans. He had the swagger of a jock, the loose-limbed walk of someone utterly confident in his physical capabilities.

How old was he now? she wondered. He'd been a few years older than Sara. Three, maybe. Or four. Fortyish, then. Give or take.

"He never married. . . . Nobody measured up to Sara."

He stopped in front of her. She wished she could see his eyes. "I got your note. What do you want?"

"To talk. About Sara."

Tightly coiled fury emanated from him. "That was a long time ago."

"I haven't forgotten. How about you?"

He shook his head. "Not here. Can I meet you somewhere?"

"How about the house?"

He hesitated, then agreed. "When?"

"An hour."

"See you then."

Chief Stephen Tanner
2003

The morning after the murder

Tanner found the murder weapon in the kitchen, on the floor in front of the sink. A wooden baseball bat. The murderer had wiped the grip.

He stood and stared at it, stomach roiling. This time, he wasn't afraid of embarrassing himself—he'd emptied his stomach the first go-around.

He fitted on latex gloves and squatted to study the grip. The perp hadn't done a very good job of cleaning it, mostly just smeared the gore around. Still, effective, he thought, noting the absence of visible prints.

The prints might have been obliterated, but every contact left something behind. Locard's exchange principle. What had this perp left behind?

Tanner moved his gaze over the floor around the bat. Bloody footprints that led from the foyer to the kitchen, then stopped here, in front of the sink. As if the perp had simply disappeared.

But she hadn't, of course. More likely she had removed her shoes, then carefully made her way from the crime scene.

She? He stopped on the thought. When had he decided the killer was a woman?

The answer popped into his head. *When Katherine McCall giggled.*

Tanner shook his head. No. He needed to keep an open mind. Doing anything else would prejudice the investigation. He shifted his gaze once more to the footprints. Large for a woman's foot. But small for a man's. He frowned and made a mental note to check the size of the shoes in Katherine's closet.

The perp had carried the bat to the kitchen, most likely with the intent of wiping the grip. The bloody trail supported that theory. She—or he—reached the kitchen, cleaned the weapon . . . then what?

The scenario unfolded in his head. With his mind's eye, he saw Kat McCall standing over her sister. The blood splatter would have been tremendous. It would have been all over her, on her clothes, her face, in her hair.

So she heads to the kitchen with the bat. First she wipes the grip, then sets it aside.

What does she use? A dish towel? Paper towels? Where are they?

Tanner swept his gaze over the floor, counters, sink. Gone. She disposed of them. How? Where?

The trash receptacle. He crossed to it. Popped it open. It'd been emptied. A clean white liner stared back at him.

He turned back to the sink, aware of his heart pounding heavily against his chest wall. Smear of blood on the edge of the counter. Another on the cabinet door below the sink. It stood ajar.

A moment later, he inched the door the rest of the way open. The cabinet was crowded. A jumble of bottles and cans of cleaning supplies, grocery bags. A brand-new, unopened box of trash can liners. Beside the box, a tall can of furniture polish had fallen backward, sending several other cans tumbling.

He stared at the hodgepodge of supplies. At this point the killer's realized she's covered in blood. She grabs the open box of trash can liners, pulls out the last one or two. She strips here, shoes, undergarments, the works. Stuffs the bloodied garments and paper towels in a bag.

She scrubs her hands, arms, face—anything that's marked with blood. Washes out the sink. More toweling to dry her arms. He shifted his gaze toward the kitchen doorway, the rooms beyond. She walks naked to her bedroom, her closet. Clean clothes and shoes.

He started in that direction, making his way slowly, scanning every inch, looking for confirmation of his theory. Anything. More blood, a handprint, anything.

He reached Katherine's room. There was no doubt it belonged to a teenage girl. A pink hurricane. Closet doors stood open, so did several drawers. That could mean something, but in such a mess, it was hard telling.

He crossed to the closet, rummaged through it. No bag of incriminating evidence. That would've been too good to be true.

What next? He closed his eyes. She's dressed. She knows she has to get rid of the evidence.

She makes her way back to the kitchen. Tanner followed the path he imagined for her. He pictured the waiting bag, moved his eyes from where it would have been, then to the rear door.

Tanner crossed to it. He found it unlocked and stepped out onto a small rear porch. A garbage can sat at the far corner of the house, near the driveway. Lid askew.

That was it. He thundered toward it, heart racing. He flipped the lid the rest of the way off. It clattered to the ground.

Not what he'd expected. Not what he'd hoped for.

He'd hoped for the obvious—a bloody bag, stuffed with everything they'd need to tie this up with a neat little bow.

"Chief!"

He turned. Guidry hurried toward him. He heard the wail of a siren. "Judas Priest! What now?"

"Miz Bell's had a stroke or something! I knocked on her door and saw her there . . . right there in the front room. Scared the crap out of me! Thought maybe—"

"She's alive?"

He bobbed his head. "Sloane's with her."

"Is she talking?"

"Not a word! That's why I figured she'd had a stroke. Really, I thought she was dead, but then—"

"Focus, Guidry! Miz Iris will be fine."

Guidry looked confused. Tanner wanted to shake him. "You spoke with the other neighbors?"

"Yes, Chief."

"I need your help here." He nodded and Tanner went on. "The other neighbors, anybody see or hear anything last night?"

It was a short block, the list of neighbors was woefully small. Miz Bell across the street. An empty rental next to her, the Hingles, a family with young kids, next to her. Ms. Russell across from them. She was single, went out a lot.

An empty lot on the McCalls' left, the old cemetery tucked into the bend in the road, on the right.

Guidry opened his notebook. "Barbara Russell saw headlights. Late. Thought she heard car doors slamming."

"Doors? Plural?"

He checked his notes. "Yup."

"Time?"

"One a.m., she thought. She'd gotten up to get a couple Tylenol."

"Nothing earlier?"

"She got home ten, ten thirty. Lights were still on over here. Said she didn't pay much attention—she'd a had a couple cosmos and just wanted to get to bed."

"What about the Hingles?"

"The entire family was in bed by nine thirty with the exception of Bill. He's conducting interviews today and wanted to review the applicants' resumés while the house was finally quiet. His words."

"And?"

"He was aware of some activity over here. More than usual, he said."

"What the hell does that mean?"

"Vehicles passing. Headlights."

"He didn't look out the window? See what might be going on?"

"Nope. Said he wishes he had now. Turned in around midnight."

Tanner frowned. "Somebody had to have seen something. Somebody—"

He bit the last back, remembering what Trixie had said earlier about Miz Bell calling in. Something about Katherine McCall. Things going on over at the McCall place.

Tanner shifted his gaze. The ambulance had arrived; the EMTs were carrying the woman out on a stretcher. Sloane was watching over their progress like a patient mother hen. All the time in the world.

He scowled at Guidry. "Go get Sloane. Tell him if doesn't get his ass over here right now, I'm going to shit a load of purple bricks to bury him under!"

Wisely, Guidry didn't comment and set off to retrieve his colleague. Tanner headed back into the house, to the kitchen. Where were those clothes?

And then he knew. The washing machine. Of course. He looked around. This was an old house, built at least a century ago. Before fancy washers and dryers went in large, well-appointed laundry rooms.

A lot of these old places had them hooked up in garages or sheds. Some on screened-in porches.

He shifted his gaze to the window above the sink, to the detached garage beyond, then started out the door. Guidry and Sloane met him at the bottom of the steps.

Tanner brushed past them; they followed like a couple of lost puppies. "Where're we going, Chief?" Sloane asked.

Guidry didn't give him a chance to answer. "Have you called the sheriff's department? Are they on their way?"

"No. I didn't call them."

Guidry looked at him as if he had gone daft. "We can't do this without them."

"The hell we can't."

"We don't have the manpower, Chief. The technical expertise—"

"That's bullshit. What technical expertise? I've

been trained in evidence collection. So have you. The crime lab does the rest."

Tanner opened the garage's side door, stepped inside. Flipped on the light.

Nestled just inside the door, on a cement pad, was what looked like a fairly new washer and dryer.

Guidry pressed on. "But this, Chief . . . I don't think—"

Blood. A swath of it. On the side of the washer. *Bingo.*

Guidry fell silent. Sloane cleared his throat. Tanner crossed to the washer, lifted the top.

The tub was empty. A moment later, he saw the dryer was, as well.

Chief Stephen Tanner
2003

The afternoon after the murder

Jeremy Webber agreed to bring Katherine in for an official interview. Instead of meeting in the broom closet they'd converted into an interview room and holding cell, they sat in Tanner's office.

Tanner eyed Kat McCall. Her demeanor was odd. Not quite right. Jittery. Dry-eyed. Strange. She seemed closer to nervous laughter than to tears.

He'd asked Guidry to sit in, take his own notes.

He signaled him now. "Grab Miss McCall a box of tissues. She may need them."

"I'm okay."

Fricking weird. "Get 'em anyway."

A moment later, Guidry set the box on the table, then returned to his post by the door. He'd positioned himself to have a clear view of McCall.

"May I begin?"

Webber nodded. "We're all yours."

He looked at McCall. "Do you prefer I call you Katherine? Or Kat?"

"Kat, I guess."

"When we talked at the scene earlier, you said you didn't touch your sister's body."

"I didn't."

"What about the stains on your hands?"

She looked at her hands, frowning. They were clean, free of what he'd seen earlier.

"Do you remember me asking you about them?"

She shook her head. "No."

Why hadn't he documented that? A flicker of panic settled in the pit of his gut. *A mistake.* "You had bloodstains on them. You must remember that."

"She doesn't, Chief. Let's move on."

"Let's go through this morning, step by step. Okay?"

She nodded.

"What happened first?"

"I woke up."

"You have an alarm clock?"

"Yes. I hit the snooze. A whole bunch. I hate school mornings."

Not animated. But conversational. "Go on."

"I grabbed my stuff and headed for the bathroom."

"At that point, did you notice anything different about this morning?"

She shook her head.

"It wasn't too quiet? Did you call hello to your sister, nothing like that?"

"No. Most mornings she left early for school. She might have hall duty or a student conference. Stuff like that. Besides, I was still mad at her."

Jeremy frowned. Tanner hid a smile. *That's right, sugar. Give it up.* "Why were you mad at her?"

She hesitated a moment. Tanner was certain the next thing out of her mouth would be a half-truth or a lie. "She wouldn't let me have my friends over."

"When?"

"Last night."

"Let's switch to last night. When's the last time you saw your sister?"

"Dinnertime."

"Which was?"

She shrugged. "Around six, I think."

"You ate together."

"No."

"No?"

"I told her I wasn't hungry. I had a candy bar in my purse. I ate that."

"And she was okay with that?"

Again, she shook her head. "She was pissed. She told me if I didn't eat with her, I wouldn't eat. And that I had to stay in my room. No TV or anything." She paused. Glanced sheepishly at Webber. "She didn't know about the candy bar."

"So, you stayed in your room all night?"

"Yes."

"What about Sara? What was she doing?"

"I don't know. She does her thing. Grades papers, whatever."

Present tense. Earlier she referred to her in the past. "You didn't hear anything."

"No."

"Nothing at all?"

"I was listening to music. On my iPod."

"You had headphones on?"

She nodded.

"What time did you go to sleep?"

"Eleven. Maybe twelve. I didn't think about it."

"You didn't say good night to your sister?"

For the first time she looked upset. Her bottom lip trembled. She lowered her eyes and shook her head no.

"Why not?"

"I don't know." She mumbled the words, eyes still fixed on her lap.

"Sure you do. You can tell me, I have a son near your age. Luke. Do you know him?"

"I don't think so."

"So, I get how it can be."

Webber touched her arm. "Your words, Kat. Just be honest."

Oh yes, Tanner thought, be brutally honest with me.

Kat lifted her gaze. Met his. "She sent me to my room, so I stayed there."

"To punish her."

Jeremy touched her hand, answering for her. "Don't put words in her mouth."

"Of course. But you were angry with her."

"Wouldn't you be?"

"I don't know, would I?"

"Yes."

She totally didn't get this, Tanner thought. Her sister was dead, she was a suspect, and yet here she sat, all attitude and entitlement. Is that what happened when you were catered to your whole life?

"Back to this morning. You showered and dressed. How long did that take?"

"Thirty minutes, or so. My hair was giving me fits. I finally just had to pull it into a ponytail."

Tanner recalled her sitting on the step, the breeze stirring her long brown hair.

"It wasn't in a ponytail earlier."

She stared blankly at him. Webber frowned. Tanner could tell that he, too, remembered her hair hanging free.

"When did you change it?"

"I don't know. I don't remember."

"So, you were running late. You left the bathroom and—"

"Grabbed my backpack and iPod and—"

She stopped then. Her throat worked; her eyes turned glassy with tears. Jeremy covered her clenched hands with one of his. "I'm right here, Kit-Kat. You're safe."

"I found her. There. By the—" She looked at her cousin. "I don't want to talk about this."

"You have to, sweetheart. To help the police find who did it."

She started to cry. They were the first tears Tanner had seen from her and they weren't much. A few trickles down her cheeks.

Tanner glanced at Guidry. He saw by his expression that he was thinking the same thing —manufactured emotion.

"What then, Miss Katherine?" Tanner asked softly. "I know it's hard, just tell me what happened."

She drew a shaking breath. "She was there, by the front door. I think I screamed."

"You think?"

"Yes, I'm sure I did."

"You told me the other day that your sister had

taken your phone away. Why'd she do that, Katherine?"

"To punish me."

"For what?"

She looked away. "Nothing."

"She took your phone away just because?"

"Yes."

"Let's move on, Chief Tanner."

Tanner took another tack. "Did she have a boyfriend?"

"There was a guy she saw sometimes."

"Who?"

"Another teacher. Danny something."

He looked at Jeremy. "Did she say anything to you about this Danny?"

Jeremy nodded. "Danny Sullivan. He's a coach over at Tammany West High School."

He directed his attention back to Kat. "Was it serious? Between them?"

"I don't know." She made a face. "We never talked about it."

"Why the face?"

"I don't like him."

"Why's that, Kat?"

"He acts all friendly to me, like we're going to be best friends. Then he steps in and tries to act like he's my dad or something. It's gross."

"Why?"

"He doesn't mean it. He just does it to impress her."

"That's harsh, don't you think?"

"He just wants her money. I told her that."

"When?"

"The first time I met him."

"Did he come by the house?"

"Sometimes."

"When was the last time?"

"I don't remember."

"Think back, Kat," Jeremy said. "It could be important."

"They had an argument. A couple nights ago."

"About what?"

"I don't know. I heard Sara crying. He drove off in his big, stupid truck."

"What did you do after he left?"

She blinked. "What do you mean?"

"Did you check on her? Try to comfort her or ask what was wrong?"

"No."

"Why not?"

She hesitated. Long enough that even Webber noticed. "I was grounded. So I stayed in my room like she told me to."

"Grounded?" Tanner worked to keep his expression neutral. "That's why she took your phone, isn't it?"

"Yeah, I guess."

"Why'd she ground you, Kat?"

"Stupid stuff. Same as always."

"Nothing special this time?"

160

She rubbed her palms on her thighs. "No."

"Stupid stuff, what does that mean?"

"My grades. Keeping my room clean. My friends."

"The friends she wouldn't let you have over?"

She nodded. "She didn't like them. Thought they weren't *good* enough for me."

"Anybody stop over last night?"

"To see me?"

Odd. "Anybody at all."

"Not that I heard. Like I said, I had my earbuds in."

He purposely gentled his tone. "Are you sorry? That you didn't say good-bye to Sara?"

Her eyes filled with tears. "I want to go home, Cousin Jeremy."

Tanner ignored that. "Did you love your sister?"

She started to cry. "I want to go home."

Where was home? Tanner wondered. The little cottage with blood spattered on the walls? Obviously, the fact that she didn't have one hadn't sunk in.

Her cousin put his arm around her. "I think that should do it for now, Tanner."

"I'll need to interview you, Webber."

He nodded, expression grim. "Anytime."

Tanner watched the two walk away. Katherine McCall had killed her sister in a fit of rage. He had no doubt about that. Now he just needed the evidence to prove it.

Chapter Eighteen

An hour later, Danny arrived. Kat was waiting on the front porch and stood while he walked toward her. She wasn't certain what to expect from their chat, but it had been obvious in the parking lot that he would have preferred this not happen.

"I remember you driving a pickup," she said as he neared her.

"Still have it for hunting and hauling." He pushed his sunglasses to the top of his head. "Putting gas in it was killing me."

"You want to go in?"

He glanced at the door, then shook his head. "Rather not, if you don't mind."

A series of images flashed through her head: The baseball bat, shiny red bow affixed to the grip. Sara on the floor, lying in a pool of blood. Figures grouped around her bed, chanting. Demanding justice.

Why had she suggested they meet here? If he was a killer, it wasn't safe. If he wasn't, it was thoughtless and cruel. She motioned to the two wicker porch chairs. "I'm fine out here. Have a seat."

He nodded tersely, crossed the porch and sat. Kat hesitated a moment, then followed. "Can I get you something to drink? A bottle of water?"

"Thanks, no."

They fell silent. She wished she had prepared what she wanted to say to him. The order in which she would say it. Suddenly, winging it didn't seem like such a good idea.

"Here," he muttered, and held out an envelope.

Kat looked at it. She thought of her letter-writing fan. The last letter she'd received. She told herself that Mrs. Bell was watching, that she was always watching. Her fingers shook. She lifted the flap.

Pictures of Sara. One with a group of students, beaming at the camera. Another of her accepting an award. And another, just a close-up of her smiling.

Kat trailed her fingers across the last, caressing. She couldn't speak for the lump in her throat. She missed her so much it hurt.

"When—" She cleared her throat. "When were these taken?"

"The spring before—"

He didn't finish. He didn't have to, the words hung in the air between them. *Before she was murdered.*

He indicated the one with her students. "She'd won that award, remember?"

Kat didn't. She frowned, trying to remember.

"Tammany West Teacher of the Year," he said. "It was a really big deal."

Kat's vision blurred with tears. *Teacher of the Year. A big deal.* Had Sara tried to share her good news with Kat, only to find her too self-involved to listen? Or had Sara, disgusted with her little sister's horrendous behavior, not even bothered to try? Either possibility hurt terribly.

"I was such an asshole back then. I didn't even—" She looked down at the photos, then back up at him. "She loved teaching so much. And she was so good at it."

He didn't reply. The tears rolled down her cheeks. Kat rubbed them away. "I thought you hated me," she said.

"I did." He spread his fingers. "Don't anymore."

"Why not?"

"We're both victims, Katherine."

She hadn't expected this. Had expected this meeting to be confrontational, acrimonious, the way it had been with Ryan.

Of course, she hadn't accused him of killing her sister. Yet.

"But earlier, at the school, you were angry. I could tell."

He looked sheepish. "I was. I don't know, it was a shock, hearing from you like that. I had to process."

She got that. God, did she get it. Ten years later and she was still processing.

"I blamed you," he said. "For a long time. In a way, that was easier than not knowing who did it. I could hate you. For taking her away from me. I could hate the system that set you free."

All that hatred and anger, she thought. She curved her arms around her waist. It could eat a person alive, from the inside out.

"What happened to change your mind?"

"Therapy." He laughed self-consciously. "Don't tell anyone, okay? People like me aren't supposed to need help. Gotta be strong, invincible. It's part of the jock image. I just . . . I realized—"

He fell silent and Kat reached across and covered his hand with one of hers.

After a moment, he cleared his throat. "You didn't do it, Kat. The justice system didn't fail. It worked."

She shook her head. "I can't believe what I'm hearing you say. I was sure you were going to be like everyone else in this town, wanting to see me hang."

"I started remembering the good things Sara had said about you. Not the ones she'd said out of frustration and anger, but the rest of the time. She loved you very much."

He squeezed her fingers, then released them. Kat fought tears. Danny Sullivan, an ally? A friend? Could it be?

"Thank you," she said softly. "Do you have any questions for me?"

"You came back to find out who did kill her."

It wasn't a question. She answered anyway. "Yes."

"And now Tanner's reopened the case."

She nodded.

"Good," he said. "Sara deserves justice."

She froze. "What did you say?"

"That Sara deserves justice. Why? What's wrong?"

"Nothing. I—" She turned toward him, wanting a clear view of his face. "It's hard to put the past behind me. I keep wishing I'd done things differently."

He nodded, looking sorrowful. "Me, too. I wonder, if I hadn't asked for that loan, if we hadn't fought, would she be alive today? Would she have been safe in my arms that night?"

The loan, Kat remembered. It was addressed during the trial. A brief line of questioning.

He looked down at his hands, clasped in his lap, then back up at her. Something in his eyes was far away. "I never should have asked to borrow money. It gave her the wrong idea. About me. My feelings for her." He sighed. "She was sensitive about having so much. She didn't like being rich."

She didn't, Kat realized. Sara had enjoyed simple comforts, the quiet life of a small-town teacher. She'd wanted children. To raise them in Liberty.

"Chief Tanner never made much of that fight," she said softly.

"There wasn't much to it." He lifted a shoulder. "Couples fight, Kat."

He fell silent a moment, then met her eyes, and there were tears in his. "I loved Sara. She meant more to me than any business proposal. Then she was dead. And I couldn't take it back."

He fell silent again. And so did she. This time, it dragged on.

Finally, he broke it. "Would it be weird if we became friends?"

Kat smiled. "I think Sara would've liked it."

She went to give the photos back; he shook his head. "They're for you. Keep them."

"But—"

"I have others."

For a long time after he left, she sat, photos in her hands, lost in thought. Ten years ago, she had left with nothing. A suitcase of clothes. A few photographs of her parents. She had wanted to leave Liberty, her life here, as far behind as possible.

Jeremy had taken care of it all for her. Had everything packed up, put into storage. She wanted it now. The stuff from her past. The memories. And the truth.

Kat shifted her thoughts to Danny Sullivan. Was she crazy to trust him? He could be lying. A murderer, desperate to keep his secret buried. Or to gain her trust.

She almost laughed at her own thoughts. Danny hadn't killed Sara. She would bet her life on it.

Maybe you are, a little voice inside her whispered.

Suddenly chilled, she hugged herself. Sara had been keeping a journal. She'd begun after their parents' death, at first as a way to make sense of her feelings. The police had claimed it didn't exist, that it had been yet another thing Kat had invented to try to divert them.

But it had existed. And she wanted it, whether it contained secrets that would lead to her killer or not.

It contained Sara's secrets. Her hopes and dreams. Their lives together. Kat couldn't physically have her sister back, but she could have this piece of her heart.

She meant to find it.

Danny Sullivan
2003

The afternoon after the murder

Danny Sullivan looked like a man who had been to hell and back. His eyes were puffy and bloodshot, his face pale. His usual confidence had been replaced by despair. By all appearances, he was a broken man.

"Danny," Chief Tanner said, taking the chair directly across the folding table from him. "Thank you for coming in. I know how difficult this must be for you."

He nodded. Though he didn't speak, Tanner noticed his throat worked, as if he was trying to hold back tears.

Tanner went on. "Guidry here is going to take notes, as am I. If you don't mind, we'd like to record this interview."

"Record?" He shifted his watery gaze between him and Guidry. "Why?"

"For your protection. And ours. It's important that we move the investigation forward as quickly as possible, before the trail gets cold. It's imperative we don't miss anything. Do you understand?"

"Yes." He rubbed his hands against his thighs. "Whoever did it . . . I want . . . you have to get them, Chief Tanner. They can't get away with this."

Word had spread like wildfire through Liberty. Of Sara McCall's murder. Of Wally's. The phone had been ringing off the hook. People were freaking out. He'd had to call in all the volunteers to calm them down. If he could quell fears by dispelling—and stopping—rumors, it would make this investigation go much more smoothly.

"We will, Danny. You and Sara were dating. Is that correct?"

"Yes."

"For how long?"

"Six months. But we were friends before that. We teach together. At Tammany West High."

Present tense. It hadn't sunk in yet. Tanner went on. "Was it serious?"

"Yes." He cleared his throat. "I was going to propose."

"Did she know?"

"No. I mean, we'd talk about getting married, but not specifically. I'd gotten the ring. I—" He choked on the words.

"I'm sorry," Tanner said again. "How long have you had the ring?"

"Three weeks."

"But no set plans on when you were going to pop the question?"

"No. I . . . I wanted to wait until things with her sister calmed down."

"Explain."

He spread his fingers. "It was an unhappy time for Sara. Kat was making her crazy. Lying. Acting out. I worried some of it was my fault."

Tanner waited; after a moment, Sullivan went on. "Kat doesn't like me much."

"Why's that?"

"I think because I tried to step in sometimes. To help Sara out. Be a father figure."

"And that didn't work out so well?"

"Not at all. She resented me for it." He lifted a

shoulder. "I always wondered if she might have been afraid I'd steal her sister from her. You know, since she lost her folks. Of course now . . ."

"When's the last time you saw Sara?"

"At school. Yesterday."

Tanner nodded. "What about Katherine?"

"Our paths don't cross much. Even when I visited Sara. Kat wouldn't come out of her room."

"Where were you last night?"

He looked surprised. "Home."

"Alone?"

He nodded. "It was a school night."

"What were you doing?"

"Same things I do most weeknights. Ate dinner, watched some tube. Worked on lesson plans, stuff like that."

"Lesson plans? I thought you taught P.E.?"

"Believe it or not, Chief, even P.E. teachers are required to make them."

"Could I get a copy of those?"

"Of course."

Tanner flipped through his notes, then looked back up at Sullivan. "When was the last time you were over at the cottage?"

Sullivan frowned. "Sara's?"

"Yes."

He thought a moment. "A couple days ago."

That jibed with what Katherine had said. "What did you do?"

"Watched TV. Talked."

"That's it?"

Tanner held his breath. Would Sullivan offer up that he and Sara had fought? Considering that the woman was now dead, it would be a bold admission.

And then he did. "We had an argument."

"What about?"

Color flooded Sullivan's face. "I'd asked to borrow some money. It was a stupid thing to do. It was unmanly."

Tanner didn't comment, though he agreed with Sullivan's assessment. "What did you need the money for?"

"A business opportunity. With Dale Graham."

"The LSU basketball star."

He nodded, expression miserable. "It hurt her feelings for me to ask. She accused me of wanting her for her money. I tried to assure her that wasn't true. I begged her to believe me. That I loved her."

"And did she believe you?"

"She told me she needed time. To process."

"And that's it?"

"Pretty much."

Tanner narrowed his eyes. "Kat overheard the fight. Your version sounds pretty tame compared to hers."

"I can't help that. Mine's the truth, Chief."

"So, she refused to loan you the money?"

"No. She said she had to think about it. Talk to her cousin Jeremy."

"Will Webber corroborate your story?"

"I don't know if she ever talked to him. It was the last time I saw her. She wanted time and space, I gave it to her."

"You make yourself sound like a helluva guy, giving her all that 'time' and 'space.' "

"It's true, Chief. After screwing up so bad, I owed her that, don't you think?"

"Maybe your story's only half true. Maybe, when she refused you the loan, you thought you'd play your trump card. You got her the ring, you popped the question. But she said no."

"That's not what happened! I already had the ring, I'd been planning—"

"You flew into a rage—"

"No!"

"—and killed her."

He launched to his feet, expression horrified. "You can't seriously think I had anything to do with Sara's—Don't you get it? I loved her. She was my future. I honestly have no idea what I'm going to do with my life now!"

He was trembling, looked near tears. Tanner pointed at the chair. "Sit back down, Sullivan. I believe you."

He sank back to his chair. Dropped his head into his hands.

"Your story's gonna check out, right? With Graham and the loan? The date you bought the ring? The lesson plans."

"All of it, Chief Tanner. Every last thing."

Tanner nodded, pleased with himself. With the way the investigation was proceeding. "Good. I'm going to grab a Coke from the machine. You want anything?"

"A Coke would be great. Thanks."

A couple minutes later, he set the red can in front of Sullivan. He watched as Sullivan popped the top and took a gulp. He opened his own and took a leisurely swallow. "The wife doesn't like me drinking these. Too much sugar, she says. But the diet ones taste like crap."

"You got that right."

He took another swallow, then set the can aside. "Let's talk about Kat and Sara McCall's relationship again. Had it worsened recently?"

Tanner figured any sympathy or loyalty Sullivan might have felt for Kat McCall would be gone now that he knew she had tagged him.

Sullivan rolled the can between his palms. "They had a big blowup. Less than a week ago."

"What about?"

"Sara found out that Kat had been lying to her. Said she joined the softball team at school, but it was all a fabrication. Just a story so she could hang out with her friends."

"Did you say softball?"

"Yes."

Tanner's head filled with the image of the baseball bat, covered with gore. *Connecting the dots.* Tanner didn't smile, though he wanted to. "These friends, do you know any of their names?"

"I know the crowd. I could give you a list of names."

"I'd appreciate that. Tell me some more about this fight."

"It was pretty ugly. Sara grounded her. Took away her car, phone, everything. Kat said she hated her. That she wished she were dead. She screamed it at her, actually."

Tanner straightened. "Excuse me?"

"That she wished . . ." Sullivan's words trailed off; his eyes widened. "My God—" He shook his head. "You don't think Kat could have—No way, right?"

"Why not?"

"They were sisters and it . . . Sara was all she had left."

Except for the McCall fortune, Tanner thought. She would have that, all of it. "What was Sara's reaction to the fight? To having her sister say that to her?"

Sullivan looked sick. "She was really upset. Mostly, though, about the reason for the fight. The lying. She felt helpless. And completely lost." He glanced away, then back at Tanner. "She was . . . looking at boarding schools for Kat."

That was it. The why. "Boarding schools?"

"She didn't want to do it but thought it was her only choice."

"Had she told Katherine yet?"

"I don't think so. But I don't know for sure."

"Did Katherine have a boyfriend?"

He hesitated. "Maybe."

"What do you mean by that?"

"Sara wondered. She'd asked her, but Kat denied it."

"But she still suspected. Why?"

"Just getting those vibes from her. Plus, she didn't believe anything Kat said to her anymore. She's a liar, flat out."

A liar. With a fortune to inherit. Friends and maybe a boyfriend she didn't want to leave.

Tanner nodded to himself. People had murdered for less. Much less.

Chapter Nineteen

Thursday, June 6
8:00 a.m.

Kat contacted Jeremy about her and Sara's things. He sounded surprised by the call.

"It's all in a storage locker in Mandeville."

"Could I stop by and pick up the key?"

"Sure, but—"

"What?"

"Are you sure you're ready for this?"

"No," she replied honestly. "But I'm going to do it anyway."

"It's June, Kat, and today's supposed to be a scorcher. Let me make a few calls, I'll hire a couple guys to do it for you. Some of those boxes are really heavy."

She didn't know what kind of flower he thought she was, but she routinely schlepped sixty-pound bags of wheat and maneuvered hundred-quart bowls of bread dough. Kat smiled. "I've got this, Jeremy. No worries."

"I'll help you. Let me look at my calendar and—"

"Jeremy," she said softly, "you've already done so much for me. I can do this. I *need* to do it."

His silence told her he disagreed. That he wanted to insist, but knew it would get him nowhere.

So he did what she had known he would. "I'll bring you the key."

"I'll pick it up." When he started to argue, she cut him off. "I've got nothing but time right now. Just tell me when and where."

Jeremy met her outside the Lakehouse restaurant on the Mandeville lakefront. A historic building in the classic Creole style, it had been turned into a restaurant and event venue, the double galleries used for al fresco dining. Quintessential south Louisiana, with sweeping views of Lake Pontchartrain, the property dotted with ancient oaks and azaleas, gardenia and camellia bushes.

He was on his cell phone, so she waited while he finished his call.

"I will," he said. "Keep me posted."

"That was Tish," he said as he ended the call. "She asked me to tell you she has information about the waterfront property and will call you later."

"Thanks." She motioned the restaurant. "Breakfast meeting?"

"Hammering out the final arrangements for next week's party." He smiled. "I'm making it official. I'm running for state senate."

"Jeremy! Congratulations!" She hugged him. "You'll win. I know you will!"

He hugged her back. "I expect you to come. To the party."

"I don't think that's such a good idea."

"I do."

"The focus needs to be on you. I'd be a distraction."

He caught her hands. "You're family. The last thing I'm going to do is try to hide you, like a dirty secret. How can my opponents make a big deal out of something I fully acknowledge?"

Kat wasn't convinced but she agreed anyway. "Okay, then. If it's what you want, I'll be front and center, for all the world to see."

"Good girl."

He retrieved a key from his pocket. "Here you go. Locker one-two-zero. Mandeville Storage on Highway 22, near Beau Chene."

Twenty minutes later, she rolled up the storage container's metal door. A wall of boxes faced her.

Kat saw right away that Jeremy had been right. If she wanted to get this done today, she was going to need help. But she wasn't about to bother Jeremy again. Maybe Danny could help her? She could pay a couple of his jock students to do the heavy lifting. Maybe one of them had a truck. If not, she could rent a U-Haul for the day.

It took one call. Danny showed up with a couple football players who had failed health class. She didn't need to rent a trailer, because Danny had insisted on swinging by to pick up his truck.

Working together, it took less than an hour to get the boxes moved from the locker to the truck. Forty minutes after that, the teens had the boxes unloaded and stacked in her front room.

As she paid the boys, she noticed Luke across the street. Talking with Iris Bell. He looked her way, lifted his hand in greeting.

She waved back, a strange catch in her chest.

"Is that Luke Tanner?" Danny asked.

"It is. You know Luke, right?"

"It makes me feel old, but he was one of my students. A heck of a ballplayer."

"How about a cold drink?" she asked the teens.

They refused and tore out, obviously delighted to have been given the rest of the morning off. But Danny took her up on it.

"Water good?" she asked.

"Water's perfect."

He followed her inside, then stopped cold. "It still smells like her."

It did. The boxes, she realized. Her sister's things.

She didn't comment, she couldn't. She fixed them both a glass of iced water.

Kat handed him his. He took it, expression pinched. "Are you okay?" she asked.

"No, I don't think so. I need air."

They went back out to the front porch and sat on the steps. Kat gave him space, knowing how it felt to be ambushed by the past.

Finally, he looked at her. "Do you ever think about the point where your life came to a screeching stop?"

"Yes. God, yes. All the time." She looked away, then back. "That's why I'm here."

He laughed without humor. "Look at us. Pathetic."

Kat realized she didn't feel that way, not anymore. "Only we can change that. That's what I'm trying to do."

"Will you help me?"

She swallowed hard. "Yes. Of course I will."

They sipped their waters in silence. As he drained his, the ice clinking against the empty glass, he checked his watch. "I should go. Can't leave jocks on their own for too long."

She smiled and stood. "Thanks for everything."

"If you need help going through all that stuff—"

She put him out of his misery. "You already helped enough. But I appreciate the offer. More than you know."

He opened his mouth as if to say something, then closed it and started again. "What do you hope to accomplish here, Kat? You've lived without this stuff for ten years, what can it matter now?"

"I've got to put the past behind me," she said. "How can I do that if I don't confront it? On every level."

"It's only stuff," he said.

"Memories," she countered. "Open doors." She paused. "And I thought maybe I'd find answers in her journal."

He looked startled.

"You knew she wrote in a journal, didn't you?"

"No, I don't think I did."

"Really? That surprises me."

"Why would I, Kat?"

"It was a big part of her life. She'd been religious about it since our parents' death."

"You noticed because you lived with her. She never mentioned it to me."

His demeanor had subtly changed. He seemed aggravated. Anxious.

Was there something in the journal he didn't want her to see?

181

A moment later, he explained. "Wow, thinking about Sara having a journal feels so weird. So personal." He smiled ruefully. "She probably wrote about us. Our relationship. When we were . . . intimate."

Of course. She felt like an insensitive idiot. "Sorry, I . . . didn't think. If I find it, I promise not to pry."

She noticed he couldn't quite meet her eyes and she felt bad for him. How would she feel in the same situation?

Totally exposed.

"Thanks. I appreciate that." He cleared his throat. Handed her his glass. "Can I call you sometime?"

"I'd like that."

Even as she murmured the words, her gaze drifted across the street to Luke. She caught herself and jerked her attention back to Danny. "Thanks again."

"I'll call you. We can get a cup of coffee."

"Sounds great."

As he pulled away from the curb, her cell phone sounded. It was Tish. "Good news," she said. "The owner of the property on the water's agreed to sell. All we need to do is come up with the right number."

Kat McCall
2003

Seven days after the murder

Kat sat across the kitchen table from Jeremy. She gazed down at her wilting bowl of cornflakes. He'd awakened her early. To talk before he left for work. It didn't matter. She'd hardly slept since Sara's death. She would doze off for an hour here and there, then awaken screaming for her mom. Or Sara. Terrified. Certain someone was hiding in the closet or under the bed, waiting for the moment she fell back asleep to pounce.

During those small snatches of sleep, she was tormented by nightmares. Bloody ones. In them she lost everything and everyone she loved.

They mirrored her every waking moment.

"Kat, we need to talk."

She lifted her gaze from the cornflakes. "Okay."

"You're in a lot of trouble, sweetheart. They're going to arrest you."

"Why? I didn't do it!"

"You're their only suspect, baby." He reached across the table, covered her hands with his. "You've got to help us help you. Can you do that?"

"Yes, anything. I'll do anything."

"You need to tell the truth."

"I have. I swear!"

"You were locked in your room?"

"Yes!"

"Honey—" He paused. "That doesn't sound like Sara. She wouldn't lock you in and not allow you to use the bathroom."

Kat's eyes filled with tears. "But she did."

"Your story keeps changing. Things just don't add up."

"I get confused. It doesn't seem real."

"Okay, sweetie, you've gotta level with me here. Promise?"

She nodded.

"Sara told me she thought you were seeing some guy. Are you?"

Kat stared at him, the blood beginning to pound in her head. A drumbeat sounding the refrain *tell him tell him tell him* . . .

But she couldn't. Ryan loved her. He was all she had left.

"No," she whispered, shaking her head. "No one."

He looked frustrated. He tightened his fingers over hers. "Maybe he did this, Kat. Have you considered that?"

Kat thought of that night, in the car. But they'd only been joking around. He'd never do something like that. She knew him.

"Baby, listen. They're going to arrest you, they have enough evidence—"

"But I didn't do it! How can they have—"

"It's called circumstantial evidence, Kat. Enough of it can convince a jury."

He looked so deeply and for so long into her eyes, she wondered if he was trying to read her mind or mesmerize her.

"Give me something here. Give me a name. If he loves you, he wouldn't want you to be arrested. Would he? He wouldn't want you to be in trouble?"

She lowered her eyes, shook her head.

"That's right, he wouldn't. Give me his name, sweetheart."

"No," she said again, pulling her hands back. "I don't have a boyfriend."

"Dammit, Kat! You're not thinking clearly. This is your life we're talking about."

Ryan was all she had left. She wasn't about to lose him, too.

"Danny did it. I know he did!"

"But the police haven't found anything on him."

"I told them about their fight." Her voice rose. "And I heard his truck!"

"Couples fight, that's not enough. And first you said you didn't hear anything, then you said you did. They don't believe you and he denies it."

Kat sat back, searching her memory. Everything from the past couple months was a blur. Between the lies and sneaking around, the alcohol and weed, she hadn't been paying attention. Nothing jumped out.

But then something did.

Her expression must have changed, because Jeremy sat forward. "You remembered something. What?"

"Sara wrote in a journal every day. She talked about it. Even suggested maybe I should try it. That it might help me work through stuff."

"Okay. And?"

"And if she'd found out Danny was an asshole, I bet she would've written it in there."

Chapter Twenty

Thursday, June 6
11:30 a.m.

Luke didn't know how it was up north, but down here, in a town the size of Liberty, a lawman, especially the chief—or in this case, his stand-in—was expected to sit awhile. Visit. Talk about the weather, family or politics.

Iris Bell had decided on family, but Luke didn't doubt that if he gave her the opportunity she'd work her way around to the other categories.

He took another sip of the tea. It was too sweet. Old school, he thought. Before all the fancy flavored and herbal teas, before people thought about how many grams of sugar they ingested in any given day.

His attention drifted once again to Katherine's place. She and Danny Sullivan had arrived with a couple teenagers and a pickup loaded with boxes. The teens had carried them in, then taken off. She and Sullivan had talked for a while before he'd driven away.

Interesting. Her sister's old boyfriend. Boxes that no doubt had been in storage. She'd told him what she meant to do; she sure hadn't wasted any time getting about it.

He wondered if she'd learned anything he could use.

"Can I get you another glass of tea?"

He jerked his attention back to Iris Bell. "No, ma'am. But thank you."

"It's lovely you stopped by, Chief. How's Margaret?"

She had him confused with his dad. "Stephen is my dad, Mrs. Bell. Margaret's my mother."

She looked at him wide-eyed, then blinked. "Such a lovely woman."

"Thank you." He set aside the glass. "I wanted to ask you a few questions about the night Sara McCall was murdered."

"Oh dear." She brought a hand to her throat, to the strand of pearls he had never seen her without. She toyed with them. "Such a horrible thing."

"Yes. Awful."

"Whatever happened to her?"

"Who?"

"Sara? She was a sweet girl."

"Sara was murdered."

"Yes, I know."

"Did you mean, what happened to Katherine?"

"Yes, that's right." She smiled brightly. He had the sense that the lights were on, but nobody was home.

"Do you remember that night?" he asked.

"Yes, I do." She seemed suddenly, completely lucid. "So many cars that night. So many visitors."

"What do you mean, so many cars? All at once?"

"She was dating that fella. Didn't like him much."

"Who? Miss Sara or Katherine?"

"Miss Kat used to climb out the side window. I told Sara."

"You did? When was that?"

"I think I told her." She frowned. "Or did she tell me? I know I saw her."

"The boyfriend you didn't like, do you know his name?"

"Dark hair," she said instead. "Good-looking." She shook her head. "Slick."

That could be Ryan Benton or Danny Sullivan. "Any chance you can recall his name?"

"It'll come to me. He was there that night."

"Did you say the boyfriend was there that night? The night Sara was murdered?"

Iris shifted her gaze across the street. "Someone's moved in. It looks like a lovely young couple. I wonder if they have children."

"Not a new couple. Miss Katherine's back. Remember, you called me about the vandalism? The graffiti spray-painted on the front of the house?"

Again, she blinked. "That's right." She shook her head. "I forgot for a moment."

Luke leaned forward. "Think back to that night, Mrs. Bell. It could be really important. You said a boyfriend was there that night. Was it Danny Sullivan? Or Ryan Benton?"

She frowned. He sensed her struggling to remember, to make sense of her own addled thoughts. "I wondered why he was visiting so late."

"Who, Mrs. Bell?"

"Yes, who?" She toyed with the pearls once more. "I'll have to ask my girl, maybe she'll remember."

The woman who had greeted him and brought them tea. Viola, her part-time housekeeper/sitter. From the corner of his eye, he saw her at the screen door, peeking out, checking on her charge.

"You said you saw many cars that night? Did you recognize any of them?"

She nodded. "Do you think a plant would be nice?"

"A plant?"

"From my garden. A welcome gift for my new

neighbor." She turned to look across the street, at the now-empty front porch. "Or would cookies be better?"

He'd gotten everything out of her that he was going to, at least for today. "Why don't I go ask?"

She smiled brilliantly. "Good idea, Chief."

He stood. "Thank you for the tea, Mrs. Bell."

She tried to stand. The screen door squeaked open and Viola stepped out. She smiled apologetically. Almost as if it were she who had wasted his time. "Let me help you, Miss Iris."

"Thank you, Viola." She turned her gaze back to him. "And Stephen, please tell Margaret I said hello."

Instead of correcting her again, he smiled. "I will."

Viola crossed to the edge of the porch. "She's not having a good day. Some days are like that. Try back another."

"I will, thanks." He nodded and glanced back. The old woman was gazing up at the sky and humming to herself. What about that night was locked away in her brain, inaccessible except for brief moments of clarity? Enough to have cast suspicion in a direction besides Katherine's, he decided. Already, he had fragments to go on.

Luke crossed the street. Kat must have seen him coming, because she opened the door and stepped out onto the porch.

"Hey," he said as he reached her.

"Hey."

"Mrs. Bell wants to know, would you prefer a plant from her garden or cookies? For a house-warming gift."

"Are you serious?"

"I am. But she's probably already forgotten she asked me to find out."

"You've launched your investigation, I see."

"And so have you. Did Danny pass?"

"I don't know what you mean."

Of course she did. He thought of what Iris Bell had said. A man had been at the cottage that night. He had been visiting late.

That man could have been Danny Sullivan.

"This isn't a game, Kat. Don't forget that."

"Not to worry. I have the feeling you won't let me." She folded her arms across her chest. "If there's nothing else, I've got boxes to start going through."

"Speaking of, what's up with that?"

"What do you mean?"

He could tell she was irritated. "The boxes. What're you looking for?"

"It's my and Sara's old stuff. It's been in storage."

"I gathered. Looking for anything in particular?"

"Sara's journal."

He frowned. That's the sort of item the prosecution loved. "I never heard anything about a journal."

"I told your dad about it. Told my lawyer, too."

"One wasn't introduced into evidence, which tells me they didn't find one."

"But she kept one. She started journaling after our parents' death."

"I believe you. But maybe she stopped long enough before the murder that it had no relevance for either side."

"I know she didn't."

"How?"

"She told me so. She wondered if she could turn it into a book one day. Something about coping with loss."

"When'd she tell you that?"

"I don't remember exactly. But it wasn't that long before her death. I remember wondering what she wrote about me. Worrying about it. Because I was so bad."

He smiled. "You tried to find it and read it, didn't you?"

She flushed. "I thought about it, but I guess when it actually came down to doing it, I didn't want to know."

"Who else knew about her journaling?"

"I thought everyone knew, but I just learned Danny didn't."

"Or so he said."

"Yes."

"He knows you're looking for it?"

"He does now."

She glanced at her watch. "Sorry, but I've got to go. I'm meeting Tish Alexander at the real estate office. The owner of the Riverview property's agreed to sell."

"Congratulations."

"Thanks. But I've gone through this enough times to know that celebrating before all parties have signed on the dotted line is a big mistake."

Chapter Twenty-one

Thursday, June 6
2:00 p.m.

"Hey, Trixie," Luke said. "Messages?"

"Nothing important." She handed him three message slips. "One's from your mom, reminding you it's lasagna night. She's setting a place for you."

He never missed his mother's lasagna. Her maiden name was Furelli, and she had the food gene that came with it. He flipped through the others, then tucked them into his pocket. "Trix, I'm going to need the logbook from the night Wally Clark was killed."

She seemed to freeze. "The logbook? Why?"

He could have pointed out that he didn't have to explain why, but that wasn't the way this place ran. "I'm reopening the McCall homicide."

"I know, but Wally—"

"Was killed the same night. His also went unsolved."

She looked genuinely confused. "But Sara McCall's murder was. Kat McCall—"

"Was found innocent," he said sharply. "Which means, in the eyes of the law—and therefore the world—she didn't do it. The case was unsolved."

She flushed. "I'm sorry. It's just that your father—"

"I'm not my father, Trix. I need you to remember that."

"Yes, sir."

He gentled his tone. "What's wrong, Trixie?"

She shook her head. "Do you think your dad missed something?"

"Fresh eyes. It's only fair to Officer Clark and both McCalls."

"Only fair," she whispered. "Yes."

"Who was on desk that night?"

"I was. I used to . . . I worked nights when the kids were little. So I could be home with them during the day while Pete was at work."

Her gaze drifted to a point beyond him, the expression in it far away. "That was the worst night of my life. Wally and Sara McCall, both of them." She met his eyes. "Your dad was beside himself. I'd only seen him like that once before."

When Stevie died. "It must have been difficult for you."

She nodded and lowered her eyes. He noticed her hands were shaking. "I don't have access to the old logs, they're in storage. Your dad has the key."

"Thanks, Trix." He laid his hand on her shoulder, gave it a reassuring squeeze. "I'll get it from him."

His parents still lived in the house he had grown up in, a small, raised Creole cottage on Front Street. He let himself in. It smelled of his mother's home cooking, the way it had his whole life. "Mom," he called. "It's me."

She appeared at the door to the kitchen. "Hi, sweetheart. Perfect timing."

When it came to food, he had impeccable timing. He crossed to her and gave her a big hug, then kissed her cheek. "Where's the old man?"

"Staring at the news. Grumbling about the state of the world."

Of course he was. "How's he feeling today?"

She smiled. "Today was a good day."

Luke headed for the living room. He found his dad just as his mother said he would.

"Hello, son."

"Pops." Luke took a chair. "What's up?"

"World's getting more screwed up by the day." Luke didn't comment and he went on. "More than a murder a day over in New Orleans. Can you believe that?"

Unfortunately, he could. Gang on gang. Cities across the country had the same problem.

"Got a question, Pops. Where would I find the logbook for the night Wally was killed?"

"I can tell you whatever you need to know."

"I'd rather read it."

He grunted. "Sheriff's department has it."

"They don't. Your testimony, that's it."

"Should be enough."

"You taught me better than that."

That brought the hint of a smile to his craggy face. "Damn right I did."

"Dinner, you two."

His dad struggled to his feet, and they made their way to the dining room. They sat, taking the same chairs they had all his life, his dad at the head of the table, his mother at the opposite end, Luke to his dad's left, the chair across from his empty.

Stevie's place.

Some nights he barely noticed the empty spot, others it shouted at him. Tonight it remained mercifully quiet.

After grace, Luke dug into layered pasta, waiting for the first bite to hit his taste buds and send him swooning. It didn't have its usual effect, and he laid his fork aside.

"Pops? The McCall case, you ever hear anything about Sara McCall having a journal?"

"There was no diary."

"Katherine McCall says there was."

"So she said back then." He frowned. "We went through that place with a fine-toothed comb, there was no journal."

"Like I said, McCall believes there was. She's looking for it."

He frowned. "We couldn't have missed that." He looked at his wife as if for confirmation, and Luke was struck by the vulnerability of it. His dad didn't do that. His dad's word was law, he needed no one to help him make up his mind.

She sent Luke a warning glance, then reached across and covered her husband's hand with hers. "No way you could have missed it."

They ate in silence for several moments.

"What do you think, Pops, if there was a journal, maybe the perp lifted it?"

His dad paused, fork of pasta halfway to his lips. Luke could almost see him thinking: the perp. The person who had beaten Sara McCall to death. But if that murderer was Kat McCall, why was she looking for it now?

"They're in storage," his dad said suddenly.

"What's that, Pops?"

"The logbooks. I'll get you the locker key before you leave."

Chief Stephen Tanner
2003

Two days after the murder

Jeremy Webber sat across the table from him. Waiting.

Tanner eyed him, took his time. The ball was in his court. His party, his pace. And he didn't want to rush this one.

"Thanks for coming in, Webber. I know this is a difficult time for you."

"Anything I can do to help catch the bastard who did this, I'm all in."

How would he respond if he told him they'd already caught her? "What can you tell me about Sara and Katherine's relationship?"

"What do you want to know? They were sisters. Sara was put in the unenviable position of having to raise her little sister after their parents' death."

"It was a turbulent relationship, wasn't it?"

"The last year or so, yes."

"Why was that?"

He looked incredulous. "Kat became a teen. Teenagers can be difficult. Surely *you* know that, Chief Tanner."

Because of Luke. They had almost come to blows more times than he could even remember. The whole town knew. And it was damn embarrassing.

Tanner didn't allow the thought to cross his face. He changed tack. "How would you describe your relationship with Sara McCall?"

"Mine?" Webber looked surprised. "Cousins, of course. Friends. She used me as a sounding board. After her dad died . . . she needed a father figure, I guess. Someone she could turn to for advice."

"So she confided in you her worries about Katherine?"

"Yes."

"That she was thinking about sending her to a boarding school?"

"Who told you that?"

"Danny Sullivan. Is it true?"

"Yes." He nodded. "Sara was upset about the idea. She couldn't believe it had come to that. But she was at the end of her rope."

"What precipitated the decision? The straw that broke the camel's back, so to speak."

He hesitated. "I don't know if there was one thing. They had a big fight recently. It was pretty ugly."

"Had she told Kat about the boarding school?"

"The last time we spoke, no."

"And when was that?"

"About a week. Six days, maybe."

"How do you imagine Kat would react to that?"

He hesitated. "Not well."

"She'd be angry?"

"I see where you're going with this, but you're wrong."

"Answer the question, please. Would Katherine be angry at her sister if she decided to send her away to school?"

"I believe so."

"She might even fly into a rage?"

"She didn't do this."

"Why so sure?"

"I know her. She's going through a tough time, but she's not a killer. Plus, Sara was all she had left. Her only family."

"Except for you." He didn't respond and Tanner went on. "Tell me more about this fight of theirs. What was it about?"

He spread his hands, expression helpless. "Kat told Sara she'd joined the girls' softball team at school, that she had practice every day after school."

"But that was a lie."

He inclined his head. "Sara bought wholeheartedly into the story. She was excited that Kat was taking an interest in something. She took her to the sporting goods store to buy everything she needed to play. Sara was crushed when she learned it was all an elaborate hoax to spend time with her friends."

"Of whom Sara didn't approve?"

He laced his fingers. "Yes. Sara confided in me she was afraid Kat was dabbling in drugs."

"And what did you tell her?"

"To get her tested."

"Drug abusers will say and do anything to keep using, isn't that right, Mr. Webber?"

"I don't know. I've heard that, but—"

"What would you say if I told you Sara was beaten to death with a baseball bat?"

All the color drained from his face. "A baseball bat?" he repeated, his voice choked. "Are you certain?"

Tanner laughed, the sound harsh. "That's not something I could make a mistake about, Mr. Webber. And I certainly wouldn't make it up."

Tanner let the information sink in a moment before he went on. "Poetic justice, maybe. Certainly, highly coincidental. Sara being beaten to death with what I believe was the symbol of the 'straw that broke the camel's back.' "

"She didn't do it," Webber said, though he didn't sound as convinced as before.

"What about a boyfriend? Did she have one?"

"Maybe. Sara suspected."

Same thing Sullivan had said. "Did she give you a name?"

"No. It was just another worry."

"It?"

"That she was becoming sexually active."

Sex, drugs and rock 'n' roll. The three mortal enemies of every parent. "What do you think, Webber?"

"It's definitely possible. She's seventeen. A beautiful girl. Rebelling."

"Let me pass something by you. Sara and Kat get into a big fight. Maybe she's found out about the boyfriend. Maybe there're drugs or alcohol involved. Sara confronts her sister. Tells her she's had enough, she's shipping her off to boarding school. Kat's furious. Her sister is taking everything away from her. Her friends. The boyfriend. The partying and drugs. Or maybe she thinks her sister is trying to get rid of her. So she can start her own family with Danny Sullivan.

"Rage boils up in her. She doesn't mean to kill her sister. But the bat's right there. And once she starts hitting Sara with it, she can't stop."

"No."

"All the pent-up anger spilling out. At her sister. But at her parents, too. For going out that night. For getting killed. For destroying her life. And she takes all that anger out on her sister, Sara."

"I know Kat, she couldn't do that."

Webber's voice shook. Because he could see it going down that way. Because he didn't want to.

Tanner pressed on. "Think about it. She's covered in blood. But she's in her own home. It's easy. She strips naked, cleans up best she can and goes to bed. Like nothing happened."

"So where are the clothes, Chief Tanner?"

"She dumped them someplace."

202

"She doesn't have a car."

Tanner made a mental note to have his deputies begin scouring every garbage bin, drainage ditch and unimproved lot within walking distance of the McCall place. "Sure she does. She takes her sister's."

"You think you have this all figured out, don't you? Well, you're wrong."

"Fine." Tanner folded his big hands on the desk in front of him. "Who do you think did it?"

"Sure as hell not Katherine. A stranger. Or an acquaintance. A student with an axe to grind. Maybe someone who heard about Sara's money. Thought she'd have a safe at the house—"

"Went to rob her? Big problem. Nothing was stolen. And it wasn't a sexual predator, because she wasn't sexually assaulted." When Webber didn't respond, he pressed on. "Who had a lot to gain from Sara McCall's death? Only one person. Her sister, Katherine."

"This is all circumstantial."

"That's okay. Because it's a lot of circumstantial. And it's good."

"Maybe she did have a boyfriend. A really bad guy. And he did it?"

Or they planned it together.

Tanner wasn't about to say that aloud. Not yet. He inclined his head. "Maybe so."

"She's more malleable than she seems. Easily duped. She's been so sheltered."

203

"That makes sense." Tanner stood. He held his hand out; Webber took it. "She'll talk to you, Jeremy. See what you can find out. She might be protecting someone who doesn't deserve her loyalty."

"I will. Kat didn't do this, Chief. I promise you that."

Chapter Twenty-two

Tuesday, June 11
6:00 p.m.

A week passed without incident. Not with her existing bakeries. Not with Liberty's small mind. A week without threats, property damage or baseball bats.

Tish had been by with paperwork for her to sign. The owner of the Riverview property had accepted her offer. The inspection was next week. Kat had begun interviewing contractors about the build-out.

She'd spoken to Jeremy and Danny almost daily. Danny had invited her to coffee twice. She had accepted once, though sitting there with him had felt weird. He had offered to escort her to Jeremy's announcement party tonight, but she had refused. She wasn't going.

She had seen nothing of Luke, but had almost

called him several times to see how the investigation was going. Each time she had stopped herself. He would contact her when he had something to share, and the truth was that her desire to talk to him was about more than the investigation.

And that was somewhere she had no intention of going.

Digging through the boxes had been slow going. Each thing she unpacked held a different memory. And every memory had been precious. The unicorn figurine her dad had bought for her in Greece, the shells she'd collected on a family vacation to Destin, Florida. Photographs. The shirt she'd been wearing when she'd gotten her first kiss. A favorite blouse, a dress Kat remembered wearing to an eighth-grade dance.

She'd unpacked Sara's hair ornaments. A lot of them. In various colors and designs. Sara had long, honey blond hair and she'd almost always worn it pulled away from her face.

Jeremy had even packed up all Sara's cosmetics. The scent of her sister had spilled out when she'd opened that box, wrapping around her like a hug. She'd lost it then, crying so hard and for so long that her eyes had been puffy and bloodshot for twenty-four hours.

Slow going because with every new item she stopped and remembered. Sometimes she cried. Sometimes she laughed. At yet others, a stillness had fallen over her as she allowed herself to wonder, "What if?"

Was she moving forward? Exorcising the demons of her past? Or was she simply picking at scabs, so many of them she would be left bleeding and raw forever?

The knock on her door surprised her. She glanced at her watch, then went to the door, peeking out the sidelight before she opened it.

Luke? She ran her fingers through her hair, an involuntary attempt to smooth it, before she swung open the door. "This is a surprise."

"I'm here to pick you up."

She glanced past him, another involuntary action, half expecting him to be with backup, here to arrest her. "Pick me up?"

"For Jeremy's party."

Kat noticed then how nice he looked. Light blue button-down shirt, open at the throat. Pressed khakis. Freshly shaved.

"I'm not going."

"Sure you are. With me."

"Did Jeremy put you up to this?"

"All my idea. Can I come in?"

She stepped aside so he could enter, then closed the door. "I'm not going," she said again.

"He's your cousin. Your only family. You need to be there."

That's what Jeremy had said. She disagreed.

This was Jeremy's moment, she intended to let him have it without the past intruding.

She told Luke so.

He shook his head. "He can't hide you orthe past. You need to be front and center from the start. That way when things heat up during the election, his opponent can't use you as a weapon against him."

She hesitated. He saw it. "I'll wait while you get ready."

Kat pictured it: A room full of the Northshore's movers and shakers. People who had known her parents, worked with her father, with McCall Oil. People who knew her whole story. Whispering as she walked by. Exchanging glances.

She didn't know if she could do it.

"I'll hold your hand the entire time," he said.

Kat shook her head. "How do you do that?"

"What?"

"Read my mind."

"Not your mind," he said softly. "Your eyes."

Nothing he could have said would have affected her more. "It'll take me a few minutes. I have to shower, too."

"No problem. That'll give me something to think about while I'm waiting."

She grinned at that, then hurried to get ready.

Kat decided on a simple sheath in a deep pink. Strappy sandals. Her mother's pearls. For courage. She fixed her hair as best she could, added a bit of blush, mascara, lip gloss.

She was a baker, not a socialite. Truth was, she had damn little in the way of clothes to choose from and only a vague idea if what she was wearing was appropriate for this kind of event.

He stood when she entered the room. She saw by his expression that he thought she looked good, he didn't have to tell her. But she hoped he would anyway.

He did. "Wow. You look spectacular."

"You're sure?" She looked down at herself, then back up at him. "My mother always knew just what to wear, how to wear it. But I—"

"You look perfect, Kat. Trust me."

She smiled. "Thank you."

"Before I forget." He reached into his jacket pocket. "I found your earring."

He held it out. A diamond fleur-de-lis. The real thing, not costume. Lovely.

"It's not mine." She handed it back. "Where did you find it?"

"By your car. The other day."

What she'd seen him picking up. "Do you think—"

"It was left by your vandal? Maybe. You recall seeing anyone wearing these?"

She thought a moment, then shook her head. "Sorry. But it looks expensive. How many people would own a pair like this?"

"Over here? You'd be surprised. And since Katrina, fleurs-de-lis have become really popular."

"Can I see it again?" She studied it another moment, then handed it back. "I guess it won't do me much good to be on the lookout for its mate, will it? Women don't usually wear a single earring."

He laughed. "No, I suppose they don't."

He offered his arm and they headed to his car. He helped her in, then went around to the driver's side. "Ready?" he asked as he fastened his safety belt.

"As I'll ever be."

They arrived at the Lakehouse fashionably late. A banner had been strung across the upper balcony: WEBBER FOR STATE SENATE. Clusters of balloons decorated both the entrance and upper balcony.

Luke opened the door for her. She stepped out, smoothing her hand over her dress. "Do I look as nervous as I feel?"

"A few nerves can be a good thing."

"Nice save." She smiled. "Thanks."

"You're welcome."

They crossed to the restaurant. Supporters spilled out and onto the grounds. The atmosphere was exuberant, celebratory.

Kat realized quickly that if she had wanted to melt into the woodwork, she had chosen the wrong dress. The great majority of the women wore black; she stood out like a peacock in her pink.

She wanted to turn and run in the opposite direction.

As if sensing her thoughts, he caught her hand, laced their fingers. His hand felt strong and warm, and she clung to it.

"The little black dress memo must still be in my in-box," she muttered.

He laughed. "Making a statement, Ms. McCall. I like a lady with guts."

"Let go of my hand and I'm out of here."

He tightened his fingers around hers. "Let's find Jeremy and Lilith."

They wound and wormed their way through the throng of people. Kat was acutely aware of the way conversations would stop as people caught sight of her, of the hush that fell over them as she passed. And of their excited whispers when they thought she was out of earshot.

She realized this hadn't been a good idea, but also that to turn and run would be a worse one.

Luke, as promised, kept hold of her hand. She clung to it. Not wanting to come hadn't been about Jeremy at all, she realized. It had been about her.

So much for guts.

"You're here!" Jeremy exclaimed when he saw her. He gave her a big bear hug.

He turned to his wife. "Look, Lilith. Kat made it!"

"Good girl," she said and hugged her, though she had the distinct feeling Lilith wished she hadn't come. The other woman felt as she did, Kat thought. That her being here was a distraction.

"I'm giving my speech at eight," Jeremy said. "Downstairs in the main room. I want you right there by my side."

"I don't know, Jeremy. I don't think—"

"You're family. My family. I need you there, Kit-Kat."

She looked to Lilith for support; the other woman wouldn't meet her eyes. So she reluctantly agreed. A moment later, the two were off, back to glad-handing and fund-raising. She and Luke went in search of the bar.

They found it. And Danny Sullivan.

He'd obviously had several drinks. "I thought you weren't coming," he said.

She realized then how this must look. He'd asked her to accompany him and she'd begged off, now here she was with Luke.

"I'm sorry, Danny. I changed my mind at the last minute."

"I changed her mind," Luke said softly.

The words were territorial. As if he was staking his claim, telling the other man to back off. She flushed. It hadn't been like that. Had it?

Danny's gaze dropped to her and Luke's clasped hands. "I see that."

She wanted to explain. Or did she? She felt bad that she had hurt Danny's feelings, but she liked her hand nestled in Luke's, liked the fantasy that they might have a chance at romance.

Dangerous thinking, Katherine. Stupid.

Moments later, Luke put a glass of champagne in her hand. She drank it, then another. They roamed, ending up on the balcony, gazing at Lake Pontchartrain.

The bubbles felt celebratory. They tickled her nose as she sipped, then went straight to her head, making her deaf to the whispers and blind to the glances.

"It's time," he whispered against her ear.

She nodded and let him lead her downstairs. Jeremy and Lilith were already on the dais; he waved her over, smiling broadly.

She had to let go of Luke's hand. She crossed to the dais, took Jeremy's outstretched one. He kissed her cheek and she took her place, standing behind him to his left. In that moment, looking out at all those faces, many of which she recognized, the truth came crashing in on her.

It was they who should be squirming. Reluctant to face her. They who accused her. Who continued to accuse her after the jury's acquittal. They who sent anonymous letters, who vandalized her home and vehicle, who made threats.

And one, a killer, who should be very nervous indeed. Because she wasn't going to stop until she flushed him out.

Jeremy began. "Welcome, friends and supporters! Thank you for coming out tonight to celebrate with me and my family. My beautiful wife, Lilith. Who I couldn't do this without."

They kissed to thunderous applause. Lilith beamed at him, and Kat was struck again by what a perfect couple they made.

"And to my family," he said when the clapping had subsided. "My cousin Katherine McCall. Family is everything. And on that platform, on those values, I intend to run for senate of the great state of Louisiana!"

The assembled group once more broke into applause. And her presence was forgotten. If her history was going to hurt Jeremy's chances at winning a state senate seat, it wasn't in evidence now.

He was smart. And charismatic. Never a misstep, it seemed. He was holding the crowd in the palm of his hand.

She shifted her gaze from him to Luke. Their eyes met. He smiled and the curving of his lips affected her like a caress. Her pulse fluttered; she warmed.

What would making love with Luke be like? Tender or frenzied? A slow burn or a white-hot blaze?

Kat jerked her gaze away, afraid everyone would know what she was thinking. Read her eyes, the way Luke seemed able to do. That they would feel the sexual pull between them.

How could they not? she wondered. It was electric.

She forced her thoughts in another direction. To Sara's killer. Was he here? Watching her and secretly laughing? Making his plans?

And what of her letter-writing fan? Was he here? Were they one and the same?

She studied each face. Her gaze landed on Danny Sullivan. He was staring at Jeremy, his expression malevolent. As if he *hated* him. She caught her breath, loudly enough to earn a glance from Lilith.

Kat looked apologetically at her, then back at Danny Sullivan. And discovered he was gone. Something about that felt wrong, ominous.

She suddenly understood Lilith's three gates.

Kat skimmed the crowd for him, working to hide her panic. She came up empty.

Applause jerked her back to the moment. Jeremy had finished his speech. She clapped and smiled appropriately, hugged her cousin, all the while thinking of Danny. Of the animosity that had emanated from him.

Luke found her. "What happened up there?"

"Did you see Danny Sullivan leave?"

He shook his head. "Why?"

"I just have this feeling . . . he was looking at Jeremy so strangely. As if he wanted to hurt him."

Luke's expression changed. "Let's fan out, see if we can find him. You check upstairs and the bar, I'll hit the men's room and the perimeter. Meet me back here."

Danny was nowhere to be found. Kat rubbed her arms, chilled. "Maybe I imagined it," she said.

"Do you think you did?"

She paused, then shook her head. "No. But I don't know if I trust myself right now."

"Let's get some air."

He caught her hand and they crossed Lakeshore Drive to the lakefront. It was a lovely night. The moon big and bright, the breeze off the lake making the June night feel milder than it was.

They strolled on the pathway, holding hands, not speaking. He stopped under the canopy of one of the ancient live oaks that dotted the lakefront.

"Kit-Kat," he said softly, turning to face her. "I like that." He trailed a thumb down her cheek. "It suits you."

"We can't see each other, Luke. We both know that."

"Do we?"

Those eyes of his were sucking her in. As was his touch, the warmth emanating from him. She laid her right hand on his chest. Beneath her palm, his heart thundered.

She had put it there in an attempt to push him away; instead it drew her closer.

She struggled to sound reasonable. "Think this through, Luke. My past, who your father is. It would never work."

"I'm my own man."

"We can't escape the past."

"I'm not trying to."

He lowered his gaze to her mouth and her heart seemed to stop with anticipation. She involuntarily curled her fingers into the soft fabric of his shirt.

"Stop running, Kit-Kat."

"For all you know, I could be a cold-blooded—"

"You're not."

"You don't know that. Maybe this, me being back, is a sick power trip. Forcing myself down Liberty's throat. Laughing at them behind their backs."

"I don't think so." He moved his hands from her shoulders to her upper arms, drew her closer.

"Get involved with me, I may bludgeon you to death. I may—"

He kissed her.

She resisted for a nanosecond, then she melted into him. Letting go, trusting her body in a way she hadn't allowed herself to since her seventeenth year.

It was heady. And exciting.

It scared her to death.

Because, in that moment, the past disappeared. Melted away. And she was fully present, in this man's arms. Nothing else mattered. Nothing could intrude.

She felt his cell phone, attached to his hip, go off. It vibrated against her side. But still he held her. Still he kissed her.

On the fourth alert, he muttered under his breath and broke away. "Tanner," he said, voice thick.

They stood so close Kat could hear the panicked voice on the other end of the line.

Her house was on fire.

Iris Bell
2003

Two days after the murder

Iris Bell prided herself on her seventy-five years of life. She'd raised her kids right, taken care of home and husband, weathering the ups and downs with grace. A husband's unfaithfulness. A child's cancer. The loss of loved ones. She understood her place in the world. She understood she was the glue. That all women were.

But the world had gone to hell in a handbasket. Until death do us part had become meaningless. The family home was an outdated concept. Today, parents chased jobs from one place to another, toting their kids with them. Both parents, leaving their children to raise themselves with fast food and video games.

"How are you today, Mrs. Bell?"

She looked at the woman, dressed in white. "Do I know you?"

"I'm Amelia, your nurse."

Iris blinked and looked around her. "Where am I?"

"Lakeview Regional Hospital. Remember? You arrived two days ago."

"That's right." She plucked at the blanket, wanting to ask another question but having the feeling it was something she should already know.

"There's someone here to see you."

Iris shifted her gaze to the doorway. Not Ned. Not one of the kids. Chief Tanner. And he'd brought her flowers.

She waved him in. "Aren't you the sweetest man. I'll just get a vase for those."

She moved to climb out of the bed, but the nurse stopped her. "I've got them, Mrs. Bell. You stay where you are." She took the flowers—Iris realized they were already in a vase—and set them on the table beside the bed. "I'll just leave you two alone to chat."

"Thanks for stopping by," Iris called after her, looking back at Chief Tanner. Such a big man. Why in the world did he even need to carry a gun?

She tipped her face up to look him in the eyes. "I'll get a crick in my neck, better come have a seat. And wipe your feet, I just mopped the floor."

"Yes, ma'am," he said, looking startled. She smiled at the way he carefully sat, as if he might break the chair. That chair had survived a lifetime with her Ned, it would survive this little visit.

"I have a question for you, Chief," she said.

He took a small spiral notebook and pen out of his coat pocket. "Yes, ma'am."

"Whatever happened to dinner at the table at five thirty, the entire family in attendance?" She leaned forward. "With hair combed and hands washed."

"Times change, Miz Bell."

"And what about worship on Sundays?"

"I don't know, ma'am."

"Hell in a handbasket," she said. "And now this."

"Pardon?"

"You're here because of all the goings-on over at the McCall place."

"Yes, ma'am. I'd like to ask you a few questions about that, if you feel up to it?"

"Of course I am. Right as rain, dear." She smiled at him, waiting.

"Sara McCall is dead. Somebody killed her."

"Oh dear." She brought a hand to her throat, then dropped it back to her lap. "I was afraid something like this might happen."

"What do you mean, Miz Bell?"

"The way they were always fighting." She shook her head. "It wasn't right. Not at all."

"Who was always fighting?"

"Miss Sara and Miss Katherine. She was a wild one."

"Who was a wild one?"

Iris narrowed her eyes. "Are you being deliberately thick, Chief Tanner?"

A smile tugged at his mouth. "Actually, I am. I can't assume anything. It wouldn't hold up in court."

She nodded, pleased. "Very well, then. I'll be specific. I meant Katherine. Always causing her sister fits."

"Fits?"

"Lying. Sneaking out at night. Hanging with a bad crowd."

"How do you know all this?"

"Now she'll never forgive herself."

He leaned toward her, pen poised over his notebook. "What do you mean, Miz Bell?"

"Katherine wished her sister were dead. And now she is. Why, Chief," she said, "your hands are shaking."

He flattened them against his thighs. "Too much coffee this morning."

He cleared his throat. "How do you know Katherine McCall wished her sister was dead?"

"I heard her say it. Just the other day."

"Tell me about that."

Poor man, she thought, now his voice was shaking. "They were arguing. Out on the porch. I couldn't help but overhear."

"Your hearing must be very good."

"They were shouting."

"Do you wear a hearing aid, Miz Bell?"

She scowled at him. "That doesn't mean I can't hear, it makes me hear better. And if I need to, I turn it up."

"Did Sara McCall confide in you?"

"The other day she came over and asked if I'd seen any boys around the house. I could tell she was real angry."

"Had you? Seen any boys?"

She shook her head. "No."

"When was this fight you overheard?"

"That same afternoon. After Miss Sara stopped by. They were on the front porch. Screaming at each other."

"How long ago was that? Try to remember, Miz Bell."

Iris brought a hand to her throat. "My pearls!" she exclaimed. "They're gone."

"It's okay, Miz Bell. The hospital has them. Your wedding ring, too."

She gazed at her left hand. It looked naked. Shriveled and old. Not like her hand at all.

"My ring, too?" she whispered. "Why would they do that?"

"For safekeeping."

"You'll get them back for me, Chief?"

"I will." He laid his big hand over hers. "I promise."

Strong and steady. The way a leader was supposed to be. "Thank you, Chief Tanner. You're a good man."

"Can we talk about Sara and Katherine McCall's fight again?"

"They had a fight?"

"You were telling me you heard them arguing. On the front porch."

Iris frowned. "What did they fight about?"

"I was hoping you could tell me."

"Can I offer you a glass of iced tea, Chief? You sound parched."

"No, thank you, ma'am." He closed his notebook and stood. "It's been lovely visiting with you."

Iris tipped her face up to his. "I saw Miss Sara crying. Right over there on the porch steps. Poor baby seemed like she had the weight of the world on her shoulders."

Iris shook her head. "Such a shame. And now Miss Katherine has to live with it."

"With what, Miz Bell?"

"To wish things like that and have them come true. I don't know that I could."

Chapter Twenty-three

Tuesday, June 11
10:15 p.m.

Kat cried when she saw it. Black smoke swirling up to the sky, angry flames devouring Sara's pretty little cottage. Stealing another piece of her past.

The Liberty Volunteer Fire Department had arrived with the ladder and pumper trucks; their lights bounced crazily off the surrounding homes and other vehicles. Like a life-size pinball machine.

Luke braked and she jumped out of the vehicle. The heat slammed into her, the smoke stung her eyes and nasal passages. She ran toward the house; Luke grabbed her around her waist, dragging her back.

She fought him. "Let me go!"

"There's nothing you can do!"

"No." She struggled. "I have to try!"

"To what?" He forced her to meet his eyes. "Save things you've lived without for ten years? Clothing that can be replaced?" He moved his hands to her shoulders. "Let the firefighters do their job, Kat. It may not be as bad as it looks."

Word had spread and neighbors began to gather. Jeremy and Lilith arrived. He called her name. She turned and ran to him.

"Why, Jeremy?" she cried. "I can't bear it!"

He caught her in a bear hug. "I don't know, sweetheart. I'm so sorry."

She pressed her face into his shoulder. "I shouldn't have come back. It was a mistake."

"Don't say that. You belong here. This is your home."

"I haven't belonged here since Mom and Dad died." She tipped her face up to his. "What will I do now? Where will I go?"

"You'll stay with us," he said. "As long as you need to."

Luke joined them. "Fire's extinguished. You got lucky, Kat. Mrs. Bell saw the fire early on and called 911. The firefighters were able to contain it to the front, right side of the house, which was probably the point of origin as well."

"Does it look like arson?" Jeremy asked.

"Of course it was arson," Lilith snapped. "Wake up, Jeremy."

Kat flinched at her words. They hurt. Jeremy tightened his arm around her shoulder in silent support. "We don't know that for sure," he said.

Lilith looked annoyed. Luke stepped in. "No, we don't. Firefighters are inside now, looking for evidence. I contacted the state fire marshal's office; they'll get word to their investigator for this area." He turned his gaze to Kat's. "We'll get this sorted out."

She swallowed past the lump that formed in her throat. She looked up at her cousin. "I've ruined your big night, Jeremy. I'm so sorry."

"You didn't ruin anything. Understand? This isn't your fault."

"Thank God you weren't home," Lilith said. She glanced back at the smoldering cottage and shuddered. "This is why we live behind gates."

Gates. Danny's image filled her head, his malevolent expression as he gazed at Jeremy. *Could he have done this?*

"Yes," Luke agreed, "thank God. Jeremy, Lilith, why don't you head home? There's nothing you can do here. I'll bring Kat later."

Jeremy shook his head. "We can wait, it's not a problem."

"My car's here," Kat said. "I can drive myself."

"I don't think you should." Jeremy looked at Luke, as if for support. "This has been horrendous for you, you're understandably upset. The last thing I think you should be doing—"

"I'll be fine." She squeezed his hand. "I promise."

"I'll make certain she gets there safe," Luke said. "I'm not sure how long it will take to finish up here."

Jeremy wanted to argue, Kat saw. But Lilith wasn't making a secret of the fact she wanted to go home. In the end, Lilith—and Luke—won.

Kat watched them drive off, then turned to Luke. And found his gaze on her. The memory of their kiss filled her head, momentarily pushing aside the vision of flames against the night sky.

"You can stay with me," he said softly. "I'll take the couch. I promise to be a perfect gentleman."

Somehow, that appealed more than the thought of Jeremy and Lilith's luxurious home. But they both knew if she stayed with him, he wouldn't be on the couch.

"I don't think that's such a smart idea."

"I could change your mind about that."

He could. She searched his gaze. "And I want you to, I really do. But I've given this town enough to talk about tomorrow morning."

He nodded. "Jeremy and Lilith's is the perfect place for you. You'll be safe there."

Locked away behind gates. In her head, she heard the clang of them shutting behind her. She shuddered and rubbed her arms. "What if I'd been home?"

"I don't think he meant for you to be."

"He just wanted to scare me?"

"That's one theory. Scare you enough to send you packing. Once you're gone, he figures this whole thing will die down again."

"And another one?"

"Just another attempt to punish you, because in his opinion, you got away with murder."

"Like the graffiti and anonymous notes."

He nodded. "Although arson certainly kicks that up a notch. I have one more theory." He held her gaze. "Firefighters said the blaze started in the front room of the house, Kat. The front room."

"Okay, so—" She bit the words back, realizing what he was getting at. "The boxes," she said. "All our things from back then."

"Yes. And among those things, maybe a journal. In which a murder victim shared all the most intimate details of her life. Her innermost thoughts and feelings. Her secrets."

A murder victim's secrets. Of course. The last thing the killer would want to come to light.

Danny. Kat pictured the way he had looked at Jeremy tonight. As if he hated him.

As if he hated her.

"Danny knew what I was looking for. When I told him, he acted upset, then claimed not to know Sara journaled. And acted embarrassed at the idea that she might have written intimate things about their relationship."

"Which could be true."

"Yes, but he left the party early. And angry."

"Who else knew about the boxes and what you were doing, Kat?"

"You and Danny." She ticked off on her fingers. "Jeremy and Lilith. Maybe the high school boys who helped me move the boxes. I don't remember what I said in front of them." She thought a moment, searching. "My Realtor, Tish. I think I mentioned it when she called one day."

"Of those, who knew you were looking for Sara's journal?"

Kat thought a moment. "All of them but the high school boys. I didn't tell Lilith directly, but I assume Jeremy would have told her."

"And I haven't been quiet about what I've been doing. Reopening the case. Interviewing people."

"Ryan," she said. "Bitsy."

"The sheriff's department. My department. Your neighbors." He paused. "I asked my dad about the journal. He said they looked, that they couldn't find it. In his opinion, it didn't exist."

"So I just made the whole thing up."

"That or she stopped journaling."

"She didn't."

"There were a lot of things about your sister's life you weren't aware of."

It was true. It stung anyway. "Maybe your dad didn't look hard enough, because he didn't care if he found it."

"That doesn't make sense."

"Sure it does. Why work hard when you've already got your murderer locked up?"

She let that simmer a moment, then met his eyes. "Or when you're trying to protect someone else. Maybe even trying to protect yourself."

"That's just silly, Kat. My dad didn't kill your sister."

"Silly? Really?" Her voice shook; she realized how close to the emotional edge she was but continued anyway. "Maybe this whole thing is a figment of my imagination? A product of my silliness?"

"You seriously think my dad might've killed your sister?"

His incredulous tone, the way he arched his eyebrows in disbelief pissed her off. "I haven't crossed him off my list."

"He was the law."

She saw he was trying to control himself. Be patient. Understanding. Perversely, she wanted to push him until he lost it. "Cops abuse their power every day."

"You're tired. Upset. After a night's sleep you'll see things more clearly."

"Maybe you're the one not seeing clearly? Maybe your old man buried the truth?"

"Tomorrow we can discuss this rationally."

She grabbed his arm. "Your dad never looked further than me for a suspect. Why is that?"

"Because you looked guilty, Kat. Damn guilty."

His words affected her like a slap to the face. "Maybe you should join the Tar and Feather Kat McCall Club with everybody else in this shitty little town?"

"I don't think you're guilty. But there was a lot of circumstantial evidence. That's all I'm saying."

"Maybe your dad set the place on fire because he was afraid I'd find the journals, proving I *didn't* do it and making him look like a fool? I don't think the mighty Chief Stephen Tanner would enjoy the taste of crow."

"Stop it, Kat."

She shook with anger. "What would all the good folks of Liberty think if they learned their supercop was just a bumbling country lawman who was in way over his head?"

"Enough!"

"Not nearly. Not—" She turned on her heel and marched to her car. "I'm done."

He caught up with her. "C'mon, Kat. I'll drive you to Jeremy's."

"Not happening." She yanked the car door open. "Thanks for the memorable evening."

He caught the door, preventing her from closing it. "I'll follow you to Jeremy's."

"You can do whatever you want."

He bent to look her in the eyes. "You're going to feel pretty silly about this tomorrow morning."

"I hope so," she said. "The door, if you don't mind."

He slammed it, then strolled to his vehicle, parked on the street, blocking her car. The minute he was in and had moved his vehicle out of her way, she took off.

Chapter Twenty-four

Wednesday, June 12
12:35 a.m.

Luke followed her to the entrance of Jeremy's neighborhood, then turned around to head back to Liberty. He flashed his headlights as he did, which Kat figured was damn nice of him, considering. He'd warned her she would regret the things she'd said in the morning.

She regretted them already.

Truth was, she had regretted them even as she had been lashing out at him, attacking him through his father, as if it had been Luke who had caused her all this pain. But she hadn't been able to stop herself.

What she had really wanted to do was curl up in his arms and cry.

Kat rolled up to the gate and lowered her window for the security guard. He had the deeply lined face of a man who had spent his life outdoors. He looked at her strangely and she realized she must look a fright.

"Hello, miss." Pity in his tone. "Where to tonight?"

She opened her mouth to tell him, then shut it. *She had to go back.*

"Miss?" the guard said, pity now concern. "Are you all right?"

"Sorry, I—Never mind. There's something I have to do."

Kat shifted into reverse and backed away from the surprised guard. She saw him writing down her plate number and hoped he didn't call the police. More involvement with the law, she didn't need.

She swung into the turnaround and seconds later she was again on Highway 22, this time heading back toward Liberty. She might be cracking up, but she had to go back to the cottage. Kat laughed out loud, the sound a degree south of scary. Might be cracking up? Serious understatement. But she had the strong feeling she would find answers there.

She reached Liberty, took the winding road to the cottage. The emergency vehicles were gone; porches were dark, indicating the neighbors had all gone in to bed. A lone car was parked in front the cottage. One identical to hers.

Danny.

He stood beside his Fusion, gazing at the structure, its charred facade. He turned when her headlights sliced across him.

She pictured Danny's expression as he'd gazed at Jeremy earlier that night. Hatred. Jealousy.

Keep driving, Kat. If this is anything, Luke will take care of it.

She parked behind him instead, got out and joined him beside his car. "What are you doing here, Danny?"

"I heard about the fire. I had to come see for myself."

"Did you? Have to come see?"

"That's what I said."

"Where were you tonight?"

"You know where I was." He slid his gaze over her. "You and your date."

His tone dripped contempt. For her. Luke. Jeremy. "Why'd you leave early?"

"It was time to go. Why so interested?"

"Take a look." She motioned the cottage. "Why do you think?"

"That's bullshit." He turned and grabbed his door handle.

She caught his arm, stopping him. "Why'd you leave the party early?"

"I promise you, you don't want to do this."

For the second time that night a man was warning her to stop before she went too far, and for the second time she ignored the warning. "I saw your face when you looked at Jeremy tonight. It looked like you hated him."

He laughed, the sound uneven, slurry. "That a crime?"

"Did you do this to punish him? Or me?"

"Fuck off."

"Why do you hate Jeremy? What did he do to you?"

"B'sides ruin my life?"

His words ran together and she realized that the drinks he'd had at Jeremy's party hadn't been his last. He was drunk.

If she hadn't been so close to the edge herself, she would have noticed before now. She would have seen the ugliness creeping into his gaze.

She did now and took a step back. "Forget it, I'm just upset. I shouldn't have said that. Any of it."

"Yeah, you're right, you shouldn't have."

"We can talk tomorrow, I—"

"I want to talk now." He grabbed her arm and jerked her against his chest. He bent his head close to hers, breathed deeply. "You smell like her."

Kat worked not to panic. "Let me go, Danny."

Instead he anchored her to him, one hand at the small of her back, the other at the back of her head. "How can that be?" He drew another deep breath, this time with his face buried in her hair. "She's been gone ten years."

"Let me go," she said again, softly, working to keep the panic out of her tone. "And we can forget this ever happened."

She felt him stiffen and knew immediately she had said the wrong thing.

"Forget?" he said. "I can't forget!" His voice

rose. "I can't get the picture of her out of my head. The foyer . . . all that blood. Her face crushed—"

He had been there. In the foyer.

Instead, he moved his hands to her upper arms, gripping so tightly she cried out in pain. "Don't you get it?" He shook her; her teeth rattled. "I-don't-want-to-see-it-anymore!"

Had he been standing over Sara with the bat, shaking with rage? Screaming at Sara the way he was screaming at her now? Eyes wild, spittle flying from his mouth.

Was this rage the last thing Sara had seen?

"Little bitch!" He shook her again. "You ruined everything! It should have been you lying there, not her!"

He wanted her dead.

She started to struggle. She realized she was sobbing. "Let me go. Please, Danny, let me go!"

Instead he slammed her against the side of his car, her neck snapped back and her head hit so hard she saw stars. He was on top of her then, she couldn't breathe. She fought to get her hands between them, to push him away.

He kissed her neck and ear, slobbering on her as he continued his tirade. "I figured maybe you and me. Maybe I'd get my McCall that way. But he did it again, didn't he? Jeremy, that son of a bitch.

"Turned her against me . . . told her she was too good for me. That I only wanted her for her money. Fuck!" he screamed. "Stupid fucking loan!"

Iris Bell's front light snapped on. Startled, he relaxed his grip. Kat used the opportunity to knee him in the groin, then as he doubled over she scratched him across his cheek. Her hand came back sticky with his blood.

She figured if she didn't get away and he killed her the way he'd killed Sara, at least she'd have the bastard's DNA under her fingernails.

He bellowed and swore. Kat broke free. Light spilled across her neighbor's porch as the woman opened her door.

"What's going on over there?"

"Call 911!" Kat screamed, running to her car. She yanked the door open and launched herself inside.

A moment later, she sped off, Danny Sullivan a crumpled heap in her rearview mirror.

Chapter Twenty-five

Wednesday, June 12
1:45 a.m.

Luke's cell phone went off at the same moment someone pounded on his door. He answered the cell and made his way to the front of the house. "Tanner."

"Luke, it's Cindy. There's been some trouble at the McCall—"

He flipped on the porch light and peered out. Kat, looking like a crazy woman.

"Mrs. Bell called it in. A woman screamed—"

He opened the door and Kat fell into his arms.

"Send Reni," he said. "Keep me posted."

He scooped Kat up and carried her to the living room. He sat on the couch with her cradled in his lap. She curled into him, sobbing and shaking.

"I've got you," he said softly, rocking slightly. "When you're ready, tell me what happened."

She nodded and pressed her face into his shoulder. The sobs stopped first, the trembling minutes later. Still she clung to him, not speaking, not easing her hold on him.

Finally, her grip lessened. She whispered something he couldn't make out.

"What, sweetheart? I can't hear you."

She tipped her face up to his. "Danny. He was there."

"Where? Jeremy's?"

"The cottage. I went back. I shouldn't have . . . I had this feeling . . ." She drew in a shaky breath. "He was there. At the front gate, staring at the cottage. Everyone else was gone."

And she got out of the car. The very worst thing she could have done.

Luke silently counted to ten. Let her talk, he told himself. The same as he would any victim.

237

Pretend she wasn't someone he was growing to care for.

He couldn't. Not completely. "Perpetrators often return to the scene of their crime. To relive it. To get off on it again." He shifted so he could look directly into her eyes. "Promise me you won't do anything so stupid again?"

She nodded. Horror crept into her eyes. "I realized he was . . . the one. And then I was so scared. I was afraid he was going to kill me, too."

"Wait a minute, what do you mean, kill you, too?"

For several moments, she didn't speak. When she did, her voice was hushed. "I think he killed Sara. He was talking about that night."

"I need to get my notebook. Are you okay now?"

When she nodded, he eased her off his lap and onto the couch beside him. She shivered. He grabbed the afghan and wrapped it around her shoulders. "Can I get you anything? Water, soft drink?"

"I'm fine."

But she clearly wasn't. She looked lost, sitting there, being swallowed up by the overstuffed couch and bulky afghan. "Okay, I'll be right back."

He returned a minute later to find she hadn't moved. He'd brought her a glass of water anyway and set it on the coffee table in front of her. She didn't seem to notice it was there.

"Ready?" he asked. She nodded. "You said you were afraid he would kill you. That you now believe he killed Sara. Tell me why, Kat. Don't leave anything out."

"He said . . . he said he couldn't get the picture of her out of his head."

"What picture?"

"Dead. On the foyer floor. He mentioned the blood. Her . . . crushed face." The last came out a whisper.

Luke thought back to the trial notes he'd read. Sullivan had testified for the prosecution. Witnesses were not allowed to be trial spectators, so he wouldn't have seen the photos that had been entered into evidence. His father might have shown Sullivan a picture, but to what end? And if he had, why no mention of it in his case notes?

That left one option. Sullivan had been there.

"What else did he say? It's important, Kat."

"That it should have been me who was dead."

He looked at her hands. She had them clenched so tightly, her knuckles were white. He took them. They were ice cold and he rubbed them between his. "Did he say what that meant?"

She shook her head. "No."

"And that's it?"

"I don't know, I—He went sort of crazy. He grabbed me and . . . shook me. He was yelling.

About not being able to forget. And I couldn't stop thinking about Sara. If that was the last thing she saw, his screaming at her like that . . ."

She shuddered and he curved his hands protectively around hers. "I tried to get away. He shoved me up against the car."

The dress's scooped neckline dipped and Luke saw them. Bruises. Like purple fingerprints on her skin.

He wanted to howl. Felt the primitive reaction rise up inside him. The intensity of it shocked him.

"What else?"

"He said something about Jeremy," she said. "That he hated him. That he ruined everything."

"What does that mean, everything?" He heard himself. The words sounded tight, completely controlled. As if he wasn't counting the moments until he could tear Sullivan apart.

"That Jeremy turned Sara against him. Because of the money."

She fell silent. His mind raced. He hadn't heard back from Cindy. He wondered if Reni had picked Sullivan up at the scene or whether he'd been gone by the time he got there.

She shuddered. "He screamed something about the loan. The fucking loan, he called it."

The loan. It'd come out at the trial, a minor line of questioning. Nothing at all.

Judging by what he was hearing now, it was definitely something.

"That's when Mrs. Bell's light snapped on. If it hadn't—"

"But it did. You're safe now."

She looked down at their joined hands, then back up at him. "I thought he—" She choked on the words, then tried again. "I scratched him. So if he killed me, I would have DNA evidence under my fingernails."

His cell phone vibrated. He stood and answered. "Tanner. What do you have?"

"Reni caught Danny Sullivan fleeing the McCall place. He had to give chase, but has him in custody now. What do you want us to do with him?"

"Book him with resisting arrest. I'm on my way in.

"They have Danny," he said softly, reholstering his phone. "I've got to go in and question him. And I need you to come with me."

Fear raced into her eyes. "Me? Why?"

"Gotta get your nails scraped and your bruises photographed. Just in case we need the evidence." He held out a hand. "And now's better than later."

She took his hand and he eased her to her feet. And against his chest. She met his eyes. "Luke?"

"Yeah?"

"I'm sorry. For what I said earlier."

"I know." He bent and kissed her lightly. "It's going to be okay."

Chapter Twenty-six

Wednesday, June 12
3:15 a.m.

Luke sat across the table from Sullivan. He looked like shit. Pale. Bloodshot eyes. Disheveled. But it was the bright red scratches across his right cheek that Luke couldn't take his eyes off.

He fought to keep his fury at bay. Frankly, he didn't think he was going to be too successful at that.

Reni stood by the door, facing Sullivan. To note his every blink, twitch or grimace.

Luke glanced at the tape recorder on the table. Old school. No fancy video hookup here at the Liberty P.D.

"Officer Reni read you your rights?" When he agreed, Luke went on. "What were you doing over at Kat's place tonight?"

"I heard what happened. That it had caught on fire. I wanted to see for myself."

"How'd you hear?"

"How?"

"Yes. How?"

"The sirens."

Luke arched an eyebrow. "The sirens?"

"I was at the E-Z Serve. Gassing up. I asked the dude what was going on. He told me."

"Which E-Z Serve?"

"On 22, right before Marina Del Ray."

Luke made a note. "And the 'dude' knew which house was on fire?"

He nodded. "And I went to see for myself."

Luke pretended to skim his notes. "Why, Danny?"

"You know, because of Sara."

"No, I don't know."

"I loved her. I never got over her."

"Is that why you attacked Kat? Because you never got over her sister?"

"I didn't attack Kat."

Luke arched his eyebrows. "No? Your face is telling me differently."

His hand went up to his cheek; halfway there, he dropped it. "She attacked me. Came at me like a crazy woman. Kneed me in the balls, for God's sake."

Luke lowered his eyes so Sullivan wouldn't see the fury in them. "That fire tonight, it wasn't any accident. Somebody torched the place. Would you know anything about that, Danny?"

"I want a lawyer."

"You're entitled. Do you have someone in mind? Or do you need a phone book?"

"Phone book."

Luke looked over his shoulder at Reni and signaled for him to get the book, then turned back to Sullivan. "While Officer Reni retrieves that, let me offer you a different scenario about tonight's events. When you saw Kat and Jeremy, you were consumed with anger or jealousy and left the party early. With a plan."

"I left because I was bored."

"To torch Kat's cottage. Destroy the evidence. And pay them both back, for whatever sin you imagine they committed against you."

"How many drinks did you have tonight, Tanner? One too many, I'm guessing."

"You went back to the scene," Luke continued, "after everyone else had left. To admire your handiwork. Or make certain it was done."

"That's nuts."

His dismissive tone didn't match the panic that raced into his eyes. Luke leaned forward. "What did you hope to achieve, Sullivan? Besides making certain Sara McCall's journals would never be recovered."

"I don't know what you're talking about."

"Of course you do. Kat told you about them. What could we have found in those journals? Maybe a reason for you to have wanted her dead?"

Sullivan leaped to his feet. "I'm not saying another word until I have a lawyer!"

"Sit your ass back down. You're not going anywhere."

Reni returned with the phone book. He dropped it on the table in front of Sullivan. "Stay with him, Reni, make sure he gets that call made."

"You got it, Sarge."

As Luke left the room, he glanced back. Sullivan was staring at the Yellow Pages, looking for all the world like he might puke.

"And Reni? Get Mr. Sullivan a Coke and a paper towel. He's got a long frickin' night ahead of him."

Chapter Twenty-seven

Wednesday, June 12
5:30 a.m.

Kat opened her eyes and found Luke gazing at her. "Hey there," he said softly. "You looked so comfortable, I didn't want to wake you."

She smiled. "I was dreaming. And it smelled like you. I opened my eyes, and here you are."

He trailed a finger along the curve of her jaw. "That desk chair seems to fit you a whole lot better than it fits me."

She looked around. His office. He'd told her to wait for him.

"I think we better go get those nails scraped."

For a moment, she didn't know what he meant, then it all came crashing back down on her. Her cottage in flames. Danny shoving her up against his car. Her raking her nails across his cheek.

"Danny?" she whispered.

"In the cage. Waiting for his lawyer."

She pulled in a deep breath. "It really happened, didn't it?"

"It did. And so did this."

He bent and kissed her. Softly at first, testing. Then deeply. Kat gave herself over to it. Wishing she could hide here, in Luke's arms.

But she couldn't. She'd done a lot of hiding in the past ten years, and it hadn't landed her anywhere good.

She ended the kiss and gazed at him, taking in his face.

"What are you thinking?" he asked.

"That I don't know what to make of all this."

"Then don't." He smiled. "One day at a time, tiger."

"Tiger? Where'd that come from?"

He straightened and held out his hand. She took it; he helped her to her feet, drew her close. So close their bodies brushed each other. All she would need to do was lean slightly forward and she would be in his arms.

"Because of the sweet job you did on Sullivan's face. Those scratches aren't going anywhere anytime soon. Plus, he told me you kneed him in the nuts. Good job."

She smiled. "I could do it again, just say the word."

"I'd love to see that, but you have a date with the parish crime lab in Covington."

Chapter Twenty-eight

Wednesday, June 12
6:00 a.m.

The lab tech was waiting for Kat; the process of scraping her nails took less than fifteen minutes. As the tech scraped, bagged and tagged the debris from each nail separately, he chatted with her. Even though it was weird—like a manicure gone noir—the chatter helped relieve the weirdness.

"Done," the young man said. "You can wash your hands. Feel free to scrub under your nails."

"Thank you." She smiled and stood. "That's a huge relief."

He smiled back. "Thank you, for making my night."

"Pardon?"

"It's nice to have someone to talk to. I'm usually doing this to dead people."

From there, a female officer photographed her bruises. The woman was matter-of-fact but incredibly kind. When Kat commented on it, she replied that working with victims of sex crimes took an especially sympathetic touch.

Kat was about to say that she wasn't a victim of a sex crime, but then she remembered: Danny kissing her, licking her neck, slobbering all over her. The memory turned her stomach. The realization of how much worse it could have been took her breath. She could have been one of the dead people the tech usually worked on. Or the shattered victim of a rape.

Back in Luke's SUV, she stared out the side window as he barreled toward Liberty.

Luke glanced at her. "Are you okay?"

"I'm okay." She met his glance. "Thinking about how lucky I am."

She didn't have to explain. He reached across the seat and squeezed her hand.

A couple miles outside of town, Luke got the call that Danny's lawyer had arrived.

"You up to driving?"

"Absolutely."

"You'll go directly to Jeremy and Lilith's. No side trips or last-minute hunches."

It was the first time she had thought of them, and she glanced at the dashboard clock. Nearly eight. If they'd noticed she hadn't made it there, Jeremy would be worried sick.

"I mean it," Luke went on. "No getting hunches and turning around. Promise me."

"I promise. Though with Danny in jail, I'm not too worried."

Luke turned onto his street. She saw her car ahead, parked in front of his house. He pulled up behind it and turned to her.

"He might not have done it, Kat. So, until we

know for sure, you play it safe. No more detective work."

"Don't worry, I think I'm done with that."

She climbed out of his car and into hers. After one last glance back at him, she pulled away from the curb. As promised, she headed for Jeremy and Lilith's place.

Not that she had any interest in doing anything else. She was exhausted. She felt grimy and couldn't get the smell of smoke out of her head. Or Danny's fury as he shook her. The murderous expression in his eyes.

Fear sent chill bumps racing up her arms. He was in jail, she told herself. He couldn't hurt her, couldn't hurt anyone again.

Sara.

A lump settled in her throat. Was that the last thing Sara had seen while alive on this earth? Hatred and rage? From the man she had trusted? Who she had thought loved her?

That hurt. Terribly. It made her angry. She hoped he'd fry for it.

"He might not be the one, Kat."

No, she thought. Luke was playing it safe. She understood. It made sense. But she knew in her gut that Danny had done it. How else could he have seen Sara lying dead in the foyer? He'd set the cottage on fire in an attempt to destroy the journals, to keep his secrets hidden forever.

But why not simply steal them? He'd known she

wasn't home, that she wouldn't be for some time.

She pushed that thought away. No, Danny had wanted to hurt and punish her. Terrorize her *and* destroy the evidence.

Her cell went off, startling her. With one hand, she fumbled in her purse for it. Not in her purse, so where—

Then she remembered: she'd tossed it on the front seat last night. It must have fallen on the floor or between the seats.

Kat checked her rearview, then pulled to the side of the road. She followed the sound and found the device, tucked up under the front passenger seat.

She grabbed it up too late. Jeremy, she saw, and redialed. "Jeremy," she said when he answered, "sorry, the phone had fallen—"

"Where the hell are you?"

She was taken aback. "What?"

"We were worried sick."

"I'm sorry, I didn't think—"

"Apparently not."

It'd been a long time since she had been treated like a rebellious child, and Kat resisted the urge to act the part. "Danny Sullivan attacked me last night."

The silence was stark. Deafening.

"My God, Kat. I'm—What happened?"

She told him about heading back to the cottage, finding Danny there and confronting him.

"He was drunk," she said. "And whatever I said pushed his buttons and he . . . lost it."

"Are you all right? Did he hurt you?"

"No. I managed to get away."

"That son of a bitch—"

"There's more, Jeremy. He killed Sara."

The silence again. This time almost breathless. "I don't understand . . . Did he confess?"

"No, but he said some things . . . He was *there,* Jeremy. He saw her lying there, dead. Said that he couldn't get it out of his head."

"You should have called me." He sounded shaken. "I would have come to get you."

"I went to Luke's."

"Oh. Right." He cleared his throat. "I was on my way into the city, but I'll turn around and meet you back at the house."

"No," she said quickly. "Danny's in jail, and I'm fine. I'm going to shower, then lie down. I'm exhausted."

"Are you certain? I don't mind rescheduling—"

"No, please. We can talk tonight."

He wanted to argue; she sensed it in the long pause that followed her words. But she wasn't up to it. And she didn't think it'd be fair to interrupt his life more than she already had.

"Luke is interviewing Danny now, then meeting with the arson investigator. We'll know more tonight."

He sighed. "Okay. But keep me posted."

"I will. I'm sorry I worried you, Cousin Jeremy. I love you."

Again the pause. "I love you, too, Kit-Kat."

Chapter Twenty-nine

Wednesday, June 12
8:20 a.m.

Lilith had left Kat a note, directing her to the guest room. She'd laid out a robe and a change of clothes. All the toiletries she might need.

Kat stood under the shower, letting the hot water sluice over her, washing away the smell of the smoke and the sensation of Danny's hands and mouth on her body. Washing away the ugliness of the night before.

As she wrapped herself in the thick terry robe, Kat realized she was starving. She made her way back down to the kitchen. Although the coffeepot beckoned, the last thing she really wanted was to wake her brain back up.

She needed to give the hamsters up there a break.

She crossed to the fridge, surveyed its contents. She thought about grabbing a yogurt, but decided on a sandwich instead. Turkey, cheese, wheat bread. Avocado. When she finished building it, she poured herself a big glass of orange juice.

"Where were you last night?"

Kat jumped, nearly choking on her first bite of the sandwich. *Lilith. On the keeping room couch, nearly hidden by its high, cushioned back and mountain of pillows.*

"You scared the life out of me! I didn't realize anyone was here."

"I see that." As if realizing how harsh that sounded, she added, "I'm working from home this morning." She laid aside her papers and stood. "Can we talk?"

"Of course."

"Sit. Enjoy your sandwich."

Kat sat at the breakfast counter. Lilith stood and made her way to stand directly across the counter from her. Like a counselor preparing to interrogate her witness.

Do you swear to tell the truth, the whole truth, nothing but the truth, so help you God . . .

It was obvious Lilith hadn't spoken with Jeremy since they had talked, but Kat was curious about what the other woman had to say. She took another bite of the sandwich, waiting.

"Liberty is a small town, Kat." She smoothed a hand over the granite countertop. "And small towns have tongues that like to wag."

Kat nodded and Lilith went on. "Jeremy is embarking on the most important journey of his life. It's what he's been working for, what *we've* been working for, all along." She looked Kat directly in the eyes. "You understand that, don't you?"

"I do, Lilith. If this is about last night—"

She held up a hand, stopping her. "You're a grown woman. If you want to play patty-cake with the town sheriff, it's none of my business. But because what you do reflects on Jeremy, it is my business."

"Someone saw my car at Luke's all night."

It wasn't a question, but Lilith answered anyway. "Yes."

"I can explain."

"Please, don't. I think you should leave Liberty."

"Are you kidding me? You know why I'm here, how important it is."

"And you know how important this moment is for Jeremy. I'm asking you to do it for him."

"Because someone saw my car at Luke's?"

"Not just that, Kat. The vandalism to the cottage. The resurgence of talk about the murder. The reopened case. Now the fire. Jeremy has been so good to you. He was good to Sara."

Kat stared at Lilith, stunned. And hurt. It felt like a betrayal. On the most elemental level.

Lilith must have read the emotion in her eyes, because she reached over and touched her hand. "I hope you understand, Katherine. This isn't about *you*. It's not personal."

Her attempt at warmth. It felt like a chill wind. Kat pulled her hand away, hurt becoming anger. "It's *you* who doesn't understand, Lilith. You haven't spoken with Jeremy, have you?"

"This morning. Before he—"

"Danny Sullivan's in jail. He attacked me last night. That's why I was at Luke's house, Lilith. Not for what you so delicately called patty-cake. In case you're interested, I was also at the Saint Tammany Parish Crime Lab getting my nails scraped and getting these documented."

She pulled aside the collar of the robe Lilith had provided, revealing the bruises. Lilith gasped and Kat went on. "But that's not the really big news. It looks like we might have our guy, Lilith. The one who killed Sara."

Lilith's entire countenance changed, from righteous determination to shocked disbelief. She brought a hand to her chest. "But I—Oh my God, Sara's killer . . . but who? Danny Sullivan?"

"That's right, good-old-boy Danny. So maybe having me around awhile longer will be a good thing. Bring in the sympathy vote. Poor Jeremy Webber, his only family, falsely accused."

Lilith didn't apologize, but Kat didn't give her the opportunity. She wrapped what was left of the sandwich in a napkin and left the room.

Chief Stephen Tanner
2003

Two days after the murder

Tanner stood as Lilith Webber entered his office. Petite, dark-haired, she was not so much beautiful as stunning, one of those women who knew how to work with what the good Lord had given them. The bit of research he had done on her revealed an impeccable pedigree: Uptown professional family, Sacred Heart Girls' Academy, under-graduate degree at Tulane University, Loyola law school, associate at Thomas, Mouton, Price and Dunne.

"Mrs. Webber," he said, motioning the chair in front of his desk, "thank you for coming in this morning. Please, sit down."

She did. He saw that she clutched a hand-kerchief in her left hand.

"I can't believe this has happened," she said.

"None of us can, Mrs. Webber."

"We moved over here to . . . get away from all the crime. And now, look. This is worse than anything that happens Uptown. Much worse."

That wasn't actually true, but he wasn't about to correct her. He also wasn't about to tell her that in his estimation, this crime had nothing to do with community and everything to do with family.

"Jeremy said . . . he told me . . . Sara was beaten to death with a"—she choked back a sob—"a baseball bat. Is that true?"

"It is, Mrs. Webber."

"Oh, my God." She pressed the tissue to her nose. "I don't know if I'll ever sleep again."

"We'll catch the person who did this, I promise you that."

"Thank you." She wiped her eyes. "I'm sorry, I'm just so distraught."

"I understand. And I'll try to be as quick as possible."

"Today's my anniversary," she whispered. "Jeremy and I were married six months ago today."

He didn't comment, and she brought the hankie to her face once more. Her diamond caught the light and winked at him. Biggest damn diamond he'd ever seen. It'd been the talk of the town for a while.

"Daddy used to call me his little steel magnolia. He and Mama both, they said I came out of the womb knowing what I wanted and how to get it." She lifted her tear-soaked eyes to meet his. "And I did, Chief."

"Why are you telling me this, Mrs. Webber?"

"Because I thought it was true. But you can't control everything. Life . . . things happen and suddenly . . . everything changes."

She began to cry. A knot formed in his throat. He cleared it away. "I'm so, so sorry."

"The day before yesterday, I was looking forward to my anniversary. Making plans. How can I feel safe now?"

"You'll feel safe again, Mrs. Webber. Time heals all wounds, isn't that what they say?"

She nodded again, visibly pulling herself together. "Of course. Everything will be fine. Of course it will." Something about her tone conjured the steel magnolia her parents had called her. "How can I help you, Chief?"

"Let's start with Sara and Katherine's relationship. What are your thoughts there?"

"When Jeremy and I first started seeing each other, they seemed really close. It was sweet. But that began to change."

"How long ago?"

She thought a moment. "Months before the wedding. On my wedding day, there was all sorts of drama. Kat's behavior was horrid. I felt so sorry for Sara."

And for herself, too, he thought. "Did Sara confide in you?"

"Not at all."

"Really? Considering your ages and relationship through Jeremy, that surprises me."

"My life was across the lake, hers was here. Between my planning our wedding and being a new associate at the firm, we didn't have time to get to know each other that well. I'd thought with us living over here now, that she and I might . . ."

She let the thought trail off. "She confided in Jeremy. And he confides in me. It's been really hard on him. A burden, what with trying to manage their estate for them and their personal problems. Most people just think he's lucky to be part of McCall Oil; they don't understand the headaches that have come with it."

"He called it that? A burden?"

"God, no." She shook her head vehemently. "He's never complained, not once. That's my observation." She looked away, then back, her eyes wet with fresh tears. "He loves those girls. Sara particularly. And now"—she brought a hand to her mouth, taking a moment to compose herself—"he's planning her funeral."

"I understand Sara was seeing someone, another teacher from the high school."

"Yes. Danny Sullivan."

"Do you know, was it serious?"

"I think it was. I think that's what she told Jeremy."

"Had you met him?"

"Yes. Several times."

"What did you think?"

"I had my reservations."

"Why's that?"

"Because she was such a wealthy young woman. You have to be careful when you have so much. I hate to be harsh, but people aren't always honorable."

"As much as you wish they were."

"Yes."

"Jeremy was concerned as well?"

"Yes. He was thinking about hiring a private detective, just to make certain Sullivan was on the up-and-up."

"Any reason in particular for that?"

"Not that I recall."

"What about Katherine, did she have a boyfriend?"

"Not one she was talking about."

"What do you mean by that?"

"Sara thought she might be sneaking around with someone."

"Did she talk to you about it?"

"No. Again, she and Jeremy talked. She was considering boarding school for Kat." She leaned slightly forward. "I was afraid of how Kat would react to that."

"Afraid? Why?"

"Of what she might do."

As if realizing how that sounded, she pressed her lips together and sat back.

Tanner decided to face the comment head-on. "Do you think maybe Sara did tell her? And that she reacted . . . badly?"

"You're asking me if I think Kat could have killed her sister?"

"Yes."

She shifted her gaze ever so slightly. "I don't want to think that."

"But you believe it's possible?"

"I didn't say that, Chief Tanner. And I won't."

"Then what will you say, Mrs. Webber?"

"That in a rage people can do monstrous things, ones they would have never thought possible." She looked down at her hands, folded in her lap, then back up at him. "And that scares me."

She thought the girl had done it. That Katherine McCall had flown into a rage and beaten her sister to death. Because of her husband, she couldn't say it, but it scared the hell out of her.

Tanner stood. "Thank you for coming in, Mrs. Webber. I appreciate your time."

"You're very welcome." She followed him to his feet. "Can you tell me, what's going to happen next, Chief Tanner?"

"I think we'll be making an arrest. Soon. And then you'll be able to sleep again, Mrs. Webber."

Chapter Thirty

Wednesday, June 12
10:00 a.m.

Luke recognized Sullivan's lawyer from his television ads. Frank Pierre. Ambulance chaser. Sullivan was going to need a lot more firepower to wiggle out of this.

Luke shook the attorney's hand. "Good to

meet you. One of my officers, Gene Reni."

They shook hands as well, then they all sat.

Pierre began. "Chief Tanner, I believe we have a huge misunderstanding here."

Luke arched his eyebrows. "Really? Those gouges in your client's cheek are a misunderstanding?"

"Mr. Sullivan can explain."

"I'm looking forward to it." He turned his gaze on Sullivan. "You have a story you'd like to tell me?"

Pierre jumped in again. "Not a 'story,' Sergeant. The events of the night as they happened, the truth."

Luke wanted to retch. "Of course." He turned to face Sullivan. "Danny, you've got my attention."

Danny laid his hands in his lap. "What I told you earlier, about how I ended up at the cottage, was the truth."

Luke flipped open his notebook. "Why don't you repeat it for Mr. Pierre? I'm sure he'll want to hear it from you."

"I was gassing up at the E-Z by the marina. I'd heard the sirens and wondered what was happening. I asked the dude inside and he told me the McCall cottage had caught on fire. I went to see for myself."

Luke noted a couple changes in detail. "The station attendant called the cottage by that name? The McCall cottage?"

"Yeah."

"You didn't mention that before."

"Didn't I?" He scratched his head. "Must've slipped my mind."

"You didn't find that odd? That this random 'dude' knew where the fire was and that it was the McCall place?"

"Not really. At the time anyway. It's a pretty famous place around Liberty."

"That E-Z Serve is located in Mandeville."

Sullivan lifted his hands, palms up. "I don't know what else to tell you. He knew."

"Let's move on. Why did you want to see for yourself?"

"Because of Sara. Because I'd loved her. It was her place. We spent a lot of time there together. Isn't that enough?"

He had tears in his eyes. Luke might have been moved to sympathy if Sullivan hadn't proved himself a scumbag just a couple hours ago. "When you arrived, who else was there?"

"Nobody."

"But you had just heard the sirens."

He shook his head. "Heard them. But not 'just.'"

Sullivan looked at his hands, then back up at Luke. "Kat shows up. She's acting weird. Combative. She makes all these wild accusations—"

"Like what?"

"That I started the fire. That I hated her cousin Jeremy. Crazy shit."

"How'd you respond?"

"At first, I just figured she was upset. Overwrought. I tried to calm her down."

"How'd you do that, Sullivan? By grabbing her and shoving her against your vehicle?"

"That's not the way it went down. Not at all." He spread his fingers. "When I wouldn't engage, her behavior turned . . . sexual."

Luke's gaze sharpened. "Excuse me?"

"She came on to me. In a big way."

Police brutality. Perhaps there was a time and a place. Like now.

He smiled grimly. "What does that mean, 'came on to' you, 'in a big way'?"

"She grabbed my crotch. Started rubbing it. Rubbing herself against me."

"And you went from angry to willing sex partner"—he snapped his fingers—"just like that?"

"I'm only human."

Luke was beginning to doubt that, but he kept it to himself. "Did you even question why she went from contentious to amorous?"

"I should have, I realize that now." He shrugged. "She was a wild chick all those years ago, I figured she still was."

"So you just went along for the ride?"

"Like I said, I'm only human."

"Then what happened?"

"We're really going at it, you know. Right there, against my car. But I'm like, 'Babe, we need to go someplace. This can't happen here.' "

Luke held up a hand. "Wait. I thought you were only human? Along for the ride?"

"Yeah, at first. But no way I was going to do it there. I'm a high school coach, I've got a reputation to protect."

Luke gazed impassively at him, all the while imagining his fist smashing into that smug face. He consoled himself with the fact that Sullivan's precious reputation was about to take a big trip south.

"So, you try to inject a bit of reason into the moment."

He nodded. "But next thing I know, I'm getting kneed in the balls. I double over and she scratches the hell out of my face and starts screaming for help."

Luke sat a moment, letting Sullivan's words settle around them. He glanced at Reni, then back at Sullivan. "Wow, this story is so different from the one McCall told me. According to her, you attacked her. She drove up to the cottage, you were there. She got out of the car, she was angry, suspicious of your motive for being there. When she began to question you about Sara and the past, you lost it."

Luke flipped back in the notebook. " 'He went

sort of crazy,' " he read. " 'He grabbed me and shook me. He was yelling.' " Luke flipped forward a page. " 'I tried to get away. He shoved me up against the car.' " Luke lifted his gaze. "Why do you think she said all that?"

"At first, I didn't know what was happening. I was . . . stunned. But now I realize she was setting me up."

"Setting you up? Why?"

"To hurt me. To hurt my reputation. Because she hates me. Because of the past. Because of Sara. Because I testified against her."

"Revenge, Sergeant," Pierre said. "One of the oldest motives in the book."

Using the past against her. A brilliant choice. "Revenge because you testified against her?"

"Seems right to me."

Sullivan leaned back in his chair, looking way too comfortable. Luke decided to turn up the heat. "Pretty much everyone in Liberty got on the stand for the prosecution. You think she wants revenge on them all?"

He shrugged again. "Maybe so. I hear she's been making the rounds. Getting up in folks' faces."

"What folks?"

"Folks. But she especially wanted to punish me. Because Sara turned to me for counsel about her. Because I tried to step in, be a father figure to her. She resented it."

"Why didn't you tell me all this earlier?"

266

"I didn't think you'd believe me."

"I don't believe you, Danny."

The lawyer stepped in. "I'm not surprised. You do have a personal interest in this case."

Luke turned to the lawyer. "What did you say?"

"I understand from my client that you two are dating."

"We attended her cousin's party together. Does that constitute dating?"

"You tell me, Sergeant."

Instead, Luke turned back to Sullivan. "So, you're telling me that the sobbing, hysterical woman I talked to was faking it."

"Yes. Everybody knows she's a liar."

"Was she also faking the bruises on her arms, neck and chest?"

"Pardon?"

You had to love digital cameras. Luke nodded at Reni, who slid him a manila envelope. Luke extracted two photos. Laid them in front of Sullivan.

"Bruises," he said. "They look like fingerprints, don't they, Sullivan?"

"I didn't touch her."

"So she bruised herself. As part of her plan to frame you. Is that what you're telling me?"

Pierre looked at him. Sullivan flushed. "If it happened, it must have been when I was trying to get her off me."

"I thought you were only human? That you two

were . . ." He flipped back a couple pages and read. " 'Really going at it . . . Right there, against my car.' "

"Not then. After she clawed my face."

Luke cocked an eyebrow. "Let me get this straight." He glanced at the notes. "She knees you, you double over, she claws you and screams for help and, at the same time, you have to fight her off."

"Not exactly like that, but yes."

"I'm having a hard time picturing this."

"Wacky, right? Like I said, she's a wild chick."

"I have another scenario. If I may?"

He glanced at the lawyer, who nodded. "You were drunk. And angry. You asked her to accompany you to Webber's party and she chose to go with me instead."

"I was just being friendly."

"Friendly? Like when you grabbed her and shook her? So hard you left the imprint of your fingers on her skin?"

The lawyer cleared his throat and Luke refocused. "You left the party early, you got a can of gas, maybe even at the E-Z Serve, and you used that gas to set her house on fire."

"Because she didn't go to a party with me? That's pretty lame, Tanner."

"I think you were counting on getting friendly with Kat McCall. To cover your ass." He leaned forward. "You wanted to get a peek at Sara's journals, didn't you? The ones Kat told you she was looking for. The ones Sara wrote in every day, without fail. The ones where her true feelings have been etched forever. Maybe the reason she wouldn't marry you was in there."

"Shut up, Tanner."

"What about the loan?"

"What loan?"

"The one you asked Sara for. The one she refused to give you. The one that caused the big fight the two of you had only days before her murder."

"What are we talking about here?" Pierre asked. "Tonight? Or ten years ago?"

"Both."

"Unacceptable. This line of questioning has nothing to do with the reason my client is here tonight."

Luke ignored him. "Did you or did you not tell Kat McCall tonight, as you were shaking her, that you couldn't get the image of her dead sister out of your head?" He referred to his notes. "You mentioned the blood on the foyer floor and her crushed face."

The lawyer sputtered; Sullivan paled. Luke went on. "My question to you, Danny, is how did that image get into your head in the first place?"

Sullivan stared. His mouth worked, but nothing came out. Luke smiled grimly. "Wasn't in the newspaper, not on TV. Witnesses aren't allowed in the courtroom. So, when *did* you see her like that, Sullivan? After you beat her to death?"

"No! Kat set me up! To clear her name." He turned to his lawyer. "None of it's true!"

"What was the loan for, Mr. Sullivan?"

"I was going to open a basketball training facility. With Dale Graham."

"The former LSU point guard?" He nodded. Luke continued. "What were you doing the night of the murder?"

"I don't know . . . it was ten years ago!"

"Really?" Luke arched his eyebrows. "The woman you loved, who you planned to marry, was murdered, and you don't remember where you were or what you were doing?"

"I was home, like I told your dad. What I was doing, I don't remember. Watching TV, doing laundry, the usual shit I do on a school night."

"No alibi?"

"I didn't need one. Your old man never asked me."

Luke curled his hands into fists, angry. *Because his dad figured he had his perp in hand. Kat had been judged and found guilty before she'd even been arrested.*

"Well, I'm not my old man and I want one now."

"You must be joking," Pierre said. "It's been ten years."

"Some things you don't forget, right, Danny?" Luke looked him dead in his eyes, holding his gaze. "And there are some things so horrific you just can't get them out of your head."

Luke looked at Reni and nodded. Reni stood. "Back in the cage, Sullivan."

"But—" He looked at his attorney. "I have to stay?"

Luke answered for him. "Oh yeah, you have to stay. We're done for now."

Chapter Thirty-one

Wednesday, June 12
10:45 a.m.

When Luke emerged from the interrogation room, he found his dad waiting for him.

"Is that Danny Sullivan in there?"

"It is." He changed the subject. "What can I do for you, Pops?"

"I heard what happened. About the fire."

"Figured. How about I buy you a cup of coffee?"

His dad agreed and Luke led him to the break room and the coffee. It looked like Trixie had just made a fresh pot. "Perfect timing."

Luke poured his dad a cup, using the Fraternal Order of Police mug he had been using for years, then poured himself one. "Let's sit in here."

They did. His dad sipped, then grunted in

271

appreciation. "Your mother only lets me have decaf. Without caffeine, what's the point?"

Luke nodded, took a sip. And waited for the questions to come.

They didn't take long. "What do you think about the fire? Is it looking like arson?"

"Yeah, it is. I'm meeting with Caleb Green in a little bit."

"Too bad she wasn't home."

Luke stiffened. "I hope you don't mean that."

At Luke's expression, he had the decency to look embarrassed. "You didn't see what I did. I puked my guts out, it was so bad."

"I saw the photos, Pops."

"They're nothing in comparison." He brought a trembling hand to his head. "It haunts me. I wish I could get it out of my head. But no matter how I try, no matter how many years pass, it's still there."

Basically the same thing Sullivan had said to Kat. But his dad had been there. He'd had a reason to be there.

"Got a question for you, Pops. Back then, when you were investigating McCall's murder, you look closely at Danny Sullivan?"

"Danny?" He frowned. "Interviewed him, of course. Is that why he was in today?"

When Luke didn't answer, he went on. "Sullivan was in love with her. He was devastated by her death."

"But her sister wasn't?"

"Frankly? No."

"But you did check his alibi, right?"

"Of course. I wasn't a rookie, son. Love, hate, greed, the unholy trinity of murder."

"What was it? His alibi, I mean?"

"It's in the case notes."

"No, it's not. I checked. In fact, I didn't see much about Sullivan. Or anyone else."

Color flew to his dad's face, making him look healthier than he had in months. "I should have expected that from you."

"What's that?"

"Criticism."

"Look, it just seems like—" He bit the words back. Nothing would be gained by picking apart his dad's conduct on the case. Nothing would be changed. "Never mind."

He scowled. "No. I want to know. It just seems like what, son?"

"You really want to go there?"

"Hell yes, I do."

"Okay then, you stubborn old jackass. It seems like you never looked at another suspect. Never pursued anyone besides Katherine McCall."

"That's bullshit! I interviewed everyone with a connection to Sara McCall. Anyone who might have had a beef with her."

"But what did you ask them? The case notes, where's Sullivan's alibi? What about the loan he asked Sara for? Did you follow up on that?"

"Didn't need to. Everyone confirmed what I already knew."

"That she was guilty."

"If it walks, quacks and shits like duck, it's a goddamned duck!"

His dad almost never took the Lord's name in vain; that he did so now indicated just how close to the edge he was. Luke pressed him anyway. "What about the journals—"

"There were no journals. We looked."

"How hard?"

"Hard enough!" He brought his fist down on the table. The salt and pepper shakers rattled. "I don't have to explain myself to anyone, including you!" He struggled to his feet. "I came down here to offer my help, not be interrogated by my own son."

Luke stood. He held out a hand. "Let's get this solved, Pops. Once and for all. We'll do it together. Then you can let it go. Don't you want some peace?"

"I want respect!" he shot back. "I've earned it."

"You've always had my respect," Luke countered, suddenly angry. "How about you show me some for once? *I've* earned it."

When his dad didn't respond, Luke sucked in an angry breath. It was a bitter pill. One Luke had swallowed too many times to count.

He wasn't going to swallow it this time.

"Stevie's gone. I'm it, Dad. The only one you have left."

"This isn't about your brother."

"Bullshit. Everything between us, since the day he drowned, has been about Stevie."

"What do you want me to say?"

"Just admit it. You blame me. Tell me you don't."

"That's crazy talk."

He couldn't say it. The truth of it cut like a knife. "I tried to save him. I couldn't. I'm sorry."

"This woman has you mesmerized."

"It's not about her! What about justice? What about the truth?"

His dad made a slicing motion with his hand. "I know the truth! Come to your senses, boy. Until you do, I'm done with you."

Truth was, he'd been done with him since the summer of '92.

Luke bit back the things he wanted to say and watched his dad hobble out. A broken old man struggling to keep his head held high.

Luke muttered an oath. But before he could chase after him, Trixie buzzed him. "Caleb Green, line two."

He took one last look at his dad, then answered. "Caleb, how you doing, man?"

"Okay, dude. It's been awhile."

Luke had worked with the Saint Tammany Parish arson investigator a few years back, when he was still with the sheriff's department. Someone had been torching small rural churches with mainly African-American congregations.

Luke still marveled at what Green had deduced about the perpetrators and their actions from charred remains. Green had explained that he read a fire, its origin and path, what it left behind, the same way Luke read any other crime scene. They all had stories to tell, you just had to understand the language.

They'd caught the perps—a couple country boys, fueled by hatred, weed and Jack Daniel's.

"That it has," Luke agreed.

"I was surprised to learn you moved to the Liberty force."

Luke heard the "why?" in the question. He didn't address it. Instead, he asked, "You at the scene?"

"I am. Looked it over, ready to process. Thought you might want to walk through it with me."

"Absolutely. On my way."

Luke pulled to a stop behind the man's SUV. Green hopped out and came to meet him. They shook hands.

"What have we got?" Luke asked.

"No doubt arson. But you already knew that."

"True. I was hoping you could tell me something I didn't know."

Green nodded, narrowing his eyes. "This screams first-timer. Total amateur."

They started toward the cottage, to the right front corner. "Fire originated here, as you probably figured by the damage. Our perp used gasoline. Take a look."

They both crouched down to peer under the raised home. Green aimed his flashlight beam. It landed on a red gasoline can.

"The offender saturated this area with the fuel, then tossed the can under the house. He might have assumed it would be consumed in the fire, or maybe he didn't care."

Green tipped the flashlight beam up. The fire had destroyed the subflooring nearest the point of origin, the damage radiated out from there, like the legs of a spider.

"This is interesting." Green straightened. He indicated the window directly above. "Our perp knew enough to break the window. The draperies caught and the oxygen fueled the fire."

Luke gazed up at the window, picturing the room beyond. The living room. The stacks of boxes. *Not so amateurish after all.* "You've talked to the firefighters?" he asked.

Luke knew the drill. Unlike a typical crime scene, where processing physical evidence came before witness interviews, the arson investigator flipped that. Since fire destroyed evidence, first-hand accounts could mean the difference between solving the crime and not. That meant interviewing anyone who had been at the scene early. Firefighters. Witnesses. Even the press.

"On my way in. Everything they told me supports what I see here. The color of the flames, the smoke. The way the fire spread."

"And the gas can," Luke said, then looked at Green. "What about motivation?"

"Without my crystal ball, I'd say this was personal, not random. If you've got a perp who just likes to watch things burn, he's going to use a lot more accelerant. For those guys, the bigger and hotter, the better."

"So, what's our perp doing here?"

"Making a statement. Getting the owner's attention." Green lifted a shoulder. "In my opinion."

"That sounds about right."

"Whose house?"

"The most hated woman in Liberty, Louisiana." At the man's expression, he asked, "You remember the McCall murder? Happened about ten years ago. Young teacher bludgeoned to death. The victim's sister was charged but acquitted at trial. Most folks believed she got away with murder."

"No recall, man."

Luke nodded. "We have one other theory, that somebody wanted to destroy evidence in the house. Evidence located in boxes in that room.

We have a suspect in custody. Prints off the gas can would be helpful."

"If there're any to be had, it'll be this afternoon. Pretty slick if they matched up to your suspect."

"That it would be," Luke responded. "Nice and easy. Just the way I like it."

Chapter Thirty-two

Wednesday, June 12
12:40 p.m.

His dad may not have seen the need to check out Danny Sullivan's story, but Luke sure as hell did. He tightened his fingers on the steering wheel. He was still stunned over his dad's refusal to admit he was wrong. That in a rush to judgment, he'd pegged Kat as Sara McCall's killer and hadn't looked any further. He had prejudiced the case from the get-go.

Luke sighed. It was ironic that the one thing his dad wanted from his son was respect, and it was the one thing he'd always had. Until now. The past was over and done. Unchangeable. But to not own up to your mistakes after the fact? That wasn't the man he'd thought his father to be.

A sign indicated Dale Graham's Hoops Center lay a mile up ahead. Minutes later, he turned into the center's drive, parking next to the only other vehicle in the lot, a Lexus sedan.

Dale Graham had parlayed his four years playing for LSU into a damn good life. Nice home, solid business, endorsements, respect. He'd never made the pros, but that hadn't mattered. Louisianians loved their sports, idolized their teams and never forgot their heroes. And Graham had been one of those.

Luke climbed out of his vehicle and took in the building. Basically a warehouse with a fancy facade. Nice land out here in North Covington, rolling hills, lots of trees.

He crossed the gravel lot. Graham was expecting him and appeared at the double glass doors. "Sergeant Tanner?"

"Good afternoon," Luke said when he reached him. "Thanks for seeing me."

They shook hands. Graham showed him in. "Let's go to my office."

Luke followed him, taking it all in. It was a first-class facility. High-tech. Tricked out. All the bells and whistles. "Impressive."

"Thank you. Here we are."

The office wasn't more than serviceable. Luke suspected Graham didn't spend that much time in it. One wall was covered with framed photos, many of them from Graham's days playing ball. The others appeared to be of some of his students.

On his desk sat a framed photo of his family.

Two kids, pretty wife. Blond. Luke shifted his gaze to Graham's. "Tell me about the Hoops Center."

"We give kids the competitive edge they need to play junior high and high school ball."

"Junior high? High school?"

"It seems crazy, I know, but the competition around here is fierce. Especially for a basketball slot. Any given school only has eleven to thirteen spots. That's it. It's not unusual for hundreds to try out. Some kids have the natural ability. We help develop those God-given gifts. Those kids have a chance to play college ball."

"And everybody else?" Luke asked.

"Those are the kids who just love the game. They just want to play. We teach them the skills that make up for what God didn't give them."

"Slick. Wish you were around when I was a kid."

"You played ball?"

"Football. Made the LSU team, but screwed it up."

"Too much partying and not enough studying?" When Luke nodded, Graham grinned. "We couldn't have helped with that."

Luke laughed. "Good old-fashioned rebellion."

"You wanted to talk to me about Danny Sullivan?"

"Yes. How do you two know each other?"

"Oh, man, we go way back." He smiled. "We're both local boys. Played on the same school teams, both studied P.E. at LSU. Good guy."

"Ten years ago, you offered him the opportunity to partner with you in this venture, is that correct?"

"He asked for the opportunity."

"Come again."

"We were friends. I talked about it. He asked." Graham lifted a shoulder. "I gave him first shot to come up with the cash."

"How much?"

"Seventy-five grand."

"That's a lot of money for a high school P.E. teacher to come up with."

"Not if you're married to a McCall."

"Or engaged to one."

"Yes."

"What happened?"

"Sara McCall was murdered. And I found another partner."

"Wow, that's cold."

"It was business, Sergeant. And with Sara out of the picture, he wasn't going to come up with the cash."

"And you had other interested parties."

"Exactly."

"When did you tell him you were moving on?"

"Shortly after. He took it hard. Begged me for more time. I considered it, but—" Graham shifted his gaze, expression uncomfortable.

"But what?"

He hesitated. "He's a good guy and I'd known him for ages. But I had concerns."

"About?"

Again, he hesitated. "He likes the casinos a little too much."

Luke sat up a bit straighter. "What does that mean, exactly?"

"Just what it sounds like. He's gotten himself in trouble a few times."

Luke made a note. "That doesn't sound like good partner material."

"He was marrying McCall money. I wasn't worried."

"They weren't engaged, were they?"

He shook his head. "But he had the ring. He said it was a sure thing."

The only sure things in life were death and taxes. Betting on anything else as certain was a fool's wager.

Graham must have been thinking the same thing, because his expression became pensive. "Poor guy. He's never been the same."

"Let's back up a minute. Before Sara McCall's murder, how did Danny seem?"

"About?"

"Life. His girlfriend, this business opportunity."

"Happy. Excited and enthusiastic. Anxious, too."

"Why?"

"He really wanted to make it work."

"Did he seem desperate?"

Graham frowned. "No. Never."

"And after her murder?"

"Brokenhearted. In shock."

"That was a pretty big rock Danny bought her. How do you suppose he paid for it?"

"Don't know. Financed it, maybe. Won big one night. She may have even bought it. I never asked."

As far as he knew, nobody had. Luke paused a moment, reviewing his notes. He lifted his gaze, met Graham's. "Do you think Danny could have killed Sara?"

He stared at him a moment, obviously shocked by the question. "No," he finally said. "Hell, no."

"Why not?"

"He's not that guy. He loved Sara. Besides"—he leaned forward slightly—"she was his ticket, you know?"

"His ticket?"

"To the good life. Work a little, play a lot."

Luke stood. "Thank you, Mr. Graham. I appreciate you answering my questions."

He followed him to his feet. "Anytime, Sergeant."

"You talk to Danny much anymore?"

"We see each other from time to time. Like I said, he was never the same after Sara's death. He got bitter."

They exited the office. "Do you know, does he still like the casinos?"

"Oh yeah. I actually ran into him at Beau Rivage a couple months ago."

"Beau Rivage? Nice place."

"Danny always liked nice things."

Graham walked him to the front of the facility. "Can I ask you something, Sergeant Tanner?"

"Sure."

"Why all the questions about Sara McCall's murder? I thought they caught her killer."

"She was acquitted."

He opened his mouth as if to say something more, then must have thought better of it, because he shut it again.

Luke crossed to his vehicle and climbed in, thinking of what Graham had said. Sara McCall had been Sullivan's ticket to the good life. Little work, a lot of play.

But what if Sara McCall had said no? To the loan? The marriage? All of it? How would Sullivan had reacted to it all slipping away? Would he have been angry? Enraged? Enough to take a baseball bat and beat her to death?

Maybe so, Luke thought. The line between love and hate was razor thin. And just as sharp.

Chapter Thirty-three

Luke figured he had just cause for a search warrant of Sullivan's home and vehicles. The judge figured otherwise. After being denied the request, Luke decided a drive over to the Mississippi Gulf Coast casinos was in order. He'd start with the Beau Rivage Resort and Casino in Biloxi, then, if need be, he'd move on from there. The casino manager, Tom Phillips, had agreed to meet with him.

The Gulf Coast had opened up to casino gambling in the 1990s, with local law restricting them to mobile marine vessels. The industry's answer to that had been fixed floating barges. After Katrina's complete devastation of the coast, that law had been changed.

Luke remembered the Mississippi Gulf Coast before gaming arrived. Sleepy. Picturesque. The poor man's riviera it had been called. Casinos had changed all that, bringing glamour, headline shows and, most of all, money.

He preferred it before all the bright lights, though he suspected he was in the minority.

Luke used the hour's drive to make calls. Caleb

Green was first. The only news he had was bad news: they'd pulled several good prints from the gas can. The problem was none of them matched Danny Sullivan's.

So much for nice and easy.

He dialed Kat next. "Hey," he said when he got her voice mailbox. "I have some news. Call me back."

Luke arrived at the resort. Thirty-two-story hotel, casino, championship golf course, high-end shopping and dining. He'd stayed here a few times when he'd come to catch a show. The first had been Willie Nelson, the second Cirque du Soleil.

Tom Phillips had given him directions to his office. The gorgeous brunette manning his reception area looked more Vegas than Gulf Coast and he couldn't help but notice her legs as she escorted him to Phillips's office.

"Can I get you anything?" she asked.

"I'm good. Thanks."

"C'mon in, Sergeant Tanner," Phillips said, standing. "Have a seat."

They shook hands. Luke wasn't sure what to expect, but had secretly wondered if the man would be a Robert De Niro or Joe Pesci look-alike. No such luck. Instead, he was a pleasant-faced, gray-haired man in a really sharp-looking suit. "Thank you for seeing me."

"You said you wanted to ask me a few questions about Danny Sullivan."

"That's right. He's a casino patron?"

"Longtime patron. For as long as I've been manager here."

"How long is that?"

"Since 2003. Stayed to oversee the rebuild after Katrina."

"You're made of tough stuff."

"You have no idea."

Something about the way he said it brought forth the Mafia, Joe Pesci image again. "What kind of gambler is Danny Sullivan?"

"Let's put it this way, over the years he's lost quite a lot of money with us."

"And won a lot as well?"

"Enough to keep coming back."

"But the house always has the advantage. Right?"

"We make no secret of that."

"Does Sullivan have a problem?"

He steepled his fingers. "Could you be more specific?"

"With gambling. A problem. As in an addiction."

"We in the industry don't like that term, Sergeant. I prefer to say that it's ceased to be fun for him."

Phillips slid a pamphlet across the desk. *When the Fun Stops—Understanding Compulsive Gambling.*

"What's this?"

"A product of our compliance with the AGA code of conduct for responsible gaming."

Danny Sullivan had issues. "Do you remember when Sullivan was last in?"

"I remember clearly. April first."

"And why so clearly?"

"It was April Fools' Day and we had to eject him from the casino."

"What happened?"

"He got into an argument with a blackjack dealer. Made a big scene. Accused the house of cheating him. Security escorted him out."

"Is he welcome back?"

"Not anytime soon."

Luke digested the information. "And the other casinos along the coast?"

"Nobody wants trouble."

"Which means?"

"Currently, Mr. Sullivan is barred from all Gulf Coast gaming establishments. Like I said, nobody wants trouble."

Luke lowered his gaze to his notebook, organizing his thoughts. "Did he ever threaten anyone here at the casino."

"With physical violence?" Luke nodded and Phillips steepled his fingers in thought. "He's gotten verbally abusive a few times. When he was losing. When he's winning, however, he's quite magnanimous."

"Aren't we all?"

"True."

"Did you ever have to break his legs?"

His lips lifted into a small smile. "We don't do that, Sergeant. You've seen too many movies."

Luke smiled, though something in the man's gaze made it clear that he would do whatever it took to protect the casino and its assets. Tom Phillips didn't put up with bullshit. "I had to try."

He glanced at his watch. A Rolex, Luke noted. The glance told him he was now on the clock.

"Just a few more questions. Can we go back in time now? To 2003?" Phillips agreed and Luke went on, "Do you recall anything about Sullivan from that time? Anything at all?"

"Actually, I do. He won big one night. Big, like forty thousand bucks. Sullivan was the type to keep playing."

"That's what the compulsive ones do?"

"Yes. Win and lose fortunes, some of them. At least, what a fortune would be for them." Phillips paused. "But this night he stopped. It was late. Maybe two a.m. He enlisted my help in convincing the owner of the resort's on-site jewelry store to come in and open up for him."

Luke knew what was coming next: *He bought an engagement ring.*

Phillips confirmed it. "He used every penny of his winnings. He was over the moon about it. Went around the casino showing it off. His excitement was sweet."

Sweet, a rare occurrence in a casino, Luke suspected. Certainly memorable.

"He showed it to so many people, we gave him an escort out. We were afraid somebody might jump him."

"Did he marry that girl?"

Phillips's expression changed. "Not any girl. McCall Oil's older daughter. But no, he didn't. I'm sure you know how that story ended, Sergeant Tanner." He stood. "I'm sorry, but I'm out of time."

Luke followed him to his feet. "Thank you. You've been very helpful."

Five minutes later, he was on the road. Time for round three with Sullivan. He phoned in. "Reni, it's me. Contact Sullivan's lawyer. Tell him we're bringing his client back in for questioning. One hour."

Danny Sullivan
2003

One month before the murder

Danny stepped into the casino, breathed it all in. The flashing colored lights, like a carnival midway for adults. The sounds, the clinking of coins dropping into metal trays, the whirl and snap of the one-armed bandits, the occasional whoop of joy and the hum of conversation. And the smells, cigarette smoke—casinos, one of last bastions of smoking in public places—old-lady perfume, cloyingly sweet or heavy with musk, and hope. The thing that drove them all.

Or desperation. Depending on the night.

He couldn't stop himself.

But he shouldn't have to. He won more than he lost. A lot more. He was a good strategist and the cards loved him. It's how he planned to buy Sara's ring. He'd already picked it out. It sat in the store's display window, winking at him. Three full, sparkling carats. If you wanted a prize like Sara McCall, you had to pony up. She was worth it.

Maybe tonight would be the night. He'd win big enough to snag the stone, then the girl.

Danny frowned slightly at the whisper of doubt that wormed its way through him. What if she said no? What if she never understood this rush, the one that took him as he stepped up to the blackjack table? The high of winning?

He'd suggested bringing her several times. She'd shot the idea down. The last time, she had looked at him strangely.

Suspiciously. Like *he* had a problem.

He hadn't liked that. Not one bit.

Her parents had been killed on their way home from the Gulf Coast casinos. Like that was the casinos' fault. The gaming industry's.

She'd change her mind, he assured himself. After they were married. After she saw how good he was at this. After he told her how he'd afforded the beautiful ring on her finger.

She would be proud of his skill. Awed by it. She might even grow to enjoy gambling as much as he did.

Danny made his way to the cashier's cage. The woman, Angelle, recognized him and smiled. "Mr. Sullivan, it's good to see you again."

"Good to be back." He took out his wallet, extracted the five crisp hundred-dollar bills he'd gotten at the bank that afternoon. Not his local branch. No, he'd gone into Covington. He hadn't wanted to run into a neighbor or colleague. What he did in his free time was nobody's business but his own.

She assembled his chips. "Good luck, Mr. Sullivan."

Luck? Screw that. He had skill.

Instead of saying so, Danny slid her a twenty-dollar chip. "Thank you, Angelle. See you in a few."

She did see him in a few. But not for the reason he had hoped. To buy more chips. And more chips. Danny didn't get this. It wasn't right.

Tonight, the cards didn't love him.

In fact, it was almost as if they were plotting against him. He stayed on nineteen, dealer got twenty. He stayed on twenty, dealer pulled black-jack. He took a hit on fifteen and went bust. Hand after hand.

The more he lost, the more he drank. The angrier he got. And the more determined. This was *his* night. He was meant to win. He deserved it. He'd stayed away for a month.

He drained his available cash at the ATM. When that happened, he used his credit card.

Until it was declined.

Bleary-eyed, he gazed at Angelle. "That can't be right. Try again."

"I'm sorry, Mr. Sullivan, but—"

"Try it the fuck again."

He hadn't meant to raise his voice that way. Or use that language. The booze, he thought. The cards. Not him.

Someone touched his arm. He turned. Tom, the casino manager. His buddy.

"Is there a problem?" he asked.

Angelle answered. "Mr. Sullivan's card was declined."

"A computer glitch," he said, turning to Tom. "You know me, I'm good for it."

Tom's face puckered with regret. "I'm sorry, Mr. Sullivan. Casino policy."

"That's bullshit, Tom. And you know it."

"We could offer you a room. No charge, of course."

A room? What the fuck was he going to do with a room? How was he going to win his money back in a room?

Furious, he thought about asking Angelle for his

tip back. All of them. How much had he given her over the past year? A couple grand, for sure.

Angelle wouldn't meet his eyes. Embarrassing. Fucking embarrassing.

"I'm marrying Sara McCall, did you know that? McCall Oil. I'm going to have more money than God. You'll be glad we're friends."

Tom's expression shifted subtly. Respect. Understanding. He nodded at Angelle.

"Three hundred, Danny. Because we're friends."

Chapter Thirty-four

Wednesday, June 12
5:00 p.m.

From the road, Luke tried Kat again. And again left a message. He was fired up.

Kat hadn't killed her sister. But there was a good chance Danny Sullivan had. He had opportunity. And motive. When she'd turned down his offer of marriage, the good life he'd counted on evaporated right before his eyes. He'd flown into a rage. The bat had been there. He'd grabbed it and swung.

Crime of passion. Temporary insanity.

When it was over, and he'd gazed at the bloody mess, he'd realized what he'd done.

Now Luke just had to get him to admit it.

When he walked into the station, he found Reni waiting. He looked anxious. "What's wrong?" Luke asked.

"Somehow, your dad got wind of this. I just got off the phone with him."

"What did he say?"

"He wants in on the questioning. He ordered me to come pick him up and to inform you that you are not allowed to question Sullivan until he arrives."

What the hell was his old man up to? Luke frowned. "What did you tell him?"

"I said I would, Sarge. He's the chief."

"He's on medical leave. I'm senior officer, you take orders from me. Is that understood?"

"Yes, sir."

"So, let's do this."

"But, what about your dad? Should I call—"

"When you don't show, he'll figure it out."

They entered the interview room. Pierre looked pissed, Sullivan strung out. Edgy. Jail did that to you. Luke greeted both men and sat. He popped a fresh tape in the recorder.

Luke began. "Let's get right to it, shall we?" He looked directly at Sullivan. "I've had the opportunity to talk to a few people about you, Danny. Found out some interesting things. Some real interesting things."

Sullivan didn't respond and Luke went on. "I spoke with your old friend Dale Graham."

"What does he have to do with this?"

"Then I spoke with Tom Phillips. You know Tom, the casino manager at Beau Rivage?"

Luke saw apprehension rush into Sullivan's eyes, but his response was pure bravado. "Yeah, I know him. And Dale. So what?"

"You're a high school teacher and coach, Danny. How've you managed to keep this problem a secret for so long?"

"I don't know what problem you think I have. I like to play my luck every once in a while. Big deal."

"What's your game?"

"Blackjack."

"Twenty-one," Luke said. "You're pretty good at it, aren't you?"

He nodded, looking pleased with himself. "I am."

"How long have you been gambling, Danny?"

"A long time." He arched his eyebrows. "Again, so what?"

"Tom Phillips described you as a guy who wins and loses fortunes. Would you call that accurate?"

The corner of his mouth lifted. "Yeah," he said. "I would. You have to play big to win big."

"And you live by that adage?"

"I do."

"Was courting Sara McCall 'playing big'?"

Something sneaked into his gaze. Like admiration. "I was in love with her. I don't consider love a game."

"Nice sentiment. Kind of romantic."

"I'm a romantic guy."

"You are. I saw a photo of that ring you bought her. Wow, what a rock."

"A symbol of how much I loved her. I wanted her to know."

He'd said almost exactly the same thing in court. Luke recognized it from the transcripts. "Mighty big rock for a high school teacher to be able to afford." He paused. "How'd you pay for it?"

"Why does it matter?"

"Maybe it doesn't. Maybe I'm just curious."

"I bought it with winnings."

"One night's winnings?"

"Yes."

"That was quite a night for you? You remember it, right?"

"Oh, yeah. It was one of the best nights of my life."

"How much did you win?"

"Forty thousand."

"Dude. That's like a year's salary."

"Back then, more than."

"And you stopped playing. You took your winnings."

"Even though I knew I could make it bigger."

"You think?"

"I know." He leaned forward. Animated. An addict recalling his high. "I was white-hot that night. I couldn't lose."

"I can't imagine how that feels."

"No, you can't. It's just crazy."

"What happened then?"

"I'd seen this ring. In a jewelry store there, at the resort. I cashed out and bought it."

"Showed it around to all your friends there. Bragged how you were going to marry Sara McCall."

His satisfied smirk slipped a bit. "I wasn't bragging. I was excited."

"Another sure thing?"

That caught him by surprise. "I . . . I wouldn't have bought the ring if I didn't think she'd say yes. But I wouldn't put it that way."

"Let's talk about the other big thing going on in your life back then. Dale Graham. The opportunity to go into business with him. Tell me about that."

Sullivan glanced at his lawyer, then back at Luke. "He and I were friends. Old friends. He had this idea to open up an athletic training facility for kids on the Northshore. I thought it sounded like a winner."

"A sure thing?"

"Yeah, I did think of it that way. And it's proved out."

"Without you."

"Obviously."

"And you were fed up with teaching."

"It gets old. You should try it."

"No thanks. They wouldn't let me bring my gun."

Sullivan snickered. "True, that."

"So you approached Graham about the partnership, not the other way around. Isn't that right?"

"That's not the way I remember it." He lifted a shoulder. "Why does this even matter?"

"He wouldn't have approached you. Because he was worried about your gambling."

"That's bullshit. He offered me the in. If he was worried, why'd he do that?"

"The McCall name. The McCall money."

"That's nuts."

"You didn't tell him about your relationship with Sara McCall?"

"Sure, I did. We were together."

"Isn't it the truth that you bragged to him about marrying Sara McCall? That you told him it was a 'sure thing'? Those are Dale Graham's words, Danny."

He'd become flustered. "I don't know why he would have said that."

"According to your old friend Graham, Sara McCall was your ticket to the good life."

"I loved her."

"How much was the partnership going to cost?"

"Seventy-five thousand."

"You were more than halfway there that night. With your winnings."

He said nothing. Luke went on. "But you used it to buy the ring."

"Because I loved her."

The statement lacked conviction. "I contend that the ring was a gamble. You were upping your ante. Putting it all on the biggest jackpot of all. The McCall fortune."

Luke leaned forward. "But she said no, didn't she? To it all. The loan. The marriage proposal. All of it."

"What does this have to do with the other night?" Sullivan looked at his lawyer. "Why do I have to answer these questions?"

Luke didn't give Pierre a chance to respond. "Why do you hate Jeremy? Did he tell her about the gambling? When you asked her for the loan? Did he dig a little, find out your secret? Did you see it all slipping away? When you showed her the ring, and she turned you down. Everything you'd worked for. Dreamed of. Gone.

"Did you fly into a rage? The baseball bat was there, wasn't it? Propped against the wall. You grabbed it and swung. Isn't that right?"

"No!"

"In a fit of rage. You didn't mean to kill her. You were blinded by fury. That's how the image of her got into your head. Of her lying in a pool of blood."

301

"That's not what happened! I swear!" He looked at Pierre. The lawyer's expression was almost comically rapt.

"For a moment, did you think of romancing Kat? Of getting the McCall money that way? Is that why you were so angry when she showed up at the party with me? Why you set her house on fire—"

"No, I swear I didn't!"

"—why you attacked her? The way you attacked Sara? Because you saw it all slipping away? Again?"

"No!" He brought his hands to his face, breaking down. "That's not the way it went down! I was there that night. But I didn't kill her!"

The interview room door flew open. They all looked that way. His dad stood in the doorway, pale and shaking. "Son, I need to speak with you. Now."

Chapter Thirty-five

Wednesday, June 12
5:45 p.m.

Luke excused himself, then led his dad to his office. He was pissed and worked to get a grip on the emotion as he shut the door behind them, then turned to his father. "What the hell, Pops? It couldn't wait?"

"What are you up to?"

Of all the things he would have expected his old man to say first, none of them had been that. "Questioning a suspect. Danny Sullivan."

"I ordered Reni to come pick me up." His hands were curled into fists. "He was to inform you to hold off until I arrived."

"You're on medical leave, Dad. I'm acting chief until you're officially cleared to come back to work."

"You instructed Reni to disobey my direct orders."

"At this time, Reni takes orders from me." He felt as if he were speaking to a belligerent child. "I'm acting chief while you're away."

"I'm right here, dammit!"

Luke frowned. "You're not up to this."

"I'm just sitting in."

"I can't let you do that. It'll undermine my authority."

"Any authority you have came from me, boy. I'm the chief!"

The things Kat had said about his father the other night raced into his head. "Who are you trying to protect?"

"Who would I be protecting? That's ridiculous."

"You're either protecting someone or trying to cover something up. That's the way it seems, Pops."

"I should take your badge! My own son,

trying—" He burst into a fit of coughing. His face reddened as he tried to control it. "Trying to destroy me!"

"Danny was there that night. He admitted it just now. A moment before you interrupted us. He was there at Sara's place, the night she was murdered."

Coughing shook his dad again. Luke wondered if it was all an act. A ruse to get his way.

"That's . . . not . . . possible."

"He has a gambling addiction. McCall was his ticket to easy street. What if she turned him down? Think that might be cause for him to fly into a rage? The kind that can lead to murder?"

His dad just stared at him, mouth working, hand gripping the back of the desk chair.

"Why didn't you find any of this? Because you didn't look?"

His dad didn't have answers, and Luke shook his head. "All my life I looked up to you. I figured I didn't measure up, that I'd let you down. Now I'm starting to wonder if it's you who doesn't measure up. You who let me down."

His dad didn't meet his eyes. Luke took the lanyard with his shield from around his neck and dropped it on the desk. "Take it back. The authority. The badge." He followed with his side-arm. "My gun. It's all yours, old man. I'm done."

Luke strode from the office, not looking back even when he heard the chair slam against the wall. Let his old man throw a temper tantrum. Luke had grown up on them. More than six decades of life under his belt, and he could still act like a two-year-old.

He was clear to his car when he heard Reni behind him. "Sarge, wait!"

He stopped, looked back. "Not anymore. I quit."

"But your dad—"

"Is a pigheaded old son of a bitch. I'm through with him."

"No, Luke. Your dad, he collapsed."

Chief Stephen Tanner
2003

Five days after the murder

Tanner couldn't sit still. He paced in front of his desk, sat, then popped back to his feet. Jeremy was bringing Kat in for another round of questioning. Everything was riding on this. He couldn't screw up.

This time, he was prepared. The scene had been processed. He'd interviewed both the victim's and the suspect's friends, family, co-workers. Neighbors.

Things weren't looking good. Not for young Miss McCall.

Tanner paused, drawing in a deep, calming breath, then slowly releasing it. Jeremy had hired the top criminal defense attorney in the entire Gulf Coast region to represent her. Robert Henry Clay III. He'd gotten more fish off the hook than Johnny Morris, the bass master himself.

Tanner knew he'd better bring his A game. Otherwise that shark would eat him like a guppy.

Trixie buzzed him. "They're here."

"Put 'em in the interview room. Offer 'em cold drinks, coffee, whatever. I'll be out in five."

Tanner used the minutes to organize his thoughts and shelve his nerves. He could do this. He didn't need the sheriff's department or anybody else to help him do his job.

Fact number one: Kat McCall hated her sister. She had publicly wished her dead. She resented the fact that Sara controlled her inheritance. If her sister were dead, she would have it all.

Fact number two: She had been lying to Sara for weeks. Telling her she was going to softball practice when in actuality she was hanging out with friends she had been forbidden to see.

When Sara found her out, they'd had a huge argument. Sara had taken away her phone, car and computer, then grounded her for the foreseeable future.

Fact number three: Sara McCall had decided to send her sister away to boarding school. The way Tanner figured it, that was what had sent Kat McCall into a rage. She had beaten Sara to death with the very bat they had fought over.

It made perfect sense. She had the means, the motive and the opportunity.

In addition, the manner of death fit the crime. This wasn't the impersonal work of a stranger. This had been personal. Fueled by rage. Hatred. The fact that the perp had pulverized Sara's face. That she had continued to beat her after she was dead.

Tanner smiled tightly. *You're on, Stephen. Do this thing.*

A moment later, he stepped into the interview room, his gaze landing on McCall. She looked young. And scared. The lawyers stood to greet him. Webber introduced him to Clay, whose appearance was the antithesis of the tall, commanding figure he'd expected.

Instead, Robert Henry Clay was short and disheveled. Towering over him, Tanner decided that he was the shark, about to gobble up the unsuspecting attorney.

They shook hands. Tanner turned to Webber. "I'm sorry, Jeremy, but I'm going to have to ask you to leave. Conflict of interest."

Fear raced into McCall's eyes. She grabbed his hand. "Cousin Jeremy, no."

"She's a child, Tanner. And as her only living relative, I'm now her guardian."

Tanner appreciated his concern and told him so. "But you know as well as I do, in the eyes of the state of Louisiana, at seventeen Miss Kat here is an adult. And she has good counsel. She'll be just fine."

"I'll take good care of her," Clay said.

Webber bent down and kissed the top of her head. "It'll be okay, Kit-Kat. I'll be right outside that door."

She watched him go, flinching slightly as the door clicked shut.

Tanner began. "I appreciate you comin' in, Miss Katherine. I know how awful, and how scary, this must be for you."

She nodded, swallowing hard.

"But you don't have to be scared. This is a formality. Do you understand what my job is?" he asked.

"To find the person who killed Sara," she whispered.

"That's right." He smiled. "And to do that, I need to gather all the information I can about what happened. Think of the crime as a puzzle with many pieces. I'm collecting all the pieces, so I can get a clear picture of what happened."

"Yes, sir."

He saw Clay glance at his watch. *Check away, Mr. Big City Attorney, but I have no intention of rushing this.*

"When I questioned you last time," he continued, "you told me you were home all night, the night Sara was murdered."

"I was."

"You never left?"

"No, sir."

"When did you last see your sister?"

"Five thirty. Six."

He nodded. "That's right. And what did you say you talked about?"

She drew her eyebrows together. "I don't remember exactly what I told you, but we didn't talk much. She said dinner was ready and I told her I wasn't hungry."

"And that's it."

"Pretty much. Then I went to my room."

"Because you were grounded."

Tanner made a show of flipping through his notes, though every word she'd said to him was burned onto his brain. He'd scoured through the notes every night since the murder.

"Refresh my memory, why were you grounded?"

"Just because."

He glanced at the notebook again, then back up at her. "Last time, you said your sister was punishing you because of your grades and not keeping your room clean, and because she didn't like the people you were hanging with. Do you stick by that?"

When she agreed, he went on. "No phone, no TV. No computer."

"Yes."

"But she didn't take away your iPod."

McCall frowned. "No. I was listening to it that night."

"Why do you think she let you keep it?"

"I don't know."

"That seems odd to me, Katherine. Does it seem odd to you?"

Clay spoke up. "It may seem odd to you, Chief, but that's what she said happened. Can we move on?"

He was in control of this interview, not Robert Henry Clay. And he was going to prove it. "Those reasons you gave me for Sara grounding you, you weren't being truthful, were you?"

"Yes, I was."

"Not according to your cousin or his wife. Not according to Miz Bell across the street. What's the real reason she grounded you?"

Kat flushed. She glanced at her lawyer, then back at him. "She found out I'd been lying to her."

"About joining the girls' softball team?"

"I guess."

"Yes or no?"

"Yes."

"And when she found out, you had a huge fight about it. Right on the front porch. A witness said you were screaming at her."

She pressed her lips together and nodded.

"Yes or no?"

"Yes," she managed.

"Why did you lie about that?"

"About joining the softball team?"

"Yeah. Why? You have something better to do?"

She was searching for an answer. He saw it in her eyes. "Not really."

"Not really? You just lied to you sister for the fun of it? Created this big ruse about softball for . . . nothing?"

"I didn't want to tell her where I was."

"And where were you?"

"With my friends. Hanging out."

"Your friends?"

"She didn't like them."

"Names?"

She looked at Clay. "Do I have to say? I don't want them to get mad at me."

"You do," he replied. "They won't be angry, go ahead."

"Dab Holt. Sheila Thompson. Joe Patron. That group."

"And they'll confirm what you're telling me?"

"Yeah, but—" She hesitated. "I didn't hang with them every minute. Only some of the time."

Fact was, he'd already talked to the folks in that group. Kat McCall did hang out with them, but in the last three weeks they'd seen her only sporadically. They'd also confirmed that she hated her sister, had complained bitterly about Sara controlling her inheritance and had even wished her sister were dead.

"Okay, Miss Katherine. You're lying to your sister so you can hang out with kids she didn't approve of, only most of the time you weren't with them. So what were you doing those afternoons?"

"Nothing." She crossed her arms over her chest. "Just hanging out."

"Alone?"

"Yes. Alone. Why don't you believe me!"

Tears flooded her eyes. He'd bet his badge they were manufactured. "Because you're a liar, Miss McCall."

"I'm not. Really! I just—"

"You just admitted lying to your sister. Your guardian. Not a little white lie. A big lie."

"She was always watching everything I did! I just wanted to do what I wanted to!"

"Did you want that badly enough to kill her?"

"No! Please, stop saying that!"

"And you lied to me. Why'd you do that?"

She stared, a deer caught in headlights. "You know why."

"You have to tell me."

Moments ticked past. Clay gently nudged her. "Kat? It's okay to tell him."

"Because it would . . . make me look guilty."

"Are you guilty? Did you kill your sister?"

She shook her head. "No, I did not."

He changed tack. "You found your sister the next morning?"

"That's in the record already," Clay said. "She called 911."

"So, you know how she died?" She nodded, head down. "It wasn't a quiet crime, Kat. She would have screamed—"

"Tanner—"

"The sound of the bat hitting the body. Of bones breaking."

"Tanner! Enough!"

"But you heard nothing?"

She lifted her head, looked blankly at him. Then she blinked. Twice. "I had my earbuds in. Listening to music."

"On the iPod your sister conveniently didn't take away from you. Do you remember who you were listening to?"

She thought a moment. "No."

"Were you listening to the same artist the whole time?"

"I don't think so. I like to skip around."

"Tanner," Clay interrupted, "is this really taking us anywhere?"

"And you never left your room. Never got hungry or thirsty—"

"Established," Clay said.

She answered anyway. "I told you before, I had a Snickers and a bottle of water. Besides, I couldn't leave the room."

Tanner jumped on that. "Couldn't?" he repeated. "What do you mean?"

"She locked me in."

Tanner nearly choked on his own spit. "Your sister locked you in your room?"

"So I wouldn't sneak out."

"Sneak out? You didn't mention that before. Had you been sneaking out?"

"I didn't say that. She was afraid I might."

Caught again. Kat McCall was a liar. Just not a good one. "You're saying you didn't leave your room, but you tried to?"

She looked at Clay, as if confused. The attorney stepped in. "Less obtuse, if you don't mind."

Tanner hid his annoyance. McCall was confused because her lies were beginning to overlap. "My question is, if you didn't try the door, how did you know it was locked?"

"I just knew."

"Did she lock you in every night? That doesn't sound like the Sara McCall we all knew."

"No. Never before."

Beside her, Clay involuntarily sputtered.

Tanner's lips twitched. "So, why that night?"

"I don't know."

"You don't know? Really, no clue? Your sister locks you in your room once, only once ever, and it just happens to be on the same night she's killed?"

Her eyes filled with tears. "I don't know why! It's true, I swear it!"

Clay interrupted. "I need a moment alone with my client."

Just bet you do. He had them on the run, and her attorney knew it. All this business about being locked in her room had been news to him as well.

He stood. "Certainly. Can I bring either of you anything?"

Kat asked for a Coke, Clay a bottle of water. Tanner exited the room, closing the door behind him.

Webber stood in the hallway. He looked anxious. "How is she, Chief?"

"Truthfully? Man, she's in a world of trouble."

Webber didn't pursue more information, which was for the best. He wouldn't have shared more anyway.

Tanner went for the drinks. When he returned, Clay was in the hallway with Webber. They were ready for him.

Tanner handed Clay the drinks. He took them, smiling slightly. "May I ask you a question, Chief Tanner? How many murder investigations have you worked?"

"A few. Why?"

"Just curious."

Tanner knew what he was suggesting, what he was trying to do. Undermine his confidence. Make him doubt his direction. Tanner followed him into the interview room, shoulders squared,

315

spine stiff. Well, that wasn't going to happen. Not this time.

Clay handed McCall her Coke. She popped the top and took a long drink. Tanner saw that her hands were shaking. Her face was deathly pale.

For a split second, he felt sorry for her. Then he pictured her sister's bludgeoned body and any sympathy he might have had evaporated.

He gave her another moment to drink, then began. "We're almost done, Miss Katherine. I just want to be certain I have every piece of the puzzle." He cleared his throat, thumbed through his notes, then lifted his gaze to hers.

"Did you wish your sister were dead?"

"No," she said, the sound breathless.

"Not ever?"

"I'd get mad at her, but I didn't want her to die."

"So, what if I told you not one, but several people told me that you verbally wished she were dead. That if she were dead you'd have all your money and be able to do whatever you wanted."

She wrung her hands. "I didn't mean that for real. I'd get mad and say stuff, stupid stuff, but I didn't really want that."

"So you admit you said more than once that you wished your sister were dead?"

"Yes. But—"

"A few more questions." He gentled his tone, slid a box of tissues across the table. Thumbed through the notes again. "Sara locked you in your room."

She whimpered. "That's right,"

"I get that. I just have one question." He frowned. "If Sara locked you in, how did you find her the next morning?"

"What?"

"I mean, if the door was locked, how did you get out?"

She shifted in her seat. She looked at the ceiling, then the floor, then at her attorney, as if for help. When none was forthcoming, she looked back at him. "It was unlocked in the morning. I figured Sara unlocked it before she went to bed."

He shook his head sadly. "Be honest with me, Kat. Let's make this simple. Your sister never locked that door, did she?"

"She did. I—"

"You made that up. In the hopes it would be an alibi? Isn't that right?"

"No, no—"

"Just like the whole earbuds thing is your attempt at covering your tracks?"

"No." She brought her hands to her face, then dropped them. She suddenly looked angry. "Did you even talk to Danny about that fight I overheard?"

"I did. It was nothing."

"It wasn't!" She fisted her fingers. "Sara was crying!"

"Couples fight," he said softly. "And women cry."

"I might have heard his truck. That night."

"But you said you had your earbuds in. That you couldn't hear anything."

"I must've taken them out to go to the bathroom."

"But you were locked in."

She looked a hairbreadth from falling apart. "That's right. That's when I realized she'd locked me in. I pounded and called for her, she didn't answer."

"What time was that?"

"I don't know." Her voice rose. "I figured they were making out or something."

Tanner frowned. "But you said they had been fighting. Just days before. Violently enough so that you believe Danny Sullivan killed your sister?"

"Maybe they were making up. Why won't you believe me?"

"Your sister told you she was going to send you to boarding school, didn't she? Is that why you did it?"

"Sara wouldn't have done that to me. She wouldn't. She was my sister."

The crazy thing was, he wanted to believe her. He secretly felt sorry for her. He'd known little Kat McCall all her life. He'd attended her parents' funeral.

But none of that changed the facts.

He extracted two brochures from a manila envelope. He laid them side by side on the table in front of her. Blue Ridge Academy in Charlottesville, Virginia, and Christ Church School in Greenville, South Carolina.

"These were on your sister's nightstand."

Kat stared at them a moment, throat working. With a low keening that sent gooseflesh up his spine, she doubled over, sobbing.

Clay stepped in. The interview ended. Tanner watched them go, the two men all but carrying her out.

The door eased shut behind them and Tanner sank back to his chair. He dropped his head into his trembling hands. Tears stung his eyes and he knew if he let go, he'd bawl like a little baby.

First Wally. Then Sara McCall. Now Kat. He didn't sign up for this. He didn't want it.

But the only way to escape this nightmare was to see it through.

Chapter Thirty-six

Kat opened her eyes, disoriented and groggy. She stared at the window, the sunny day beyond. For a split second, she wondered where she was. And how she'd gotten here.

Then she moved and pain shot through her left shoulder and neck. And it all came crashing back. The fire. Danny. The crime lab. Lilith, scolding her.

Luke. His arms around her.

She rolled onto her back and gazed at the play of light and shadow on the ceiling. After the confrontation with Lilith, she'd been unable to sleep. She'd tossed and turned, her mind racing. The thought of going through the cottage had been repugnant. She'd wondered if she'd ever be ready. She had considered sticking a For Sale sign in the yard, pulling up stakes and heading back to Portland.

Not now. She would not be driven out. She would not run away. And she sure as hell wasn't about to be intimated by this coward, whether it was Danny or someone else.

Her phone pinged and she retrieved it from the

nightstand. Two messages waiting. Both were from Luke. She hadn't even heard it ring.

She listened to the first. *Met with the arson investigator. Found the gas can under the house. He's checking it for prints.* In the second, he said he had news and to call him.

But what surprised her more was the date and time on the display—June 13, 9:50 a.m.

She'd slept for twenty-four hours.

Kat dialed Luke back, got his in-box, left a message and scrambled out of bed, wincing at each movement. She hurt all over. From her head to her toes. She hobbled to the bathroom, relieved herself and started the shower. While the water warmed, she brushed her teeth, then stripped. And caught sight of herself in the mirror. The bruises shocked her. Their number and color. Dark and ugly.

She trailed her fingers over them, tears stinging her eyes. She blinked, thinking of her sister. The horror she had gone through. Aching for her.

Kat closed her eyes. "I promise you," she whispered, "I don't care what it takes, or who I have to go up against, I'm not going to stop, Sara. Not until the one who did this pays."

Thirty minutes later, showered and dressed, Kat started downstairs. Halfway down she stopped. Lilith and Jeremy were home. They were arguing.

"What did you expect?" Lilith said. "Don't be an idiot."

Kat froze, shocked. She had never heard Lilith speak that way. And to direct it at Jeremy was unfathomable.

"Why are you being such a bitch?"

"I thought you wanted this!"

"I do, dammit!"

"Then why do you continue to do everything in your power to fuck it up?"

"Nice, Lilith. Thanks for the vote of confidence."

"You really expected people to welcome her with open arms?"

They were arguing about her, Kat realized, horrified. It was her fault. She took a step backward, up the stairs.

"She may even be a thief."

Kat stopped on that.

"For God's sake, Lilith. You're being ridiculous."

"I'm missing some jewelry."

"Talk to the housekeeper. Or take a look at yourself."

"What's that supposed to mean?"

"It wouldn't the first time you lost something, then blamed it on someone else."

"Right. At least I take care of my shit instead of whining about it like a little girl."

"Like I said, you're good at pointing the finger at someone else."

"I hate you."

"The feeling's mutual."

Kat pressed a hand to her stomach. Lilith resented her. She thought so little of her, she would suspect her of stealing from them? And Jeremy. He hated his wife. He'd called her a bitch.

Kat suddenly realized their voices had grown closer. *They were heading her way.* Heart pounding, she turned and ran as quietly as she could back up the stairs. She didn't want them to know she'd overheard them. It was going to be difficult enough, knowing what she did, for her to look them in the eye. But if they knew, it would be impossible.

She reached the landing. Figuring there was no way she could make it back to her room without them seeing her, she stopped and turned, hoping it would appear that she had just arrived there.

They came into view. "Good morning," she called.

Lilith looked up, expression suspicious.

Jeremy smiled broadly. "You were so quiet, we didn't even realize you were here."

"I can't believe I slept so long."

She reached the bottom of the stairs and he wrapped her in a bear hug. He released her, but held her at arm's length. "My poor baby. Are you okay?"

"I'm fine. Shaken but—"

"Dear God."

Jeremy was staring at her. Kat followed his gaze. Her shirt's boatneck had slipped, revealing the bruises on her left shoulder.

Jeremy's face flooded with angry color. "That son of a bitch. I'll tear him apart."

She straightened her shirt. "I'm fine. Really."

"You're not." He frowned. "Those bruises—"

"Are nothing. It could have turned out lots worse."

He could have killed her.

As if Jeremy was thinking the same thing, he squeezed her hand. "I'm grateful, too. If anything happened to you, I don't know what I'd do."

"He's in jail, Cousin Jeremy. He can't hurt anybody from there."

"Thank God," Lilith murmured.

Kat didn't look at Lilith. She couldn't, and hoped it wasn't so blatant that the other woman noticed. "I'm going over to the cottage now, to get a look at the damage."

"Come and have something to eat first," Jeremy said. "We'll keep you company."

"I can't," she lied. "I'm meeting Luke there. In fact"—she glanced at her watch—"I'm already late."

"Have you heard anything yet?" Jeremy asked, falling into step with her.

"It was definitely arson. They're going to see if they can get prints off the gas can they found under the house."

"Keep me posted, okay?"

She said she would and he walked her to her car. She opened the door, but he stopped her before she climbed in. "You heard us fighting, didn't you?"

She hated to lie to him, but she just couldn't admit she had. Maybe later, but not now. "You were fighting? Is something wrong?"

"No. We're both under a lot of pressure right now and it's got us sniping at each other. No big deal."

"I hate you."

"The feeling's mutual."

"I hope I'm not the cause of your stress."

"Of course not. It's this running-for-office thing. It's a big step."

"A very big step," she agreed.

He smiled then. "The truth is, you're like a ray of hope for me." He glanced over his shoulder. Lilith had appeared on the porch. "I'll let you go. Keep me posted, okay?"

She said she would and started to back out. He stopped her again. "Be careful, Kit-Kat. I'm worried about you."

She smiled. "I'm worried about me, too."

As she drove off, she glanced in her rearview mirror. Lilith had joined him. They stood with their arms around each other. Once again the united front.

Kat turned her gaze back to the road. Were they apologizing now, Kat wondered. She'd heard of couples who fought viciously, saying unforgivable things to each other in the heat of the moment, then apologized just as passionately and moved on until the next blow-up. She never would have thought Jeremy and Lilith had that kind of relationship.

That they had each other's back, yes. That they would plunge a knife in it, no.

Jeremy Webber
2003

Ten days before the murder

Jeremy had to admit, unequivocally, he was a happy man. Not even thirty years old and he owned a big, beautiful home, was a rising star at a prestigious law firm and had a brilliant, beautiful wife. He had it all, and the future looked as bright as the sun.

That hadn't always been the case. Though he often reminded people of his connection to McCall Oil, he wasn't truly family. He wasn't blood, and without that, the keys to the kingdom would never be his.

When he was ten, his mother had finally gotten the guts to leave his abusive, no-good old man. She'd packed them both up and run to her wealthy sister in Liberty.

He hadn't realized at the time what that was going to mean for the course of his life, and how being in the McCall fold would change everything.

They'd been very generous toward him, had bought him his first car, paid for his schooling, even left him some money and property when they passed. His uncle Peter had treated him almost like a son.

Jeremy had learned the full extent of his uncle's faith in him only after his death. He'd appointed him, fresh out of law school, the executor of their estate, a position that paid him a fat yearly stipend.

Lilith tapped on his office door, then poked her head in. "Love, Sara's here to see you."

Sara stepped in and he stood, smiling warmly.

"Why didn't you call?" He came around the desk and hugged her. "We could have prepared lunch."

"Could we speak privately?" She looked apologetically at Lilith. "It's really personal."

"Of course. Can I bring you anything?"

"No, but thank you."

Though Lilith's expression remained unchanged as she backed out of the room, Jeremy knew that the request had hurt her feelings. It upset her that neither of his cousins had warmed to her.

"Come sit down," he said. "Tell me what's up."

Sara nodded and took a seat on the small, dark leather sofa. It wasn't until that moment that he realized she was upset.

He sat beside her. "What's wrong? Is it Kat again?"

"It's always Kat." She let out a long breath. "But not just Kat this time."

He waited. When, after a couple moments, she didn't say more, he prodded her. "You can tell me anything, you know that. I'm here for you."

She twisted her fingers together. "I feel like a complete idiot. I thought . . . I'd hoped . . ."

Again he waited. This time she continued without a nudge. "I thought I was in love. Or maybe, I think I am."

"Danny?" She nodded. Her eyes filled with tears. "Did you two have a fight?"

"No. But—" She cleared her throat. "He asked if he could borrow some money."

"Oh, boy."

"I know, that's the way I felt."

"What did he need it for?"

"To open an athletic training facility. He said it's a great opportunity. A former LSU player came to him with the offer; he gave Danny the first crack at partnering with him."

"Did he say who the player was?"

She shook her head. "And I didn't ask."

"How much money are we talking about?"

"Seventy-five thousand. Cash."

"That's a lot of money."

"That's what I told him and he—" She bit it back.

"What?"

"He reminded me I was worth millions. That seventy-five grand was nothing to someone like me. We fought and he said . . . he said if I loved him, I'd do it. That my hesitation meant I didn't believe in him."

"That pisses me off. I thought Danny was a stand-up guy."

"But—" She looked hopefully up at him. "This doesn't mean he's not, does it?"

"I don't know what to tell you." He paused. "Did he show you a business plan?"

From her expression he saw that Danny hadn't. "Look, ask him for one, I'll look it over."

"He said time was of the essence. If he waited too long, he'd lose the opportunity."

Jeremy frowned. Either Sullivan was pulling the wool over her eyes, or somebody was pulling the wool over his. Business moved fast, but not that fast.

"You're right to be cautious. I'm going to do a little checking around. In the meantime, you stall him by asking for a business plan."

"What do you mean, check around? Like, check up on him?"

He covered her hands with his. "Sweetheart, what do you really know about Danny Sullivan?"

"Jeremy, we're . . . we're talking about marriage."

Jeremy worked to hide his dismay. "You haven't been seeing each other that long."

"Six months. We get along really well. We're both teachers."

"Did he propose?"

"No. But I think . . . I have this feeling he will."

"And you'll say yes?"

"I think so. Or at least I did, before this." She hugged herself. "I need your opinion on something." She paused, drew deep breath. "It's about Kat. I'm thinking of sending her to boarding school."

She could have knocked him over with a feather on that one. He wondered if Sullivan had been the one who'd planted that seed. Get rid of the annoying little sister so they could concentrate on their romance.

Jeremy thought better than to say that out loud. "What brought this on? I thought things were better?"

"I thought so, too." She twisted her fingers together. He could tell this decision was agony for her. "I just have this feeling. That she's . . . up to something."

"Her grades are good?"

"Fine. Not great, but fine."

"And she's playing softball?

"Yeah."

"Then what?"

"How do you know if a kid's doing drugs? I should, I'm a high school teacher. But it's different when it's your own family."

"Shit, Sara. That's big." He ran a hand through his hair. "Drug-test her. Take her to a doc-in-the-box or buy a home test at the drugstore."

"I feel bad about doing that. She'll think I don't trust her."

He laughed without humor. "You don't. And that's okay. She needs a mother, not a best friend."

"But I'm not her mother! I *should* be her best friend, we're sisters."

"Sorry, Sara, but the drunk driver who killed your folks changed all that. For the time being, you're the only mama Kat has."

She nodded and stood. "I needed that. Thanks."

He got to his feet. Gave her a quick hug. "That's what I'm here for."

She started toward the door, then stopped. "I really might want to do this."

"Send Kat away?"

"No, marry Danny. Lend him the money. It's different when you're married. It'll be our money, not just mine. Our life he's investing in."

A flicker of panic settled in the pit of his gut. This could change everything. "Please, for your sake, Sara, don't agree to anything yet. You're a very rich woman. I want to protect you."

"But I have enough money, right?"

"Of course. Sara, c'mon."

"I mean, that I can get to quickly? I forget what that's called."

"Liquid assets," he said. "Of course you do."

He walked her out, then frowned as her car disappeared from view. Did she? he wondered. Have enough liquid cash? He hadn't been paying attention. Not enough attention, anyway.

He turned back toward the house. Lilith stood in the open doorway, expression concerned. "Is everything all right?"

"Fine, baby." He forced a smile. "Never a dull minute with those two. I'll tell you about it over lunch. How about the club?"

Chapter Thirty-seven

Thursday, June 13
10:50 a.m.

Kat stood on the sidewalk in front of her cottage. The pretty yellow on the side to her right was charred, marred by ugly fingers of black. Someone had deliberately done this. To frighten or punish her. To destroy evidence. Whatever. She flexed her fingers, fighting her warring emotions. Anger, despair at the loss. Determination. Interestingly, not fear.

Not fear. Kat smiled grimly. A step in the right

direction. She wouldn't run. If Sullivan, or someone else, thought that by destroying her house, he would destroy her, he had seriously miscalculated.

Kat pushed open the gate and started up the walk. She reached the stairs and climbed them to the porch. Careful to avoid the most burnt areas, she made her way inside.

The smell hit her first. Horrendous. She brought a hand to her nose. A dirty fireplace on a humid day. Times a thousand. And visually, it was strange. Dark and light. To her left, untouched by the fire. To her right, consumed by it. Her gaze went to the foyer floor, to the bloodstain. The flames had eaten it. But gone no farther.

As if Sara herself had stood in their way.

Maybe she had.

The worst damage had been to the living room. Kat went farther inside, picking her way carefully toward the living room. She stopped in the opening, surveyed the damage.

The boxes sat, charred tombs, their contents destroyed. All the photos. Sara's personal items, hers. Mementos of her childhood.

Their past. Her past. Dead now. Gone.

She felt suddenly ill. Light-headed and queasy.

Kat turned and hurried from the house. Across the porch, down the steps. She sank onto the bottom step and gulped in the fresh air. It was just stuff, she told herself. She didn't need it. She had her memories; no one could take those from her.

The queasiness passed. The blood returned to her head. It could have been worse. If Iris Bell hadn't seen the flames and called 911, how much longer would it have burned before the fire department arrived?

Iris Bell. Kat glanced up. A car was rolling slowly past, both driver and passenger gawking. Kat's gaze slid from the car to Mrs. Bell's porch. The old neighbor stood on it, staring her way.

Kat jumped to her feet and started toward her. "Mrs. Bell," she called when she was close enough to be heard, "it's Kat McCall."

The woman squinted at her. "Katherine," she said, "have you come to visit me?"

"I have. Is now a good time?"

"Lovely," she said. "I have tea. And cookies."

The woman's big, round glasses magnified her eyes, making them huge. Holdovers from an era before her time, Kat thought.

"Thank you," she said and climbed the steps. "I'm sorry I haven't been over to say hello sooner."

"That's fine, child. How's Sara this morning?"

"Pardon?"

"Such a shame. About the fire. Why do these things happen?"

"That's what I'm trying to figure out, Mrs. Bell. Did you see anything?"

"See anything?" she repeated.

"Last night. Over at the house."

"Cars coming and going. Lots of visitors. I didn't feel so well."

Kat was confused. "Visitors? Last night."

"So many." She motioned to the screen door. "Let's visit inside. The air smells this morning." She wrinkled her nose. "I don't like it."

"It's from the fire."

"The fire?"

"My house caught fire last night, Mrs. Bell. You called 911. I was hoping you saw something that might be of help."

"Of course. Come in."

Mrs. Bell insisted Kat sit in the front room while she got the tea and cookies. She could hardly sit still and jumped up to help the woman as she returned with a tray, which shook slightly as she carried it.

Kat took it from her and set it on the coffee table.

"Thank you, child." She handed Kat a glass of tea, then passed a plate of cookies. Animal crackers, Kat saw. She selected a bear, and thinking of what Luke had said about her being a tiger, bit off its head.

"Did you happen to see anything, Mrs. Bell? Last night?"

"I saw your house on fire. I called the fire department."

"Thank you, Mrs. Bell. You probably saved it."

She blinked those huge fish eyes, as if seeing her for the first time. "Oh my, it's Miss Katherine."

"Yes. It's Kat McCall."

"You've been giving your sister fits, you know."

"My sister? But—" Then she realized that Iris Bell's mind was jumping back and forth in time. Instead of correcting her, Kat decided to go with that. "I know I have, and I'm sorry about it. I've changed."

"That's good." She nodded. "I told your sister what you were up to."

"What I was up to?"

"Sneaking out at night." She wagged a finger at her. "That boy's too old for you."

Was that how Sara had found out about Ryan? Why Sara had locked her bedroom door that night?

Kat frowned. But the bathroom window she had crawled in and out of was on the side of the house out of view of this one.

So how had the woman known about Ryan?

She decided to ask her. "How did you know about my boyfriend?"

"My sweet girl told me."

Her sweet girl?

"She brings me flowers. And figs. I love figs. Do you enjoy them, dear?"

"No, ma'am, they're not my favorite." Kat

leaned forward. "Your sweet girl, when did she bring you figs?"

The woman thought a moment. "Before I got sick. Not after. I didn't see her after. I don't know why."

When she got sick. Her stroke? Maybe. And what figs? When did they ripen?

"When you got sick, are you talking about your stroke, Mrs. Bell?"

"My stroke." She nodded. "Yes. My sweet girl found me—" Her eyes widened; she looked at Kat in horror. "That was the night your sister . . . awful. Horrible."

"I didn't do it, Mrs. Bell. I didn't kill my sister."

"Of course not. How could you? You were locked in your room."

Surprise rippled over her. "How did you know that?"

"I suggested it to your sister. I'm sorry, dear, but I had to. That was a bad boy you were seeing."

"You told Sara about him?"

She nodded. "I don't like to be a busybody, but I was worried about you. We both were."

"You and who else?"

"My sweet girl. She told me everything. She was very worried about you." The woman wagged a finger at her. "He's too old for you. And fast. Boys like that can ruin a girl."

Kat leaned forward. "Who is your sweet girl, Mrs. Bell? What's her name?"

"I've been asking myself that same question. It's on the tip of my tongue, but—"

"Please, Mrs. Bell, try to remember. I'd love to go thank her for worrying about me."

"My memory . . . Oh, dear . . ." She nervously smoothed her housedress over her knees. "I used to remember with that children's rhyme. You know the one."

"No, Mrs. Bell, I don't. How does it go?"

"You know . . ." She lifted her fingers and wiggled them. "The itsy-bitsy spider—"

"Bitsy Cavenaugh? My friend Bitsy?"

"Yes!" The woman beamed. "Such a sweet, sweet girl. Whatever happened to her?"

Kat didn't answer. She reached between them and caught the woman's hand. "Was Bitsy over the night Sara died?"

She frowned. "Yes. So was he."

"He? My boyfriend Ryan? He was here?"

She laughed. "Silly. He visited Ms. Sara."

Kat's heart began to thump uncomfortably. Bitsy had been in love with Ryan. She'd been spying. That's how Sara had discovered what she'd been up to. It's why her bedroom door had been locked.

Ryan had been at the house the night of the murder; Bitsy had been right across the street.

"You said you saw a lot of visitors that night. Who?"

"I don't know. A lot of cars. Wally drove by more than once."

"Wally?"

"Officer Wally. I haven't seen him lately. Have you?"

Wally Clark had been killed the same night as Sara. He had been by their place.

"He used to stop here every once in a while, check on me if he saw a light on. He hasn't in a while."

"I've got to go, Mrs. Bell. Thank you for the tea and cookies."

But when she went to stand, Mrs. Bell refused to release her hand. "I saw you sneaking out again. That night. I called the police."

"But I didn't, Mrs. Bell. I was locked in my room, remember?"

"Out the back," she insisted.

"Was Bitsy still here?"

"Heavens, no! It was the middle of the night."

"But you said she found you."

"I did?" She shook her head. "That couldn't be right."

"Could it have been a man you saw?"

"A man? Maybe. That fellow your sister was seeing. He took out the trash sometimes."

From the back of the house. "Danny Sullivan," Kat said. "That was his name."

"Yes. He seemed like a nice-enough young man."

"Was he there that night?"

"He might have been. I didn't feel so well."

"He drove a big truck back then? Used to toot the horn when he arrived? Think back, Mrs. Bell. Was he there that night?"

The pressure flustered the old woman. She suddenly seemed anxious. Visibly more confused. She brought her hand to her pearls, nervously working them. "A terrible thing. Terrible."

"What, Mrs. Bell?"

"The fire . . . the cars, so many visitors. Poor, dear Sara. I can't imagine."

"I have to go, Mrs. Bell. But I'd love to come by and chat again. Would that be okay?"

"That'd be lovely." The woman blinked up at her. "Bring Sara along. I haven't seen her in ages!"

Chapter Thirty-eight

Thursday, June 13
11:55 a.m.

Kat made her way across the street to her car. She slipped inside. She started it up, turned the air on high. Her hands shook; her thoughts raced.

Bitsy was the one behind Sara finding out about her and Ryan. Iris Bell had done the actual deed, but it had been Bitsy's machinations that had made it happen. She had befriended the old woman so she could spy on her. Monitor her and Ryan's comings and goings.

Ryan had been at the cottage the night Sara died.

And Bitsy knew it. She had seen him there. That's why she'd been so nervous at lunch. Why she'd threatened Kat. Ryan had been at the cottage. And Bitsy was afraid he'd done it, that he'd killed Sara.

Betrayal welled up in her. What had Bitsy seen? Ryan going into the house. Maybe leaving as well, covered in blood.

No. Surely if that had been the case, she would have turned him in. She couldn't have been that blinded by love. Could she?

No, she thought again. But even if Bitsy had known nothing more than that Ryan had been at the house but had reported it to the police, Kat might not have been arrested. It might've been enough to keep the trial from happening.

What else might Bitsy have seen? Danny? A stranger? Information that maybe, just maybe, could have led to the real perpetrator?

Kat flexed her fingers on the steering wheel, betrayal replaced by anger. She could have gone to prison. Could have been convicted of first-degree murder.

How could Bitsy have said nothing?

Kat grabbed her phone and dialed Jeremy. He

answered immediately. "Is everything all right?"

"I'm fine. I need to talk to Bitsy. Face-to-face. Do you know where her office is?"

"I haven't a clue. But Lilith would."

She heard the concern in his voice. She didn't address it. "Thanks, Jeremy. Talk to you later—"

"Wait! What's going on?"

"I need some clarification on something Iris Bell told me. No worries."

Kat didn't give him the opportunity to ask more and hung up. She immediately tried Lilith. The woman sounded more apprehensive about giving her information than her husband had.

"Her shop's in Mandeville, at the Trailhead," Lilith answered. "Is there something I can help you with?"

"You just did, Lilith. Thank you. In case the shop's closed, any idea where she lives?"

"I don't like the way you sound, Katherine. I don't know if I feel comfortable—"

"For heaven's sake! Bitsy knows something important about the night Sara died. She was with Iris Bell, she—"

"First Danny Sullivan, now Bitsy? Are you trying to implicate everyone?"

"Mrs. Bell said she saw a number of vehicles at the cottage that night. Ryan Benton's among them! Bitsy knew but said nothing! She's protecting him!"

"Why can't you just let all this go and live

your life? You were acquitted, be glad and move on."

Lilith's words affected her like a slap to the face. "You really think I did it, don't you? You think I got away with murder."

"I didn't say that."

"You didn't have to. Never mind, I'll use the phone book."

"Danny Sullivan contacted an attorney from our firm. He claims you're trying to pin the murder on him, to clear your name."

"What? The man attacked me! He said he saw Sara dead . . . Iris Bell said—" Kat realized what she was doing and stopped dead. "I don't have to explain myself to you. And by the way, I'm not a thief!"

Kat hung up and tossed her phone on the passenger seat, furious. Hurt. She shifted the Fusion into drive and pulled away from the curb. Did Jeremy think she'd done it as well?

She shook off the thought. No, no way. He *knew* her. That she wasn't capable of such an act.

It would break her heart to believe otherwise.

The Mandeville Trailhead was located in the heart of Old Mandeville and just six blocks from the lake. Charming, with pavilions, an amphitheater and kids' splash fountains, and circled by shops, restaurants and even a place to rent bicycles to pedal the Trace.

Kat found Bitsy's shop. And as she feared, it

was closed. "By Appointment," the sign read. She peered through the window. Elegant with a hip edge. Shelves of design books. A few select pieces of furniture, lamps, mirrors, decorative pieces.

She lifted her gaze, taking in the building's facade. Picture of the past, constructed to be a live-and-work concept, storefront at street level, condo above. One of her Good Earth locations occupied just such a storefront.

What were the chances Bitsy lived above?

The proprietor of the chic dress shop next door came out for a smoke. As she lit up, she looked at Kat. "You looking for Bitsy? Or Ryan?"

"Bitsy. Does she live upstairs?"

"She did. Moved about a month ago."

"Do you know where?"

"Her parents' old place, I think. She's been remodeling for more than a year." She lifted a shoulder. "I don't have any idea where it is, though."

Kat did. She'd spent a lot of time there as a kid.

The woman blew out a stream of smoke. "The apartment's for rent, you should see it. Gorgeous. She knows her stuff."

"Yes, she does. Thank you."

"She's in the shop a lot. You want me to give her a message?"

Kat glanced back. "No, thanks. I'll catch her later."

• • •

The Cavenaughs' "old place" was a sprawling estate on Millionaires' Row in North Covington. It encompassed ten acres and backed up to the Bogue Falaya River, had a horse barn and a garage specially built to house Peter Cavenaugh's car collection.

The estate had gates, but they stood open. Kat drove through and up the winding drive. It had changed little since the last time she'd been here, and memories came flooding back. Happy times. Carefree. Before her parents' accident. Before everything had changed.

Merlin was parked in the circular drive in front of the house. She didn't know what kind of vehicle Ryan drove, but there wasn't another in sight.

Perfect. Just her and Bitsy.

Kat stopped behind the Mercedes and climbed out. The flower-scented breeze stirred her hair. It was way too pretty a day for the confrontation she knew was coming. For the ugly emotions simmering inside her.

She crossed the drive, then the veranda. She rang the bell.

Bitsy opened the door, her smile fading. "What are you doing here?"

"I think that should be obvious, Bits. Looking for you."

"Now's not a good time."

345

"Sorry about that." She ducked past her into the house. "Wow," she said. "It doesn't even look like the same place."

"What do you want, Kat?"

She faced her old friend. "Where were you last night? I didn't see you at Jeremy's party."

"Ryan and I stayed in." She folded her arms across her chest. "And no, we didn't set your cottage on fire. If that's what you're wondering?"

"Where were you the night Sara was murdered?"

She paled. "You're being ridiculous."

"Am I? I just had a lovely chat with my neighbor. You remember Mrs. Bell. You were so kind to her, Bits. What a humanitarian. Bringing her flowers and figs."

"I want you to leave."

"Did you know, I was so stupidly in love with him, I was ready to run away with nothing to be with him. Lose my inheritance. But he made no bones about it, he wasn't going anywhere without my money. I was his ticket out."

"He doesn't need my money. He's very successful."

"R and B Imports. What does the B stand for? Benton? Or Bitsy?" Kat could tell by her expression that she had lent him the money to open his business. She could almost feel sorry for her. Almost.

"All that's not why I'm here. I don't really care

if you want to throw your life away on some-one like him—have a ball. He was there at the cottage, the night of Sara's murder."

"You're crazy."

"We both know I'm not." She took a step toward her old friend. "I could have gone to prison. And you said nothing."

"What about you? You never whispered a peep about your precious boyfriend. Why not?"

"If I'd thought, even for a minute, that he'd done it, I would have shouted it from the roof-tops."

"Really? You're so certain of that? Then why're you back here now? Accusing him. Now conveniently remembering conversations where you 'claim' he talked about killing her."

"Because I was young and really stupid. I thought he was joking around. I loved him. And I thought he loved me. We were going to head off into the sunset together."

"Get over it."

"Was Ryan the last person to see Sara alive?"

"He didn't kill her."

"How do you know? Did you see anyone else there?"

"It's time for you to go."

"If he didn't kill her, why was he there, Bits?"

"I went to convince your sister I was a good guy."

They both turned. Ryan stood in the door-

347

way. Bitsy ran to him; he caught her in his arms.

"I find that hard to believe."

"It's true. And she was alive when I left."

"Can you prove it?"

He laughed. "I don't have to. And you can't prove I was there."

"Yes, I can. Iris Bell told me. She knows. About both of you."

"Iris Bell is a confused old lady. She can't recall the fact of what happened the day before, let alone ten years ago."

He was right. Even if the woman told Luke just what she'd told her, it'd never stand up in a court of law.

"Good-bye, Kat."

His lips lifted in the smile she used to find so attractive. It just seemed smug to her now. He and Bitsy deserved each other.

Her cell phone went off as she walked to her car. She saw it was Jeremy.

"I thought you'd want to know," he said. "Luke's dad's in the hospital. Lakeview Regional."

Bitsy Cavenaugh
2003

Two days after the murder

Bitsy heard the rumble of the Mustang. The slam of the car door. In a minute the bell above the Sunny Side's entrance would jingle.

And in he would walk.

She held her breath, waiting for her first glimpse of him. She had known he would be here. Most Saturdays he was. The ones he missed bitterly disappointed her. She would sit, laptop open, papers spread around her, looking to all the world like she was studying.

But in reality she waited. Hoping and praying. That maybe this time he would *see* her.

When he didn't show, she would feel stood-up. Hurt. Then angry. But today, of all days, she had known Ryan Benton would come.

The bell jingled. She lifted her gaze. He started toward her and her heart lurched to her throat. He had this strut, this way of moving that shouted: *I own the world, it's mine.*

He mesmerized her.

She stared at him as he approached, mouth going dry. She imagined his eyes meeting hers, his lips lifting in that cocky smile that made her nipples tighten.

But this time, like every time before, his gaze

349

slid right past her, to his friends in the booth directly behind hers. Sheila and Dab. Joe and Sam. His core group.

"What's happening, dudes? Make room."

"Where've you been?" Sheila's voice. Hushed.

"Around."

But Bitsy knew. All his secrets. She smiled to herself.

"What's everyone's problem?" he said. "Cheer the fuck up. It's Saturday."

"Have you heard?" Sheila again.

"What?" He sounded annoyed.

"Kat's sister is dead," Sheila whispered. "Somebody murdered her."

Bitsy held her breath. She needed to hear his response for herself.

"Get the fuck outta here."

"It's true," Joe said. "I heard it was a real mess."

"Somebody said old man Tanner puked when he saw the body."

"When?" Ryan asked. Was that a tremor she heard in his voice? What did that mean?

"The other night."

"Thursday," Dab offered. Why does it matter?

They didn't know about him and Kat. But they suspected. Bitsy had heard them talking. They figured he had screwed her. A couple times even. But Ryan Benton didn't get any more involved than that, they said.

Joe snapped his fingers. "Ryan? Shit, man. Are you okay?"

"Yeah, I'm cool. Hungry. Where's our waitress?"

"Maxie!" Dab called. "Got an order over here."

Dab's mom ran the Sunny Side. Lots of times Dab waited their table. Bitsy knew for a fact she didn't charge them for a bunch of the stuff they ordered.

The girl hurried over. She, like everyone else, didn't notice Bitsy. *The funny-looking girl sitting alone with her laptop.*

"Sorry," Maxie said. "It's been a little hard to focus today. What can I get you, Ryan?"

"A couple sausage biscuits. And an orange juice. Large."

Bitsy opened the database and typed in what he ordered. Most times he got them with egg and cheese, too. Sometimes with a side of cheese grits.

She wondered why the change today.

"I tried to call Kat," Dab whispered. "Didn't get an answer."

Bitsy smiled. *Of course not. Katherine was grounded. She'd lost her phone and computer.*

Ryan knew that. But he wasn't talking.

"Do you think she's okay?" Sheila asked.

"I'd be so scared. He could have killed *her.*"

"Just think," Joe said, "a murderer. Right here in Liberty."

"Doesn't seem real," Ryan said. "A total freaking nightmare."

"I had Ms. McCall for English a couple years ago. She was pretty cool."

"I wonder how he did it?"

Bitsy realized that she was listening so intently she had forgotten to breathe. She did now, horrified when it came out as a gasp. No one seemed to notice.

"If Tanner puked, it must have been bad."

"I wish I knew."

This was her chance. *Do it, Bits.*

She turned around in the booth and peeked over the top. "I know."

All their eyes went to her. Ryan swiveled. His face was so close she saw the gold flecks in his brown eyes.

"What's your name?" he asked.

"Bitsy. Cavenaugh."

"Yeah." He nodded. "I've seen you around."

She almost swooned. *He had noticed her. If Kat hadn't gotten in the way, maybe she and Ryan would have been together already.*

"You say you know how Sara McCall was killed?"

She nodded, glanced furtively around, then lowered her voice. "With a baseball bat."

Ryan flinched. His friends seemed to freeze.

"How do you know that?" Dab asked.

"My folks." She lowered her voice. "They talked to her cousin Jeremy. We know the family real well."

Ryan cleared his throat. "You want to sit with us?"

"Really? Sure."

Bitsy came around the booth and scooted in beside him. There was barely enough room and she ended up pressed snugly against him. Her heart beat so heavily, she feared he would hear it. That they all would.

"I'm Ryan," he said, smiling brilliantly. "This is Sheila, Joe and Sam. You know Dab."

"Sure. Hi."

"What else did you hear?" Dab asked.

Bitsy looked around her once more, then leaned in. "This is all supposed to be top secret. You can't tell *anyone*. You've got to promise."

"We do," Ryan said. "Right, y'all?"

They agreed. She nodded. "Okay. Kat found the body."

Sheila squealed. "Oh, my God! Gross."

"Wow," Ryan muttered, "that's really fucked-up."

"Her cousin Jeremy's finding her a lawyer."

"A lawyer? Why—"

"She was there. Right? And they always suspect the person closest to the victim."

They all fell silent. Dab broke the silence first. "Kat hated her sister. You know how she always said—"

"No way," Sheila said. "She couldn't do *that*. Could she?"

"Of course not. No way."

"Can we talk about something else?" Ryan said. "This just isn't cool."

Ryan's sausage biscuits arrived. He dug in, as if he didn't have a care in the world.

The waitress looked strangely at Bitsy, as if seeing her for the first time. Bitsy had always imagined it would be this way if she was with Ryan. No longer invisible.

"Can I get you something?" she asked.

"I'm good, thanks."

Ryan ate and the others chatted. Bitsy sat quietly, just letting it all swirl around her. Eventually, they all stood to leave. Bitsy collected her laptop, papers and check to pay for her meal.

"I'll get that," Ryan said, plucking the bill from her fingers.

"Really?"

"Yeah, sure." He looked at the amount and left it and a tip on the table. "Can I walk you to your car?"

"Sure," she said, smiling shyly. "I'd like that."

They exited the Sunny Side. The rest of the group was already in their cars.

"Where're you parked?"

"Over there." She pointed. "The BMW."

"Sweet wheels."

"Thanks. Sixteenth-birthday present."

"Sweet," he said again. "How old are you, Bitsy?"

"Seventeen."

He walked her to her car and opened the door for her. She slid inside, looked up at him. If he kissed her, it would be perfect.

He smiled instead. "Maybe I'll call you sometime, Bitsy Cavenaugh. Would that be okay?"

She looked up at him, cheeks hot. She nodded. "You want my number?"

"I tell you what. I'll give you mine, instead. You got a pen?"

She did. She handed it to him.

He took it and her hand. He turned it palm up, wrote his number across it. His smile widened. "Better not tell your mama whose number that is, she won't like it."

Mama wouldn't notice. Nobody noticed.

He leaned down. "I promise I won't tell anyone what you said."

"Thanks."

"Call me if you hear anything else. Okay?"

She said she would, then watched him walk away. She looked at her palm, the numbers scrawled across it. Her and Ryan Benton. It was really happening.

And all it had taken was Sara McCall dying.

Chapter Thirty-nine

Thursday, June 13
1:55 p.m.

Kat drove there as fast as she dared. Still it took all of forty-five minutes to reach the Mandeville hospital. She parked and ran in. "I'm looking for Stephen Tanner."

The volunteer checked her directory, then looked up, expression sympathetic. "Intensive care. Second floor."

Kat thanked her and hurried for the elevators. They dumped her at the ICU waiting room. The last bastion of hope. Exhausted, hollow-eyed families. Hushed conversations. Tears. Then the occasional fresh recruit. Someone like her, just rushing in. Wild-eyed and worried.

She'd been here before, had done this vigil for a loved one. After the accident, for her mother. Her dad had been killed instantly, but her mom had hung on for two days.

Luke saw her at the same moment her gaze found him. He stood and she crossed to him, feeling suddenly awkward. Would he find it odd that she was here? As odd as she now did? She'd all but flown here, as if it were her loved one in need. Her emergency.

How could she have grown to feel so strongly about Luke in such a short period of time?

"Jeremy called me," she said. "What happened?"

"The doctors aren't sure. He collapsed. He's conscious but groggy."

He shifted his gaze to a point behind her. She looked over her shoulder. A woman. His mother, she realized. They had the same eyes.

She was obviously distraught. And judging by her expression not happy to see Kat. "Katherine, have you met my mother, Margaret?"

"If I have, it's been years. Hello, Mrs. Tanner."

The woman greeted her, then turned to Luke. "The nurse said we could go in for a short visit, one at a time."

"You go," he said.

She nodded and headed that way. Kat watched her go, then turned back to him. "I should go. I just wanted to let you know—"

She stopped. Everything she wanted to say sounded lame. As close as she suddenly felt toward Luke, she wasn't family. The fact was, they hardly knew each other.

"If I can help in any way, just let me know."

"I will." His eyes crinkled at the corners in that way she found both attractive and infuriating. "C'mon, I'll walk you to the elevator."

They reached the bank of elevators. The center car's doors slid open. He stuck a hand in, to hold them open. "I have so much to tell you," he said. "But now's impossible."

"I have things to tell you as well."

"If it looks like I can sneak away for an hour, I'll call you. Is that okay?"

"Perfect."

He stepped away and the doors swooshed closed. As the car descended, Kat wondered what the hell she was doing. She didn't date cops.

And she certainly didn't fall in love with them.

Chapter Forty

Thursday, June 13
2:30 p.m.

Kat swung by the cottage to pick up some things, then headed back over to Jeremy's. When she got there, she found him loading an overnight bag into the trunk of Lilith's Jaguar.

"What's up?" she asked.

"Jackson. A deposition. I'll be gone a day or two." He slammed the trunk. "You'll have the run of the place. Lilith's in Houston. Girls' trip. Martinis and the Galleria. It's going to cost me a fortune."

Saved by shopping, Kat thought, relieved to be spared the awkwardness of facing Lilith without the buffer of Jeremy.

"Taking the Jag, I see."

He grinned. "Lots more fun to drive."

He gave her a quick hug. "I'll only be a phone call away."

"I'll be fine."

He searched her gaze, obviously unconvinced. "The timing sucks, I know, but—"

"Really, Cousin Jeremy. I'm okay."

He nodded, turned and opened the car door. "How's Luke's dad?"

"In ICU. He collapsed and they're not sure why. Don't worry, I'll take good care of the place."

"I know you will." He slid behind the wheel; she caught a whiff of Lilith's perfume. "If you need anything, help yourself. And if you need to move some things over from the cottage, the keys to the Tahoe are in the console."

"I might do that, thank you."

She watched him drive off, then headed inside. The house was quiet. Museum-like, she thought as she crossed the grand foyer, her sandals slapping softly on the marble floor. She flipped on lights as she went, more for the comfort than the light.

Her cell phone rang as she reached the kitchen, and she answered, grateful for the distraction.

"Kat, it's Tish."

She hadn't heard from her Realtor in several days. And truthfully, the purchase of the River-view property had been the last thing on her mind.

"Hi, Tish." Kat laid her car keys on the kitchen counter, then set her purse beside them. "What's up?"

"I'm afraid I've got some bad news. You lost the property."

Kat's heart sank. "How can that be? My financing's in place, what could be—"

"The owner pulled out. Took it off the market. Not only do they not want to sell, they're not even offering the property for lease. I'm really sorry, Kat."

Kat pulled a chair away from the table and sank onto it. "But they accepted my offer. They signed the agreement—"

"In the end, they own the property and can decide not to sell. They're returning your good-faith deposit. In addition, they've offered to reimburse you for all your out-of-pocket expenses."

Kat wanted to cry. To bawl like a baby. Not over losing the property. After the past couple days, she had begun to wonder if opening a Good Earth here was even a good idea.

It was another slap in the face. Another door slammed.

"They found out who I was, didn't they?"

"They didn't say that."

"Of course not," she said. "I could sue them if they admitted it."

"I'm sorry," she said again. "I think the property on the square is still available, if you'd like to take a second look at it?"

"Who owns it?"

"The property on the square?"

"No, the one on Riverview."

"An L.L.C." Kat heard shuffling papers. "R and B Properties, L.L.C."

Ryan and Bitsy.

"Thanks for letting me know, Tish."

"Should I check the availability of the property on the square?"

"No. I'll let you know if I change my mind."

Kat ended the call. She dropped her head to her hands. Not the end of the world, she told herself. Why open a store in a place she was despised? What had she been thinking? It seemed so ridiculously naive now. Waltz into Liberty, expose Sara's killer and instantly earn the love and respect of everyone.

She lifted her head. Maybe she didn't want their love and respect anymore. This wasn't about her. It was about justice for Sara, and she'd achieved that, right? Danny was in jail. Luke would pull together the evidence needed for an arrest and—

What if Danny didn't do it?

Ryan. He'd been at the cottage the night of the murder. He'd admitted it, then all but dared her to prove it.

"Iris Bell is a confused old lady. She can't recall the fact of what happened the day before, let alone ten years ago."

The bastard thought he'd gotten away with murder.

And now he and Bitsy had sabotaged her planting roots here.

A sudden thought occurred to her and she redialed Tish. "Hey," she said when the woman answered, "it's Kat. When did this thing with the sale happen? Was it today?"

"Not more than thirty minutes before I called you. Why?"

"Just curious. Thanks."

That had only been half true: yes, she was curious, but there'd been nothing purposeless about the question. Ryan and Bitsy had quashed her deal after she'd confronted them about the murder. They figured if they could scare her off, they could keep their deep, dark secret hidden.

Kat stood. She would bet one or both of them were behind the graffiti that had greeted her arrival in Liberty, the baseball bat that had followed, the vandalism to her car, the arson.

She just needed proof.

Chapter Forty-one

Thursday, June 13
4:30 p.m.

Kat decided to take Jeremy up on his offer of the Tahoe. She meant to follow Bitsy; she figured being in a vehicle other than her own would keep her from being recognized.

This might be the craziest thing she'd ever

done, launching her own superstealth P.I. thing. But Bitsy and Ryan were guilty as sin, and she meant to prove it.

She tugged the baseball cap a bit lower on her face and slid on her sunglasses. The late-afternoon sun was blinding. The timing was perfect. She hoped to catch Bitsy leaving her shop for the day; if that didn't pan out, she would head out to R&B Imports in an attempt to tail Ryan.

What would Ryan do if he caught her? She remembered his temper, the way fury could ignite in him at nothing more than a wrong word or look, and tightened her fingers around the steering wheel. She didn't want to be on the receiving end of that anger ever again.

Kat pulled into a parking spot in front of a snowball stand called the Sugar Shack. It afforded her a clear view of Bitsy's design shop. The lights were on inside; she saw movement.

Luck, she saw several minutes later, was with her. Bitsy emerged from the shop with another woman. They carried what looked like sample books. As Kat watched, Bitsy helped the woman load them into her car, then went back to the shop. The lights inside snapped off and a moment later Bitsy reemerged, locking the door behind her.

And started across the street, heading right for her.

Had she been found out already?

Kat slid lower in her seat. Bitsy was on the phone; she appeared deep in discussion. She held out her keys and the vehicle directly to Kat's right beeped.

Not Merlin. An Infiniti. Very sleek.

She'd parked right next to Bitsy's vehicle.

Kat grabbed her purse and turned to her left, started digging through it, as if searching for something. She heard Bitsy's voice, the sedan's door open, then slam shut, the engine roar to life. From the corner of her eye, saw the black vehicle pull away.

Kat counted to sixty before following. So she wouldn't be completely obvious—and to give her runaway heart a chance to slow down. She pulled into traffic, two cars behind Bitsy, and managed to maintain that distance despite the dinnertime traffic.

Bitsy swung into the Northlake Shopping Center lot, turning toward the far end and Cafe Toile.

Kat followed her into the center's lot, but turned in the opposite direction. She parked, and saw Bitsy climb out of the Infiniti and cross to the cafe's entrance, where Ryan was waiting. They embraced and headed inside.

For dinner. Perfect. That should tie them up for an hour, at least.

Enough time for her to do her thing. Kat wheeled out of the parking lot, pointing north, toward Covington. She'd made a list of incriminating evidence: black spray paint, spool of red ribbon, gas cans, fleur-de-lis earring. And anything else. She figured she'd know it when she saw it.

She reached Millionaires' Row and the entrance to the Cavenaugh place. She rolled past the main drive and turned onto the gravel lane that led to the stables. Here her vehicle would be out of view of the main house. She would enter the house through the kitchen. If Bitsy had any household staff, they would have left for the day. She knew Bitsy didn't have dogs, because she was allergic to them.

Which left an alarm system. They hadn't had one, back in the day. Not for the main house, anyway. The car barn had been a different story. It'd been wired to the hilt. If Bitsy had one now, she was screwed.

Cross that bridge if you come to it, Katherine.

Ignoring the butterflies in her stomach, Kat climbed out of the SUV and made her way to the house. The Cavenaughs used to hide a spare key under a flowerpot on the back steps. Old habits died hard, but if she couldn't find a key, she would break a window.

Breaking and entering. What she was about to do was so illegal. And so reckless. She wondered if anyone would bail her out of jail if she was caught.

The sun hadn't set, but the light had begun to

change, to soften, bleed out. Kat reached the steps, darted up them. She peered in the door, looking for an alarm panel, relieved when she didn't see one.

You're on the clock. Get moving.

The key wasn't there. She tried above the door, window ledges, under the steps. Nothing.

Her heart sank. She'd been certain it would be there. She eyed the panes of glass in the French door. She'd never purposely broken a window before and wasn't sure how to do it. A rock? Her elbow. She realized she should have brought along a flashlight or some other tool to do it with.

Try the knob, Kat.

It turned. The door eased open.

Her heart seemed to lurch to her throat. Taking a deep breath, she stepped inside. No alarm panel, red light flashing. No bone-chilling growl. Just . . . silence.

Kat thought of Lilith, with her three gates and state-of-the-art alarm system. What would she say about this?

The enormity of what she was doing, the impossibility of her mission hit her. Where did she start? A spool of red ribbon? A can of spray paint? Really?

The stupidity of it came crashing down on her. But it was too late. A light came on at the front of the house. The slam of a car door from the back.

How could they be home already? She glanced at her watch, panicked. They wouldn't have had time to eat. Order, maybe but not—

They had gotten food to go.

She was trapped.

Kat looked frantically around her. She had three options: the powder room off the back porch, the pantry to her right . . .

Or exposure.

She chose the pantry. One of those big, old-fashioned ones. But with nowhere to hide. If either one opened the door, she would be caught.

She eased the door closed just as the light came on in the kitchen. Kat heard the crackle of paper bags. A moment later the snap of the back door shutting.

And . . . silence. Moments passed. The sound of plates and utensils being set up.

"Red? Or white?"

Ryan's voice.

"I don't care."

Sulky, Kat thought.

"What do you want me to say, Bitsy?"

Exasperated. Pissed off.

"There's nothing you can say."

"I can't erase my past. Sorry, babe."

He didn't sound sorry at all.

"You weren't in love with her?"

"I've told you before. No."

"You were with her for her money?"

"Yeah, I thought she'd be my ticket out. I was a kid. I'm not anymore."

"How do I know you aren't with me for my money?"

Sulky had become whiny.

"I'm tired of having this discussion, Bitsy. Either you trust me or you don't. Stay with me or not."

The sound of a wine bottle being uncorked, liquid being poured.

"Don't you think we have bigger problems right now, Bits? Like the fact that psycho bitch is trying to pin Sara's death on me?"

Normally Kat would have taken offense at the label, but considering she was hiding in a pantry, eavesdropping, she supposed it fit.

"I won't let her," Bitsy said.

"Yeah? And how do you stop her? That damn old busybody. She just—"

Iris Bell.

"—needs to die. How old is she, anyway?"

"Like ninety."

"She's an addled old lady. Even if Tanner questions us, how far could it go?"

"Nowhere." Her tone became coaxing. "I wouldn't let anything happen to you. I love you too much."

Kat rolled her eyes. *Please.*

"I love you, too, Bitsy Cavenaugh."

It went silent. Kat imagined they were

embracing. Moments later, the sound of eating, then after a while dishes being set into the sink.

Ryan broke the silence, tone nonchalant. "You never told me you saw me there. At the cottage. Why?"

"It didn't matter."

"Maybe it does to me."

"I didn't care why you were there."

"So, if I tell you I killed her, you won't care?"

Kat held her breath. The silence seemed to stretch on forever.

"Of course I'd care. But you didn't do it."

Kat wondered if he did confess, right now, whether Bitsy would even accept it. She suspected she would choose instead to stay completely in denial.

"How do you know, Bitsy?"

Something in his tone made her frown. As if Ryan was testing Bitsy. Giving her an opportunity to confess.

Kat brought a hand to her mouth. *What if Bitsy had done it?*

"What did Sara say to you that night?"

"That I was a loser. That she'd see me dead before she'd allow me to ruin her sister. *Bitch*."

The way he said the word sent a chill up Kat's spine. Ten years after the fact, and he was still angry over it.

He went on. "I laughed at her. Reminded her

that Kat would be eighteen soon, then we could be together whether she liked it or not."

"What happened then?"

Silence. Long. Pregnant.

"She told me she was sending her away. To boarding school. She laughed at me. And I knew then why Kat hated her so much. And I told her so."

Kat had the sense Bitsy was hanging on every word.

"I saw the bat. I looked at it." He lowered his voice. "I thought about doing it. Pictured it in my head."

Kat realized she was holding her breath. She could see twenty-year-old Ryan grabbing that bat and swinging it. She could picture him in that kind of rage.

"We could run away," Bitsy said. "Just go. You and me."

Kat was reminded of herself, all those years ago, begging Ryan Benton to leave it all behind. Run away with her.

And as he had all those years ago, he refused.

"And leave what we have here? No fucking way. I've worked too hard for what I have. And so have you."

"We'd have each other?"

Hurt. Hope.

But that wouldn't be enough for Ryan Benton. Not now, not ever. She almost felt sorry for Bitsy. She understood. She had been there.

For a long time after the pair left the kitchen, Kat sat in the corner of the pantry, knees to her chest. Afraid to move. Imagining the fury she had heard in Ryan's voice directed at her.

Eventually, the kitchen light went out. She heard the two moving around upstairs. The low hum of a television.

She checked the time on her phone. After ten. Fully dark outside. She stood; her legs and back protested. She opened the door, peeked out. All clear, she saw.

She activated her phone; the screen illuminated. As she turned to close the pantry door, a spot of red caught her gaze.

A spool of shimmery red ribbon.

Chapter Forty-two

Thursday, June 13
10:30 p.m.

It took all of Kat's self-control not to break into a run, tear down the steps and across the yard. It wasn't until she locked herself in the Tahoe that she fell apart.

Stupid. Crazy. On so many levels.

Terrifying. What if they'd caught her? The police would have been the least of her worries.

She looked down at her lap, at the spool of

ribbon. She had taken it on impulse. As proof.

It looked identical to the ribbon that had been tied into a pretty bow around the bat's grip.

Kat started the vehicle, carefully turned around and headed down the gravel lane, not turning on the lights until she reached the main road. She glanced down Bitsy's drive as she passed. Red taillights. One of their vehicles, backing out of the garage.

They'd heard her and were coming after her.

Heart in her throat, Kat floored the SUV, not easing off until she was confident they weren't following her. She breathed deeply, willing her heart to slow. Reassuring herself she hadn't been found out.

What to do now? Kat glanced at the dash clock. Ten thirty. It seemed so much later. Like the middle of the night.

Luke. She needed to recount what she'd overheard, tell him about the ribbon. He would know what to do.

Not the hospital, she thought. She would drive by his house. If his vehicle was there, she would go to the door.

It was there. The lights were on. Kat parked in front, climbed out. She saw the front blinds move. He had seen her.

She reached the front door, rang the bell. He opened it; she stepped inside. And into his arms.

Kat wrapped her arms around his waist, laid her head against his shoulder. It fit perfectly, nestled in the crook of his neck.

"Thank you," he whispered.

"For what?"

"Being here."

Simple. Honest. Vulnerable. She couldn't have wished for anything more.

"How's your dad?"

"Out of ICU. Mom stayed with him."

"Do they know what—"

"Not yet. He's scheduled for an MRI in the morning."

"Is there anything I can do?"

"You already did it."

She stood on tiptoes and kissed him. He kissed her back. They stood that way for minute after minute, exploring each other's mouth. Learning how the other felt and tasted, how they advanced and retreated. Long, drugging kisses that left Kat's legs weak and her head light.

She hadn't come here for this. So many other things had been at the forefront of her mind. Now there was nothing else on it.

He lifted her off her feet; she curved her legs around his waist and he carried her to the bedroom. He laid her on the bed but didn't move to meet her there.

She gazed up at him. "What's wrong?"

"I don't want to move too fast."

She smiled and reached for him. "I don't think you could."

The mattress dipped as he joined her on it. Their mouths met again, this time with more urgency. Their hands searched, explored. They tugged at clothes, greedy to feel skin against skin. Body joining body.

When he entered her, she cried out. It was as if she had been waiting all her life for this moment. For this man.

Afterward, they lay facing each other, hearts slowing as urgency became contentment. For long moments, they simply gazed at each other. Kat studied him, learned his face, every crease and nick. The small curved scar at his right eyebrow, the one on the bottom of his chin.

She touched the one at his eyebrow. "How did this happen?"

He smiled. "Dog bite."

She touched the other. "And this one?"

"Fell off my bike."

She smiled, imagining him as a little boy. "How old were you?"

"Eight."

"For both?"

"Mmm-hmm."

"Who would have thought being eight could be so dangerous?"

"Not nearly as dangerous as nine."

She started to ask what he meant, then

remembered the photo of his brother. "That's how old you were when your brother drowned."

"Yeah." He ran his hand over the dip in her waist, the curve of her hip. "Any scars I should know about?"

"Mine are all on the inside."

He kissed her. Saying without words: *I'm sorry. I understand. I'm here.*

He rested his forehead against hers. "Dad collapsing today, it was my fault. I pushed too hard."

Kat wanted to assure him it wasn't, but she let him talk. There would be time for assurances later. "What happened?"

"We fought. Right before it happened. I was questioning Sullivan, he barged in."

Luke rolled onto his back, gazed up at the ceiling. "I told him I didn't respect him anymore. Then I quit. Gave him my gun and badge."

"I'm sorry."

"After Stevie died, Dad changed. At least toward me. We didn't hang out the way we had when Stevie was alive. Used to be, we'd all go fishing, he'd throw the football with us, take us into New Orleans to see the Saints play. It all stopped."

She smoothed her fingers over his heart, wishing she could take away the hurt.

"For a long time, I tried to make up for losing Stevie. Tried to be the best at everything, to make him happy again. After a while, I just got angry." He met her eyes. "Rebelled. Turned into a regular hell-raiser."

Anything to get his dad's attention, she thought. She wondered if she was a part of that rebellion.

She propped herself on an elbow to see his face. "What about now, Luke?"

"I thought I was over it. That I'd made my peace with it. Until the last few days. You . . . this case . . . He's not the man I thought he was." He paused. "So I walked away. I heard the chair go over. But I thought . . . I didn't even look back."

She felt his regret. The depth of it. She understood how that felt. How it could eat at you.

"Don't do this to yourself." She trailed her fingers across his stubbled jaw. "He knows you love him."

"Does he?" He caught her hand, brought her palm to his mouth. "I'm sorry."

"What for?"

"For what my dad put you through. For the things he missed, the mistakes he made. You were right. You looked guilty, and he looked no further. You know, I never questioned the kind of law-man he was. I always thought he was a good one."

"One case doesn't change that."

"Thank you for that." He kissed her. "But I found some things out so . . . easily. If he'd even looked—" He bit the rest back. "About Danny."

She held her breath, waiting.

"He had—has—a gambling problem. He paid for her ring with winnings."

"Sara didn't know. If she did, she wouldn't have seen him anymore. Because of Mom and Dad."

He nodded. "I think he asked her to marry him, and she turned him down. And then he lost it."

"And killed her." Her voice shook. "That's what you're thinking, isn't it?"

"He was there that night. He admitted it. I didn't get an opportunity to question him further because Dad burst into the interview room."

"That must be what he wanted the loan for, gambling debts."

"No, the loan checked out, just the way he said. But that doesn't change the fact that he saw your sister as his ticket to easy street."

The way Ryan had thought of her.

Ryan. The things she'd overheard. The fury in his voice. Bitsy.

Luke must have seen something of it in her expression. "What?" he asked frowning. "Is something wrong?"

"No. It's about tonight. I—"

Her stomach interrupted her, growling loudly. He laughed and it growled again.

"Sorry," she said, cheeks hot. "I didn't eat."

"C'mon then. Let's take care of that." He rolled off the bed and held out his hand. "We can talk while you're eating."

He offered her one of his T-shirts. And because her feet were cold, a pair of his socks.

"I look ridiculous," she said when they reached the kitchen and she caught a glimpse of herself in the window.

"You look adorable. Sit." He pointed toward the kitchen table. "And I'll see what kind of grub I can whip up quick."

He opened the refrigerator and started poking around. "I've got some leftovers. Gumbo. White beans and shrimp. I could whip up an omelet or—"

"How about oatmeal?"

"Oatmeal," he said, looking back at her, cocking an eyebrow. "Really?"

"I love oatmeal. It's cozy."

"Cozy? I like that. Coming right up."

He prepared her a huge bowl, way more than she could eat at one sitting. With nuts, raisins and cinnamon sugar, it looked delicious. Kat told him so and dug in.

He turned one of the chairs to face her, and straddled it. "Earlier, what did you start to tell me?"

"You're going to be pissed."

"That's not the opening I hoped for."

"Ryan was there, at the cottage, the night Sara died."

He was suddenly still. "How did you find that out?"

Kat filled him in on everything Iris Bell had said, including the number of cars, seeing Wally drive past and, then, about Bitsy. And finally, about Ryan. "She said Ryan was there that night. I confronted him and Bitsy. He admitted he was there, but told me I'd never prove it."

"Dammit, Kat! I thought you were going to leave the investigation to me?"

She took a final bite of the oatmeal and pushed the half-full bowl away. "That's not the part you're going to be pissed about."

"Great. There's more."

So she shared the rest, as simply as possible.

"You broke into Bitsy's house—"

"Not quite. The door was unlocked, so I just let myself in."

"And hid in the food pantry—"

"I thought I'd have more time to look around—"

"What the hell were you thinking?" He stood, crossed to the window, then turned to face her again, pinning her with his angry gaze. "Not only was that illegal, it was stupid. And pointless. What did you hope to find, ten years after the fact?"

"I had a list. Gas can—"

"Which was left at the scene—"

"Fleur-de-lis diamond earring—"

"You were having lunch with Bitsy, how could she have lost hers while vandalizing your car?"

"Black spray paint—"

379

"Would prove nothing. I have a can or two in my garage."

"Okay"—she threw up her hands—"I admit it. It was stupid! But I found something."

"Other than the things you just told me about?"

"A spool of red ribbon. It looks like the same ribbon that was wound around the grip of the bat. It was in the pantry."

He was quiet a moment. "That could be useful. If we established it's the same ribbon. And if we could lift a print from the bow or the bat. But it doesn't prove Ryan or Bitsy had anything to do with Sara's murder."

"Then why would either one of them try to scare me off by leaving the bat?"

"Lots of reasons. For one, Bitsy could be threatened by you being here. Because of your and Ryan's past history."

"I took it."

"What?"

"The spool of ribbon. It's in the car."

Luke massaged his right temple. She caught her bottom lip, watching as he struggled to get a grip.

"I'm guessing by your expression I shouldn't have done that."

"You contaminated it, Kat. Even if we establish it's the same ribbon, we can't use it. It's your word against theirs. And you acquired it illegally."

"I could take it back. Sneak in and—"

"God, no." He sat back down. "Let's focus on the facts. When you confronted Ryan, did you ask him why he was there that night?"

"Oh, yeah. He told me he meant to convince her he was a stand-up guy. He didn't convince her, though." She leaned forward. "Tonight he and Bitsy were fighting. She asked him about that night, his being there."

"And?"

"Sara told him he was a loser. That she would never allow us to be together. He said he saw the bat, that he thought about using it on her."

"Do you think he did?"

Kat shifted her gaze, putting herself back in that moment. "He had a temper. This . . . chip on his shoulder. He would have been furious when she called him that." She nodded. "Yes. I think he could have. But why wouldn't he have admitted it to—"

"Bitsy? His fiancée? He'd be afraid she'd either run, turn him in or someday blackmail him into staying with her."

"What do you think? Did Danny do it? Or Ryan?"

"It's odd, but their motivations are similar. Sara was Danny's ticket to the good life, you were Ryan's."

"That's what I was thinking earlier."

"I'll bring them both in for questioning." His cell phone went off and he answered. "Tanner."

381

He listened a moment, eyebrows drawn together in concern. "Okay, I'll be right there."

"Is it something with your dad?" she asked when he ended the call.

"It is. And he's asking for me."

"You have to go."

"Yes." He kissed her. "I'm sorry, I can't ask you to go with me."

"It's okay. I understand."

"Stay. I'll be back as soon as I can."

Chapter Forty-three

Friday, June 14
6:08 a.m.

For Luke, it was a long, tense night. His dad had been agitated, his heart rate all over the place. They'd had to sedate him and administer an antiarrhythmic drug to try to regulate his heart.

Although the treatment had the desired effect, neither Luke nor his mother had left his side. Morning now, the hospital hummed with activity. Breakfast being delivered, meds administered, doctors making their rounds.

"Morning," the nurse said cheerily as she entered the room. "I'm Karin. I'll be taking care of the chief today."

She crossed to the bed, checked his vitals. "Rise

and shine, Chief Tanner. It's a beautiful day. And you have visitors."

He stirred, opened his eyes. She smiled sympathetically at them. "Everything looks good. The doctor will be in shortly."

"Hey, Pops. You gave us a bit of a scare last night."

"Sorry 'bout that." His dad's voice was thick. "Help me sit up, boy."

His mother took over, cooing and fussing with the pillows. Even as weak as his dad was, Luke could tell the coddling was driving him crazy.

He smiled to himself. Oh, yeah, his dad was feeling much better.

"Luke?"

"Yeah, Pops?"

"Need to talk."

His mother signaled him with a small shake of her head. Luke squeezed his dad's hand. "It'll wait, Pops. I'm not going anywhere."

"But I might be." He looked at his wife.

She hesitated a moment, then agreed. "I'll get us some coffee, Luke."

She bent and kissed her husband. "I'll let you two talk. Just promise you won't get yourself worked up."

After hugging Luke and giving him a "go easy on him" look, she left the room. Luke pulled the chair closer to the bed.

"Last night, Mom said you were asking for me?"

He nodded and motioned him closer. Luke bent his head.

"Afraid cancer's back," he whispered. "They . . . worried it might have spread to my brain."

Luke's gut tightened at the thought. "You don't know that, Pops. This could be nothing more than—"

"I'm not stupid, son."

His dad was scared. Luke saw it in his eyes. He squeezed his hand. "It's going to be okay."

"Might not be." He lowered his gaze. "Have to . . . tell you—"

"Dad—"

"Got to set things right. Just in case."

A lumped formed in Luke's throat. "About the other day, I shouldn't have said those things. I was angry. I—"

"No. You were right. I screwed up. The McCall case, I didn't—"

"It's just one case, Pops. We all make mistakes."

He chuckled, the sound weak and raspy. "I must be sick. Yesterday you were ready to kick my ass."

"We'll work this out. We don't have to do it now."

"Yeah, we do. I did some things I'm not proud of. Things that—"

Luke could hardly hear him and bent his head even closer.

"I don't want to carry around anymore. I don't want to go to my grave this way."

"Dad, you're not going to your grave. Not yet."

"Let me . . . talk. I need to . . . do this." Luke agreed and his dad began. "What you said the other day, about me, you and Stevie . . . it broke my heart. I don't . . . blame you for Stevie." His voice thickened. "I blame myself. I should have been there. I was supposed to take care of you. Protect you. I didn't."

His voice cracked. "Every time I looked at you, I hated myself a little more. So I pushed you away. Turned to alcohol. For years, the booze . . . my life revolved around it. Because it numbed the pain."

Luke couldn't believe what he was hearing. His dad? An alcoholic? How had he kept it hidden?

"Did mom know?" he asked.

"She did. Threatened to leave me if I didn't dry out. Remember the summer the two of you spent a month at Grandma Wells's house?"

He did. And he remembered his mother crying a lot.

"So I sobered up. For a while. Then I'd fall off the wagon, go on a bender. One that would last a week. Or several months. The last time was the night of Sara McCall's murder."

When he spoke again, he sounded like a man consumed by regret. But one on a mission, as well. "Wally called that night."

Luke didn't hide his surprise. "The night he was shot? That wasn't in the report."

"I was drunk. I couldn't . . . I couldn't remember what he said. Truth is, I didn't even remember him calling."

"Then how—"

"His number, in my cell phone. And Trix. He told her he had talked to me. That he gave me the description of the vehicle at the side of the road."

He started to cry. Quiet tears of shame. They rolled down his cheeks. "He may have asked me to assist, I don't know. If I hadn't been drunk, it would have gone down differently. Wally might still be alive."

It could have changed everything. "So what did you do, Pops?"

"I lied. I convinced Trix to lie, too. Begged her. So no one would know. About me. How I failed Wally."

Luke let it all sink in. It was one of those life moments when everything synced. Past and present, fact and feelings. And as it all clicked into place the truth emerged, both staggering and freeing.

"The description of the vehicle?" Luke managed.

"Made it up. Doctored the log." He paused. "You don't have to say anything, I see the disappointment in your eyes. I've never forgiven myself. Or taken another drink."

Luke didn't know what to say, so he simply caught his dad's hand. Curved his fingers around it.

"I broke my oath," he went on, voice wobbling. "And Wally's shooter was never caught."

And for ten years it had been eating at his insides.

"What about the McCall case?" Luke asked softly.

"Something came over me. Like I had to prove something to myself, the sheriff's deputies I'd lied to, and everyone else. That I had the chops. That I wasn't just a good old boy with a badge."

He cleared his throat. "But I promise you, I didn't have a doubt in my mind that Kat McCall got away with murder. Not one doubt. Until yesterday."

He cleared his throat, struggling, Luke suspected, to return to familiar footing. "You say Danny Sullivan was there, at the McCall place that night. He admitted it?"

"He did. Though he claims he didn't kill her."

"And you say he's got gambling issues?"

"Pretty significant ones, from the sound of it."

"I should have known that. I screwed up. Big-time."

"We all do, Pops. The question is, where do we go from here?"

"Let's make this right."

Luke nodded. "We'll do it together. Get it solved."

His dad laid his head back against the pillow. Sagging. Exhausted.

Luke got to his feet. "We'll talk more later. You need some rest."

"Bullshit. Sit your ass back down." He closed his eyes for a moment, then turned them back on Luke. "I've been thinking about Wally. A lot these days."

His voice thickened and Luke offered him the cup of water.

"You're fussing as much as your mother."

"I heard that."

Luke turned. His mother stood in the doorway, a cup of coffee in each hand, her gaze on her husband. With such affection. He wasn't sure how—or why—she still loved him after all these years, but she did. That was the kind of love, the kind of marriage, he wanted someday. Somebody who could put up with his crap and still love him. It was possible. He believed it because he saw it in action.

He thought of Kat and wondered if she believed in it, too.

"The doctor's on his way in," she said. "I just spoke with him. They've scheduled you for an MRI."

Luke started to stand, his dad caught his hand. "I need you, son. Get your badge. Talk to Trixie. She'll give you whatever you need."

The doctor arrived. Luke released his dad's hand, then bent close. "I will, Pops. We'll get it done together."

Luke found Trixie at her desk. "How is he?" she asked first thing.

"Okay this morning. He had a bad night. They've got him scheduled for an MRI this afternoon."

"What can I do?"

"Right now, you're doing it." He paused. "We need to talk, Trix. Can you come into Dad's office?"

Apprehension raced into her eyes, but she nodded and stood. "Sure thing."

Luke closed the door behind them. His badge was on the desk, right where he'd left it. He clasped it onto his belt. "My weapon in the gun safe?"

"Yup. Glad you're back."

He smiled. "Me, too."

She folded her hands in her lap. "You're not firing me, are you?"

"Nope." He sat, looked her square in the eyes. "Dad told me about Wally, what he asked you to do."

The color drained from her face. She dropped her eyes. "Maybe you should fire me."

"You did what your boss asked."

"I could have refused. I should have."

Luke heard the regret. The self-loathing. Same as he'd heard in his dad's voice.

"Wally was a decent man. And for his killer to never have been caught, it's just not right."

Luke agreed. "That's why, knowing the truth now, I want to reexamine what happened that night. How clearly do you remember what Wally said to you?"

"Pretty clearly. I've gone over it so many times in my head. I even wrote it down, so I'd always remember the truth."

Luke nodded. "That's good. Very good."

"I have it here. If you want—"

"Thank you, Trix. That would help."

She went to her desk and retrieved a small, worn spiral notebook. It was held together by a rubber band. She handed it to him. He noticed that her hand shook.

"I knew your dad had a drinking problem. It hadn't interfered with work much, but I'd covered for him when it had. Small stuff. Forgetting to do things. Missing something. I understood. Couldn't judge. I mean, after what happened to Stevie, how could I? If it had been my son, I don't know if I could've gone on."

She fell silent, the expression in her eyes raw. Like it had happened yesterday. "Once it was done," she said softly, "I felt like I couldn't go back."

"It's okay, Trixie. I get that."

She sank back to the chair. Tears rolled down her cheeks. "I always hoped I'd have the chance to tell the truth."

He unwound the rubber band, opened the notebook. And began to read. The facts were there, as he knew them, as were snippets of conversation from that night. She and Wally had chatted. He'd mentioned his girlfriend. And the McCall place.

But the notebook served as a sort of journal, as well, recording ten years of second-guessing and regret.

He shifted his gaze to Trixie. "It was a 'vehicle' at the side of the road, not a sedan. He never mentioned a color or make." She looked down at her hands, then back up at him.

"He'd already talked to your dad, he said." She wrung her hands. "I asked if he'd been by Louanna's. I was craving one of those strawberry-filled doughnuts she made. I asked if he would bring me a couple."

She fell silent and he prodded her. "Then what, Trix?"

"He said he would, then I heard his sirens pop on, then a moment later go off. He said, 'Oh, no worries, be back at you in a few.' I always thought he was just being Wally, you know. Friendly. Now I wonder if it meant something else. Like 'Never mind.'"

No worries, cancel that.

"Why would he do that?" Luke asked.

"This is what I figure. He was calling in to report something suspicious, then it wasn't anymore. He recognized the car. Or the driver."

Luke nodded. "That makes sense to me, Trix. Did you ever talk to my dad about that?"

She shook her head, looking miserable.

"How long was your conversation?"

"A couple minutes, tops."

He nodded. "May I keep the notebook?"

"Of course." She looked away, then back. "I always thought it was too weird that Wally and Sara McCall were murdered on the same night. Do you think the same person could have killed them both?"

"I do, Trix."

"Not Katherine."

"No, not Kat." He stood. "I've got to head back to the hospital. You can reach me there."

She looked up at him, eyes welling with fresh tears. "Can I stay in here for a minute, please?"

To collect herself. "Of course, Trix. Take as long as you need."

Chapter Forty-four

Friday, June 14
8:30 a.m.

Kat awakened on top of the world. She and Luke were lovers. It felt completely and utterly right, in a way nothing had before. How could something so good have grown out of something so horrible?

The day was overcast and gray, but at the same time the world had never looked so beautiful.

She showered at his place, changing into a shirt and shorts she had in her car. She left him a note, then headed for the cottage. She'd noticed the gardenia bushes in the garden there were spilling over with blossoms.

Nothing smelled quite as heavenly as gardenias; Kat had decided Miss Iris would enjoy having some.

When she reached the cottage, Kat went inside for scissors and a bowl. Gardenias had short stems; the trick was to float the blossoms in a bowl of water. And to not touch the petals. Once touched, the snowy white blossoms browned.

Kat carefully clipped a bunch of the blossoms, setting them in the bowl. When she got to her neighbor's, she would fill it with water. They would last for days, filling the room with fragrance. With the amount of blooms on the bushes, she would be able to keep the old woman in gardenias for weeks.

She laid the shears on the porch step and headed for her neighbor's. The woman's living room light was on; Kat could hear the TV. She knocked on the door. She got no answer and knocked again, loudly. "Mrs. Bell," she called, "It's Katherine, from across the street."

She still got no response and Kat realized the woman couldn't hear her over the television. Kat smiled to herself. *Yet she could hear a pin drop across the street.*

Kat shifted the bowl of flowers and tried the door. It was unlocked, and she opened it and poked her head inside.

Fox News. Another scandal in Washington.

"Miss Iris, it's Katherine." Still no answer. "I've brought you some gardenias."

Kat stepped inside. She saw the woman, in the recliner in front of the news. She had the remote in her hand. She might be asleep, though over the years, Kat had wondered if the woman ever slept.

"Can I help you?"

Kat spun around, nearly dropping the bowl in surprise. The woman on the porch behind her wore nursing whites. "I'm Katherine McCall, from across the street. I've brought Miss Iris some flowers."

"She'll be so pleased." The woman smiled. "I'm Viola. I help Mrs. Bell out a few days a week."

"I think she's asleep. I called out, but she didn't answer."

"Asleep?" The woman chuckled. "Not likely. She gets pretty wrapped up in her Fox News." She waved Kat in. "Let's get some water on those blossoms."

"I can just leave them with you? If she's busy—"

"She'd be very disappointed if she didn't get the chance to thank you and visit a bit."

And visit a bit. Kat smiled. "I would hate for her to be disappointed."

"Go say hello. I'll get those."

Kat nodded, handed her the bowl and headed into the living room. "Good morning, Miss Iris," she said brightly. "How are you today?"

She came around the recliner and not wanting to startle her, touched the woman's shoulder lightly. The woman's arm flopped over, the remote slipped from her hand.

Kat sucked in a sharp breath. Miss Iris wasn't sleeping. She was dead.

While Kat called 911, Viola checked Miss Iris's pulse. Kat had known she would find none. Just as she knew the EMTs, the coroner and the police were all a formality. There would be no reviving her neighbor.

Neither she nor Viola cried. They sat together on the porch step, waiting for the ambulance and police.

"She's at peace now," Viola said. "With her Ned."

"I'm sorry to say, I didn't know her that well."

Viola smiled. "Some folks found her too crusty. An opinionated busybody. And she might have been. But she also had a heart of pure gold."

Kat heard the sirens. "Did she have kids?"

"And grandkids. They all live out of state. They come see her every once in a while, but not that often. They're busy, I don't blame them. Her daughter offered to buy her a place near them, but she refused to leave Liberty. Even to go see them. She was planted here. In Liberty and this house."

The ambulance arrived and Viola directed the EMTs inside; they reappeared moments later. The pair, a man and a woman, tromped back out to the porch.

Viola looked at them. "She's gone to her reward," she said.

"Yes, ma'am," the man agreed. "Coroner's on the way. Police, too."

"And here they are now. Y'all have a nice day."

Kat followed her gaze. A hearse rolled up the block, followed by a Liberty cruiser.

She and Viola stood. The Liberty coroner, who was also the local mortician, climbed out the passenger side of the vehicle. His driver also served as his photographer and body mover.

The cruiser pulled up behind the hearse and Luke climbed out. At the same moment, the sun peeked out from behind a cloud.

Oh yeah, she thought, she had it bad. Real bad.

Chapter Forty-five

When Luke learned from Reni that Iris Bell had died and that Kat had called it in, he figured he'd better make the scene himself.

Some circumstances were just too odd to ignore.

He joined the coroner and they walked together to the porch. Kat stood waiting, and Luke found it difficult not to stare at her like a horny teenager. The night before had been pretty damn spectacular.

"I didn't expect you today," she said when he reached her. "How's your dad?"

"Better. Having an MRI this afternoon. Kat, this is Charlie Pride, Liberty's coroner. Charlie, Katherine McCall."

"Yes, that's my real name," he said, smiling. "Good to meet you, Ms. McCall."

He turned to at Luke. "I'll go in and see Miz Iris."

"I'll go with him," Viola said.

Luke nodded and turned back to Kat. "I can't stop thinking about last night."

"I can't either."

She actually blushed. He wanted to trail his finger over her rosy cheek but slipped his hands into his pockets instead.

He smiled. "So, how did you come to be over here this morning?"

"I thought she'd enjoy having some of my gardenias. I'd noticed them yesterday. I came over, knocked, heard the TV and tried calling out, but—"

"She didn't answer."

"Yes. I was in the process of going in when Viola arrived."

"The door was unlocked?"

She nodded.

"And Miss Iris was dead?"

"In her recliner." Kat's eyes welled with tears. She blinked at them, making a sound of embarrassment. "I feel so stupid, I hardly knew the woman."

He squeezed her hand. "She'd had a long, full life, Kat. She was ready to go."

"Luke?"

Charlie stood at the door. "Could you come here a minute?"

"Sure." He told Kat he'd be right back. He passed Viola on the porch. He frowned at her expression.

"What's up, Charlie?"

"I think Miz Iris had a little help passing on."

"Excuse me?"

"I think she was murdered."

The man could have knocked him over with a feather. "No way."

"You take a look. I'm a coroner, not a pathologist or detective."

Luke did, squatting in front of her. Purple and red splotches. On her lips. Her face and eyes. Petechial hemorrhages. An indication of suffocation.

Luke sat back on his heels, stunned. Somebody had murdered harmless old Mrs. Bell.

Maybe not so harmless. Not to everyone.

It couldn't be a coincidence. Yesterday Kat had pried information from Mrs. Bell about the night Sara died. And now she was dead. Someone had felt it necessary to silence her for good.

He lifted his gaze. "You were right, Charlie. Looks like we've got ourselves a crime scene."

Kat took it hard when she heard the news. She sank to the porch step. Dropped her head into her hands. "My fault," she said.

"It's not."

"I got her killed. Asking questions. Confronting people."

"Listen to me." He sat on the step beside her, took her hands in his. They were as cold as ice. "You did nothing wrong."

She searched his gaze. "I just talked to her yesterday. When did . . . do you know when it happened?"

"Sometime last night or early this morning. Rigor and lividity suggest ten or twelve hours ago. Pathologist will get an internal temp."

"Who did you talk to about this, besides me, Ryan and Bitsy?"

"No one else."

"You're certain?"

"Yes." She pressed her lips together. "They killed her to keep her quiet. She knew their secrets."

Her eyes widened as if she'd just thought of something. "Danny's still in jail."

"Yeah, he is."

"So he couldn't have killed her."

"That's right."

"I forgot to tell you something. It . . . last night, it didn't seem important. But now—" She curved her arms around her waist. "Oh, God. It was Ryan. Or Bitsy."

"Okay," he said softly, "calm down. Just tell me."

"I parked by the stables. There's a gravel road, just beyond the main drive to the house. I figured I'd be less likely to be seen."

She dragged in a broken-sounding breath. "I didn't leave the house until it'd been quiet a pretty long time. I heard the TV upstairs but it was totally quiet on the main floor. I didn't even turn my headlights on until I reached the main road. But when I passed the main drive, I glanced that way and saw one of them leaving the house."

"Which one?"

"I don't know. One of the cars, backing out of the garage. I thought they were coming after me and I panicked."

And hauled ass out of there.

"But they didn't follow you?"

"No." She brought a trembling hand to her mouth. "And last night, when they were arguing, Ryan said that she, Mrs. Bell, just needed to die."

Luke stood. "Reni and I are going to finish up here, then I'm bringing in Ryan and Bitsy. They have explaining to do."

"What should I do?"

"Go to Jeremy's and wait." She made a sound of frustration and he glared at her. "I need to be certain you're safe."

"I'm fine."

"Kat, someone out there was willing to kill a confused old woman to keep their secret safe. You're the one who's stirring it all up. So how much do you think they'd like to get rid of you?"

He was glad to see the fear that shot into her eyes. "C'mon, I'll walk you to your car."

She climbed in, rolled down the window. He bent. "Straight to Jeremy's. Nowhere else."

She agreed. He watched her drive off. As he walked back across the street, his cell went off. It was Frank Pierre. Danny Sullivan wanted to talk.

Chapter Forty-six

"Mr. Pierre. Danny." After greeting both men, Luke sat. He and Reni had processed the Bell scene, canvassed the neighbors; Luke had contacted Miss Iris's next of kin. That had been the hardest part. Explaining that their mother was dead. And that it looked like she had been murdered.

But she lived in Liberty, her daughter had said. That doesn't happen there.

It had given Luke a glimpse into how his father had felt all those years ago.

"We heard about your dad," Pierre said. "How is he?"

"Out of ICU. Having tests today."

"We wish him well."

"Thank you. I appreciate that." He set the recorder up. "Ready?" Sullivan nodded and Luke hit RECORD.

"When we last met, you admitted you were there the night Sara McCall was murdered. Is that correct?"

"Yes."

402

"And today you're here to set the record straight?"

"That's right."

"To confess to the murder of Sara McCall."

"No! I didn't kill her!"

"Why do you want to talk now?"

"I should have come forward with this years ago."

"Why didn't you?"

He lowered his eyes. "Because I was afraid. I'd already lost Sara, I couldn't lose my job, too."

"My heart bleeds, dude." Luke met his gaze. "Here's what I think. You know you're in a shitload of trouble. In the heat of the moment, you admitted on tape that you were there the night Sara was killed, but my dad's health crisis gave you the opportunity to come up with a story. And time to get it good and memorized."

"No! What I'm going to tell you is the absolute truth."

And nothing but the truth. Luke had heard that one before. But in this case, considering the turn of events, this time it could be true.

"Okay, Danny, let's hear it."

Danny Sullivan
2003

The night of the murder

Danny parked in front of Sara's cottage. He'd spent the last two days reeling from her rejection. Raging over Jeremy Webber's interference. Plotting how to win her back—and crush Webber.

Danny didn't get it. He'd thought the ring would sway her. He thought he'd pop the question, dazzle her with the rock and all her worries about his gambling would melt away. It'd had the opposite effect. They'd fought. She'd sobbed that he didn't know her at all.

He'd given her a couple of days, then called, begged her to see him. Finally, she'd agreed he could stop by. He'd heard the tiniest quiver in her voice. The hint of longing.

She loved him. He knew she did. He could convince her they were meant to be together. That he would give up the casinos. He would promise her. For her, he would do anything.

He climbed out of his truck. Took a deep breath. He had considered that instead of giving him another chance, she meant to give him the final heave-ho. Had considered it, but not dwelled on it. He couldn't go there. He didn't have a Plan B.

He smoothed a hand over his freshly cut hair. He'd dressed carefully, wearing the khakis and the white Oxford cloth shirt she liked best. Hat in hand, he thought. He hated the feeling. That he was begging. Wrong-side-of-the-tracks Sullivan crawling back to the Uptown have-it-alls.

He shook his head. Sara wasn't like that. She wasn't like Webber or her crazy sister. Whatever she wanted, he told himself. Anything. She was worth it.

He climbed the porch steps, crossed to the door. He stopped, patted his pocket to make certain the ring was there. He knocked. The door wasn't closed tightly and eased open. Probably Kat's doing, he thought. Everything was these days.

"Sara," he called. "It's me. Danny."

She didn't answer and he pushed the door wider. Something on the floor caught his eye. He stared at it, frowning. What the hell was that? A piece of a sandwich? And drops of something dark. He called out again, pushed the door the rest of the way open and stepped inside.

Then he saw. He realized.

Blood. A lot of it.

His stomach raced to his throat. He brought a hand to his mouth, holding the sickness back.

Sara. In a broken heap. Nearly unrecognizable.

He turned and ran. Across the porch, down the walk. He yanked the driver's door of the pickup open and hauled ass inside. Only then did the howl of pain rip from his chest. Not Sara. His sweet Sara . . . She didn't deserve this. Who could have—

He dropped his head into his hands, rocking back and forth, moaning. What to do . . . who to—

The police. He had to call the police.

Danny snatched his phone from the center console and flipped it open. They would find who did this. They—

Would think he had done it. Maybe. Because she had turned him down. The marriage proposal. The loan. They'd interview Jeremy, folks from the casino, Dale Graham. It'd all come out.

And if the cops named him a person of interest? The school system would want to distance themselves, as quickly as possible. Parents would demand he be removed from his post.

He'd be ruined.

Danny dragged a shaking hand through his hair. He was sweating, he realized. His heart racing, thundering against the wall of his chest.

No one had to know he'd been here. The street was dark. No one had been by. He could just go now. Drive off.

Coward. Weasel.

He knew it was true. But he told himself he couldn't help Sara. That nothing would help her. Now he had to protect himself.

Danny started the truck and eased away from the curb, not even putting on his headlights. He had to put as much distance between him and this as possible.

Chapter Forty-seven

Luke propped the baseball bat in the corner of the interview room. The corner directly across from where he would first ask Bitsy, then Ryan, to sit while he questioned them. The bright red bow seemed to grin at him.

He hoped it would taunt one of them. If it had been their handiwork, they would be unable to ignore it.

A neat trick developed by the Behavioral Science Unit of the FBI.

Luke had timed the sequence of events carefully, sending one of his officers to retrieve Cavenaugh first. While she was being interviewed, that same officer would retrieve Benton. When she was leaving, she would see her beloved waiting to come in.

And all manner of fears and anxieties would beset her. And Luke would have them both right where he wanted them. Of the two, Ryan seemed the more likely to have done it, but this game was still anyone's.

Luke stood and held out a hand as she entered the room. "Ms. Cavenaugh, thank you for coming in."

"It's not like I had a choice."

She shook his hand. He noted hers was clammy. "Have a seat."

She did. He indicated the recorder. "I'm going to tape this interview."

She made a sound of disbelief. "You've got to be joking?"

"Not at all, Ms. Cavenaugh. This isn't a joking matter."

She shifted her gaze. Caught sight of the bat. He saw it in the shock that rippled across her face.

She jerked her gaze back to his, but didn't mention the bat. She laid her small, expensive-looking clutch in her lap. "I know what this is about."

"You do?"

"Let's not play games, Sergeant Tanner. I know you and Kat are romantically involved. So, of course, she's told you that she spoke to her crazy old neighbor, who supposedly told her both Ryan and I were at the cottage the night Sara was murdered."

"Is it true?"

"No. Absolutely not."

So that was the tack they were going to take. Deny now, and let him try to prove it.

Only now, Iris Bell was dead.

It pissed him off.

"Of course, you can only speak for yourself."

"Pardon?"

"About being there that night."

"Of course," she said quickly. "But Ryan and I have talked about this. He told me he wasn't there."

Lie number one. "And you believe him."

Her fingers tightened on the clutch. "Absolutely I believe him."

Number two. "Let's just focus on you, if you don't mind?"

"Certainly."

"What was your relationship with Iris Bell?"

"I had no relationship with her."

"None?"

"None."

"You didn't befriend the old woman so that you could spy on your friend Kat McCall? Because you felt she stole your boyfriend?"

"Did she tell you that? Pathetic. Ryan and I had never even met at that point."

"But you'd seen him. And considered yourself in love with him."

"Poor Kat," she murmured. "She's either obsessed or delusional."

Luke kept his thoughts to himself, though not without effort. "How badly would you like Kat to disappear?"

"Excuse me?"

"Leave Liberty. Get out of your and your fiancé's hair."

"For all I care, she can hang around forever."

He smiled. "C'mon, Ms. Cavenaugh. Be honest, she's thrown your perfect little world into turmoil."

"Turmoil? I don't think so." She laughed lightly. "Yes, she's been an annoyance. An irritation. So what? Life's full of them."

"Have you threatened Katherine McCall? In any way?"

Her gaze skittered briefly toward the bat, then back to him. "No."

"Didn't send her anonymous letters? Graffiti her home? Anything like that?"

"No."

"Didn't threaten her with a baseball bat?"

Again, her gaze flickered to the bat, then away. "No."

He gave her a moment to ask about it—the elephant in the middle of the room—but she didn't. The bat with its pretty bow was the last thing she wanted to talk about.

"Have you heard the news? About Iris Bell?"

She frowned. Apprehension crept into her expression. "No, what about her?"

"She's dead."

"Oh my God."

She looked shaken. He commented on it.

She visibly pulled herself together. "She was a nice lady. It was a shock, that's all."

"I thought you didn't know her?"

"I didn't say that. I said we didn't have a relationship."

"Why do you think someone would want her dead?"

"I don't know what you mean. Surely she died of natural causes."

"No, unfortunately not."

"I don't understand."

"Iris Bell was murdered last night."

Bitsy went white. Luke continued. "It wasn't a robbery, nothing was taken. And she didn't have a big life insurance policy. Nothing like that."

She didn't comment. The silence stretched between them. Luke leaned slightly forward. "Where were you last night, Ms. Cavenaugh?"

"Home. We both were."

"I'm only asking about you. All night?"

"Yes."

"Can anyone confirm your whereabouts?"

"Ryan. Of course. He was with me. All night."

"Never out of your sight?"

She nervously bit her lip. "That's right."

"And your cell phone records will confirm that."

She didn't know, he saw it in her eyes. In the twitch that had developed in her left.

Ryan had left the house. It had been him Kat had seen backing out of the garage.

"Are you thinking what I'm thinking?" he asked.

"I have no idea what you may be thinking," she said stiffly. "I'm not a mind reader."

He tipped his head, studying her. "I'm thinking what an odd coincidence this is. The very same day Iris Bell tells Kat that she saw Ryan Benton at the cottage the night Sara was murdered, she ends up dead."

She stood. "I think it would be better if I spoke to a lawyer before I said anything further."

"Of course." He followed her to her feet. "We're done for now anyway."

Her gaze skittered toward the bat. He took his shot. "Pretty bow, isn't it? Nice ribbon."

She jerked her gaze back to his. "Pretty ordinary, I'd say. If that's all, I'll have my counsel call you."

Chapter Forty-eight

Friday, June 14
1:46 p.m.

Luke was fired up. Cavenaugh had responded just as he had expected her to. The icing on the cake had come when he walked her out and they'd run smack into Reni and Benton. It had been a moment perfectly pregnant with tension. With him and Reni standing there, all the couple had been able to do was say hello and exchange meaningful glances.

He loved it when a plan came together.

"Have a seat, Ryan," Luke said, shutting the door behind them.

"What the hell is that?"

Luke turned. "What?"

Benton pointed to the corner. "The bat. What the hell's that all about?"

"A couple of the guys. Joking around."

"Some sick joke, man."

"That's cops. Gallows humor, gets us through the day."

Benton frowned and sat. Luke got the feeling that he didn't buy the explanation, but hadn't yet put his finger on the real reason.

"I don't know what you hope to accomplish here, Tanner, but I promise you, you're wasting your time."

"Whatever." Luke sat. "Just so you know, I'll be recording this."

"Just so you and your low-tech tape recorder know, you have about five minutes. I hear one word I don't like, I'm lawyering up."

"Understood." Luke folded his hands on the desk in front of him. "I want to talk about the night of Sara McCall's murder."

"Figured as much."

"I hear you were there that night."

"Where'd you hear that?"

"You admitted it to Kat McCall."

"Did I?"

"You're a pretty cool customer, Benton."

413

"I'm not trying to be."

"Previously, you admitted to me that ten years ago you and Kat were in a relationship."

"Screwing around. Yes."

"And that you wanted her for her money."

"Until she beat her sister to death. Too freaky for me."

"What if I told you that your fiancée confirmed what Kat McCall told me. That you were there that night."

His eyebrows shot up. "Bitsy? I find that hard to believe."

"Why do you say that?"

"Because I know Bitsy. And I know the truth."

"And what is the truth?"

"Kat McCall's leading you around by your dick. And this is all a big load of crap. Are we done here?"

"Not hardly. I'm afraid I have some bad news." Luke paused for effect. "Iris Bell is dead. But you already know that, don't you?"

Benton frowned, the slightest hesitation edging into his voice. "Why would I know that?"

"She was murdered. Suffocated. Only hours after telling Kat she saw you over at the cottage the night Sara died."

Still no reaction. Luke leaned forward. "Where were you last night, Ryan?"

"Home. In bed." He narrowed his eyes. "Which

you already knew, because Bitsy told you the same thing. You're just fishing."

"I think you're lying. You wanted Iris Bell dead because she was the one person who could place you at the scene of Sara's murder."

Luke got a reaction, though not necessarily the one he wanted. Benton stood. "I'll be calling my lawyer now, Tanner."

"Sit back down, Benton. I'll bring the phone to you."

Chapter Forty-nine

Friday, June 14
2:05 p.m.

Kat sat on the top porch step and gazed across the street at Iris Bell's place. The police had left hours ago, the hearse carrying the woman's remains before that. During that time, Kat had forced herself to pack a suitcase of things to take to Jeremy's; she'd called the contractor Luke had recommended, and had begun sifting through the destruction in the front room.

But no matter how busy she made herself, she couldn't stop thinking about her neighbor. She'd gotten the woman killed, by asking questions then running off half-cocked. Impulsive and stupid.

The guilt was tearing her apart.

She dropped her head to her drawn-up knees. It should have been her. Iris Bell hadn't done anything but be a little nosy.

"Hello, Miss Katherine."

She lifted her head. The postman. Ronnie. He'd been their postman back when she moved into the cottage with Sara. She was surprised he hadn't retired by now. "Ronnie, you're still working this route?"

"Yes, ma'am. Been awhile since I've seen you."

"Ten years."

He gestured toward the fire damage. "Sorry about your house."

"Me, too. What have you got for me?"

"A bundle of forwarded mail."

She stood and met him on the walkway. He handed her the mail.

"You must be back for good."

"I'd thought so, but—" She smiled. "Thank you, Ronnie. I appreciate this."

He searched her gaze. "It's not right. Not at all. Anything I can do for you?"

She forced a smile. "No, but thank you."

He nodded, turned to go, then stopped and looked back. "For what it's worth, I never thought you did it. Just wanted you to know that."

Kat sank back to her porch step, clutching the bundle of mail. Small miracles, she thought. Little glimmers of light in the darkness. Did God send those, she wondered. Or was it just some weird, cosmic coincidence?

She lowered her gaze to the mail. She removed the rubber band that held it together and sifted through. Bills. An invitation to a friend's birthday party. Correspondence from her insurance provider.

And a legal-size envelope addressed to her by hand, no return address.

Her fan.

Kat stared at it, mouth going dry. She didn't want to open it. She didn't know if she could take any more animosity aimed her way.

But she couldn't not open it, either.

Taking in a deep breath, then letting it out slowly, she loosened the flap, slipped the single sheet of unlined paper out. The message had been written with what appeared to be the same blue pen, in the same clumsy hand.

WHO DO THE POLICE ALWAYS LOOK AT FIRST?

JUSTICE FOR SARA.

Chapter Fifty

Friday, June 14
3:15 p.m.

Luke sat back down with Ryan Benton and his lawyer. With the attorney present, Benton had completely lost the attitude. Suddenly, the man was helpful to the point of conciliatory.

"From what I could tell, Iris Bell was a sweet old lady. I have no idea why someone would want her dead. It's disgusting to me that someone would do that."

"I feel like I have a case of whiplash from your change of tune, Benton. What's up?"

He lifted a shoulder. "When you grow up the way I did, Tanner, your first instinct is to push back."

That made sense. Luke gave the guy kudos—either for honesty or brilliance. A jury would eat that up.

"Where were you last night?"

"Home. With Bits."

"All night?"

"Yes. Except for about a half hour."

This was new. "And then?"

"Up to the mini-mart for ice cream."

"At that time of night?"

"My lady has a sweet tooth."

"What flavor?"

"Chocolate chip."

"Why didn't you tell me this earlier?"

He smiled sheepishly. "I was too busy being a hard-ass."

Luke got a glimpse of why the ladies liked him. *Charming. Mercurial.* "How long were you gone?"

"Half an hour, tops."

"He has the receipt," the lawyer offered.

"I do."

Benton slid it across the table to Luke. He glanced at it. Ice cream. Ten forty p.m.

"In addition," the attorney continued, "I've called the market. They have a security tape, which they have agreed to hand over."

Luke kept his frustration from showing. This was not going as he'd hoped. "Let's talk about the night Sara McCall was killed. Were you there?"

"Absolutely not."

Luke had expected him to change his tune there, as well. Apparently, his magnanimity went only so far. "C'mon," he coaxed, "Iris Bell placed you at the scene and you admitted as much to Kat McCall."

"Both according to Kat McCall," the lawyer interjected. "My client's jilted lover."

Luke gazed at the two men. Everything he could throw at Benton now would also be Kat's word against his. And right now, Benton sounded damn convincing.

Luke wanted to mess with him awhile, just because he could. He suppressed the urge. Benton wasn't going anywhere. And neither was he. Time was definitely on his side.

"Thank you for coming in," he said, standing. "I'll be in touch."

Chapter Fifty-one

Friday, June 14
3:33 p.m.

Kat stared again at the single sheet of paper, the boldly scrawled message. The police looked at family first. Those closest to the victim. Kat knew that only too well. If no suspect emerged, they moved out from there, in ever widening circles.

Family. Her. And Jeremy. No, not him. It would kill her. But she had no one else. Just Jeremy and—

Lilith.

That was stupid. Ubercontrolled Lilith? And why? Jeremy and Lilith had been newlyweds. Kat and Sara had only just begun to get to know her.

Kat made a sound of frustration at her own malleability. She was going to take this seriously? An anonymous letter. Really?

Stupid, Kat. She got to her feet. Her fan was messing with her. The same as he always had. If her fan knew so much, why had he sent this to her Portland address?

She locked the cottage and started down the walk. Could the letter be an attempt to throw her off? She could see Bitsy or Ryan doing this.

Anger surged up in her. The bastards. Hadn't she lost enough? Now, he—or she—wanted her to distrust and fear her own family.

She resisted the urge to crumple the letter and toss it in with all the refuse from the fire. Instead, she stuffed it into her purse.

A car eased past, but for once its occupants weren't gawking at her. Today, they were staring toward Miss Iris's place.

The small-town communication network, hard at work.

"I saw you sneaking out again. That night. I called the police."

"But I didn't, Mrs. Bell. I was locked in my room, remember?"

But the woman had insisted. Out the back, Miss Iris had said.

The bloody footprints. They'd stopped at the kitchen sink. As if the killer had disappeared.

An earring. "Bitch" scratched into the side of her Fusion. The perfect red bow, tied around the bat's grip.

At the trial, the prosecutor had posed the

question: Did the killer leave the scene naked?

Of course not, he'd continued. Because the killer lived there.

Kat brought a hand to her mouth. The killer wouldn't have had to strip and leave naked, not if she could have simply changed clothes.

Who do the police always look at first?

Family. Those closest to the victim.

Another woman. There was only one.

Lilith.

Kat ran the rest of the way to the Tahoe. She climbed in and started the engine. It roared to life, oddly mirroring the way she felt inside. As if her every nerve ending, every instinct had just come to life.

She had Jeremy's house to herself. If there was anything there to be found, she would find it. She would tear the place apart if she had to.

As she drove, her thoughts raced. Why would Lilith have done it? The woman had everything. She'd been a newlywed, new house, new career, bright new life. Why chance losing it all?

Kat flexed her fingers on the steering wheel. Or was she suspicious of Lilith because she didn't like her? Or because Lilith had made it clear she wasn't wanted here? That she resented having Kat stirring up the past?

Kat didn't think so. It all fit. The journal, for one. That's why it had disappeared. The "why Lilith would do it" had been written in those pages. Ryan would have had no cause to steal it. Nor would Bitsy. Not a stranger. Danny would have, but he was no longer a suspect.

Lilith. *No one else was left.*

Kat's thoughts were flying. She glanced at the speedometer and saw that she was as well. Going sixty in a thirty-five. She slowed. Focused on the road and traffic.

She reached the first gate. The old security guard from the night of the fire. The same pitying expression. But this time she didn't turn around.

She made her way to the second gate. Then the third. She hit the garage door opener and the door rumbled up.

She rolled inside. Jeremy's Mercedes. That's right, he'd taken Lilith's Jag.

Kat let out a long breath. She lowered the door behind her. Quiet, save for the thunder of her racing heart and the sound track playing in her head. She swung her door open, started to climb out, then stopped. How long had Jeremy and Lilith had this SUV? Ten years? They kept it for Jeremy's occasional excursions to hunt in Mississippi or trips down to Lafitte to fish.

She clambered back in, popped open the glove box. The user's manual. Proof of Insurance. Certificate of registration. A few receipts.

She moved on to the console. The spool of ribbon winked up at her and she hesitated. Not twenty-four hours ago, she had convicted Ryan and Bitsy; a day before that, Danny Sullivan.

You're losing it, Kat. You've let the fan into your head. He's messing with you.

Dammit. She didn't know what to believe, what was true and what was not. She snatched up the ribbon. And caught her breath.

A gun.

Kat stared at it. She knew nothing about guns, except that they scared her.

Lilith was a security freak. Three gates. A gun in every vehicle. Maybe even in her bedside table. It wouldn't surprise her.

Hands shaking, she picked it up. Heavy. And cold against her palm. She quickly laid it aside. Dug through the rest of the console's contents. Nothing. Stuff. The kind of stuff that accumulated over years of driving.

Kat replaced the contents, pausing at the gun. Was it loaded? Probably, though she didn't even know how to check. She put it back where she'd found it and headed into the house. She knew exactly where she would start.

The master bedroom.

She reached it. A room fit for a king and queen. A giant four-poster bed. A separate sitting room. Two huge walk-in closets, a His and a Hers. She'd never realized Jeremy was so vain—he had at least fifty suits. Two dozen pairs of shoes.

Lilith's walk-in was almost double the size and had an island in the center, its granite top big enough to lay out a suitcase. Drawers, shoe racks. Kat turned slowly around, almost dizzy at it all.

Kat began with the drawers. Forcing herself to go slowly, resisting the urge to dig through, tumble and toss garments. If this didn't pan out, she didn't want to have burned her bridges and lose access to the property.

Or to Jeremy's life.

He wouldn't believe her, not without proof. She had to find something.

She came up with nothing. She returned to the bedroom proper. Tried both bedstand drawers. Again, nothing. Not even the gun she had been certain Lilith would have had tucked there.

The dresser proved just as disappointing. The woman was almost obsessively neat. Lilith would notice an uneven line, a garment with the slightest rumple.

The opulent master bath was next. Who lived like this? Kat wondered. A chandelier above the huge whirlpool tub? A built-in dressing table? Lilith must look at herself in the mirror here, as she applied beauty products and cosmetics, and feel like royalty.

Mirror, mirror on the wall . . .

Lilith, the wicked queen. Kat smiled grimly and headed for the dressing table. And there, in a small crystal dish, she found a single fleur-de-lis diamond earring.

Bitch. She pictured the word, etched onto her

brain, the same as it had been into the side of her car.

Her instinct told her to snatch it. But she remembered what Luke had said about contaminating evidence. She slid her iPhone out of her back pocket and snapped several pictures of it there, sparkling up at her from Lilith's dressing table.

She needed that journal.

Reinvigorated, Kat picked up her pace. Among some boxes stacked in the far corner of the closet, Kat found a jewelry case. Costume jewelry, Kat saw. Faux pearls, high school class ring, holiday accessories. Jewelry Lilith wouldn't be caught dead wearing, not anymore.

Kat rifled through the contents. And stopped when her gaze landed on it. A key. Old-fashioned. A skeleton key.

Kat retrieved her phone once more, took several shots of it nestled there, among Lilith's things. Tears stung her eyes. She wanted to weep. She fought the tears back, remembering. The words burned onto her brain: *"Your sister locks you in your room once, only once ever, and it just happens to be on the same night she's killed? . . . If Sara locked you in, how did you find her the next morning? . . . Your sister never locked that door . . . You made that up. In the hopes it would be an alibi . . ."*

All questions that had tormented her for years.

And now she knew.

She knew.

Kat's tears dried. She was ending this now. The bitch had murdered her sister. And she was going to make her pay.

Luke could take it from here. He *needed* to take it from here. Smiling grimly to herself, she called up a photo of the earring and messaged it to Luke's phone, then sent him two of the key.

He would understand. And waste no time.

She couldn't leave the key, she thought. It was too important. Kat hurried back to the island, to the drawer of scarves she had seen. She plucked a small one from the stack. Using the scarf, she lifted the key, folded the fabric around it and tucked it in her pocket.

Carefully, she restacked the boxes, then backed out of the closet, scanning the interior, looking for the slightest imperfection. Anything that would tip Lilith to the fact she had gone through her things.

She needn't have bothered.

"So, I was right. You *are* a thief."

Lilith. Kat whirled around. Surprise became dread. She had a gun. And it was pointed at Kat.

"Surprised to see me?"

"I thought you were in Houston with girl-friends."

"Obviously." She gestured with the gun. "What were you doing in there?"

"Seeing how the other half lived."

Lilith laughed, the sound brittle. "You are the other half, stupid."

Kat responded with a question of her own. "So, how come you're here instead of in Houston?"

"To check up on my *loving* husband. Figured he'd take the opportunity to shack up with his girlfriend."

The untrustworthy never trusted anyone. It explained the gates. The guns. Lilith understood just how evil people could be.

"Didn't think I'd catch the poor little rich girl stealing from us."

"Knock it off, Lilith." Kat started past; Lilith stopped her. "What's in your pocket?"

"None of your business. You're crazy."

"And I have a gun. Empty your fucking pockets."

Kat reached in the empty one first, pulled out the pocket, wondering what she was going to do. Could she drag this out? Would Luke get the photos? Would he try to call or immediately head this way?

Would Lilith shoot her where she stood?

Kat reached into the other pocket, eased out the scarf. The key slipped from its fold and fell to the floor.

Lilith looked at it, then lifted her gaze to Kat's. "Now you know," she said simply.

Fury choked her. "Why?" Kat managed. "What did she ever do to you?"

Lilith Webber
2003

The night of the murder

Lilith stared at Sara in disbelief. They stood at the edge of the foyer. Just minutes ago they had been sitting on the couch, attempting a heart-to-heart.

But Sara was refusing to be reasonable.

"After all Jeremy's done for you," Lilith said. "I can't believe you would do this to us."

"What about what I've done for him? What my family's done for him?"

Sara was angry. Her cheeks were pink, her voice shaking.

But Lilith was, too. She tried to control it, the way she controlled everything, but it was leaking through the cracks. "You and your sister," she all but hissed, "always needing something! Always coming crying to him! You have no idea how difficult it is for him."

"And he gets a fat paycheck for being there for us."

"Like that's enough compensation—"

"Oh, I think he's been getting plenty."

Rage rose up in her. Lilith squeezed her hands into fists. "Danny's a no-good gambler! Don't you get that?"

"I love him. He'll change. He—"

"They never change."

"He's going to rehab. He promised."

Lilith counted silently to ten. She didn't want to beg, but she would do whatever was required to make this right. "Please . . ." She held out a hand. "Don't do this. Try to see my point of view."

"I can't let this go, no matter how much I want to. I love Jeremy, but I've already begun making arrangements."

Her control snapped. "Love? You love him? That's such bullshit!"

Sara's expression hardened. "I think it's time for you to go."

"No."

"Excuse me?"

"We're your family."

"I have my sister. *She's* my family."

"Crazy little bitch, she'll be pregnant before she's eighteen. And if she's not already on drugs, she will be soon."

"Get out!"

Sara whirled around, started toward the door. Lilith's gaze fell on the baseball bat, propped there in the corner. Why wouldn't Sara understand? What of *their* plans? What of *their* future?

She grabbed the bat, curled her fingers around the grip. She wouldn't allow her to take it all away from them.

Lilith's vision went red. She swung. The bat connected with Sara's shoulder.

Sara screamed. The force of the blow sent her stumbling sideways.

Their plans. Lilith hit her again. That blow sent her to her knees. Sobbing, she tried to scramble away. *Their future.*

Sara pleaded. The more she did so, the more enraged Lilith became.

"Why—"

A horrible cracking sound.

"won't—"

Blood splattering.

"you—"

In her eyes. Her hair.

"understand—"

The bat slipped from her fingers. Lilith looked at her hands, her legs, her feet. She was covered. Dripping.

She shifted her gaze to Sara. Realizing. Seeing. *What had she done?*

Chapter Fifty-two

Friday, June 14
5:20 p.m.

Kat stared at Lilith. She realized she was crying and wiped the tears from her cheeks.

"I didn't mean to kill her," Lilith said. "I didn't mean to. It just happened."

Kat shook her head. "Just happened?"

"She refused to understand. To see reason."

"She wanted to marry Danny."

"I was so angry. She wanted to take everything away from us."

Suddenly Kat remembered. Calling Lilith to get Bitsy's address. Telling Lilith that the neighbor had seen vehicles at the house that night. A woman leaving. "You killed Iris Bell, didn't you?"

"She was ready to die. She didn't even fight me."

"You can't argue your way out of this, Counselor. You're a murderer. A cold-blooded killer."

Lilith frowned. "Sara refused to see reason, just as you refuse to. I'm going to have to shoot you. Right here."

"In your master bathroom? You won't get away with it."

"You were robbing us."

"No one will believe that."

She laughed. The sound sent chill bumps up Kat's spine. "But they will. Just like they believed you killed your own sister. They'll actually *expect* it."

"But I didn't. Luke doesn't believe it. He won't. He'll know what I was looking for. And what I found."

Hesitation crossed her features. A hint of worry. "He'll have no proof."

"I sent him pictures. Right before you showed up."

"Sure you did."

"I'll show you. On my phone."

"Keep your hands where I can see them!"

Kat could almost see Lilith's mind working. Weighing her options, separating fact from fiction. Sizing up her own chances.

She was going to die, Kat thought. There was nowhere to go. She took a step back. Toward the closet. If she was fast enough, maybe she could lock herself in. She could charge the other woman, but she'd shoot.

"He's probably on his way. He'll find the key. And the journal."

"No. You're a liar and a murderer. Everyone knows it." Lilith cocked the gun. "This will work. It has to."

Kat threw her arms over her face. The shot resounded. Then another and another. The mirror shattered, spraying glass.

But she wasn't hit.

Lilith was. The woman lay in a heap on the cool marble, a pool of blood growing around her.

And Jeremy stood in the doorway. Gazing at his wife. The gun slipped from his fingers, landing with a thud. He shifted his gaze to her, his expression devastated.

With a cry, Kat ran to him.

Chapter Fifty-three

Jeremy took her into his arms and held her. Kat held him just as tightly. She wasn't sure who was shaking more.

"She's been acting so strangely . . ."

"She killed Sara. She confessed. I found the bedroom key—"

"My God—"

"Why are you here? How did you—"

"Her friend Carol called. Told me she didn't show up. I tried her phone . . . so many times. I thought she'd been kidnapped. Or murdered."

He started to cry. Kat led him out of the bathroom. He sank onto the bed, dropped his head into his hands. His shoulders shook.

"I dropped her at the airport, but it turns out she never got on the plane."

He lifted his eyes to hers. "I don't understand."

"She thought you were having an affair. She said she meant to catch you in the act. Instead, she caught me looking for evidence of her guilt."

He drew in a shuddering breath. "I don't know what happened to her. She'd become someone I didn't know."

Apparently, she'd always been someone he didn't know. Kat's heart broke for him.

Kat heard the scream of sirens. So did he. He met her eyes, the expression in his pleading.

"I had no choice, right? She was going to kill you. I couldn't let her hurt you."

"You had no choice," Kat agreed. "She killed Sara. She admitted it to me."

"Oh my God," he said again. "I found this. The console of her car." He dug the crumpled receipt out of his jacket pocket. "I was going to confront her with it. Ask if she was the one who had been sending you those horrible letters . . ."

Kat took the receipt. From a local sporting goods chain. A receipt for a baseball bat. Dated June 1, two days before she arrived in Liberty.

In the next instant, Luke and the rest of the cavalry arrived.

Chapter Fifty-four

Wednesday, June 26
10:45 a.m.

Kat arrived at the Lakehouse early. She parked, flipped down her visor to check her appearance in the mirror. Bags under the eyes minimized; sleepless nights masked with bronzer and a little extra blush; lip color to add a bit of life. All good.

435

Jeremy had called together a small group of his supporters and a few members of the local press to make his announcement official. He was withdrawing his name from the state senate race. For reasons obvious to everyone.

This gathering would be a solemn affair, none of the celebratory goodwill of just a couple weeks ago.

So much had happened since then. The twelve days since Lilith's confession—Kat preferred to mark it that way—had been nightmarish. The police had interviewed and reinterviewed both her and Jeremy. There were still so many unanswered questions—such as who had set her house on fire and who had been the author of the anonymous letters she had received. Obviously, Lilith hadn't sent them—she wouldn't have wanted to challenge her to return to Liberty to seek justice for Sara—even if she had tried to scare her off with the bat, graffiti and vandalism to her car.

The police didn't like dangling threads. Nor did she, but she had been there. Had heard the words from Lilith's very own lips. They could question her a hundred times; her story wasn't changing.

In the end, the Mandeville police had coordinated with Luke and the St. Tammany Parish Sheriff's Department as well. Lilith's death had solved another decade-old murder, that of Officer Wally Clark.

Lilith had shot Officer Clark. They'd run ballistics on the gun she had trained on Kat—and had gotten a match.

The media attention had been intense. The local and regional outlets had jumped on the story, the national news had followed. She'd even gotten an interview request from the *Today* show and HLN's Dr. Drew.

She'd respectfully declined all offers. She wasn't interested in looking back with them, only in moving forward.

Kat took one last glance at her reflection, then slid out of the car. She intended to stop in, wish Jeremy the best and go. This was his party, not hers.

Besides, Luke hadn't wanted to let her out of his sight. Kat smiled as she darted across Lakeshore Drive. Truth was, he was still a little pissed that despite him warning her of the danger of her running a private investigation, she'd done it—again—anyway. And almost gotten killed.

Secretly, she liked the way he held her now, as if he couldn't bear losing her.

Kat entered the restaurant through the bar. Long and narrow, a few tables in front, the bar on the right, a mirror behind it, running the entire length. Entry to the dining room at the far end, on the left.

The bar was empty, not even a bartender, though the door to the stockroom at the far end was open, and someone could be heard moving around inside. Kat started for the dining room entry. As she neared it, she caught a movement in the mirror.

Jeremy, she saw. And Tish. She opened her mouth to call out, then shut it as Jeremy pulled Tish into his arms and kissed her. Not a friendly peck on the cheek—a passionate kiss between lovers.

Kat stared at the reflected image in shock.

Lilith had been right. Jeremy was having an affair.

Feeling like a voyeur, Kat stepped back, then turned and hurried outside. She stepped beyond view of the doorway and sucked in a deep breath. To clear her head. To shake off the ominous feeling in the pit of her gut.

This meant *nothing*. People had affairs. They broke their marriage vows. It happened all the time.

Fixing a smile on her face, she stepped back into the bar. The bartender emerged from the storeroom, arms full of bottles. "Hello," Kat called out. "Is Jeremy Webber here yet?"

"In the dining room."

"Thanks." With a small wave, she went that way.

Jeremy was there, by the front window, studying his notecards. Tish was nowhere to be seen.

He caught sight of her. "Kit-Kat."

For the first time ever, the pet name from him rankled. "Cousin Jeremy."

He gave her a quick hug; she caught a whiff of perfume. "Are you okay?" she asked.

"As well as can be expected. Certainly, this isn't what I'd like to be doing today."

"I understand." Kat heard the click of Tish's heels on the stained concrete floor. She turned to look at her. Lipstick freshly applied. Hair combed.

"Tish," she said, forcing warmth into her voice. "It's good to see you."

"You, too." She glanced at Jeremy, then back at Kat. "Just here to show my support."

Kat bit back what she wanted to say and cleared her throat. "I'm not staying, Jeremy. But I wanted to tell you how sorry I am. You would have made a wonderful state senator."

Or at least she had thought so until today.

"What's wrong?" he asked, a small frown forming between his eyebrows.

"Nothing. Exhausted, that's all."

He searched her gaze. "You're certain?"

She squeezed his hand. "You worry too much. I'm fine. But if I stay, I'll have to perform and I'm just not up to that right now."

He hugged her. "I understand. I'll call you later."

Kat had cleared the front door before she glanced back. And found them watching her go, the strangest expressions on their faces.

Kat lifted her hand and they both smiled. Simultaneously. Automatically.

Moments later, as she started up her Fusion, a realization popped into her head: Tish Alexander hadn't been at Jeremy's party the night of the fire.

Chapter Fifty-five

Wednesday, June 26
11:10 a.m.

Kat found Luke in his office. "Do you have a minute?" she asked.

He smiled. "For you, many minutes."

She didn't smile and crossed to the chair in front of his desk, sank onto it. "Jeremy is having an affair. With Tish Alexander."

His eyebrows shot up. "And how did you find that out?"

"I caught them kissing."

"Maybe it wasn't—"

"It was, trust me. He was performing exploratory surgery with his tongue."

Kat sensed Luke digesting the information, thinking it through. "He's just a man, Kat. Not perfect. It doesn't change anything."

"I know. That's what I told myself, but—"

"Lilith thought he was cheating?" When she

agreed, he continued. "It doesn't change the fact that she killed your sister. Right? She confessed."

"Yes. And he saved my life. She was going to kill me. I have no doubt."

Luke agreed. "He didn't have a choice but to pull the trigger. You said so yourself."

Then what was bothering her? The fact he pulled the trigger three times? His shock and tears after?

Or that she felt like she couldn't trust him anymore?

"Okay, Kat." Luke leaned forward. "What's going on in that beautiful head of yours?"

"Do you have that receipt? The one for the bat, that Jeremy found in Lilith's car?"

He frowned. "It's in evidence, yes."

"Can I see it?"

The frown deepened. "Why?" He reached across the table and caught her hands. "Kat, it's over."

"I know, but I . . . never really looked at it. Please?"

He studied her a moment, then nodded. "I'll have Trix get it for you while we're at lunch."

They stopped at her desk on the way past. Luke made his request, Trix nodded and held out a FedEx envelope. "This came for you. Just a moment ago."

"Toss it on my desk. I'll see to it when I get back."

• • •

Trixie had gone one step further—she made a copy of the receipt for Kat. Luke had handed it over with a deep frown and a warning not to do anything stupid.

What could she do? she'd countered. As he said, it was over.

But it wasn't, Kat thought. Not for her. Not since she had seen that kiss.

Kat told herself she was simply putting her doubts to rest. Considering the circumstances, that was fair. She wasn't being disloyal to Jeremy. She was being honest to her feelings.

She pulled into the shopping center parking lot and drove around the perimeter to the sporting goods store. She'd studied the receipt. Lilith had purchased the bat on June 1, two days before she'd arrived back in Liberty. She'd paid cash. The store number. The employee number. As far as she could see, that was it.

Kat hurried from the car to the store. She went to the counter, smiling brightly at the man behind it. "I hope you can help me."

He returned her smile. His name tag proclaimed: *Scott Meyers, Manager*. "I'll try."

She held out the copy of the receipt. "Do you have any idea who might have purchased this item?"

He looked at the receipt, then at her, expression incredulous. "Ma'am, do you have any idea how many bats we sell this time of year?"

"A lot?"

"A ton."

She pointed. "Is this the employee number?"

"It is."

"Is that employee here? Could I speak to him?"

Meyers's expression turned wary. "May I ask why?"

"It's complicated. It's . . . something that's come up in my divorce. Please, it'll only take a minute."

He hesitated, then nodded. "That's Elliot. He just punched in. I'll get him."

A moment later, he returned with a gangly teenager. She had to tip her head back to meet his eyes. "Hi, Elliot. According to the number on this receipt, you sold this baseball bat."

He glanced at it. "Yup."

"By any chance do you remember who bought it?"

He laughed, then apologized. "Sorry, ma'am. But that's just a bat."

"I know. But it's really, really important." She retrieved the photo of Jeremy and Lilith that she'd brought with her. "Do you recognize either of these people?"

He studied them, then nodded. "They look familiar. Especially her."

Kat's heart skipped a beat. This was the answer she'd hoped for. "Take all the time you need. Is it possible you remember her because she was in the store?"

He squinted at the photo, then grinned. "No, I recognize them from being in the news."

"But she could have been a customer?"

"Could have been. But I don't remember. Sorry."

He handed the photo back. It'd been a long shot, but she'd been hopeful anyway. "Thanks," she said. "I appreciate—"

She bit the last back. "Could I show you one more picture?"

"Sure, I'm on the clock."

Kat pulled out her Smartphone. With a few clicks, she was at the Front Door Realty site, had pulled up a photo of Tish Alexander.

"How about her?"

The young man smiled. "Oh, yeah. I remember her. She's the kind of customer I don't forget."

Flashy. Blond. Stacked.

"Did she buy this bat?"

"She could have. But to say with certainty?" He shook his head. "Sorry."

He didn't need to say with certainty. Because Kat was certain herself. She felt it in her gut.

"Is she in a lot? A regular customer?"

"I wish." He glanced at his manager, then back at her, grinning sheepishly. "We get mostly kids and parents in. Not . . . you know."

Women who looked like Tish. "Thanks, Elliot. You've been a lot of help."

Kat made her way out of the store, hands shaking. Tish hadn't been at Jeremy's party. But she had been in that sporting goods store. She and Jeremy were having an affair. Had been having one for some time.

Coincidence. All circumstantial. Just like what she'd been charged and tried on.

Was this the way Luke's dad had felt ten years ago? This grinding in the pit of his gut? This undeniable certainty that he knew the truth?

What if she was wrong?

But what if she was right?

What would be Tish's motivation for setting her house on fire? Or for terrorizing her with a baseball bat?

To be with Jeremy. To get rid of Lilith.

Kat started the car. Turned the air conditioner on high, directing the vents at her face. She felt faint. Light-headed from the truth. Tish hadn't acted alone in this. She and Jeremy had done it together. He had a key to the cottage. He'd had the receipt, claimed he'd found it in Lilith's car. He'd had his girlfriend set the fire. But why?

Kat tightened her fingers around the steering wheel. So she would move in with him and Lilith. So he could manipulate her, set things up.

He'd sent those last few anonymous letters. The ones challenging her to return to Liberty.

He'd been the puppet master in all this.

Pulling Tish's strings. Pulling hers.

Betrayal choked her. Kat rested her forehead on the wheel. That wasn't the worst, she realized. More horrendous yet, he'd known about Lilith. That she'd killed Sara. He'd known and no doubt helped her cover it up.

She lifted her head, wiped away tears. The bastard wasn't getting away with it.

Justice for Sara. Just like he'd written.

Chapter Fifty-six

Wednesday, June 26
2:15 p.m.

Luke cruised down Riverview Street on his way back to the station. He passed the Sunny Side, then moments later, the property Kat had tried to buy.

What Kat had told him about Jeremy nagged at him. Like an itch he couldn't scratch. It was a piece of the puzzle that didn't seem to fit. Not the circumstances. Not Jeremy's story or his apparent shock and grief.

Luke figured he'd nose around a bit, see what he could find out.

He turned onto First Street, heading toward the square. His thoughts turned to Kat. Why the receipt? What did she hope to uncover? Or did she hope to prove something?

Was she, like him, trying to scratch an itch? Nosing around a bit?

Luke frowned. When she started nosing around, bad things happened to her. He glanced at his phone. He'd touched base with her a couple hours ago. She'd been distant, vague about what she was doing. Normally, he wouldn't have given it a second thought. If it had been anyone other than Kat.

What was she up to?

He reached the station, parked in one of the dedicated spots out front and climbed out of the cruiser. He entered the building. "Hey, Trix. Any messages?"

"Just Mrs. Burns complaining about her neighbor's cats pooping in her garden again."

"What did you tell her?"

"That cats have to poop somewhere and there's no law specifically aimed at roaming cats, but that we'd speak to Mrs. Martin anyway."

"Again."

She laughed and he stepped into his office. The FedEx envelope lay on his desk. He'd forgotten all about it.

It was from a law office. Thomas, Mouton, Price, Dunne and Webber.

Lilith's firm. He frowned. What could they have sent him?

He pulled the tab, slid out the manila envelope, the correspondence attached. It was from Lilith

Webber's personal assistant. Other than a greeting, closing and signature, the note consisted of one sentence:

Mrs. Webber instructed me, in the event of her death, to forward this to you.

This was it. What had been nagging at him. The itch he was finally going to be able to scratch. He ripped open the envelope. It contained a letter from Lilith.

And journal pages.

He forced himself to read the letter first. To take it slow. In the proper order.

If you're reading this, Sergeant Tanner, Jeremy will have won. But not the final battle. Oh, no. He will be exposed for a liar and a thief. And as an accessory to murder.

I killed Sara McCall, it's true. But Jeremy knew. He went back that night. To make certain she was dead. To make certain I'd covered my tracks. And to retrieve Sara's journal.

Now he wants to move on. To another love. To pretend he didn't do these things. To pretend he's lily white.

Take him down, Sergeant Tanner. And when you do, tell him I look forward to seeing him in hell.

Luke read the message twice, then the journal pages. Sara McCall had discovered Jeremy stealing money from her and Kat's trust. When he'd begun trumping up reasons that it was a bad time for her to lend Danny money or to plunk down a fat check for a fancy boarding school, she became suspicious. She'd demanded an accounting. Cornered, he'd admitted to "borrowing" from the trust. For Lilith's ring. Their new house. The wedding and honeymoon. He'd insisted he meant to pay it back. It'd been a loan.

Sara's writings painted the picture of a devastated young woman, stretched to the breaking point. The man she loved was a compulsive gambler. Her sister was a rebellious brat. And now her most trusted adviser was a thief.

But Sara, the pages revealed, had a very big heart. She told Jeremy she wouldn't press charges, that she forgave him, but also that she intended to have him removed as manager of their trust. She had been heartbroken over it.

Luke dialed Kat's cell, got her message. "Call me, now," he demanded, even as his phone chimed the arrival of a text. "Now, Kat. It's urgent."

He read the text, heart sinking. It was from Kat. *Meeting Jeremy at his place. Talk to you after.*

He jumped to his feet, responding as he ran. *Jeremy was involved. Do NOT corner him. On my way.*

Chapter Fifty-seven

Wednesday, June 26
2:58 p.m.

It wasn't until Jeremy climbed out of the Jaguar and started toward her that Kat asked herself what the hell she was doing. Her plan was more of a vague idea than an actual course of action.

Get Jeremy to confess. Record the confession with her phone. Get the hell out.

Mostly a single refrain had been running through her head, drowning out everything else:

Justice for Sara.

At the last moment she had sent Luke a text. That way, if she disappeared or ended up dead, he would know she had been with Jeremy.

Her cell phone pinged the arrival of a text. His response, no doubt. But too late to check it.

"What's up, Cousin?" Jeremy called, bounding up the steps. He had his briefcase.

Like a man renewed.

He hugged her. She had to force herself to hug him back. "How did it go this morning?"

"What can I say? I've dealt with it, and I'm moving on."

"I know you are." Kat couldn't help herself, and his frown told her he had picked up on the sarcasm.

"Is something wrong?"

"Not at all. Let's go inside, There's something I want to show you." They entered the house. "It's in my purse, in the kitchen."

He followed her in, shutting the door behind them. Her cell phone pinged again. "You need to get that?" he asked.

"It's just Luke. Responding to my text."

He frowned, looking confused. "You were a bit off this morning. Even Tish noticed. And you still seem . . ."

Understanding crossed his features. "You saw me and Tish, didn't you?"

"Saw you and Tish what? Making out?"

"We kissed, that's all."

"You were cheating on Lilith. Just like she thought."

"Do you blame me? She was a psycho. We hadn't had a real marriage in years."

"Did she know that?"

They'd reached the kitchen. He stopped and looked at her in disbelief. "Really, Kat? You're defending the woman who killed your sister? Who stood by and let you nearly go to jail for it?" He shook his head. "You're disappointed in me. I'm sorry."

Disappointment didn't begin to cover it. "Tish wasn't at your announcement party. But Lilith was."

"Excuse me?"

"I keep wondering, who set the cottage on fire? And who sent me those last couple of letters?"

He laid his hands on her shoulders and looked in her eyes. "It's over. You've got to move on."

She jerked away from him. "The receipt for the baseball bat, how'd you come to find it?"

"It was in the Jag's console. Just like I said."

"And you realized what it was and raced home, worried I might be in danger."

"You *were* in danger, Kat." He laid the briefcase on the counter. "I'd started putting the pieces together. And thank God I did. I saved your life."

"Funny thing about that receipt. I went out to that sporting goods store, they didn't recognize you or Lilith. But that high school boy remembered Tish. He remembered her very well."

"What are you saying?" He could have been a choirboy, judging by his innocent expression. "That Tish and Lilith were in some sort of cahoots? That's ridiculous."

"Not Tish and Lilith."

"Stop this right now! You're exhausted. You had a surprise today—"

"I found Sara's journal."

His expression went blank. "You couldn't have."

"Why not, Jeremy?"

"You just . . . couldn't. The police looked. They couldn't find it."

"You knew about it all, didn't you? You might

not have killed Sara, but you helped Lilith cover her tracks."

"You've lost your mind."

"The journal says it all. It was about the money," she said, taking a stab. "It was always all about the money."

"Why are you making this up?"

"Making it up?" She dug the blank diary she'd purchased out of her purse and waved it at him.

"That's not her journal."

The words landed between them.

"How would you know that, Cousin Jeremy?" she asked.

"I'm not a killer." He flipped open his briefcase. "A man does what he has to do. To protect his family. Everything he's built."

He closed the case. He had a gun in his hand. He pointed it at her. "Like now, Kat."

Jeremy Webber
2003

The night of the murder

Jeremy gazed at his new bride in horror. He'd been pacing, waiting for her to get home. She'd gone to see Sara. To convince her they had only borrowed the money. That they meant to pay it back.

"Sweetheart, what . . . My God . . ." He swept

his gaze over her. Her clothes were different. Her dark hair was matted . . .

Blood. A trickle of it down her forehead.

"What's happened? Are you hurt?"

"I killed her."

He couldn't have heard her correctly, Jeremy thought.

"She wouldn't listen," Lilith went on. "She refused to understand."

He felt sick. "Oh, baby, tell me this didn't happen."

"The bat was there," she went on. "Just there, and I took it and I hit her with it."

Deadpan. No emotion. Jeremy grabbed her hands. She'd washed them, she must have, but he saw blood under her nails.

"She was going to tell everyone, Jeremy. About the money. She was going to take it away from us."

He dropped her hands, stepped away from her. *Dear God . . . what to do?*

"I told her we'd pay it back. We'd just borrowed it. She had so much, we didn't think she would miss it. I explained it was only a short-term loan."

"Did anyone see you?"

"No, I don't think so."

"What about Kat?"

"She was locked in her room. Sara told me." Lilith rolled her eyes. "They fought again."

"This is bad."

"What are we going to do?"

"I don't know. I have to think."

"I didn't mean to kill her. I didn't, Jeremy. You have to believe me."

He started to pace. *Think . . . he had to think . . .*

"I didn't mean to hurt her." She started to cry. "It just happened."

What to do . . . think . . .

"All our plans, Jeremy. Slipping away."

"Where are your clothes?"

"In a trash bag. In the car."

It's going to be okay. Somehow.

And then he remembered. Sara journaled. Every day. When she'd confronted him about the money, she'd promised she hadn't spoken to anyone else yet.

But she would've written in her journal.

Dammit . . . this was bad . . . think, Jeremy . . .

"What?" Lilith asked.

"Her journal. I've got to go back to get it." He took a deep, calming breath, smoothed a hand over his hair. "And to make sure there's nothing . . . you might have left something . . . she might still be—"

"She's not. She's dead."

"Where's the bat?"

"I left it. But I cleaned it off. The grip."

"Give me the keys to your Tahoe. No one will recognize it. You haven't driven it around here, have you?"

"No." She shook her head. "No."

"We need to get a grip, Lilith. Calm down, deep breath.

"Good," he said as she followed his directions. "Where are the keys to the Tahoe?"

"In the kitchen. The drawer by the phone."

"Get them."

While she did, he changed clothes. Black pants, black long-sleeved tee. Dark ball cap, pulled down low.

"What now?" she asked.

"Bring me some hand wipes. I'll meet you in the garage."

He went there. From his tool chest he retrieved a screwdriver and went to work on removing the SUV's license plate.

Sara was dead, he told himself. There was nothing he could do for her, so why ruin his and Lilith's lives over this?

"Here are the—What are you doing?"

"Taking off the plate. If someone does see me, they won't be able to track us with the plate number."

"But the police. If one sees there's no plate, he'll stop you. It's too risky."

"I'll take my chances. Where's your gun?"

"Where it always is, in my nightstand drawer."

"Get it."

"Why? You don't think—"

"No, of course not. But I want to have it, just in case."

Lilith got him the gun and he put it under the seat. He made his way to Sara's, parked just beyond the cottage. The scene that greeted him was like something in a slasher flick.

Sara was dead; no need to check her pulse. Conscious of the danger of leaving a footprint, he carefully skirted the body, the blood. Doing his best not to look at her.

He felt bad about this. Really bad. Lilith hadn't meant to kill Sara; it'd been an accident. And he would make it right. Watch over Kat. Her money. Send her to boarding school, just like Sara had wanted.

The journal would be by her bed.

He made his way to Sara's bedroom. The old floorboards creaked and each time he froze, his heart lurching to his throat. But each time his fear proved unfounded. Kat was either asleep or had her earbuds in. Or both.

The journal was in her nightstand drawer, just where he had expected it to be. Careful not to leave prints, he collected it, stuffed it into the waistband of his pants.

Back in the hall, he tiptoed to Kat's door, listened. Silence. No light coming from beneath. Good. He started to inch away and his gaze landed on the key, sticking out of the lock. An old-fashioned skeleton key.

He stared at it a moment, then as stealthily as he could, he reached out and turned the key. The lock clicked back. He held his breath a moment, then drew the key out and slipped it into his pocket.

Now he needed to get the hell out of there.

Jeremy made his way out, going through the back door, around the side of the house. He hurried to the Tahoe, started it up.

Headlights came from behind him, around the curve by the cemetery. Heart in his throat, he pulled away from the curb. Liberty police, he saw. God, no. And here he was, no plates. He wanted to hit the gas, speed away, but he knew that would be the worst thing he could do.

Instead, he played it cool. Luckily, the cruiser slowed in front of Sara's place, giving Jeremy the chance to reach the end of the block and take a left.

Moments later, Jeremy saw the cruiser turn the corner behind him. He began to sweat. What to do? Where to go?

Highway 22. Get out of Liberty. Cross into Mandeville. The Liberty cop would turn around.

But he didn't. Jeremy felt the sweat of panic roll down his spine. His heart thundered so heavily, he worried he might have a heart attack. He couldn't breathe. His mind went blank with terror.

He flipped on his emergency flashers. Pulled over. With shaking hands, he drew the gun out from under the seat, lowered the window, stuck his free hand out and waved.

The wave had the desired effect. In the side mirror, he saw the cop amble his way. Wally Clark, he saw. Good guy. Real friendly.

Jeremy squeezed his eyes shut. He couldn't allow Wally to place him at the scene. And even if he gave up Lilith, he'd be charged as an accomplice. Everything would come to light. He'd be ruined. And for what?

Besides, Kat needed him. Who would take care of their little Kit-Kat, if not him?

He tipped his face out the window. He firmed his grip on the gun, tucked under his left arm. "Hey, Wally. Sorry to be causing you trouble this time of night."

"No trouble at all, Mr. Webber." Wally leaned down, grinning. "What brings you out this time of night?"

"The little woman," Jeremy said, sliding out the gun and tightening his finger on the trigger. "Who would have thought a wife could be—"

The gun went off. Wally's head jerked up and then back as the bullet penetrated. For a moment, Wally simply stood, staring blankly at him. Jeremy pulled the trigger a second time. Again, the crazy jerk of Wally's head. Only this time he went down.

"—so much trouble," Jeremy finished. Turning off his flashers, he pulled back onto the two-lane highway.

Chapter Fifty-eight

Her cell pinged again. "Give me the damn phone, Kat."

"No."

"You're recording this, aren't you?"

She was. He saw it in her expression and held out a free hand. "Give me the fucking phone."

"No."

"Or I'll kill you, then take it."

He was going to kill her anyway. But better later than sooner.

"Slowly," he said as she reached into her purse. She found the device, curled her fingers around it. Drew it out.

She heard sirens. He did, too. His expression went slack with panic.

"The phone, Kat."

"Here, take it."

She threw it at him, turned and ducked into the pantry, slammed and locked the door, backed up as far as she could. Waiting for his first kick to the wooden panel, praying it would hold.

Instead, she heard a single shot. A thud. Then shouts. Luke, calling her name.

"In here," she shouted, fumbling with the lock. She got the door open, stumbled out and into his arms.

He held her tightly. The scene beyond was chaos. Mandeville police. Sheriff's department.

"Don't look," he said. "Jeremy's dead. You don't want to see that."

Kat pressed her face into his broad shoulder. "You shot him?"

"He shot himself."

He'd had nowhere to turn.

"C'mon, let me get you out of here."

Luke led her out, shielding her from the horror of the scene. Outside, he brought her back into the circle of his arms. "I thought I'd lost you. Scared me to death."

The reality of it all, how close she had come to dying, came crashing down on her. She began to tremble. "I had a plan. Record his confession, lock myself in the pantry and call you."

He tightened his arms around her. "Worst plan ever."

And then he kissed her.

Chapter Fifty-nine

Saturday, July 20
9:06 a.m.

Kat stood at the gate and gazed at the cottage, it's yellow once again sunny, the white trim crisp and bright, the gardens replanted, the shrubbery groomed. Restored to the way it had been.

The way Sara would have wanted it to be.

She shifted her gaze to the For Sale sign planted in the yard. She could have sold it the way it had been, ugly and broken, but that had felt very wrong.

The breeze stirred her hair, bringing the sweet smell of honeysuckle. Kat breathed it in, smiling. She'd done what she set out to do. In the process, she had found her future. And the person she wanted to spend it with.

They were leaving. She and Luke. Moving to Portland. She had her bakeries, Luke an interview with the Portland P.D. Too much water under the bridge to stay, Kat thought. Too much bad history. Not just for her, for the town as well.

Iris Bell was gone, murdered by Lilith in an attempt to silence her. Lilith and Jeremy had been exposed as the real culprits in Sara's death, and those who had openly and vociferously convicted

Kat now could not look her in the eye. Others had been exposed as well: Danny Sullivan as a compulsive gambler, a coward and a liar. Even though Kat had dropped the assault charges against him, he would never again be the man Liberty had looked up to. And the well-liked Realtor Tish Alexander was in jail, awaiting trial on arson and conspiracy charges.

Yes, Liberty needed to heal. And with her gone, maybe that would happen.

In the end, seeing Luke's panicked text messages might have been the final straw for Jeremy. He'd read that Luke had the journal pages, and realized no amount of fast talking or legal maneuvering would have gotten him out of this.

Without those pages, Kat was convinced she would be dead. Jeremy would have shot her, then set about proving his innocence.

As Luke had said, her plan was the worst he'd ever heard.

Luke came up behind her and drew her against his chest. "Are you okay?"

"I am." She looked up at him. "How about you? Are you sure about this?"

"Never been more certain of anything."

"You told your mom and dad good-bye?"

He nodded. "But they promised to be out as soon as Dad is cleared to fly."

Who would have thought the wound between

her and his dad could ever be repaired? Although not completely mended, it was off to a good start.

She turned in his arms. "Let's go, then. I'm ready."

"Want one last look back?"

"Nope." Kat smiled up at him. "Never again."